A FIRE IN HEAVEN

A LORDS OF SIN NOVEL

ANGEL PAYNE

A FIRE IN HEAVEN

A LORDS OF SIN NOVEL

ANGEL PAYNE

WATERHOUSE PRESS

CHAPTER ONE

Run! No one would blame you. No one would care. *You don't belong here...you don't belong here. Run!*

The thought clung invitingly to Kira Sergenkov's mind, warming her more than the cold muck attaching itself around the rest of her body. "Fog" was what all these Englishmen kept calling the sludge, yet the stuff wasn't like anything *she'd* seen before. The disparity, however, didn't surprise her in the least. Nothing had been familiar in her life for the last four weeks.

The mighty mausoleum of a house towering before her didn't help matters, either.

The only building she'd ever seen which dared to rival this place was the White House, home of President Tyler himself. But beyond the polished brick driveway and column-framed entrance of *this* mansion, she reminded herself, no president dwelled. No influential man made world-changing decisions. A man had instead used this palace as a hiding place.

A man who had forsaken the fact he ever had a daughter named Kira.

Trepidation clogged her throat again. She was suddenly conscious of her faded walking boots, the missing tassels on her shawl, the worry-wrinkled ribbons dangling from her bonnet. She swore the holes in her thin gloves grew as she reached a trembling hand to an unsmiling footman.

Saints, she was really here. Really about to meet *him*. Had she imagined this day, even in her most far-fetched visions, but four weeks ago?

Four weeks…twenty-eight days that now represented the expanse between two lifetimes. But she shouldn't find *that* fact so hard to believe. It had only taken an hour for the only life she'd known to burn to the ground. Another two days had successfully scattered the fire's other survivors—the last of the rag-tag troupe she'd called family for eighteen years—to the four directions of the wind and then some.

And then, the most bizarre shock of all had come: the father she'd thought long dead was suddenly very much alive, very much an English lord, and very much "requesting" her presence by his side.

Kira wondered just what a child-abandoning coward would look like.

She would have to wait for an answer. Appearing at the mansion's door wasn't the looming London lord she expected, but an imposing figure nonetheless. Even with its distinctly feminine outlines of graceful posture, ruffle-edged sleeves, and multiple-layered skirts, the silhouette momentarily snatched Kira's breath away with its regal presence and commanding height.

"My Lady Kira, I presume," the shadow issued in a tone that could have been pulled from the foreboding mists themselves.

Kira averted her gaze momentarily, feeling certain she'd be more comfortable center stage at the Paris Opera. Finally, she attempted an unsteady bow. "H-How do you do," she stammered. When only a prolonged pause answered from the doorway, she grew even more painfully aware of how like a fish on land she appeared.

Of how like an outsider she felt.

She forced a breath past a chest suddenly full of a hundred knives, the blades all sharpened on memory's ruthless whetstone. But she hadn't learned to throw knives—literally *and* figuratively—at the age of five for nothing. Fury welled within her, summoning daggers of defiance. Kira jerked her spine straight and affixed her gaze back to the figure atop the entrance stairs.

Easy as pie, she inwardly congratulated herself. Oh, yes; she'd faced more intimidating strangers than this haughty housemaid before celebrating her tenth birthday—and she was more than passing proud of that claim, as well. Growing up on the front seat of a circus performer's wagon showed a person many of life's more "unique" aspects, including the inclination of folks to turn a hateful eye at anything or anyone different from themselves.

And Kira, nervously fingering one of her unruly auburn curls, certainly knew what it was like to be different.

"Well, inside with you now," the figure at last bade, punctuating with a pinched sniff. "Before those threads give you pneumonia, or worse."

The remark again rendered Kira irksomely conscious of her attire, which set off yet another flash of pride-filled indignance. She wasn't allowed half a moment to indulge the fury, however. It was barreled out of the way, flattened in the path of an enthusiastic ball of sopping fur, hurdling into her legs. Equally sodden limbs gripped her knees, her waist then her neck as the creature climbed her like a miniature palm tree. But she couldn't be angry at the invasion if she tried, especially as a five-fingered paw thumped the top of her head, and blissful primate grunts resounded in her ear.

"Well, hello to you, too." She laughed, hugging the fur

ball closer, shutting her eyes and for the briefest of moments believing the two of them were wrapped in Boston fog, instead...or perhaps an evening mist off a lake in the Carolinas, where Chico had deemed it best for the wagons to stop for the night...

"Dear God!"

Boston became London again before Kira reopened her eyes and beheld the face of the maid for the first time. Obviously, flying fur balls were deemed cause enough to descend a few steps, even in England's gray and goopy capital. From where the woman now stood, her features were clearly discernible.

Beholding her, Kira kicked up both brows in shock. The woman's height had deceived her into expecting a mannish matron, but now she gazed at the epitome of the opposite. In a simple but stylish dark-blue gown, topped by impeccably chiseled features and intricately coifed hair, the woman was dipped from head to toe in proprietous English femininity—and, at the moment, in proprietous English horror, as well.

"What—is—*that*?" A manicured hand extended in shaking shock, to which Kira replied with an amused grin.

"His name is Fred. I've had him since he was a baby. His own mama was accidentally killed." She pursed a momentary frown. "She was playing around on the trapeze, just as we'd told her *not* to."

"He...it's...a *monkey*."

"Chimpanzee." Kira had no trouble slanting her expression with ire instead of grief. "Fred is a chimpanzee, not a monkey." She added in a tight undertone, "I'll thank you to inform everyone of that."

But instead of compliance, Kira was struck with a stare

of contempt. "I'll thank *you* to take that...*animal* to the barn. They can bathe it...then perhaps trim it, or something."

"They won't touch him." Despite the menace of her glare, Kira railed at herself for allowing her vulnerability to show through about this. As if the threat of *her* fury would force someone to give Fred even the respect they'd afford their dog.

But Fred was different, too. *He'd* come to accept it a long time ago. Tarnation, the imp even flaunted it.

Kira supposed that was why she'd threatened a bullet through the gut of anyone who'd tried to sell him off after the fire.

She supposed that was why she pulled him closer to her right now, and continued leveling her determined stare along with her next words.

"Fred will be staying with me," she stated calmly, but firmly. She wasn't surprised at the reacting gasp from the steps.

"I think not!" Each word was its own production of horror-filled breath.

"I think so." Kira lauded herself for the peaceful smile she managed off the side of her mouth. "He's my pet, and he goes everywhere with me."

"A *pet*, my lady, is a poodle, or—or a cat—"

"And I'm certain they're very nice pets, too."

"But—but a chimp—"

"Is infinitely more agreeable than a poodle, and more affectionate than a cat. May we come in now?"

At first, only a pair of sighs answered the continuing serenity of her smile. When no other response came except the maid's militant pivot and subsequent retreat, Kira interpreted both actions as a well-earned victory. After a quick kiss to the top of Fred's head, she ascended the stairs with a dash more confidence than she'd had ten minutes ago.

The feeling was very short-lived.

Clean. As soon as she recovered enough from a blindingly up-close view of the chandelier, that word resonated as her first impression of the mansion. The butler who stepped forward to take her shawl was impeccably clean, his face betraying no surprise at the drab garment draped over his arm—though it showed in the glint of his eyes. The marble floor beneath her feet was gleamingly clean, actually mirroring each of her steps. And the pervading scents in the air were so clean, they hurt to breathe: lye, lemon, and bleach.

There was no enticing aroma of simmering soup in the kitchen, or freshly-arranged flowers from the garden, or even the rain that seemed certain to form from the muck outside. Everything was clean and cold...and daunting.

Kira clutched Fred closer and wondered if her father might be Prince Edward himself.

She followed the maid past a winding stairway of well-oiled mahogany and into a perfectly-arranged sitting room. As they entered, the woman addressed a petite maid who was finishing her duties before a fireplace at least five feet wide, bordered by the same marble they'd just crossed in the foyer.

"Emma," the woman directed, "we shall take tea and cider in here now, and be seated for dinner in one hour."

Kira pondered if that was when she'd at last meet her father. She also admitted she didn't anticipate that encounter as eagerly as she had an hour ago.

Just as her heart formed that thought, another voice surged through her senses, swirling into her mind through the mists of memory. *Be strong...oh, please be strong, my* lipistok... *my little rose petal. Be strong for me now.*

"Mama!" Kira rasped into Fred's fur as the two maids discussed some last dinner details. "Oh, Mama, I don't know if I *can* be strong!"

But the words came again, echoing through her soul now as well, just as Mama had rasped them past smoke-filled lungs and a body crushed by the scenery flats she'd been trapped under. The backdrops, Kira recalled with a wince, which had depicted London Town—in laughably bright colors.

There is so much ahead for you, my Kira...so much...the spirits and the saints have blessed me with this knowledge, even long before tonight. You must believe this, lipistok; *you must believe in the destiny of all this. You must believe in* your *destiny...*

But Kira had felt nothing destined about watching the last breath leave Mama's body. She'd cursed destiny through scalding tears as her mother's last farewell had echoed through her heart, growing more distant as Mama joined the spirits of the earth in a continuation of life's eternal circle.

Saints, how she yearned to indulge those tears again! But now wasn't the time to surrender. Resolutely, Kira thrust Mama's image into the back of her mind and leveled her chin as the older woman approached her again.

Fred picked that moment to squirm out of her arms and start exploring his new surroundings. As soon as he scampered off, the maid grabbed Kira's elbow and unceremoniously pulled her forward. On a surprisingly prissish gasp of her own, she sputtered, "I beg your—"

"Now let's look at you properly." The woman issued the decree as if Kira's protest had been rendered in dog grunts. She peered down her skinny nose, directly at the corresponding part of Kira's face. "You've excellent features," she said with low reluctance. "Your face *is* mostly that of a Scottney, thank God. The exotic tilt to the eyes can be explained away easily enough. Or we might have Doctor Diedrich take a look at the problem. Perhaps he can stretch the skin back in some—"

"Perhaps he *cannot*." Kira jerked back, returning the woman's insult by raking *her* with an all-over scrutiny. "How dare you," she seethed. "I want to see my father. Where the hell is he?"

The thin nose became skinny as a bookkeeper's quill. "Young lady, you will refrain from spouting your American vulgarities in Scottney Manor!"

"Perhaps my father should tell me that. The father who 'requested' I cross the entire confounded ocean to get here, then remains scarce as a damn—"

"Lady Kira, I promise you I shall fill your mouth with lye myself, and posh to the fact you're my brother's by-blow heir!"

They gasped together—the maid, as she comprehended what she'd spewed and Kira, as she gaped at the maid who wasn't the maid at all.

"You're..." she murmured in slow shock. "You're..."

Though the woman looked like she'd rather jump into the North Sea in the middle of February, she dipped a brief curtsy. Upon finishing, she kept her eyes downcast. "I am Lady Aleece, sister to your father. And I—"

"You're my *aunt*." She knew she was spared an ear beating about interrupting her elders only because she cut off what was to be the woman's apology for calling her the English equivalent of a bastard. Still, only through a great effort did Kira refrain from throwing her arms around Lady Aleece in a hug. "I've never had an aunt before," she confessed softly. "Unless one counts Sheena. She was our troupe's contortionist. She let no one else but me handle her snakes—"

"Her s-*snakes*?"

Kira repressed her grin in deference to the blanching complexion of the woman next to her. "She said I had 'the touch.' Eventually, she taught me how to feed them, too. She would say, 'Let Aunt Sheena show you how to feed a snake, *leetle Keeerrra.*'" She smiled then, as her deliberate use of Sheena's thick Ukraine accent flowed warm memories into her heart. Yes, in every manner except shared blood, she could call Sheena family...and she would remember her that way, as well.

"You...you haven't brought any pet *snakes* with you, have you?"

Aleece's trembling voice would, in another time or place, have brought on another amused grin. But not now. "The snakes are gone," Kira murmured huskily, following with a hard swallow. "So is Sheena."

They were *all* gone, she thought with searing finality. They were all gone in one way or another, whether buried beneath the charred Virginia field upon which a colorful pavilion had stood days before, or vanished beyond the steam of trains which had taken them away to other lives...gone. She would never see any of them again. The horsemen, acrobats, clowns, and other exotic misfits of the Webber's Magnificent Menagerie and Circus would never perform together again. Would never love, laugh, or live together again.

By the heavens themselves, she missed them. Yet like Sheena, they had all been *adopted* brothers, sisters, aunts and uncles to her and Mama.

Couldn't she find it in her heart to love her *real* family in the same way?

She promised herself she'd try.

With that resolution in mind, she worked her lips into a dutiful smile as Aleece, now strengthened by relief that a cobra wasn't about to slink around one of the chairs at her, approached with authoritative purpose once more. "Well, then. I promise you the curriculum *here* will not include any snakes; though I am confident you shall find your...education... both informative and enlightening."

The woman's all-too-careful phrasing sent Kira's eyebrows into curious arcs once more. "Education?" she repeated warily.

Her aunt's mouth pursed, deepening the crimps in her chin. When she turned and confronted Kira's gaze, she did so with undeviating conviction. "Yes," she asserted then, "your education. The multitude of responsibilities you must learn about the station you now hold."

"Responsibilities?" Kira's brows plummeted to join her astounded frown. "My...station?"

"Why, yes, of course." They might as well have been talking about chuck-a-luck rules, so pragmatically did the woman press on. "The station you must fulfill to the letter, if we are to succeed at this outrageous plan at all."

"Plan?" Kira echoed with deeper confusion. She sounded like she'd spent one too many hours in the sun, but until four weeks ago, the only "stations" she'd had to know about were those where she waited for trains or steamers.

Fortunately, instead of disparaging her ignorance, Aleece angled a look at her bordering on motherly understanding. Yet when her aunt spoke, each word resonated with no less conviction than an actress performing Lady Macbeth for the last time.

"You are not just a Sergenkov, anymore, Kira. You are a *Scottney*. With this name comes centuries of honor, tradition, respect—and responsibility." Indeed as if on cue, the woman raised a stately hand to the fireplace mantel, her profile forming a perfect cameo against the marblework there. "We are one of the most powerful families in the country. Our ancestors ate at Henry the Eighth's table, and laughed at Shakespeare with Elizabeth the First. We survived with distinction through Cromwell and all four Georges; I personally attended Victoria's coronation seven years ago."

A distinct pause followed. Aleece didn't look away from whatever riveted her attention on the mantel, but Kira felt compelled to offer, "The...food must have been wonderful." It wasn't hard to lace the words with sincerity, as a snarl of hunger emanated from her stomach.

Unfortunately, sincerity earned her nothing but another pursed grimace. "You are part of a *legacy* now, Kira! This is something bigger, much bigger, than you've known in the little world of your circus."

She couldn't let *that* go returned by a bit of casual banter. "That 'little world'," Kira retorted tightly, "was plenty big enough for Nicholas Scottney."

"For a time, yes," came the disgustingly breezy reply. "Nicholas was young then, and easily lured by a pretty ankle and a mysterious lifestyle." Yet then came the cautious picking-my-words tone again. "Boys *will* be boys, my dear...and they do make their mistakes accordingly."

She bit down hard on the inside of her bottom lip, hoping the pain would obliterate the stinging stab to her heart. *You expected this,* her brain drilled at her. *You expected a comment like this at some time, so why are you letting it hurt so much?*

Her heart possessed no reply. Only disorienting confusion filled the chasm of her chest. She felt just like the first time she'd heard the truth of her identity, crouched on the floor beside Mama's cot...straining to hear each of her mother's last words...

It was love, little rose petal, which brought you here...you must believe you were always loved! But your papa, in the end, he could not marry me freely, and I did not want him at a price. I refused to be known as his "kept woman," and you would not be known as his "accident."

Now, God and all His angels and spirits have rewarded me for my honor. Nicholas has sent someone for you, to take you back to your papa. And you will become Lady Kira, at last!

Indeed, here she was, living Mama's prediction to the syllable. But Mama's "gift" had been as normal in her life as sunrises and sunsets; she didn't have a qualm of perplexion at the fact she knew she'd be here a full month ago. And Aleece's words, though successfully striking their target in her heart, answered none of the questions in her head.

"But what am I doing here, then?" she at last exploded with the biggest of those questions. "If I was Nicholas Scottney's 'mistake' eighteen years ago, what makes me so high and mighty good enough for him now?"

A thick silence stretched as her reply. Then stretched longer. It seemed, Kira concluded, she was not to receive an answer, though she suspected Aleece had it in her power to render one.

The woman looked ready to weep in gratitude when the pause was terminated by, of all people, Emma. After a hurried curtsy, the maid pronounced, "Dr. Diedrich has arrived, m'lady. Shall I show him in?"

Aleece responded eagerly. "Thank you, Emma. Yes, yes."

No, no! railed Kira's head. Though enough lightning bolts of shock had been hurled at her to form a summer's worth of storms over Georgia, she wasn't too dazed to remember Dr. Diedrich was called upon to do things like stretch faces. While Aleece rushed to the doorway, she backstepped behind the Renaissance-style settee, preparing to use the heavy furniture as weaponry if need be.

"Doctor," Aleece gushed at a man who bustled his portly frame into the room with harrumphing purpose, "thank you so much for coming, with the weather about to turn so foul upon us."

"It's my pleasure, my lady, and you know it." Diedrich had the mushiest British accent Kira had heard since arriving here. He flashed Aleece an equally disgusting wink. "Gave me a reason to brush up on the old Latin."

Aleece and he shared an all-too-enthusiastic laugh. Kira, without veering her stare from them, reached and pulled Fred to her side with protective fervor.

Her pet reacted with a small cackle of delight, raising his other hand for the dance he thought forthcoming. The sound yanked Diedrich's sights her direction. Though both his bushy eyebrows jumped, he betrayed no further horror at her pet's presence—winning him a degree of respect from Kira. As the man waddled over, she chose to give the man one benefit of a doubt. But only one.

Diedrich, twitching his bulb of a nose as if smelling her caution, broke into a friendly smile. She nervously returned the look, but the doctor had begun his own once-over of her, missing nothing from disheveled hair to mud-stained hem.

He concluded, surprisingly, with an energetic nod. "Her

posture is quite commendable."

At that, Kira flashed Aleece a vindicated look. Her aunt only sighed and supplied, "I suppose we are forced to thank the theatrical experience for that."

The inside of Kira's lip fell prey to another furious mangling. It was either do that or give in to the urge to tell this witless biddy "theatrical experience" meant she was raised in a circus, not a brothel. That the only "animal" she'd ever slept with was a pillow-stealing chimp. That she'd been raised by a dozen fathers more real than the man who'd sired, then abandoned her.

"Now, dearie," Diedrich said in a business-like tone. Kira found his voice and responsibly jutting chin a source of assurance—until he continued, "What of diseases?"

"Diseases?" Kira scowled, perplexed. "What of them?"

"Are you prone to chills?" the doctor clarified in a rare spurt of clear pronunciation. "Allergies?"

"No," Kira countered, now tensing defensively. "Why?"

"Have you had the pox?" the man barreled on. "Influenza?"

"No."

"Malaria? Diphtheria? Typhoid?"

"No. No. No!"

"And your flows come regularly, I presume?"

She took no care to hide the astoundment from the stare she flung at Diedrich then—or the apprehension working its way so intensely through her that Fred hissed and bared his teeth at the physician as well. "I beg your pardon?"

"Your flows," Aleece interjected at that point, as if merely discussing ear bobs or hair aigrettes. "Your courses. Your monthlies. You...do know of what I speak, Kira?"

"Y-yes," she stammered irritably. "Yes, of course I know, but—"

"And your cycle—it occurs regularly?"

"I—I really don't understand what this has to do—"

"And you *are* a virgin?"

"It's none of your damn business!"

Oh, the eruption felt good, despite how both Aleece and the doctor gaped as if she was the heathen who'd just giggled in church. But Kira refused to lower her gaze and straightened herself to her full proud height for the first time since arriving here. Perhaps she *was* a heathen, she conceded...but only when she'd been treated like one first.

"Well," Diedrich finally muttered, "she is small, but healthy." He chortled his way through a nod. "Oh yes; *most* healthy."

"Of course I am," Kira snapped, though also gentling her tone. "But what does that have to do with anything?"

She didn't miss the brief, but explicit glance shared by her aunt and the doctor. Nor did she misinterpret the deferring bow Diedrich gave Aleece next, as if he passed some invisible, powerful scepter to her...a power the woman accepted with a great sweep of motion and a loud crunching of horsehair crinolines as she moved across the room to stand opposite Kira, firm determination stamped on her every feature.

"Your health," Aleece stated, "has everything to do with bearing strong children."

"Children?" Kira punctuated her quiet echo with a baffled scowl. Tarnation, would there be an end to the confusion she endured today?

"Yes," came Aleece's slow, melodic answer, as if she told a three-year-old why touching the stove was dangerous. "*Children*, Kira. As in Scottney descendants. The heirs to our line, and our lands."

"And you think—" As comprehension sliced through, she found herself longing for the confusion again—with agonizing desperation. "You—you expect *me* to—"

She attempted to laugh at the whole ludicrous idea, but only Fred joined in her effort, flashing his teeth and gums at her with gleeful abandon.

Kira whirled then, unable to summon any further words as a profound darkness descended on her heart, snuffing the last trace of idealistic hope she'd held there. Odd, so odd. She hadn't even known that hope was there until now, with its death. The recognition should have lessened her grief for it. Instead, she moved to a window seat overlooking a rain-drenched lawn, waited as Fred made himself comfortable in her lap, then watched three rebellious tears soak into his black-brown fur.

She'd been brought here not out of love or even curiosity. She was to be the Scottney clan's brood mare, and nothing more.

She suddenly wondered if P.T. Barnum needed any more freaks for his emporium.

"Kira."

A moment elapsed before Kira snapped her head up, realizing her name had not been invoked by Aleece this time. Nor the doctor.

Yet a man *had* murmured the greeting to her. A man who now stood watching her from a decorous distance of approximately four feet, not a wrinkle marring his tailored frock coat, satin paisley waistcoat, and perfectly cut trousers. Atop his loosely knotted tie, a face of "Scottney" features—balanced lips, aristocratic nose, high forehead—had aged to a handsome dignity, and now gazed at her in unreadable stillness.

Except for his eyes. The man's eyes examined every inch of her while appearing to take in none of her, like a hawk assessing friend or foe, though confident he could be master of either.

Kira found herself evaluating *him* in the same mode. Friend or foe? Or both? She *knew* him...didn't she?

The curiosities drove her to step closer to the stranger. "Who are you?" she softly demanded.

The slightest movement ruffled the man's lips—as if he wanted to smile, but couldn't. Or wouldn't. "My name is Nicholas Scottney. I am your father."

The words didn't surprise her. But they didn't fill her with the joy she'd fantasized about having in this moment, either. No, Nicholas Scottney's introduction only inspired her to do one thing.

Kira took another step forward, then slapped her father as hard as she could.

CHAPTER TWO

"Dear *Lord!*" Aleece gasped, joined by a bout of uncomfortable coughs from Diedrich's direction. The next instant, Kira found her shoulder caught beneath five white-knuckled talons, leading up a frilled arm, ending at her aunt's trembling glower.

"This is an outrage, young lady. An *outrage!* You shall—"

"She shall do nothing," the man ordered with low definition. Pinning Aleece with his hawk's eyes, he ordered with similar intent, "Let her go, Aleece."

"Nicholas!" she hissed. "You cannot mean to—"

"I *can* mean to." He actually released a rueful chuckle as he glanced back to Kira, rubbing his cheek. "I deserved it."

"Yes, you did," Kira leveled, ignoring yet more spluttering coughs from Diedrich.

"Well," Aleece decreed then. "Then we have a problem, Nicholas. The girl is an urchin, just as I told you she would be."

"The *girl* is eighteen," Kira interjected then, "and wants you to stop speaking about her as she's no more than the family bloodhound." She speared Nicholas with all the anguish in her gaze while adding, "Even if you are breeding her like a second-rate bitch."

"*Nicholas!*"

"Aleece, don't start—"

"That is my point! Where *do* I start? How do you expect me to present her at Saint James, let alone around this city's finest ballrooms, with that beast around her neck and those profanities on her tongue, ready to explode at God-knows-what inopportune occasion? Oh!"

With the last of the tirade, the woman dramatically pressed her fingers to her temples. "It shall take a small miracle to have her ready for presentation at all. And quite frankly, Nicholas, I'm not sure if I'm capable of the feat."

While her father drew in an exasperated breath, Kira released a relieved sigh. She knew no more about this "presentation" nonsense than she did the duties of her "station," but she was certain if either involved being called an urchin again by a pinch-nosed shrew, she wanted no part in the scheme. She wanted no part in this family at all.

She'd rather be an orphan than a brood mare.

Dr. Diedrich, however, was clearly of another viewpoint. "My dear lady," he effused, rushing over and scooping up Aleece's hands in his own, "you are far too blind to your own wondrous capabilities. I am certain if anybody in London is capable of miracles, it is you."

Kira reluctantly afforded her father a modicum of credit for joining her in a discomfited squirm as Aleece bubbled a string of ridiculous niceties back at Diedrich. Yet amazingly, her aunt became the picture of discriminating decorum the instant she swung her regard back to Kira.

After a pause filled with half a dozen exaggerated sighs from Aleece, echoed by an equal number of sour twists in Kira's belly, the woman huffed, "Well. There's much to be done, and we very well cannot do it *here*. Nearly everyone has returned to town by now; a thousand eyes shall be on us if we so much as take a step in Piccadilly."

"Haven't you retained your staff at the Yorkshire

property?" Diedrich queried.

"Why...yes," Aleece replied, turning and beaming at the man as if he'd just invented fire. And yet, the moment *was* an illumination—Kira blinked in surprise at how striking the woman could be when she chose to smile.

"Yorkshire shall give us all the space and privacy we need," Aleece eagerly continued on, swishing across the room like a child on her way to unwrap Christmas presents.

"Need for what?" Kira asked then, unable to ignore her aunt's fervency any more—nor her own stomach's deepening queasiness.

"Yes," her father concurred, cradling his chin between a thumb and forefinger. "Yes, Aleece; you're right."

"Need for *what*?" Kira pressed, bodily inserting herself into the conversation this time.

But once more, she might as well have been the family dog. "We'll need a few days on Regent Street first," Aleece rambled, "for dress fittings and whatnot. But I think we'll be ready to leave by Thursday."

"Good; good." Nicholas nodded. "I'll make the necessary arrangements."

"Will somebody tell *me* what the tarnation is being decided about my future, before I march out that hell-fired door and get on any boat I can find out of here?"

Three stunned stares swung and locked themselves upon her. Though her stomach now churned painfully upon itself, Kira returned each scrutiny with unmitigated defiance of her own. Blast, who had violated *who* around here? If being an uncouth recalcitrant remained her only method of waking these people to the truth, then by God, she'd become such a hellion.

Only Fred dared to at last interrupt the silence, whomping his hands together in delighted applause at Aleece's face, which mottled a deep red then an outraged purple.

"Oh, Nicholas," the woman wailed, "this *is* impossible!"

At first, Kira's father rendered no response to that. After a full minute passed, he closed his eyes, and at last murmured, "Aleece, I'd like a moment alone with my daughter." When his sister didn't budge, he added with pointed emphasis, "If you please."

"Perhaps I *don't* please," came the incensed retort. "Perhaps I don't please at all, Nicholas."

"Aleece—"

"And perhaps it is just time for you to admit the folly of this scheme, just as you did eighteen years ago!"

"Get *out*, Aleece," her father cut in, distinctly snarling each syllable. "Now!"

Aleece didn't utter another word, though she managed a sanctimonious glare before motioning to Dr. Diedrich and letting him escort her from the room—closing the door behind her with a lady's version of a slam, of course.

Leaving Kira alone with the stranger who was her father.

One look at Nicholas showed he was none too comfortable with the situation, either. After darting a nervous look Kira's direction, he paced across the room to the towering window, lingered for a moment at the dark-green velvet drapes, and then pivoted back toward the fireplace.

Despite the room's stuffiness, Kira shivered. She moved to the couch and opened her arms to Fred, silently apologizing to her pet for all the times she'd bemoaned his all-too-eager devotion, as he burrowed against her with blissful abandon.

"I know you must be upset and confused by all of this," her

father finally began, bracing both hands to the mantel.

"That's a good start," Kira returned, her tone remorseless. "You can add 'furious' and 'starving' to the list, too."

At last, her father did turn toward her. His gaze was active with bits of dark gold light. "Duly noted," he replied, and Kira recognized his look as the same expression Mama would bestow on her when she'd done something pleasantly unexpected to earn her mother's pride.

She did *not* want this stranger looking at her like *that*.

She told him so by gathering up Fred, rising from the couch, and cutting a path back across the room again. As she did, she pronounced, "I'm your daughter, Lord Scottney, not your bookkeeper. You can no longer 'duly note' me into a category in one of your ledger books."

"Yes," he replied before releasing a perfunctory cough. "I know."

"The hell you do."

So much more than that burned to be released from her heart and soul, but Kira's mind searched in vain for the words. The paths of her life, once so clear and simple to find, were now overgrown by vines of loneliness, clogged by brambles of confusion, shadowed by forests of grief. Would she ever find her way again?

This man didn't make the quest for that answer easy. In answer to her retort, Nicholas didn't give her the thunderous scowl she expected, but a soft, almost admiring chortle. "You truly are Rose's daughter," he stated. "So full of fire; so full of life..." His voice descended to a husky murmur as he looked into the fire, the flames leaping in his eyes' sheens of faraway memories. "Passionate about everything, even your anger."

Kira didn't want to see this aspect of her father. She told

herself to look away from the flare of pure longing which ignited his oh-so-noble features. She tried to pretend the following clench of sorrow didn't start all the way at his silver-touched temples and end in the quivering fist at his side.

She didn't want to think the only person in this mausoleum to understand her anguish was her traitor of a father.

Still, before she could swallow the words back, she murmured, "You *did* love her, didn't you?"

Her father's eyes slid shut. "I loved her." The words rumbled from deep in his throat.

"Then...*why*?" Kira raised her hands in a gesture of desperate supplication. "*Why* did you let her go? Why did you let her get on a boat and leave your life forever?"

Why did you let her leave, knowing she carried your *child inside her? Why did you let her tell that child you were dead?*

Why did both of you hurt me like this, Father? Why?

As if he'd heard the accusations from her mind clearly as the rantings from her lips, Nicholas's hand rose to wrap around the mantel's overhang, as if he struggled for purchase on a ledge against a sudden blast of wind.

"Don't you think I tried to stop her?" he grated. A humorless laugh twisted his lips. "Oh, how I tried to stop her, Kira. I offered her a townhouse with servants in Mayfair, a monthly stipend better than most duchesses, a phaeton of her own, and the best tutors for you."

Kira didn't need more than ten seconds to issue her comeback to that. "She would have been miserable."

"Of course," Nicholas said with a fast shrug. "I know that now. I think I even knew it then. How your mother loved her gypsy life."

When Kira answered with a knowing nod, he went on:

"That was why I bought her the new wagon, and wrote up the promissory agreement that would see you and her very well taken care of, no matter where you ventured in the country." As he grabbed a poker to jab angrily at the waning log, his grimacing features betrayed raw defeat. "But she ripped the document to shreds, and said she had no intention of remaining in England at all."

"Of course she did," Kira returned, only realizing the importance of her statement after the words poured spontaneously out of her. *Oh, Mama,* her heart cried then, *why was it so hard for me to understand what you did? I've understood all along, haven't I? I've understood as easily as I breathe; as easily as your blood flows in my veins. You would have invited an evil* klikushestvo *spirit into your heart before selling that heart for a house or a phaeton or even a silly new wagon.*

"Your mother was a very proud woman," her father stated then, a good measure of the gentleness in his tone replaced by a tautly enunciated anger. "Because of it, she subjected herself and her child to a hard life in a foreign land." He grimaced once more. "A life that eventually killed her."

Kira's next words didn't even need ten seconds to form on her lips. "My mother," she bit out as she rose on a surge of enveloping anger, "didn't want to be your whore, Lord Scottney. You can call it pride. I call it honor."

Her father cocked a sideways stare at her. "Honor is important to me, too, daughter. And I shall tell you something now that I never told your mother: honor comes in many forms."

"Well, of *course* it does," she sallied in a mocking soprano. "How very silly of me to have forgotten, Papa dear. The greatest honor of them all is serving the great Scottney name, isn't it? Isn't that why you denied your gypsy whore and your bastard child the only two things they ever wanted from you: your love and your name?"

She wasn't certain if the reaction she sought was her father's sudden shove from the mantel and his feral-eyed advance across the room, but Kira found herself squaring her shoulders as she confronted that exact situation.

"Do you think I was *happy* about that choice?" Nicholas snarled at her, coming closer. "Do you think I *enjoyed* making it? If you do, then it's time you understood something, daughter dear."

But instead of grabbing her or even continuing his verbal lashing, her father halted. His shoulders slackened. A long sigh poured off his lips.

"When your mother told me you were coming, I'd never known a moment of such joy," he softly confessed. "And yet, I'd never known a moment of such terror. I was eighteen, Kira. *Eighteen*, the same age you are now, only without such a keen head on my shoulders. I had grown up with governesses and polo ponies; with benefactors in Parliament and estates at all corners of the country. I saw a full meal prepared for the first time in my life only when I spent my first night in your mother's wagon.

"Yes," he affirmed to her disbelieving gape, "it's true. Rose and her world were exhilarating to me; full of passions and freedoms I'd never known..."

His stare darkened in the moment before he bent to offer a tentative hand of friendship to Fred, who'd finally loped over in shameless pursuit of attention. "But it didn't take long to know I could never be a part of that world, either," he continued. "My father clearly stated I'd be a Scottney only in name if I married Rose. And without my family's money or resources, what could I do? Could conjugating "run" in Latin put food on our table? Could dancing a perfect quadrille buy my baby medicine when she was ill?"

Kira listened to her father's explanation in deliberating silence. And, she admitted reluctantly, with increasing understanding. Her father had, in his own way, done the best with the limits set upon him. How many times had she been forced to do the same, making one costume work for four different scenes, or watching Mama turn beans into culinary delights for a week straight?

"I didn't know how to be a part of her world," he went on, "and she didn't know how to be a part of mine." Even the tug on his trouser leg from a newly devoted Fred didn't assuage the searing pain from his eyes. "I made the wisest decision I could at the time, Kira. I'm not proud of it."

"But..." she heard herself asking, though her heart screamed at her tongue to stop, "you'd make the same choice all over again, wouldn't you?"

"Yes. I would make the same choice."

Kira thought herself prepared for that admission. Yet she felt herself stepping back, dipping her head to stay the distinctive sting behind her eyes. She kept moving even as her father stepped closer, as if he actually wanted to comfort her. In response, Nicholas halted again, though as he did, his jaw jutted defensively.

"I've done my *best*, Kira," he growled. "I've helped as I could, on the rare occasions your mother let me. If you'll just let me explain—"

"Why don't you do that?" she snapped suddenly, raising

her newly dry gaze to him with equal intent. "Because I'm truly at a loss for reasons why you've brought me here, Father. If things were so confounded fine the way they were, why did you summon me to provide a service you could have gotten more easily out of one of your legitimate child—"

"There *are* no legitimate children," he cut her off with a vehement sword of a tone. Yet the next moment, his voice became a rasp again. "There are...no other children at all."

Curiosity clawed at Kira to press harder, to shout the questions for which she deserved answers, but a noose of sympathy tightened harder around her throat by the minute. *Sympathy!* she thought, astounded. She actually felt *sorry* for the man responsible for putting her through this mess! Worse, an instinct deep in the pit of her belly told her Nicholas Scottney deserved that pity.

She slashed an end to those agitating conjectures by voicing the next point of logic in this debate. "Then what about my dear Aunty Aleece? Why wasn't *she* ever offered the honor of providing your precious beneficiary?"

This time, her father took the voluntary backstep. As he did, he stated past lips pressed so tight, his groomed mustache didn't move by a hair, "Aleece has no children, either."

She had no ambition left to pursue *that* enigma today. Instead, she answered on a heavy sigh, "So I am really the only one?"

"You are."

"The last hope for the great Scottney clan, is that it?"

Again, her sarcasm barely produced a twitch in her father. "That is exactly 'it.'"

Beyond her control, her lips quirked into a laugh, anyway. "*Please,* Father," she quipped, "I was born in America, not China."

"Precisely," came Nicholas's easy agreement. Too easy. "You see, daughter," he continued, "there is a quaint little law we have here in England; a law under which the Scottney holdings fall. This law says that our estate *must* fall to a male blood heir of the Scottney line."

The answer doesn't matter, so don't ask the question, she ordered herself. The next moment, her lips formed the words, "And if there isn't a male blood heir?"

"That depends. Usually after the last living member of the family has died, the government divides up the holdings and sells them. Sometimes, the government retains part of the holdings for its own uses. The other lands may fall into the hands of entrepreneurs, or even for the rail companies to destroy as they see fit."

With a piqued jerk, Kira shrugged away the strange clamp of dread around her shoulders...and the even odder sense that she actually cared half a fig about her ancestors' land.

Her land.

"I'm sorry about your dilemma," she impatiently retorted. "But it's not my concern." She stepped past her father with the same urgency and proceeded toward the door. "I just want to go home now."

She should have known Nicholas Scottney wouldn't let her go that simply. She should have anticipated the way he'd anticipate *her* words, and how he'd gather a potent arsenal of persuasion to be ready at his bidding.

Just like the mercilessly quiet tone he hurled at her back now.

"Home...to your burned-out circus, you mean?"

Kira stopped. Bit hard on the insides of her lips. Then harder. "I'm good at what I do, my lord," she stated, not pivoting by a toe in his direction. "I'm sure I can procur—"

"What? A position doing what, Kira, as an unmarried half-breed of eighteen without her own wagon or family? Will you be satisfied entering a show ring behind a horse, instead of atop it? How long will you be able to fetch water, mend costumes, scoop hay...scoop dung?"

"As long as I have to." She clamped her teeth around every syllable. "If that is what I must do, then—"

"Then you'll be miserable, sweetling."

At that, she did spin on him. "I am *not* your sweetling."

"But you *are* my daughter." Nicholas flung the parry with the confidence of a rapier-wielding Frenchman. "And though I wasn't there to share every day of your life, I know you are meant to do much more than pitch hay."

Kira coiled her stance tighter, hostility curling its way around her every muscle. "You don't know anything about me."

"Oh, but Kira, I do."

"*Stop it.*"

"You're a *Scottney*, daughter," he declared, voice rising with relentless relish, as if his rapier had just found its mark in her heart. "You are a Scottney as much as you're a Sergenkov. *Look—*" He swept a forceful hand toward the room's gilt-framed mirror. "Your very face betrays you. Our blood courses in your veins!"

With corresponding vehemence, Kira spun the opposite direction. "That doesn't mean I have to like it!"

"No." He plunged back to a composed murmur with that, rattling her almost as violently as his outburst. "No, it does not mean you have to like it.

"But it does mean you can take advantage of it."

At first, Kira said nothing. Moved nothing. She squeezed

shut her eyes, wondering why she suddenly felt like a maiden being enticed into the bathhouse by an unclean *bannik* spirit... yearning to resist; helpless to resist.

Surely enough, she opened her eyes and tilted a wary stare over her shoulder. "What in heaven's name does that mean?"

Nicholas answered by way of a cryptically quiet utterance. "Come walk with me in the garden, daughter," he requested. "I'd like to discuss a piece of business with you."

CHAPTER THREE

"No," Kira rebutted. "Why?" she revised, when realizing her father had invited her with his tone, not ordered her.

In reply, Nicholas only extended his arm to her. He held his stance that way, appearing every inch the influential lord of the realm, as he awaited her. The image, Kira swiftly admitted, only increased her apprehension of what he had in store for her on this "walk."

Only by looking to his eyes once more did she decide to comply with his hest. Again, the sensation overcame her that she looked into a mirror, for how many times had she beheld such an unquenchable hazel fire in her own gaze? Yes, she would certainly leave London with at least one new possession: the knowledge she was truly this man's daughter.

Carrying that knowledge with her now, she curled her hand around her father's arm and let him lead her out to the garden.

Though lit only by the ambient light from the mansion, the bushes, trees, and flowers brimmed with misty, peaceful beauty. Kira wished she could enjoy the scene in meandering relaxation, but gave up the fantasy as impossible. She'd be more comfortable walking here with the King of Prussia himself, she speculated as she searched for something, *anything* to say. But her brain only gave up more words laced with sarcasm and bitterness. Useless words.

"It's pretty, isn't it?" Nicholas finally asked, gesturing to the beds of tulips, irises, and other bounties of flowers they passed. He emitted a small chuckle when Kira slanted him a look, condemning him for using "pretty" to describe this natural resplendence. "Imagine this multiplied a hundred fold," he went on. "That's what awaits in Yorkshire."

Kira halted so fast and spun on him, spray flew off the bottom of her whirling skirts. "When I go *where*?"

This time her father didn't chuckle, but his face didn't detonate in surprise, either. "I told you I had a piece of business to discuss with you, Kira. Your trip to Yorkshire is involved in that business."

Kira longed to at last use her acrimony as an appropriate retort to that. But, she was loath to concede, her father's confidence captured her curiosity. What made the man so supremely sure of her compliance in his little proposition? She awaited the answer to that in glaring silence.

Nicholas didn't make her wait long. Nor did he make her wait through a fripperied prologue of discussion. Instead, he stated without preamble, "I want one year from you, Kira."

At first, she sent him a perplexed scowl as reply. But the next moment, comprehension set in. "*Sumnshehtshyj*," she blurted, and meant it. "You are insane."

"No," came the unruffled rebuttal. "I'm serious. You're already here—"

"And that makes everything easier?"

"I...need you, Kira."

"And that makes everything *all right*?"

She punctuated with a laugh which sounded musically merry—while her mind reeled in chordless chaos. Ironically, tranquility saturated the air around her. A small stone fountain gurgled contentedly nearby. Fred cooed at a bug crawling across the cobblestones. In the nearby carriage house, a man whistled a happy tune to soft-grunting horses.

Nicholas's hands descended gently to the back of her shoulders.

And Kira almost wept, for instead of yearning to bolt from his touch, she longed to whirl back around and burrow against the strength of her father's tall, strong form.

Until he leaned closer to her, and spoke again.

"One year," he offered in a murmur so beguiling, she ruled out comparing him to the *bannik* and steeled herself to battle the devil himself. "One year, Kira," he repeated in that voice surely learned from the Dark One. "I only ask for one year out of your life, in which I shall endeavor to prove how happy you can really be here."

At those words, Kira jerked away from him, jamming her arms across her chest. "Happy," she echoed. "Happy, as in pregnant with your precious heir, is that it?"

"Kira," he said tightly, "I think you may look at things a little differently—"

"When I'm back on the ship, bound for home."

"Postpone your trip, damn it!"

His growling eruption jostled Kira with no less startlement than a lunge from an unruly tiger. Still, her father recovered his composure half as fast as she, settling into his lordly mien with true English alacrity.

"Today is May the eighth, eighteen eighty-four," he stated as if his outburst had been nothing more than a sneeze. "If you are still miserable on May eighth, eighteen eighty-five, I'll see you back to the ship myself...along with enough funds to not only start a new life, but a new circus."

At *that*, Kira dropped her arms. And gawked openly at

him. Nicholas only blinked with slow, almost lazy, assurance.

Certainly she'd heard his words incorrectly, she supposed, or misinterpreted his meaning.

There was only one way to find out. Make him clarify the point.

"I'll want a full menagerie," she started cautiously. "Lions. Perhaps panthers, too. Maybe an elephant. And Arabian stallions, of course."

"Of course." The hint of a smile teased her father's mouth with that, and she thought a twinkle passed through his eyes, too. "And chimpanzees, as well," he added, finishing in a chuckle as Fred, recognizing at least that word, sauntered over and affectionately turned himself into an accessory on the man's wool-trousered leg.

"New costumes will be necessary."

"Designed in Paris," he filled in.

Kira swallowed against her heart's ecstatic outcry to that. "But I'll still need more than that to compete against Barnum and the Flatfoot shows," she pressed, proud of the prudence she smoothed over her tone. "Perhaps Levi North or Isaac Van Amburgh."

"Ahhh. 'The North Star' trick rider, and 'The Lion King' animal trainer. Excellent choices. Why don't you hire both?"

Again, Kira gaped at him. Again, Nicholas's features barely shifted in their calm resolve. As a matter of fact, the most lively part of his expression remained his eyes, which now danced with such vibrant gold light that Kira would have sworn on a sacred *nauzy* amulet that he enjoyed creating this dream as much as she.

That surety inched its way into her heart and bloomed into a smile on her lips. Her father's answering smile warmed her deeper, especially as his expression grew into a full laugh. "Ahhh, Kira, you ambitious piece of hellfire. You truly *are* my daughter."

As they walked back toward the sitting room door, Kira's lips only moved to smile wider. But in her soul, words bubbled in jubilant celebration. *Mama,* she exclaimed inwardly, knowing that somewhere, somehow, her words went heeded, *you were right! I have found a destiny far beyond what I ever dreamed, and all it's going to cost me is one year!*

The time would pass before she knew it. And then she would be on her way, free—*truly* free—to become that "ambitious piece of hellfire" as even Nicholas could not fathom...perhaps as even she could not fathom yet. For how did one make room for a million fantasies in a head which, twelve hours ago, had barely spared the space for an exhausted prayer?

As for the little "vacation" she'd have to endure to Yorkshire...

Well, Kira reasoned, she could do *anything* for a year.

Even dance with the devil.

CHAPTER FOUR

Four days later, with painfully clenched teeth, Kira berated herself for that moment of reckless optimism. Surely even a year of dancing with the devil wasn't as heinous as one hour in a well-laced corset.

She groaned as the coach jolted through yet another hole in the northbound road, giving the corset's steel enforcements permission to dig deeper into the tender flesh of her breasts, back, and waist.

It was, she admitted wryly, a "fitting" accompaniment to the increasingly suffocating bonds of her father's bizarre plan.

She tried to absorb the idyllic peace of the scenes visible past the dark-green curtains framing the wide window. True, she'd only seen such flawlessly tranquil vistas painted on stage backdrops before: lush valleys, sleepy villages, and primeval forests all rolled past her sights like a theatrically-produced dream...

Lord almighty, how she wished it was a dream. "Hell," she vented beneath her breath as the wheels slammed into another deep hole, giving the underpinnings one more hearty go at her nipples. Her agitation wasn't helped by glowering across the carriage at her aunt, who napped against the squab with the dainty—and oblivious—leisure of a cat.

She must force her thoughts elsewhere.

Kira roamed her sights back out the window. As she did, she summoned to mind her father's words of yesterday morning, as he'd escorted her to the carriage with a gentle smile on his lips and that golden twinkle in his eyes. *My England,* he'd said to her. *Scottney Hall is where you'll begin to discover* my *England, Kira. Drink it in and savor it...*

She grimaced at remembering her reply to him, grumbling she'd already seen more than she liked of *his* England, thanks to the previous three days' worth of a London shopping marathon. Silently, she'd added her doubts about her conclusions changing at all during this little sojourn.

But she should have remembered this wasn't America. She should have realized this was the land of Merlin and Titania, where ladies lived in lakes and armadas were defeated overnight, and a carriage journey *could* become a discovery of the incredible beauty she beheld now. Across ancient stone bridges they rolled, over creeks shimmering like costly satin ribbons. Beyond those, the recesses of the forests captivated the eye with a hundred different textures, as sun-dappled clearings turned into intriguing emerald shadows. In the valleys, the air swirled with the fertile earthiness of sunshine on clover, punctuated occasionally by the contented *baaas* of newly-shorn sheep.

After this world transported her mind off her physical misery for a blessed thirty minutes, the tiniest of smiles rose to Kira's lips. *All right, Father,* she conceded from behind that smile, *this* is *an impressive start.*

Her smirk dropped the instant they bounced into the deepest of the road ruts so far. "Hell," she muttered again, before belligerently deciding she'd rather die in uncouth comfort than decorous torment.

She tossed back her velvet shawl, then set about easing her breasts' agony, if only for a few moments, by manually pushing them together in order to allow soothing air down the sides of her torso. The resulting pleasure induced a blissful sigh to her lips—

Until an outraged gasp sliced into her reverie.

"Kira!" Aleece shot frantic hands to the window curtains, the brass rings clanking as she snapped the coverings shut. "For heaven's blessed sake, *what* are you doing?"

"Breathing." She couldn't help returning her aunt's gape with a mischief-inspired smile. "It's a wonderful sensation, Aunt Aleece. Why don't you try it?"

"Ladies do not touch themselves like that," came the expected huff. "Please compose yourself at once, Kira. We've already passed Harrogate, and neighbors may begin to recognize the carriage."

"Well," she returned, "perhaps we should be friendly in return, hmmmm?"

Her aunt answered that with two ascending arcs of perplexed brows. Kira didn't blame her. Her own brain didn't realize what she meant, until she'd spilled the retort. She was only completely sure of one fact: Aleece's rebuke had brought on an increasing inability to breathe which had nothing to do with her corset. She had to inhale something other than leather oil and the hair pomade coating her curls. *Now.*

The decision surged her with unignorable restlessness. Without another moment of hesitation or patience, Kira used the handle of her aunt's umbrella to deliver three thunks to the carriage roof. The vehicle started to slow, but she silently swore in agitation at the five minutes it would take for a complete stop, a proper set of the brake, and the stepping box to be brought around. Instead, she swung open the door, and used the momentum of that action to swing herself to the ground.

"Kira!" came the expected gasp from inside the carriage. "Kira, by all the heavens, what are you doing *now*!"

A small jolt of satisfied vengeance added a bounce to her step as Kira decided to lump her aunt's protest in the same category as dog grunts. "Tom," she called instead, addressing their driver as he secured the reins. "Do you and Fred have room for one more traveler up on the box?"

At first, the man only stared as if a ghost had materialized before his eyes. Kira acquitted his behavior, as well—she suspected spooky apparitions *were* more common than women hopping out of his carriage at will. "I—I beg your pardon, m'lady?" he finally replied, nervously fingering his droopy mustache.

"I'd like to ride a while with you," Kira repeated, adding a hopeful smile this time. "If, of course, that's all right."

"It's just dandy with me, Lady Kira, but—"

"Ohhh, no," came the interrupting command from the figure now craning her neck out the window behind them. "*No, Kira!* It is appalling enough you've halted us in the middle of this wilderness, exposed us to all sorts of ruffians and wild creatures as you run around in the lane like some dirty—"

"Lady Aleece." Kira issued each syllable with clipped brusqueness, appropriately underlining the ire tightening her own face. "I am not proposing to skip along beside the vehicle, but ride on the driver's box—as I watched countless young ladies do in Hyde Park only two days ago." A smile bloomed, however, as she watched her statement effectively weaken the support stakes of her aunt's conviction. "Are you telling me all of *them* were dirty and improper?" she finished with sardonic surety.

"All of *them* were not working to create a reputation," Aleece humphed.

"Or to create a baby, either."

"Good *heavens*." Aleece looked ready to swoon as Kira shared a rebel's grin with Tom and Fred. Her triumph was cut short, however—her aunt did *not* collapse, but swung down from the carriage in the same manner she'd just utilized. The woman did so with startling agility, at that.

Even so, Aleece didn't waste any time stomping back into her "Empress of Decorum" mien with fuming relish. "Enough is *enough*, young woman," she decreed while covering the last steps to Kira's side. "You are disrupting the travelers on this thoroughfare—"

"What travelers?" Tom muttered.

"Not to mention the demands of our schedule—"

"What schedule?" Kira said.

"Ohhhh, just get back in the carriage, Kira! Now!"

Kira compelled herself not to move. For if she did, she admitted, it would *not* be to obey her aunt. Saints, how she yearned to educate this woman with a few choicely selected "mandates" of her own!

But at that moment, a fresh, fragrant wind swirled around them, along with the *leshii* spirit which held dominion over that wind. With reluctance at first, but feeling her sincerity build by the moment, Kira beseeched that guardian of this forest to teach her its quietly controlled strength...fast.

"Kira, I'm *waiting*."

But even the *leshii* was no match for Aunt Aleece. Kira groaned deep in her throat as the woman strung a pointed cough along with her command, and the sad perception hit that the spirit still hadn't shown up with so much as a tiny dose of patience.

She had no choice over what she did next. Her sanity was at stake here.

"It seems you'll have to wait a while longer, Aunt Aleece," she stated as evenly and diplomatically as possible—under the circumstance of turning her back on the woman. "Because I'm certain my father would like me to arrive in Yorkshire as a *sane* human being."

She hadn't wanted to do that. Using her father as a bargaining chip somehow measured at the same level as him seeing her as nothing more than a walking womb. All the same, a relieved grin broke over Kira's lips when not a peep of protest followed her up to the driver's box.

The rest of the afternoon passed as if only minutes disappeared with the miles. With the sun on her face, the grass-scented air filling her nostrils, and Fred happily planted on her lap, Kira recognized a breeze called contentedness teasing at her heart...for the first time in almost a month.

She released a delighted laugh as they proceeded into a glen canopied by pines and carpeted by regal purple wildflowers. The road narrowed here, becoming more of a winding cart path, but the horses continued with spirited purpose, jangling their harnesses like gypsy tambourines.

"They're as enchanted as I am," Kira commented to Tom on the four magnificent grays in front of them.

The man's moustache hitched up in a smile. "Aye. They're fine animals. Your father is a wise man when it comes to picking horseflesh." He coughed nervously to fill the thick silence Kira issued as reply. "Of course, they've also been showing off for our afternoon guest. They like you, Lady Kira."

She smiled wistfully. "We had twelve horses in the Menagerie's show. I...miss them so much sometimes."

Tom merely nodded at that, but in the simple motion, Kira perceived his empathy more clearly than any contrived words.

She did not, however, expect his next gesture. With a nonchalant flick, Tom directed the reins at her. "Why don't you take them for a while?"

Kira didn't waste time voicing her gratitude to the man. She eagerly exchanged Fred for the reins, laughing louder as she wrapped the leather around her knuckles. She instantly savored the feeling of being connected to such sleek, beautiful animals again.

The newness of her equally spectacular surroundings, coupled with the familiar comfort of leading the horses, lifted her beyond herself, if only for a few exquisite minutes. From that same boundless place in her heart, she heard Tom's startled, but encouraging praise of her driving. She replied with a small but wicked smile, knowing the horses heard him, too.

"Let's show him what we're really made of, my friends!" she called, giving the horses a few inches of rein as interpretation.

The grays responded instantly, as she knew they would. With a bit more of a lead, they began to strain at the harnesses, entreating Kira to let them enjoy the untamed resplendence of the forest at an equally unhindered pace. While appreciating their zeal, Kira held them at a firm limit, especially as the path twisted with sharper and steeper frequency.

"I believe you've gained some new friends, my lady," Tom remarked amicably. "That's quite a compliment, coming from this bunch. Don't think I've ever seen them behave like this for a woman."

Kira turned to thank him for the compliment with a smile. Only Tom never received that smile. Just as Kira didn't see Tom when she turned. Instead, a wall of brown fur smashed into her face, accompanied by a gleeful primate laugh.

"Fred, no!" she yelled in protest, grabbing at her pet with one hand while securing the reins in the other. Or so she thought. Her pet, while determining it was *his* turn to occupy her attentions, turned the right rein into a tangled decoration around his left leg. "Catch!" she called to Tom, throwing him the left rein while she struggled with the rest of the mess—

Just as he leaned over to help her with the tangle, as well.

"Bloody Mary!" Tom shouted. He lunged for the liberated leather strip, nearly hurling *himself* off the box in the process. With a scream, Kira set Fred aside in order to yank Tom back up.

During those few seconds, Fred pulled himself free of the right rein. After a quick *fwwwipp*, the strap joined its mate, dragging in the road between the harness and the carriage.

Now, the grays were not only free, but frightened, thanks to Kira's outcry. Her shriek, injected into the enlivened instincts already pumping in the animals' blood, might as well have been a whip to their flanks. They erupted into full gallops with instinctual frenzy.

"What is happening!" came Aleece's panicked wail.

"Get back inside!" Tom yelled back, not taking time to trifle with the requisite niceties—for which, Kira thought, her aunt better be grateful. *If* they got out of this ordeal alive.

But suddenly—almost disappointingly—their wild ride crashed to an end. Around the next curve, the road turned back on itself, forming a cramped "S." But the horses, taking advantage of their newfound liberty, decided they preferred a more direct route through the foliage. Before Kira or Tom fathomed what was happening, the animals made the carriage *part* of the foliage, snagging themselves in low-lying bracken, and the carriage body between two pine trees.

Everything halted with breath-seizing speed.

Kira confirmed that fact firsthand, the air leaving her in an astounded rush as she was hurled off the driver's box. A mound of damp and dirty leaves broke her tumble. She observed Tom had met the same fate, landing in a leaf pile of his own beside the carriage's other front wheel.

Uncaring whether Aleece heard or not, she verbalized an oath on behalf of her throbbing bottom. The remainder of her aching joints urged her to repeat the epithet, yet at that moment, Fred came into view overhead, blithely swinging by one hand from a tree branch and emitting what sounded like a chimp's version of "Hee heeee!"

Unbelievably, Kira gave in to the strange urge to join her pet's carefree humor. As she rose, she looked over to Tom and giggled louder. If she looked half as dazed and bracken-torn as he, then she didn't blame Fred for his mirth. Her amusement only grew when Aleece leaned out of the carriage window, features given over to such wide shock, Kira was reminded of an orang-utang Fred had once introduced to her. She leaned back on one elbow and let the laughter overtake her as her aunt fell back inside the coach with a horrified moan.

She didn't stop until abruptly, Fred and Tom did. She turned, wondering what in the world had jolted a grown man and a chimpanzee into such captivated silence.

That was when she found out they'd not been mesmerized by a *what*...but a *who.*

"*Bozhy moj,*" she whispered. *My God.*

The man emerged as if created by the trees themselves, for he was certainly as looming, dark, and solid as any of the pines rising around them. He intensified that surreal image by moving nearer on broad, bold strides, though the underlying brush didn't let out one protesting crunch beneath his feet.

As for those feet—Kira's stunned survey of him began there first, with the mighty black boots which extended to the knees of his overworn black breeches. A black waistcoat went unbuttoned over his black shirt, with its collar bared wide to reveal thick black curls across the top of his chest. Thick black curls she couldn't rip her eyes from. Good Lord, Kira moaned inwardly, she had to find the only man in this country who refused to wear an appropriately tied stock!

A man who now gave them all a stare which made her belly ignite with fire, but her knees freeze colder than icicles. As those eyes of his locked upon her, Kira knew the reason why.

His gaze was just as dark and powerful as the rest of him.

She sucked in her lips and began to pulverize them between her teeth. She thought of her musings of four days ago; of how she'd carelessly compared Nicholas to the devil, but now she realized her shrewd but shallow father knew no more about being the devil than Fred did.

The devil was hiding inside a midnight-haired forest demon who appeared out of nowhere and now dominated her sights...everywhere.

And now, all the *leshii* really help her, she didn't even try to look away. She didn't even gasp as he drew his sinfully full lips back across his teeth, and demanded in a low snarl, "Who the bloody *hell* is responsible for this?"

CHAPTER FIVE

Damien saw the color drain from the girl's face even here, in the darkness of the forest. He watched her skin change from an entrancing, gold-touched creaminess to a mask of colorless terror.

Terror of him.

Oh yes, he saw the dread curling its way through this stranger with the proud stance, the eyes the color of fire itself, the hat skewed to one side of her leaf-covered head, and an African chimp playing in her smudged skirts. Christ, he thought, almost laughing, she was a regular little hoyden.

But ah God, she was a *beautiful* little hoyden.

Who was she? Where had she come from?

The answer, at least to his latter musing, came preceded by a slow squeak of broken carriage axles. Damien turned to see a traveling coach bearing the unmistakable gold and green of the Scottney family crest.

He glared back to the hoyden, who was now joined by Tom Montgomery, Scottney lackey number one.

Nausea joined the rumble of hunger in his stomach.

And suddenly, her terror satisfied him a great deal.

He watched in secretly satisfied silence as she inched tentatively forward, her jaw working to form words. "We—we did not mean—" she began, but then stopped, jerking her head as if scrubbing a mental slate clean.

"It was an accident, sir," she at last declared with

enunciated boldness, inducing Damien to fumble through a backward step of his own. The bizarre urge struck him to turn, run, and dunk himself beneath all one hundred freezing feet of Hardraw Force. Instead, he recovered enough to rock back on his left heel and form a soft, yet convincingly menacing retort.

"Well, your 'accident' drove my dinner away."

"Then we are greatly sorry, but—"

"I don't need your apology!"

The suddenly vicious turn of his tone came as a surprise. Clearly, the hoyden thought so, too. She yanked her pet closer to her side, like a London mother warning her child away from the rat man. Damien told himself the affront didn't matter. The Scottneys had already inflicted their deepest wounds to his soul.

That thought made it easy to insinuate himself next to her again, now looming close enough that he smelled the earth and pine needles clumped in her dark auburn curls. Not a trace of rose water or lilac spray emanated from her. Bloody hell. He'd never smelled a woman so damn enticing.

"What I *need*," he began then, aspiring for a threatening growl but ending up struggling through a betrayal by his own rasping throat, "is my dinner. Now..." He sidled nearer to her, condemning himself because he didn't know *why* he attempted such stupidity. "How do you propose I satisfy that need before nightfall?"

For a long moment, her only response came in the form of a madly-pulsing vein in her neck. Damien watched the vessel in nearly vampiric fascination, leaning so close that his breath now stirred her dirty, beautiful curls.

What the hell *are you doing? What the* hell *are you letting her do to you?*

Dear God, he hadn't realized how hungry he really was—in many more ways than the needs rampaging his belly. His mind brimmed with imaginings of what a hoyden's neck tasted like...of how succulent her lips would be...of how delicious other parts of her would be for a dessert feast...

The pulse in her neck halted. Just as Damien's heartbeat stopped. She jerked her gaze up to his, staring at him with a blaze of intensity in her eyes, almost as if his secret wonderings had overflowed from his brain into hers. *God, her eyes.* Damien felt as if he stared at the sun; knowing he should turn away, helpless in his unblinking state.

A voice sounded from somewhere then, but it didn't belong to the hoyden, so he shrugged the interruption away. But then *she* glanced at the speaker, and he was forced to listen, as well.

"Mister Sharpe." Damien recognized Aleece Scottney's haughty intonation without looking.

"Mister Sharpe," she repeated, chilling her tone to the temperature of St. Paul's in February. "I will thank you to step away from my niece this instant, before you find yourself being called out by Lord Scottney when he arrives on the morrow."

"Called out?" the hoyden interjected on an incredulous laugh. "Saints, Aunt Aleece, haven't they outlawed things like that in this 'civilized' country?"

"Sometimes," the woman snipped in return, "honor surpasses laws."

The hoyden laughed louder. "Listen," she leveled with distinct determination at her aunt, though her gaze delivered the same message to Damien, "if anyone picks up a gun to defend me, it'll be *me*."

Damien said nothing to that, knowing no pistols would be

have to be drawn in *this* match. He already conceded defeat to this woman—and her secret weapon of sheer shock. *Aunt Aleece.* She was Nicholas's *daughter.* And an *American*, at that.

Dear God, how the graves must be churning in the Scottney graveyard, even at a mile away in Middleham. *Nicky, old boy,* he chuckled inwardly, *you've been hiding some impressive skeletons in your fancy fine closet.*

But no skeletons could grip his blood as this amazing little Scottney did, as she spun completely back on him, affixing her gaze to him. Damn, *damn,* that mesmerizing bronze stare of hers...

"Believe what you want to, Mister...Sharpe," she stated then, in her clear yet slightly exotic English. "Though we *are* terribly sorry, and there is nothing we can do to bring back your rabbit—"

"Deer," Damien corrected. "One of the finest in the forest. I'd been watching that doe for days."

He deliberately dipped the pronunciation of his last sentence, corresponding it with a stare meant to show her just how intensely he "watched" something—or someone. In short, he intended to bring back a shade of the color he'd first terrorized out of her cheeks...for once upon a time, not *so* very long ago, he'd gleaned many a becoming blush for this look.

But the hoyden's complexion barely warmed from the ghostly hue he'd first induced in it. As a matter of fact, the diminutive creature stood there as pale and erect and silent as a specter gracing a headstone.

Bloody *hell.* He didn't need any more ghosts in his life.

"Deer," she finally blurted in response to him, though forcing the sound past her tight jaw. "Fine. Then I am sorry we made you lose your—doe, but I shall speak to my father tomorrow about making rectification to you, and—"

Before a thought of caution or control halted him, Damien threw his head back on a whetted scythe of laughter. "You'll make 'rectification' to me, will you?" he returned on the waves of a residual chuckle. "Just like that? Just because you'll ask dear Papa?"

Again, he surprised himself *and* her with the ferocity of his final two words. For half a moment, the hoyden blinked at him, confused, but recovered enough to state, "I'll—I'll work arrangements out with my father, all right? But it's none of your concern. This mess is, after all, my responsibility, and I was taught to clean the messes I make."

"Taught to—*your* responsibility?" He didn't try to hide his baffled tone.

"Yes." She gave an awkward nod, waving aside Tom and his frantically scowling protest. "I am at fault for your mishap, Mister Sharpe, not Tom."

She almost issued the declaration as if proud of her exploit—for which Damien found himself handing over the oddest reaction: a measure of admiration. Folding his arms across his chest, he returned past bemusedly smiling lips, "And how do you arrive at such an assertion?"

"Because Tom wasn't driving. I was."

"Oh, my word!" Aleece damn near shrieked her reaction, which more than justified Damien's surprised quirk of brows.

"Good stars!" the hoyden exclaimed, throwing her hands up at them both. "This is England, not China! Even here, I know 'ladies' handle the reins on occasion, if they like."

"No," Damien interceded. "No, no no. Haven't they told you yet? No reins for *Scottney* ladies." He ignored Aleece's glowering response to his sarcasm, instead lowering his tone to finish with a statement delivered directly at the hoyden. "And even ladies do not pick up *one* rein, without knowing what the bloody hell they're doing."

"What the bloody hell they're—" She speared him with a glare most women saved for occasions like insults to their hair or tea gown. "If you must know, sir, I have known 'what the bloody hell' I'm doing with a harnessed team since I was ten!"

Her chimp applauded her manifesto. Damien enjoyed the animal's charm but disdained its owner's indignance. The wench had *not* known what she was doing; otherwise, he wouldn't be assessing the bulk of her entrapped carriage now. "Then what *did* happen?"

"I told you: we had an accident."

"You mean *you* had an accident."

The glare deepened. "I beg your pardon?"

"You said it yourself. *You* were driving, therefore *you* let the situation get out of control."

"I didn't *let* anything happen. It just—happened. Fred got a little frisky, and—"

"So you were playing with your chimp and forgot about paying attention to the horses."

"Why, you obtuse, obnoxious son of a—"

"Kira!" Aleece rasped. "For God's blessed sake!"

"Let her come," Damien intervened with soft, but determined purpose. He never averted his eyes from Aleece's captivatingly furious niece. "Let her come," he reiterated. "I've taken much worse than this from the Scottneys."

He didn't expect his caustic drawl to deter her ladyship Kira (how had a hoyden gotten the name of a goddess?) in the least. She didn't disappoint him. Her pace didn't falter as she stomped forward, this time leaving her chimpanzee behind, and skewered him with an impressively hard glare.

Yet in the moment before she spoke, a glimmer of something passed through the woman's eyes—a glimmer he hadn't expected, and did *not* want. "It wouldn't have been an honor for that deer to die by your hand," she murmured, putting verbal form to that glittering, discomfiting element. "And that's why I'm glad I helped it escape, in my own way."

"Your own way," Damien echoed, only *his* tone held none of her shimmering prettiness. His voice curled out of him like smoke off a funeral pyre, potent and black. "Yes, that's what you Scottneys are all about, isn't it? Doing things your own way, damn the rest of the world."

With that smoke, he effectively dimmed the surface glimmer in her eyes, but not the flames at the backs of those sienna depths. "You're a sad and lonely man, Mister Sharpe," she stated with that same steady heat. "And I understand—"

"You understand?" Incredulity made the smoke ignite now, flaring hot and painful inside his gut, exploding into scalding intensity off his lips. "You understand nothing about me, lady."

"Then maybe you should let me try."

"Maybe you should go to hell."

He expected what happened next. He stumbled back without a fight when an unmistakable male grip curled into the back of his collar, followed by Tom's commanding growl. "I think that's enough, Damien."

"*More* than enough!" Stifling violet perfume heralded Aleece's arrival, flying ribbons and lace forming a wake behind the woman as she sliced her way between him and the hoyden. Gripping her niece's shoulders with possessive fervor, she gave Damien only one more dagger of a glance. "Stay—away—

from—her," she issued as she did.

Don't worry, came the immediate answer from Damien's mind. *Don't worry your head at all about the matter, you shrew.*

But the center of his chest clamored with another message entirely. His heart pounded out a cadence so booming and strong, it momentarily deafened his senses to any other instinct except yearning to haul this wild, weird little American to *his* side, keeping her like this forever...

Keeping her from going to the place where she'd learn not to say things like *I understand.*

In the end, Damien locked his legs and curled two fists to force that temptation into submission. No matter how different, no matter how bold or beautiful, this woman was still a Scottney—and that meant he would never touch her again.

Suddenly, he couldn't sweep a mocking bow to Aleece fast enough. He couldn't jerk a quick enough nod to Tom, letting the driver know he carried no fault against him for doing his job.

As for the hoyden...

He couldn't look at her. She wouldn't understand, but he didn't care. He *couldn't* care.

Without another word, Damien spun and paced back into the shadows from which he'd come...trying not to think how dark they now seemed...so much darker and blacker, now that he'd felt the fire of the sun once more.

★ ★ ★ ★

Heavy but rainless clouds settled early over the twilight, churning confusedly across the sky. They were a perfect image, Kira concluded, of the twisting murk inside her head.

As she trudged from the forest behind Tom and Aunt Aleece, she watched the dark mists gather against the crests of proud hills in the distance, and likened the sight to the way in which one of those thoughts mercilessly prodded the summits of her own imagination.

She was besieged by the recurring memory of Damien Sharpe. His ink-of-night eyes. His ground-eating strides. His irony-filled smiles. His exasperatingly fast tongue.

His tangible loneliness.

She couldn't stop seeing him in every dark-fingered cloud caressing those hills. She couldn't stop wondering about where he'd suddenly bounded from in that clearing, or where he'd stomped off to, wrapped in his personal clouds of alienation and pain.

Pain. Oh, yes, Kira confirmed. If she'd inherited none other of Mama's extrahuman perceptions and skills, she *had* gleaned the ability to discern the pith of a person's pain—

And Damien Sharpe seemed determined to spend the rest of his days in a mental torture chamber.

"That's *it*," Kira erupted in an irritated mutter. She couldn't stop the questions from bursting on her lips and perceived no reason why she had to, either.

"Aunt Aleece," she called, hastening her step to fall into place beside the much-too-quiet woman. "Aunt Aleece, I..."

Yet then she dwindled into unwanted but inevitable silence, twisting her mouth left then right, searching for the phrasing the woman might find most seemly for her query. Finally, realizing there probably *wasn't* a "seemly" way of approaching the questions, Kira just let her lips blurt out them out, one after another.

"Aunt Aleece, what happened back there? Who is that

man? *What* is that man? Why did you and Tom look at him like he was Bluebeard's ghost?"

"Kira," Aleece huffed, daintily scraping sweat-dampened tendrils off her face, "please; I am not normally in the habit of hiking the last half mile of this journey."

Kira twisted her lips again. And again, those lips had no option but surrender to her mind's scorching curiosity. "But what did he do to you? And why did you look like you were about to call him out yourself?"

"Damien Sharpe is none of our business, Kira!"

Somewhere during the retort, her aunt stopped and spun on her, but the actions were inconsequential when accompanied by the pure fury dominating the woman's glare.

For a moment, they both stood and blinked at each other in stunned silence. Aunt Aleece clenched her way through several hard swallows, as if forcing the "inexcusable" exhibition of her emotion back to the dark and secret spot in her soul from where it had obviously erupted. Kira acknowledged the temptation to break out in applause.

Finally, the woman finished in a decorously taut murmur, "He won't come near you again, Kira. He won't hurt you. That I swear to you. We *shall* watch over you here."

One more pulse throbbed in her neck, then Aleece turned and continued down the road with military precision. Her posture reminded Kira of Nelson's statue in Trafalgar Square. Reluctantly, she hoisted her ponderous skirts and followed once more, no other questions quirking her lips.

Yet while her mouth remained silent, Kira's mind—swiftly echoed in a little corner of her heart—shouted an odd but unrelenting question:

Who would watch over Damien Sharpe?

CHAPTER SIX

At least thirty stones' worth of well-muscled horse shifted uneasily beneath Damien again. The stallion jerked hard at its bridle, tossing its black mane into the biting wind that whipped along the high, rocky bluff at the edge of the forest.

Damien retightened his hold to the reins. "Easy, Dante," he crooned. "Take it easy."

In truth, he hardly faulted the animal for the restless intentions. If Dante intuited a wisp of the agitation riding his master's nerves and muscles this morning, it was a wonder the horse restrained itself to these mere fidgetings.

Selecting this place as a spot for this morning's meeting was not the wisest decision he'd ever made. As Damien awaited his associate, his view consisted of a dozen undulating hills spreading out on either side of him, their expanses cast from dull green to duller gray at the will of an ugly old witch sky. Atop the largest of the hills to his left, a half mile in the distance, rose a mansion house of graceful beauty, seemingly formed straight out of the surrounding forest...

His home.

His home.

Nestled in the valley to his right was another estate, forming an equally impressive scene—if one was impressed with castles rivaling Balmoral in their large, cold grandeur.

The fortress of the clan who had helped rob him of his home.

Dante began another nervous dance. Damien's attempt at restraining his mount proved only marginally successful as before; inside another minute, he knew the reason why. A smudge in the valley to the right swiftly took on a discernible form. A horse and rider approached at a determined gallop.

The cloaked figure and his buff-colored bay mare didn't slow until they had nearly cleared the crest of the bluff. As they breached the rise, Dante released a grumpy snort. The bay had gotten the exercise *he'd* begged for during the last hour. "Soon," Damien promised him, patting the stallion's neck as he waited for the other rider to wheel around and settle into a parallel position at a six-foot distance from him.

He exchanged no pleasantries with the man. They both knew the quicker they separated again, the better. One day, Damien swore, he'd be able to meet with his associate as a friend again, sharing a bracing morning ride, then perhaps a shared nip of brandy from a skin flask before heading to their respective homes.

Home.

The word knelled in his brain, yanking him back to the present faster than cathedral bells used to wake him as a lad sleeping in church. "Thank you for coming on the scant notice," he began without turning his head, instead continuing his steady vigil on the countryside, making sure nobody observed them except grazing sheep in the fields to their left, grazing cattle to their right.

"Phoebus needed a good sprint," the figure replied with winded casualness. "Besides, I expected you'd want to talk when we received word of Lady Aleece's return."

"Return," Damien repeated, realizing it took an effort to filter the anticipation from his otherwise pragmatic tone.

"Then she's back for more than a weekend sojourn."

"I'd say so. A baggage cart arrived a few hours after them with enough crates to clothe China." A grunting chuckle made its way into the man's account. "Overheard Tom in the kitchen this morn, saying he was surprised you didn't raid the cart in return for some doe they cost you with the traveling coach mishanter."

Damien released a snort of his own, though no humor laced the sound. "So now I'm a highway thief, too, just because I can't eat?"

"That's about the sum of it," came the sardonic but truthful answer. "Yeah, I'd say that is."

Dante tossed his head once more, the violence of the action directly gleaned from the course of Damien's thoughts. Quickly, Damien regained control over both the beast he rode and the beast inside his soul. *Concentrate,* he dictated at himself. *Damn it, Sharpe, concentrate on the details that matter here...on the truth to be discovered somewhere between these two empires you survey...*

On the truth that will get you home again.

The credo had kept him alive the last six months. It had filled him with hope and hate, desire, and dauntless determination. Yet this morning as the word *truth* resounded in his mind, a disturbingly persistent image marred the perfection of his dogma...a face of dirt-smudged fairy features, surrounded by a cacophony of auburn curls...a damnable hoyden's face, ruthlessly invading his attention!

"She's the reason," Damien stated then, barely restraining the growl from his voice, "isn't she? She's the reason they've broken form at the top of the season and come back like this."

"She who?"

"The American," he snapped, exasperated, until realizing his thoughts were only deafeningly clear inside his own skull. "The American," he repeated more diplomatically. "What's-her-name." As if he'd forgotten an appellation like *Kira*…as if it hadn't echoed in his head for the better part of an hour after he'd left her yesterday.

"Yeah," came the quiet, casual reply. "That would seem the way of it." Yet a subtle shrewdness underlined the man's tone. He no more believed Damien had "misplaced" Kira Scottney's name than he thought the livestock before them would stand up and break out into tavern ditties.

That detail clearly understood between them, Damien gratefully saw no reason to dwell on it, either. Still, he conceded the value of shrouding the eagerness from his voice as thoroughly as possible.

"So," he continued in a tone as colorless as the mists blurring the horizon, "she *is* American."

"Got off the boat from Boston five days ago," his associate confirmed. "Looking fairly much like a drowned rat, too, from what I hear."

"She's *no* rat," Damien retorted before any reasonable thought could intervene. No logic aided him in his examination of the defensiveness, either; only the surety that timid rodents and Kira Scottney had no place in the same metaphor with each other.

"Didn't seem so to any of us, either. Tom says she handled those horses like a professional driver, and believe it or not—"

"She's no professional, either." The interjection came with even more potent vehemence.

"But she *is*." At Damien's incredulous glance, the man continued, "That's the crux of it. Seems she grew up in a traveling show, over in the colonies. A circus, to be exact."

"A *circus*?"

"In her blood, I wager. Her mum used to be with a troupe over here. She was their gypsy star seer. You know the kind: shilling gets you a look into some fancy crystal ball; you walk away smelling like bloody incense all day."

Damien's scowl deepened. "How did the woman end up in America?"

"Still hazy on that." The man's hooded head tilted back as he no doubt angled a gaze into the clouds swirling above. "Just know that's where she landed, after his lordship got her full in the belly."

Damien allowed a grim chortle through the haze of his own astoundment. "A gypsy fortuneteller." He shook his head. "Christ. I didn't know old Nick's tastes ran that exotic."

"Neither did anybody at Scottney Hall, that's for certain. Especially when his lordship didn't marry all these years..." A long creak of saddle leather belied a squirming search for tactful words. "Well, tongues wagged, you know? Word had it his lordship was a bit 'sweet.'"

"Yes," Damien replied without inflection. "I know." He'd heard all the same gossip. But inside of a minute on each occasion, he'd also discounted all the rumorings. Hearsay and twentieth-hand knowledge could destroy a man more thoroughly than a round of cannon shot to his gut. Damien knew that with more certainty than anybody else in this county. And because of that knowledge, he hadn't heeded a single shocked whisper about Nicholas Scottney's 'sweetness' in six months—no matter how hard it had been to do so.

No matter how hard it had been, after the man had believed the worst of *him*.

Put it aside, Sharpe, his head ordered at him again. *Fires of fury will only burn you alive. Think of something else...think of going home...think of your goal...*

But to replace those flames, his mind's eye could only summon a bonfire. The conflagration of a bold, bright gaze, crackling embers of gold flecked against molten bronze heat, lifted to meet his stare with wonderful American nerve...with a stranger's unnknowing openness. Looking at him. *Looking at him.* Not realizing nobody had looked at him like that in six months, not since the rainy October morning when respectful nods and admiring gazes had turned into prejudging glances and suspicious glares.

His jaw worked through several clenching spasms before he summoned his voice again. "So," he finally addressed his companion, "what *has* caused the mighty Nicholas Scottney to acknowledge his bastard now?"

"Only the heavens seem to know," came the apology-edged answer. "And they sure as shillings aren't talking."

"That's all right," Damien said. "I've got a few theories brewing already."

"As do we all, my friend. As do we all."

Damien debated what to say next. His associate had called him "friend," and properly so. His trust in the man was complete. But somehow, sharing his hope about this latest twist of things at Scottney Hall—that perhaps the arrival of this American hellion would wedge the fissure in the Scottney ramparts he'd all but prayed for—would, like the chanting of some ancient hex, have its power negated in the telling, instead.

Right now, it was best to exercise caution. And distance. A great deal of distance. For while Kira Scottney might help him recover the key to his home, she sure as hell would never touch that key herself—nor any other keys to his life, for that matter. He'd learned his lesson about how the Scottneys twisted the keys they were given. He'd learned that lesson the hard way.

"I'll let you contact me next time," he said to his associate then. He added in a gritted mutter, "At least I hope there *is* a next time."

"There will be," came the gruff reassurance. "Of course there will be. I'll let you know in the usual manner."

"Right," Damien replied. "I'll look for the Scottney standard flown off the castle's right turret instead of the left."

A grunt of agreement served as confirmation of the plan. "More than likely I'll have news for you soon, with this Yank stirring things up."

"I hope *your* crystal ball is right, my friend." He glanced to the hooded figure who now rewound reins around hands in preparation for departure. As he did the same, Damien said softly, "And thank you."

His associate didn't render an answer. The distant gonging from Scottney Hall's bell tower provided ample explanation why. It was six o'clock, time to begin another day, and the bay would be missed in the stables before too long. The horse's rider, on the other hand, wasn't worth so much. He would easily rejoin the other nameless faces in the Scottney Hall staff army. His ears, just as anonymous, would spend the days trying to listen through the stone castle walls for even a scrap of information to help a friend who now lived his days in the pith of a black forest, riding the blurred line of distinction between "outcast" and "outlaw."

That final thought coincided with the sixth knell from the bell tower. Damien's whole body clenched hard around the echoes of the gong, now a forebodingly baritone sound, throughout his being. His arms pumped at the reins Dante now tested with nearly violent anticipation, and his own blood pumped with the craving to at last let the animal have its furious release, but he didn't slacken his grip yet. Damn it, but unseen torture irons kept him shackled to that point atop the hill—for torture was precisely the term to describe what the moment felt like, watching the sky lighten above the two empires sprawled below, imagining the awakening bustle of both households.

He wondered what ribald jokes were being related in those stables, and what spices inundated the kitchens as fresh breads and scones were pulled from hot ovens. He wondered about Henry, the stable boy who'd worked so hard to become a horse exercise expert, and whether the lad had finally heeded his advice and proposed to Elsa from the downstairs housekeeping staff. On the other side of the valley, he wondered if Fallon, Scottney Hall's kitchen cat, was plump with her third round of kittens yet. He wondered what Fallon thought of Kira Scottney's chimp.

Kira Scottney.

Kira Scottney.

He was glad his muscles still jerked in shock as his thoughts again found a way to drown themselves in the image of her. Now, Damien used that shock to encourage Dante into a full gallop, turning back across the wild, empty moor he fairly had as private ground these days, as the expanse was framed on one side by the crescent-curved border of his forest.

He had to drive her out of his head. He had to welcome the bite of wind against his face, open the heat of his thoughts to the air's consuming cold sting. He had to remember how that hoyden's father had helped sentence him to this dark solitude,

these days of relentless loneliness.
He had to make Dante run faster.

CHAPTER SEVEN

Kira dreamed about him again.

She was as certain of that fact as the arms and legs she now stretched beneath the sheets and blankets of the pink satin cloud that also did duty as her bed. She looked to the stormy sky beyond the padded window seat where Fred still dozed, using the shifting shades of pewter and black there to better recall the scenes which had dominated her mind's midnight hours...

In her dreams, he rode a stallion black as the shadows that had formed him, steed and rider moving together as one... moving with blatantly sensual grace. Kira wondered if her heart had pummeled her chest as wildly in her slumber as it did now, keeping strangely accurate time to the horse's hooves as they came closer in her mind's eye, closer, until suddenly, he pulled her up on the horse with him...

Only then, the horse transformed into a bank of clouds. The stallion's mane turned into tendrils of dark mist, curling around her toes as she began to dance on that cloud with Damien Sharpe. Her fingers curved around the hard, defined planes of his shoulders, and she worked to pull him closer as she struggled to find the light in his endlessly black eyes.

But instead, those dark depths sucked *her* in. She was helpless to move, to resist, as his presence surrounded her, smelling of earth and trees and clouds. His arms enveloped her, long and powerful and unyielding. And then...oh, and then his face descended toward hers, and his mouth slanted but an inch over hers...

"The Lord's own *sake*." She interrupted her thoughts in a frantic rasp. Kira bolted to a sitting position among the sheet and blanket confections. She dragged in several deep but shaking breaths, and she didn't dare look at the uncontrollable tremble of her fingers against the counterpane.

Three days, she castigated herself. She'd been here for three days, confound it, and hadn't successfully purged the man from her imagination yet! As a matter of fact, Aunt Aleece's cryptic comments on the road had only intensified her bizarre fascination with the brooding loner in the heart of that murky forest.

What in tarnation was wrong with her?

Because, came the next moment's all too easy reply, what she felt for Damien Sharpe was *not* fascination.

It was compassion.

Because, oh God, she knew just how frightening "alone" could be.

But he doesn't want your compassion, Kira! He wants nothing to do with you! He made that a mite more than clear in the middle of his blasted forest, don't you think? Or didn't you catch the dozen snarls he hurled at you? Or the glares that could have sent a tiger's tail between its legs? Or the way he turned and left the clearing without so much as a backward glance your way?

But before the last reverberations of that sermon could fade away in the alcoves of her mind, her heart whispered in stubborn tenacity: *I wonder what he's doing now.*

She wondered if he was alone while he did whatever that was, or if a big black horse really did keep him company. She wondered if he still scowled through the task, or if the horse could make him smile, perhaps a little. She wondered if he was warm in his cold forest. If he had something to eat for dinner, even if it wasn't fresh venison.

The only reply to her ruminations came from Scottney Hall's chapel tower clock, ringing long and deep through the morning one time, then twice—

Why couldn't she dismiss him as the beast he'd behaved?

Three, four and five times—

Why couldn't she convince herself he was an outcast from Scottney Hall, most likely for good reasons?

The questions received as empty a response from her soul as the clock's knells did during their final two rings down the Hall's vacant corridors. Attempting to fill that emptiness with *some* sort of thought, Kira propped herself higher against the pillows and looked again out the window. The mullioned glass turned the estate staff into aquatic-like globs as they moved cheerfully through their early morning duties, toting baskets of eggs here and wagons of hay there, lighting fires and chopping wood, all smiling and laughing with the useful purpose their day already possessed.

Just as her days were, not so long ago.

A frustrated sigh erupted off her lips. "Well, this is getting you nowhere, lazy *klop*," she muttered, and instantly felt those lips turn upward again. Calling herself a lazy bedbug came as easily as her frowns used to, when Mama wielded the gentle rebuke on her. If only Mama could see her now, she mused as she threw back the covers without another tremor of hesitation—

"Eeee gawwd!"

And collided straight into a five-foot meadow fairy in

maid's clothes, whose pert features now animated into an openly astounded gawk.

"Ally," Kira greeted to her personal maid—though not certain she'd get ever get used to *having* a personal maid. "Good morning."

"Yer...awake," the maid stuttered. A stack of hand towels and handkerchiefs wobbled in her grasp like over-buttered griddle cakes.

"Er...yes." Kira reached to help steady the pile, but Ally pulled back as if the linens were her personal cache of spun gold. Instead, as the maid bustled her way to the washstand beside the fireplace, Kira prompted, "I was awake at this time yesterday, as well the day before. I'm used to—"

"Well, stop it."

That prevented Kira from taking her final step out of bed. "Stop it?"

Ally, who'd now traversed halfway back across the room, reeled herself back with a wince. "I beg yer pardon, m'lady," she petitioned in a rapid mutter. "I'm given to impertinence, as Lady Trevor has properly disciplined me for in the past."

"I'll bet she has," Kira replied from clenched teeth. Yet at the confused glance Ally dared up at her, she roused a fast and friendly smile. When the maid's big green eyes widened yet further, she hurried down the mattress and over onto the settee, reaching out a hand to urge the girl to sit with her.

"*I* say you are given to honesty," Kira proclaimed while Ally landed on the cushion with a loud crackle of well-starched petticoats. "And right now, I'll value that honesty more than my right leg."

A few copper-colored ringlets fell loose from the maid's mobcap as she tilted Kira a stare blended of something between curiosity and bemusement. "Tom was right. You *are* a unique bird, m'lady."

"And you were in the middle of saying I shouldn't rise from bed when the sun rises, like everyone else." She conveyed a question in the sentence.

Ally aimed a matter-of-fact look at her polished work boots. "Well, not like a lady, that's for well certain."

"And ladies are so different than the rest of the world, that their days are kept by separate clocks?"

To her startlement, Ally's expression didn't falter by a twitch. "Of course they are." The girl believed the statement as thoroughly as the Greeks honored a lightning-tossing Zeus. "Ladies need extra sleep because they're more delicate than most persons, and in order to maintain the beauty of their skin and the health of their—"

"That's the deepest bucket of swill I've ever heard!"

As Ally's jaw succumbed to a speechless gape, Kira gave full vent to an incredulous stare. Her maid really couldn't believe the conviction with which she'd issued her words, she realized, just as she longed to laugh at the absurdity of lying about like a sow being fattened for fair just to "maintain her delicate beauty."

That image prompted a tiny giggle to her lips, after all. At first, Ally reacted with an even more shocked stare, but slowly, the beginnings of a grin teased her bow of a mouth. When Fred decided he wanted a piece of the fun, too—and demonstrated such by scrambling up the bed and promptly tangling himself in the bedclothes—the two humans broke out into full chortles. In that moment, Kira thought with a smile of contentment, the first threads of a friendship were stitched.

"Well," Ally said then, sighing resignedly, "yer awake and

ya plan to stay that way. So we should just as well see to yer toilette and dressing, too." Indeed as if fairy wings aided her, the maid flitted to her feet and disappeared into the closet to the right of the bed. "Perhaps you'd like to wear this new blue serge today," she called from the clothing-padded depths of the little room. "It's such a pretty color. Almost violet, I think. You'll look right beautiful fer yer first lessons with Lady Aleece."

Now Kira cursed herself for protesting her maid's counsel about returning to bed. "The lessons," she moaned, falling back against the pillows. "Hell. I'd managed to forget about the lessons." *Thanks to* Damien Sharpe's *visit to your dreams.*

Her schedule, if she remembered correctly, was to begin directly after breakfast with lessons in vocabulary, etiquette, posture, and dance. In a curious sort of way, she looked forward to *those* regimens. She anticipated collecting a few stunned stares from her aunt when demonstrating the denizens of Boston, New York, and Atlanta weren't such bumpkin cousins to London's nobility as she might think.

But the afternoon itinerary coiled her nerves in discomfited dread. Aleece apparently saved the more "important" subjects for then: appropriate uses and styles of correspondence, household management, and dinner party hostessing were to comprise the afternoon's program.

"Dinner parties," she reiterated aloud, shaking her head while the words felt like a foreign language on her tongue. "Why can't everyone bring their favorite stew and a jug of cider, and let's be done with it?"

"Beg yer pardon, m'lady?" Ally called, cutting into a lively tune she'd been humming.

"Nothing," Kira answered. "It was nothing, Ally." But as the maid bustled back into the room, she muttered, "Just wondering if God would listen to my request for a minor disaster to intercede on my behalf."

Ally didn't hesitate about reacting with an instant smile at that—though her expression was ignited into much more than amusement by a sudden din from the carriage court. As she rushed to the window seat, Kira and Fred leapt up to join her.

No catastrophe nearing a flood or foreign invasion filled their sights, though a body would be hard pressed to discern the difference by the sprinting stable boys, the hand-wringing kitchen maids, and a scowling Tom Montgomery, who now commanded them all back into a mob-like bunch in the corner of the courtyard opposite Kira's window.

Kira didn't hold back her reacting huff of astonishment at the man's militaristic severity. "Good God," she muttered. "What are they expecting? The four deadly horsemen?"

The next instant, she answered her own question—with a gasp which stopped halfway in her throat, wrenched to an early end by sheer shock.

He indeed could have been one of the mythical demons on horseback, so completely did his presence dominate the Main Courtyard from the moment he cantered in on a mount as big as Troy's war machine and as black as the night those ancient warriors had fought into.

His black horse. *His black horse.*

Kira swallowed but still couldn't breathe as she watched him masterfully slow the steed, then swing down from the saddle on legs sheathed in a buff-colored fabric appearing much like buckskin. Yes, buckskin, she decided with certainty the next moment; worn to the texture of touchable softness, if the way the fabric moved along his legs was any evidence. And oh, his legs...endless thighs rose from his knee-high boots, lean sinew and hard muscle blending in two captivating stretches ending in buttocks with interesting muscles in their own right...

"Dear *God*," she whispered, meaning to castigate herself with the words—meaning to tear her iniquitous gaze away from those legs; away from that man, period!

But she couldn't. She didn't. It's *him*, her senses cried in peals mixed of elation, trepidation, and heart-gripping awareness, even from the distance at which she beheld him now. *It's him.*

More astoundingly, it was him as she'd envisioned him in her dream, black eyes gleaming with the intensity of newly-mined coal, black hair whipped back by a wind as forceful as his stride across the court, approaching Tom. He carried a burlap sack in his hand with surprisingly contrasting gentleness.

"Oh, blazes," came Ally's dark grumble. "Here comes trouble."

Kira's reaction to that stunned the maid *and* her. Before she even acknowledged its approach, a giddy laugh burst off her lips.

But she didn't give either of them a chance to recover from that shock before acting on her next instinct. She yanked up the hem of her nightrail while spinning around and dashing out the door. As she raced down the corkscrew of a stairway, a shrieking Ally on her heels, more laughter bubbled past her lips.

Here comes trouble.

She'd heard that a thousand times before—when it was said about *her.*

CHAPTER EIGHT

She got to the Main Courtyard too late. Even though she took the short route through the kitchens, ignoring the dumbstruck gawks of the staff preparing breakfast there, she raced out into the cobblestoned yard to find only three stable boys assessing Sharpe's stallion with stares mixed of wariness and worship.

"Where'd they go?" she demanded breathlessly of the first youth she came to. But the boy mirrored his female peers from inside, gaping at her without a word. Ally was maddeningly right. Ladies who left their bedchambers before eight o'clock were more an oddity in this country than Mrs. Tom Thumb.

"Tom Montgomery and Damien Sharpe," she clarified this time, using the final word as an adjective in order to convey her meaning. She grabbed the lad's shoulder. "Where did they go? Tell me *now*."

"R-right m'lady," came the all-too-earnest reply at last. "O' course. They—they took 'emselves off to the Menagerie, they did." He pointed hastily in the direction of the covered portico leading to the stables. "Mister Sharpe, he found—"

"The Menagerie," Kira repeated, impatiently jerking up her hem again. "Fine. Thank you."

But she hadn't proceeded six steps in her running compliance to the boy's guidance before she skudded to a stunned stop. Through the next long moment, the only occurrence *not* jolting her heart in surprise was the sight of the three boys still standing there as she pivoted back upon them.

"Where did you say they were?" she asked her freckle-cheeked helpmate first.

"The...Menagerie, m'lady." The words were given with questioning slowness despite what Kira knew was her most intent, and often most daunting, stare. "Uh...surely ye know the lordship had his built next to the stables, rather than out in the gardens. Better that way, so we're all thinking, since we don't have to carry the food far, and those wild beasties do eat a jungle's worth o' victuals every—"

Kira didn't hear the rest. But she had the information she did need—the information so amazing, she couldn't believe it until she'd seen it. That was why she spun in the middle of the youth's sentence, vowing to seek him out and apologize for her rudeness later, and sprinted toward that portico with twice her speed as before. And twice her anticipation.

She still didn't imagine she'd receive Christmas over half a year early this morning...or in such a magnificent way.

She located the building with ridiculous ease, considering the way the onion-domed building stood out from the Tudor-accented stable houses like a Mongol on the dance floor at Buckingham Palace. Her heart thudded at the base of her throat as she traversed the winding entrance walk, inlaid with a cornucopia of colored glass stones, and then stepped across the portal—

To release one sharp gasp of pure astonishment.

Then she could only gape around her in wordless wonder.

The exotic roof, she discovered, was constructed entirely of lightly tinted glass, so that the whole area below received a bath of soothing light, much like the depths of a rainforest. Kira had no doubt, however, that such an impression came easily with the help of the trees, flowers, and vines blooming everywhere around her, thriving with the help of a pleasantly warm mist pervading the air and a glittering creation of a waterfall off to her right.

It was the most lavish production she'd ever seen; an illusion so complex and complete, *she* almost believed she'd stepped through a magical travel device and had landed somewhere deep in the West Indies. Clearly the occupants of this wonderland chose to presume that, too. Kira quickly took inventory of the room: along one wall, small brown monkeys, bright green iguanas, and even a trio of white-tailed deer romped through a labyrinth of serpentine trees and lush vines. The opposite side of the enclosure was reserved for the spacious residences of a sleek black panther and a majestically reclining leopard.

Between these two habitats flowed the stream fed by the waterfall, sprouting real waterside plants from its manmade confines, crossable at the middle via a vine-entwined footbridge. The stream concluded in a small pond that also served as bathing pool for the occupants of a soaring aviary. That enclosure resembled a kaleidoscope, so many beautifully feathered birds did it house.

Except for the large white cockatoo currently residing on Damien Sharpe's left arm.

Kira rediscovered her heartbeat in the moment she again stared at the reason she was out here in the first place. She stared down that aisle, at least forty feet long, but the distance might as well have been forty inches, so thoroughly did he dominate her sights and her being. Rugged and wind-blown, his dark skin even ruddier from his exposure to the chill morning winds, he almost fooled her into thinking she was back home and about to perform for a settlement in one of the wild western territories.

He *almost* fooled her. Frontiersmen usually weren't in the habit of accessorizing their wardrobe with white cockatoos.

Nor did they usually return her stares with such burning, unblinking attention.

"Oh, *Bokh*," she gasped. *Oh, God.* For despite all the gapes she'd received—and ignored—during her race out here, it took Damien Sharpe's gaze alone to strike a sudden and horrifying awareness into her:

She stood here sheathed in nothing but the cotton and lace of her nightrail.

It was that realization, Kira affirmed to herself, and *not* that man's continuing exploitation of the circumstance, that prompted the frantic trio of backward steps she took, coiling her arms across her chest as she did so. But even her blatant discomfort didn't stop Sharpe from staring at her like some mysterious crossbreed of the wildcats themselves, purposefully studying his next intended prey.

Only she seriously doubted a wildcat's quarry had to endure the throbbing race of her heart into her throat like this...or the terrifying rush of liquid sensation to secret places between her legs...

Kira completely spun from the man this time.

A curse seethed through her teeth when she found her exit abruptly blocked, until she recognized her savior in the form of Ally. Her maid had brought Fred and a mercifully thick satin robe.

After helping Kira into the garment with a few colorful imprecations of her own, the maid only took half a breath before commencing the next bulk of her muttered diatribe. "*What* in the blazing world are ya about? Do ya know what this makes ya look like around here—do ya? A bloody barmy American, that's what. Ya rise at the crack of dawn, then tear out into the morning like a half-deranged harpy, chasing God only knows what for God only knows what reason, and *now*—"

"I'm sure she had her reasons."

Upon the first syllable of that interruption, Kira whirled back around. The next moment, not yet balanced from *that* action, she stumbled backward by three more frantic steps. She tripped over Fred then collided into Ally, nearly toppling the three of them to the pathway in a mortifying heap.

The entire cause for her bumblings now stood forty inches away in truth, his gaze affixed to her with that same unfaltering attention. His posture emanated that same primal contemplation, and his proximity affected her in the same thought-robbing way it had when he'd first loomed over her in the forest...only the ordeal was worse now. Worse, because unlike three days ago, the man now cloaked all his thoughts and feelings behind a façade of disarmingly smooth calm and devastatingly beautiful masculinity.

"My lady," Damien Sharpe said then, dipping a slight bow—but not before flicking her a gaze that appeared suspiciously amused. "We meet again. Good morning."

"M'lady Kira." The salutation burst off Tom's lips with decidedly more urgency. "Forgive this intrusion to your morning ablutions." He finished with a pointed glare in Sharpe's direction. "Mister Sharpe was just leaving."

Not everyone present was in agreement about that, however. Unprovoked in any way except Tom's assertion, the cockatoo let out a sudden screech that prompted grimaces to each face in their gathering, even Sharpe's. They repeated the looks when Fred retorted to the bird with a hearty shriek of his own.

"Bloody Mary," Tom grumbled. "It's like a friggin' jungle in here."

"Imagine that," Sharpe quipped back, and Kira giggled. Saints, she couldn't help the mirth; no more than she could control the sense that with the brief exchange, she and this Yorkshire-style frontier man had become sudden allies in whatever this confrontation had become.

Nor could she deny the strange, sweet admission that she...*liked* that alliance.

"Cleo's probably just hungry," Sharpe said to Tom, but it was only when he raised a gentle finger to the cockatoo's neck that Kira realized he offered a defense on behalf of the creature. He went on in a murmur, this time to the bird, "It's not easy spending the night in a cold forest, is it, Princess? No, I didn't think so. But I'm happy you have such pretty feathers, so I was able to see you up in that tree this morning."

Fascinated, Kira watched the bird respond to the man's silken tone. Hesitantly at first, but with gaining trust, Cleo basked in Sharpe's soft adulation like a true member of her gender, "answering" the man with soft trills and seductive stretches. Eventually, she scooted her way up to his shoulder, where she began to gnaw on his ear with affectionate coyness.

Sharpe's reaction to the flirtation didn't fascinate Kira any more. This time, he just plain stunned her.

The man looked at the cockatoo and broke into a smile. A full, white, stop-the-breath-in-her-throat-with-its-beauty smile.

And yet, she noticed the next moment...not a glimmer of that smile ever ignited in his eyes.

"It...was very kind of you to bring her back," Kira offered then, growing more furious with her voice by the moment.

She'd performed for mayors and opera stars, even an Indian chief once, and never had trouble sputtering words out as she did now. Yet that Indian chief had never caused her to wonder how his fingers would feel against *her* body...

"Cleo is a fine animal," Sharpe answered her then, though in continuing to watch him, she heard the words as secondary sound. Her body had become a thudding cacophony from his potent nearness...from his brilliant, lonely smile.

"Y-yes," she managed to stammer back. "A white cockatoo. My father will be grateful to you for saving her life."

As much as the man had taken her by surprise with his princely smoothness, he jolted her now by shattering that mien with a caustic laugh. "Grateful," he repeated, though the word might as well have been scooped from a gutter in Whitehall. "Well, thank you, my lady. I'll hold that knowledge close to my heart."

And your horse will jump over the moon tonight, too, came the rejoinder from her heart. Deepening her surprise was the confession of how deeply that realization stung—and how maddeningly little she knew of why she had to feel this pain.

What in damn tarnation had happened around here before she arrived? And what did Damien Sharpe have to do with it, that everyone in Scottney Hall treated his gesture of neighborly kindness like a visit from a leper, instead?

And why did *she* yearn to ignore all of them and their mysterious hatred, and thank this man with much more than some silly mumbled words? Perhaps she could give him the meal he'd obviously *not* had last night, judging by the snarl from his stomach at the waft of sausage and bread from the kitchens. Or maybe the hair trim he was in need of, as he impatiently raked back the shoulder-length thickness of what used to be a more civilized appearance.

Or a hug.

God, she wondered when Damien Sharpe had last received a hug.

Tom clearly didn't share her pondering. On a stomp forward, he growled, "That's enough, Sharpe. The bird isn't a calling card, and you're no welcome caller."

At *that*, Kira refused to sit by in such docile acquiescence. She lunged forward herself, aiming at her belligerent servant, until a hand held her back. She followed the ensuing arm up to Sharpe's face, now firmly affixed with its mask of pleasant composure once more.

"Thanks for clearing up that confusion for me, Tom," he stated as if the man had given him road directions to London, not a tactless order to the door. "And I could have sworn that was my calling card on my shoulder when I left the house this morning."

Again, Kira found herself giggling. And Tom's glower worsening. "Why the bloody hell *did* you come?" the manservant snarled, resentment powering the words more than curiosity. "Why, Damien? You could have sent the bird back with one of our herdsmen, or at the least, left it at the outer wall."

"Tom," Kira interjected. "The Spanish Inquisition ended twenty years ago."

"This isn't just about the bird, is it?" Tom persisted instead. "Is it, Damien? *Why* did you come, Damien?"

Fight back! Kira goaded inwardly at Sharpe herself. *Tell the* sabahka *to go to hell! Better yet, send him there yourself!*

But Sharpe complied with neither of her pleas. The worst of the ordeal was, he looked like he burned to do so. Instead, with jaw convulsing reflexively and eyes glittering trenchantly, he gazed back at Tom, and spoke in a guttural murmur that reminded Kira more of a lad apologizing for recalcitrant behavior.

"You're right, Tom. It's time for me to go."

He didn't care about Cleo's objecting shrieks this time. Nor did he care about her frantic flappings as he coerced her to climb from his arm to Tom's. And he certainly didn't care about the battle Tom now waged to calm the cockatoo.

And again, as Damien Sharpe whirled on one heel and strode swiftly out of the Menagerie, he didn't care about affording Kira even one last parting glance.

★ ★ ★ ★

"This was a bad idea," Damien rebuked himself in a low rumble as he traversed the portico as fast as possible, back to the Main Courtyard and the comfort of Dante's saddle.

No, his mind instantly appended to the statement, *this was* worse *than a bad idea. This was an idiotic mistake, and now you'll pay for it during many days to come.*

Many days...and nights.

Nights in which sleep would elude him because he envisioned *her.*

Her...God, yes, *her,* the creature who'd appeared in the doorway of that building all hair-tousled and pink-cheeked, as if she'd bolted straight from bed to the heights of the north moors this morning. She'd been more gorgeous than he remembered, this captivating little American, with her hair spilling around her shoulders and over the bodice of her virtuous—yet quite diaphanous—nightrail.

Dear Christ, that nightrail. It would be the cause of half a dozen sleepless midnights to come, as he recalled its filmy texture against the dark copper disks encircling her nipples... then hugging the dusky triangle where her belly ended and his fantasies began...

"Christ," he emitted then, on a soft, scathing laugh. *What the bloody hell are you contemplating fantasies for, Damien? What makes you think you can afford a luxury like fantasies?*

Better than any answer his logic could devise came the melodious chimes from the chapel bell tower. Though the grand stone structure was situated nearly a quarter mile away as Cleo would fly, the reverent tune rendered silent all living things within a mile's radius of Scottney Hall. Seven thirty and all was well, the Scottneys reminded the world.

No, Damien revised to that. The Scottneys *commanded* the world.

He reached Dante and mounted the stallion with brutal speed. The horse immediately stomped on the cobblestones, reflecting Damien's tension back at him more accurately than a mirror. "Yes, boy," he murmured, slanting a grim smile. "I agree with you. Let's get out of this barmy bin."

In under a minute, morning dew and long-stemmed grass flew again from Dante's racing hooves over the open hills. The air was bracing and clean, the sky a pristine slate of periwinkle and gray. With a deep inhalation, Damien gave his equine friend another two inches of rein. This was much better, he decided as the ground flew beneath them. All was as it should be. No shrieking cockatoos. No cackling chimpanzees. No glowering Scottney Hall minions.

No nightrail-clad hoydens.

The vilest of oaths exploded off his lips at the unwelcome

resurgence of her image in his head. Again, Dante translated that rage into an even more forceful stride, turning the ground beneath them into a furious blur, threatening Damien's seat if they came upon any sizable obstacle or interruption.

Damien only gritted a challenging smile at the possibility. Truth be known, he relished the idea of being thrown clear to his arse. Hell, he'd *thank* Dante for the favor, for giving him a good jolt in the part of his body he'd been thinking most strongly with this morning. The part which he now forced to listen to his head. And his heart.

The head and heart which now told him Tom was right. He hadn't gone to Scottney Hall about the bloody bird.

CHAPTER NINE

"M'lady? M'lady! M'lady Kira, for blessed sake, yer out here in nothin' but yer nightrail!"

Kira couldn't discern if Ally's rasp carried more fear for her health or her character. At the moment, *she* cared for neither. Though she'd felt the maid rush up behind her and frantically fling the robe around her shoulders, she'd been numb to help Ally. She'd been oblivious to the weather, the day and the time, too. As a matter of fact, her senses still tried to claw their way past the feeling this wasn't *her* who stood here; that indeed, a lush paradise rose around her in reality and not her dreams...that indeed, a dark, wild-maned creature named Damien Sharpe had been reality and not fantasy.

That indeed, the effect he had on her was real.

And frightening.

At that, she sincerely hoped Ally wasn't wasting time fretting over her character. She had none when that man looked at her...as if she were naked. As if she were naked...and he was touching her that way.

Khvahtit! she vehemently ordered her mind then. *Enough! Stop it!* But though she italicized the command by jerking the quilted satin folds tighter around her, her breasts still shivered in taut new awareness; a million intense tremors still assaulted her entire body; her imagination still swirled with the remembrance of Damien Sharpe's black, captivating stare...as if he saw every midnight fantasy she'd ever had, and how to make them come true.

For the Lord's own sake! The man did *not* care about her fantasies! He'd barely held himself to basic civility when speaking to Tom, and he'd run from *this* amazing sanctuary as if it had suddenly been declared infected with the plague—though she was certain its standing as Scottney property made it even worse in his eyes.

She was also certain he beheld her in nothing but the same way. As a hated piece of Scottney property. Something to ruin for the sake of—

What?

What had happened in this beautiful piece of the world, to make people glare at each other with such ugly anger? What kept them doing so? What was so important that they considered such hatred worth the effort?

And why did she care?

The answer to at least the last query came during the trip back up to her bedroom. It came as her memory filled once more with the vision of the man's face as he'd caressed Cleo. He'd smiled that dazzling smile, unknowingly intensifying the captivating degree of his rugged handsomeness, but that happiness had never reached his *eyes*. In the depths of his gaze, she'd still looked upon an unwanted outsider, a lonely outcast.

And she realized she cared because she'd stood in his boots a hundred times in her life. Perhaps her feet had been clad in moccasins or show slippers, and she'd stood on train station porches or city boardwalks instead of a pathway in an exotic menagerie, but her footing had been the same: scared and unsure.

"Hell," she rasped...as she admitted her heart stood there even now. She crossed the room, sank onto the window seat, and let her lips repeat the oath while her stare sought out the silhouette of the forest on the horizon, where he'd most likely retreated.

"That's about the truth of it," came Ally's breathless interjection. Kira heard the maid rush around the bed, swishing muslin and scrunching crinolines as she went. "Hell—yeah, that's the best name for what we're both lookin' at, if I don't get ya dressed now, m'lady. M'lady, *please;* are ya givin' me even half an ear?"

She wanted to oblige Ally. She wished she could let the maid turn her into at least the representation of a lady, shedding all thoughts of Damien Sharpe as easily as she discarded the nightclothes he'd stared at her so brazenly in.

Instead, as Fred climbed up into her lap, she held out a hand to the maid, and softly requested, "Ally, come here." As the maid's eyes rolled, she stressed, "Please."

A grimace of hesitant understanding corkscrewed Ally's lips. "I'm *not* gonna thank myself for this," she muttered as she crossed to the window seat, dragging every stitch of Kira's clothes along with her.

Yet once the maid was seated and looked expectantly to her, Kira found herself caught in another mire of wordless paralysis. She looked back out the window, seeking inspiration from the forest demon visions which still haunted her from the distorted glass—but as usual, nothing profound or eloquent translated from her mind to her lips. Only the truth of her heart's confusion burst forward and blurted out.

"Tell me about him," she asked her friend without a note of vacillation. "Tell me about Damien Sharpe."

Crinolines and muslin rustled uncomfortably. "I—I don't know a thing about Damien Sharpe."

"Hell's bells you don't," Kira countered. "Everyone at Scottney Hall does. It's as quiet around here as if the Pope passed through."

Ally spurted out a giggle. "Damien Sharpe and the Pope have *nothin'* in common."

Kira quirked up one side of her own mouth. "Tell me something I don't know, please."

That hesitating scowl attacked Ally's face again. Only this time, the maid deflected the assault, directing it straight at Kira. Finally, she moaned, "Ohhh, I guess yer gonna hear things, anyway!" She shoved aside the crinolines to motion Kira closer, as she murmured, "Though Lady Aleece has promised to beat, then discharge anyone heard speakin' of it."

The maid glanced up at Kira as she finished. Kira looked deeply into her friend's green eyes and knew the maid didn't jest by one syllable. With that realization, she fished through the yards of material for Ally's hands, gripping them hard once she'd found them. "If Lady Trevor lays a hand on you," she vowed, "I'll beat then discharge *her*."

Ally gave a quick smile at that, but the look fell far short of the giggle Kira expected. The maid was truly risking her position to have this conversation! Kira reassured her friend she'd meant her promise by not letting go of Ally's hands, but nevertheless, drew in a long, deep breath. What *was* to be the significance of this discussion? What was she about to learn of Damien Sharpe, that Scottney Hall servants were threatened bodily and emotionally about its exposure?

Or maybe the question should be: did she *want* to learn those things now?

Her heart swiftly supplied her head with the answer to that. That reply was neither yes nor no. She had no choice. She *had* to know what force had carved out the endless chasms in that man's eyes.

"Go ahead, Ally," she prompted her friend. She gave the juncture of their hands a reassuring squeeze.

The maid took in a deep breath of her own then. "I suppose ya want it from the beginnin'." Her nod corresponded with Kira's. "All right, then. At the beginnin', Damien's was as welcome a face around here as they came."

"That doesn't surprise me. He...seemed quite familiar with everything this morning."

"Yes, well, he should be. He was over here enough when courtin' Miss Rachelle five years ago."

Kira aimed a scowl at the maid. A *deep* scowl. "Miss *who*?"

"Rachelle." Ally looked up at Kira in amazed scrutiny. "Bloody blazes. They didn't even tell ya about Miss Rachelle? Lady Aleece's daughter?"

"Aunt Aleece has a *daughter*?" A daughter. That meant she had a cousin...somewhere. That also meant Nicholas had lied to her back in London. *Aleece has no children*, he'd proclaimed with that look she'd actually pitied. *You're the only one.* And yet, the facts still didn't all fit together...

"But..." she stammered, "how did she...Aunt Aleece isn't married—"

"Anymore," Ally filled in with a sage nod. "Three weeks after she married Miles Denhope, he went to inspect one of his mines over in Gunnerside. He never came back out. It was one of the most huge cave-ins anyone remembers there."

Kira gasped. "*Bidnyahshka*. That poor woman. Three weeks a bride before becoming a widow."

"*And* a mother." The maid leveled a corroborating stare in answer to Kira's stunned gape. "Yes, indeed," she pronounced.

"Lady Aleece was already in the family way; only then, she had no family. Lord Scottney, the angel, moved her right back in to Scottney Hall. After Rachelle was born, he became a father to her in every way except truly siring her."

While the child who truly had his blood was led to believe he was dead. Whom he *treated as dead.*

Kira's mind and heart finished the statement in unison, one resonating with fury and the other resounding in sorrow. The emotions were useless to her now, she struggled to reason with herself, but she couldn't stop the sense of loss from pervading her...the sense of shock in now knowing Nicholas had *not* spent all these years in lonely seclusion, as she'd believed with such thorough pity back in London. As she'd been *led* to believe back in London.

Though she battled to say the words with civility, the best pronunciation she managed of her next words came in the form of a slow, clenched effort. "Aleece has a *daughter.*"

"*Had* a daughter," Ally corrected her one more time.

Kira's scowl returned. "What do you mean?"

At first, the maid just stared out the window, toward the deep-green blobs which were the hills toward Middleham. As she did, a strange sheen came over her gaze, and her lower lip trembled. "Just what I said, m'lady. Aleece *had* a daughter...but no more. No more. God rest sweet Miss Rachelle's soul."

"God rest—she's *dead?*"

Ally slid her eyes shut as ample affirmation. "She was... murdered."

"She was..." Kira gulped hard on a tight, pain-filled throat. "*What?*"

"Six months ago," Ally plunged on. "Six months." She shook her head and emitted a desperate, I-can-do-nothing-else laugh. "Feels like six years sometimes; things've changed so much."

"But—" Kira stammered, her mind clawing through confusion thick as London fog. "But were they sure it was—are they positive she was actually—"

"She was stabbed ten times," came the blunt rebuttal. "Yes, they're positive it was murder."

Kira's breath left her in jagged intervals. Fred picked that moment to demand she join him in a clapping game, but she shooed even her pet away, battling to accept what she'd heard as truth. She'd expected the "Scottney secret" to be some affair more illicit than her father and mother's; maybe the existence of another estranged love child, hidden away some place like the Caribbean.

Not murder. Dear God, never murder.

Kira thought of Aunt Aleece then—and admitted a new, tender understanding of the woman's vacillation between chilly aloofness and outright icy overbearance. Sweet saints, the devastation her heart must still be enduring. What grief must have flooded everyone here, this collected "family" in this majestic castle, many of them probably lifelong friends with Lady Rachelle. What rage they must all still be battling—

Dear God. What rage *he* must be battling.

"Damien," she blurted then. "*Bozhy moj*...Damien. Was he still courting Rachelle when this happened?"

"Courtin'?" Ally rejoined, her tone a surge of irony. "He was two years married to her by then."

"Oh..."

She forced out the reply, though it sounded more three syllables than one, choked out in hurting increments from her suddenly dry, tight throat. "Oh..." she finally repeated, "oh,

Damien. I can't imagine what he must have endured. What pain he must have..."

Ally's sardonic snort cut her short then—an outburst the maid had obviously tried to hold in check, though could do so no longer. "I'm afraid there aren't too many in Yorkshire who share yer sentiments, m'lady," she sneered, clearly including herself in that contingent.

"Why?" Kira fired back. "For Lord's sake, why?"

Ally preceded her answer by scooping *Kira's* hands back into *hers*. She inhaled and exhaled, her breath shaking through both, the strength of her derision clearly fleeing the information she prepared to convey now.

"M'lady...when they found Rachelle's body...Damien was standin' right over her."

Kira didn't know how long *she* took to breathe again. She only knew that when she did, it hurt. It hurt like hell. But not in her lungs. It hurt in her heart.

"Wh-what?" she at last heard herself rasp. There was more Ally had more to tell her, right? There was another conclusion to reach other than the image her mind conjured now...in blood-red detail. She was certain of it. She waited, chewing the insides of her lips and impatiently jiggling her right leg, for the maid to go on.

Ally did continue—but the details formed a horrific nightmare, not a justifiable explanation. "He was covered in her blood," she murmured, "though there wasn't a scratch on *him*. And he was just standin' there, as if waitin' for them to come find him."

"Nobody thought *that* a little odd?" Kira leapt onto the detail as if it were a trapeze platform in a show with no net.

Ally, however, wasted little time in yanking out that

support. "Apparently not," she said with a shrug. "Constable Wickins said he'd seen things like that happen before...the killer goin' into a shock after he committed the deed, or some such rubbish like that."

"But they never convicted him." Kira found another stronghold with encouraging speed; this time, she grinned with the undeniable triumph. "He's free today. They never convicted him."

"They never convicted him," Ally confirmed—though her voice lilted to clear the way for a deliberate pause. After that pause, she quipped, "But they might as well should've."

Kira glared. "What do you mean?"

"The trial was very long, very ugly, and very public." Ally leaned her head back against the wall, her expression glazing as her mind recreated those months-ago events. "Damien was one of Yorkshire's most muckity-muck citizens and businessmen, and Rachelle was his perfect wife and hostess."

"I don't suppose she learned at the Lady Aleece School for Wives and Hostesses," Kira grumbled.

"She knew her stuff because she had to put it to use every hour of the day," came the matter-of-fact response.

Ally followed that by leaning forward and pressing a finger to the window. "Follow me here fer a moment," she directed. "Ya know that blob over there is Damien's forest, right? Now, if ya trace a line from that point to the other forest, which ya can see out the east window—" She motioned across the bedroom to a smaller set of panes. "And imagine another border stretching north, nearly to Castle Bolton...all of that's Hyperion's Walk. That's the estate Damien owned the day they took him to York in handcuffs."

The maid paused in expectant stillness, as if waiting for

the fuse of her statement to burn into Kira's brain and explode in its stunning impact—which it did. "*All* of it?" Kira forced her slack jaw to form the words.

"Every last acre," Ally verified. "Until the trial."

With the qualifier, even the maid's voice dropped an octave with compassion. Kira was now positive she didn't want to hear an answer, but forced herself to ask, anyway: "What happened?"

"Well, first, the obvious. Wickins and his men never did scrape up enough evidence to convict Damien. But they speculated and implied enough to ruin him. And that they did."

The embers of the previous explosion in Kira's mind now furled their way into her soul, where the fires became molten outrage. It nearly burned away her reason, this searing wrath; yet she knew she only felt a spark's worth of what Damien Sharpe had endured in a York County courtroom a handful of months ago, when he'd lost first his queen, then his kingdom.

And at last, she began to understand the bottomless chasms of the man's eyes.

She rose from the seat and paced to the east window, taking in the vastness of the lush green horizon, dotted here and there with neat gray farmer's cottages. Plumes of equally orderly smoke curled from the structures' stone chimneys, disappearing at last on gentle puffs of morning wind.

"He lost it all, didn't he?" she murmured. She heard her voice catch and struggled to tamp the grief *she* felt just looking at those cottages. Her effort was futile. Those cottages, she thought, were filled with family he didn't have...with peace he'd never know.

"He had no choice," came Ally's disarmingly pragmatic answer. "Hyperion's Walk went without a leader for four weeks. When Damien returned, he walked into chaos. The tenants had kept up with their crops, only to find out nobody wanted them. They couldn't get credit to cover their losses, either. Damien was trusted no longer, and neither were they."

Kira squeezed her eyes shut and bit hard on the insides of her lips. "What did he do?"

"Joined the bats in his bloody bellfry, if ya ask me," came the anger-tinged reply. Ally needed no other urging to continue past the questioning look Kira tilted over her shoulder. "The dolt thought he could make everythin' all right again. He wasted another three months tryin' to do it, too. In the meantime, Hyperion's tenants were well near starvin' to death!" The maid punctuated with a violent upsweep of a hand which more than bespoke her personal concern in this part of the story.

"What happened after three months?" Kira asked with careful calmness, though she yearned to shout, *What happened, indeed? What happened to Damien's people, that they stopped trusting him, too, Ally? What happened that they tried and convicted him, even when the courts couldn't?*

"He did what he should've to begin with," Ally declared then. "He put aside his damnable pride and turned the Walk over to somebody who *could* do something with it."

Kira studied her friend's face as she approached the window seat again. "He sold the estate?" she ventured, albeit with a lilt of astoundment. The maid's affirming nod, however, came as no surprise. Still, Kira pressed, "All of it? To one person?"

"Indeed," Ally proclaimed, her tone resonating with such warm veneration that visions of the Pope swirled again in Kira's imagination.

"And such a person existed, waiting there in the wings to 'just take the place off his hands'?"

She delivered that with arms folded belligerently across her chest—which heightened her awareness of her heart's startled skip at Ally's impassioned comeback.

"Rolf Pembroke was very near a saint about it!" the maid proclaimed. "Gawwds, I don't know what they would've done over there without that man. He's an angel, that one; I'm sure of it."

"Rolf Pembroke," Kira repeated, searching her memory to confirm the name didn't tug any bells of familiarity in her mind. No, she was certain neither Aleece nor Nicholas had mentioned this person yet. The occurrence seemed odd, judging by the deepening mists of "Rolf reverence" in Ally's eyes.

"Who is he," she urged the maid, "besides a visiting angel?"

"He grew up with Damien at the Walk," Ally clarified. "Rolf's father was Chief Steward to Kenrick Sharpe, Damien's father. The boys were as close as brothers, maybe closer, even after they grew into hearty lads. They went off to London and sowed their oats together, and it's even rumored they saved each other's lives more'n a few times!"

Kira gave an appropriately impressed nod. She waited for the story to continue, expecting to next hear of Damien and Rolf's adventures as tropical pirates or riverboat gamblers.

"When they at last came back home and set themselves to serious matters, Damien worked to command the world of Yorkshire farmin' *and* Lady Rachelle's hand in marriage. Rolf built himself a small London shippin' empire. They kept seein' each other on holidays and the like, of course, even though

Rolf got himself a fine home just over in York, but they never really found the time—"

"Until Rachelle's murder."

Ally confirmed that with an emphatic hand gesture. "Rolf put a new meanin' to the word friendship then, I swear it to ya, m'lady. He was at Damien's side through every minute of that trial, exceptin' the days he saw to everyone at the Walk, of course."

"He walked on water while he did this, too?" Kira interjected, though her solemn tone conveyed she *did* pay credence to Ally's account.

"He might as well have," Ally rejoined, her own inflection expressing she balanced the words between sardonicism and seriousness. "No matter how he did it, that man went endlessly back and forth, betwixt here and York like a bloody bob toy, but he never ached or moaned about the ordeal even once."

Kira nodded once more, but hid her troublement at how much effort it took to do so with conviction. "It...sounds like they were lucky to have him," she murmured. It sounded more like the man was the second Messiah, she mused cynically, and the rest of the world hadn't discovered that fact yet.

What *wasn't* Ally telling her about the man?

"Now ya can understand a bit of the shock everyone felt when Damien first refused to sell to Rolf," the maid proclaimed huffily then. "God only knows, the deal was the solution for everybody's quandaries, especially Damien's."

"God only knows," Kira echoed, and was answered with Ally's satisfied nod. The maid was clearly pleased with herself, taking Kira's reply as an articulation not only of agreement, but understanding.

But she *didn't* understand—nor was she certain she

wanted to understand. No, Kira resolved, she never wanted to empathize with a person who dedicated themselves so wholly to the excellence of a goal, who inspired so many others in pursuing the ideal, as well, only to veer off the path when the bearings got hazy and the shimmer of gold provided an easier road.

Damien Sharpe had *not* left his path.

He'd been forced off of it.

She immediately chastised herself for that presumption. She no more knew about Damien Sharpe's financial leadership abilities than Ally knew about Rolf Pembroke's water-walking prowess—though that fact didn't stop her friend from letting out yet a stronger sigh then, followed this time by a ridiculously high-pitched titter.

"Betwixt you and I, m'lady," she followed in a conspiratorial murmur, "I've sinned on more'n a few occasions, wishin' it was *our* lands that man had cause to take over. The girls from the Walk tell me it's like waitin' on a god with Mister Pembroke. It's not just that he looks like Adonis, mind ya, because to my thinkin', they make much too much of that, but they also say he's even glorious in the mornin', as polite as a prince when he sits to the bloody breakfast table. Can you imagine that!"

Kira was rescued from having to form an answer to that when her bedroom door suddenly swung open. On the other hand, she rectified, she might have indulged in her relief too swiftly; so far, she hadn't come to associate Aunt Aleece's arrival in any room with any kind of salvation fantasy.

"Kira!" the woman exclaimed as if she'd been out sprinting on the moors, though her step didn't lag by one frantic step as she rounded the bed. "Heavens above, you haven't even begun to dress yet!"

"M'lady Aleece!" Ally vaulted up from the window seat, clutching Kira's clothes as if shielding her own nakedness. "I was just—we were just startin' to—well, and then there was a disturbance and we were out in the Menagerie, and—"

"I heard all about the disturbance, Ally," the woman snapped, her tone perfectly matching her high-necked, stiff-starched black and white day ensemble. With concurrent impatience, she jabbed one stray strand of hair back behind her right ear, then stabbed glares at both the maid and Kira.

But unlike Ally, Kira didn't genuflect her gaze one inch for the woman. "Ally's been valiantly attempting to dress me for the last hour, Aunt Aleece," she stated just as evenly. "My state of undress is my fault, not hers."

"I am aware of that as well, Lady Kira." Again, the words might as well have been woven of those black and white threads—though Aleece returned her regard to Ally with a noticeable gentleness. "Please dress her quickly, Ally. I've learned we must expedite the beginning of our lessons. It's essential we start post haste; we've much to go over in just two days."

Kira frowned as a foreboding chill seeped to her bones then, having nothing to do with the brisk wind shivering the window at her shoulder. "What happens in two days that's so darn special?"

She wouldn't have believed the phenomenon had she not witnessed it personally, but before her and Ally's eyes, Aleece transformed into another person then. A person resembling a ten-year-old about to share a delicious secret, lips curled upward in coy mystery, eyes twinkling in mischief.

"It seems that our return to Yorkshire has caused quite excitement," she divulged, pleasure resonating deeply in her voice. "And now, that excitement shall be the *right* sort, as well!"

"The right sort?" Kira lifted a baffled brow. There was a *wrong* way to be excited?

"How wonderful, m'lady Aleece!" Ally crooned. "Please do tell how!"

Aleece's smile grew ridiculously huge then. Still, she paused like an inexperienced soprano milking a dramatic moment for everything it was worth. "Rolf Pembroke has chosen to personally endorse our presence...by agreeing to join us for a formal dinner two nights hence!"

Ally gasped, then shrieked.

Kira swallowed, then swore.

CHAPTER TEN

She swore many more times during the next forty-eight hours. The epithets possessed nearly an equal number of motives—all thoroughly legitimate, Kira justified.

Her instigations ranged from Aunt Aleece's insistence on selecting every thread she wore tonight, to being ordered off the main stairwell because it had been polished to a perfect mahoghany sheen, to the realization she'd not get to visit the Menagerie before sunset due to a posture lesson that ran two hours overtime. When she finally declared to Aleece she'd been walking since the age of one and needed no further help at the task now, thank you, her escape from the room only led her upstairs, to where Ally fretted as if the Emperor of blazing China was expected for dinner. After watching the maid flit around like that for only ten minutes, Kira began to suspect Rolf Pembroke was the monarch himself in disguise.

She'd been tempted to swear twice then. But now she was glad she hadn't, for *this* moment deserved the advent more. Still, she almost laughed her way through the expletives, for they were prompted not by frustration or exasperation or a drop of fury.

Kira swore out of sheer amazement.

Standing before the three-sided reflecting glass in her dressing room, she openly gawked at the creature in the glass, certain the image was some fancy stage trickery wielded at her expense. That respectable Englishwoman couldn't be her.

That refined beauty, in the gown of quilted dark-pink satin layered with an overskirt sculpted of heavy iridescent lace, wasn't *her*. That certainly wasn't her hair, either, coiled and wound around a "crown" of fresh pink roses, then cascading to her neck in a multitude of shiny curls and satin ribbons.

"It's beautiful, Ally," she pronounced, touching fingers to the tiny, perfect ringlets at her temples. "Thank you."

"Heavens, m'lady," the maid replied on a humble giggle, "it's just a bit of a coiffure."

"It's *artwork*," Kira insisted. She straightened and again took in the whole of her reflection. She would have shaken her head with the impact of her surprise, but by no means would she risk turning Ally's mastery into disarray. "I'll be tarred and feathered," she murmured. "It *is* me, isn't it?"

Ally's contented sigh answered that. "Indeed, m'lady."

"Nothing I ever wore in the show compared to this."

"Ya look beautiful. Like a princess."

"She looks like a *queen*."

Kira swiveled a startled gaze to the doorway on the heels of her maid's similar look. But by the time her sights alighted on the dashing figure standing there, a smile graced her lips. Only Fred, who dallied with a left-over length of ribbon on the floor, missed the unmistakable surge of pride in her father's voice. Nicholas's handsome face was stamped with equal conviction; with genuine feeling this time, not some expression he'd tried to copy from Roza.

"Welcome home, my lord," Kira greeted, gracefully stretching out her hand and receiving her father's dutiful kiss on the knuckles. Again, she fought the temptation to shake her head in bewilderment. Twenty-four hours ago, she'd chortled her way through Aunt Aleece's tutelage of this action, feeling clumsier than an elephant trying to balance on a thimble. Now, the pose felt born from years of familiarity.

"Was your trip pleasant?" she queried of him then.

"Pleasant enough," Nicholas answered. "But it's good to be here now, with you." He lifted a tentative smile. "I missed you. Did you...miss me?"

Kira was tempted to answer him in the negative. Memories of her window seat talk with Ally two days ago, and the stunning details she'd discovered there, still burned strongly in her mind—but not so fresh that they stung anymore. Now, she admitted feeling confused more than hurt, and she wanted to know more about the cousin who was probably the closest thing she'd ever have to a sister. She yearned to talk about her feelings with Nicholas, when they could steal a private moment together.

Because of that admission, she answered her father as honestly as she could. "Perhaps," she hedged, trying to give an encouraging smile of her own. "Yes, perhaps I missed you a little, too."

"Good." Her father's eyes twinkled with even more charming gold lights as he kissed her hand again. "Good." He took her in from head to toe again. "My." He chuckled. "You do clean up well, daughter."

She batted him playfully with her fan. "You're not such a peasant yourself, my lord."

As a matter of fact, her father formed one of the most striking sights she'd ever seen, flawlessly turned out in his black swallow-tailed dinner jacket with matching breeches and shined ankle boots. Crisp white accouterments gave his ensemble a noble finish, from his impeccably-tied stock to his snowy evening gloves.

"Shall we?" Nicholas proposed then, offering her the crook of his arm as he turned back toward the door.

"Must we?" As she issued the discomfited mutter, she felt an elephant again. She attempted to close her fan in one fluid motion, but instead whacked herself in the face with the contraption's pearl framework.

Doing his best to hide a snicker, Nicholas replied, "Well, no, we absolutely mustn't. You may dine up here if you like. I'm certain Ally will be happy to fetch your plate from the kitchen, as soon as she's helped you change out of your gown into something more—"

"*No.*" The protest spilled off Kira's lips before she realized what she'd actually expressed by it. With a resigned sigh, she inwardly conceded the truth: that the London "couture tortures," as she'd come to call those endless fittings, had been worth every tedious moment. That being the "pretty one" of the party felt nice...very nice. And that she wasn't ready to change into "something more comfortable" yet.

With that decision, she hooked her arm to her father's with gritted determination. "Lead on, Lord Scottney. I'm not ready to say goodnight yet, no matter how torturous this...um... adventure may be."

"That, my dear," her father murmured as he molded a protective hand atop hers, "was spoken like a true Scottney."

Kira waited for her stomach to flip over into a disturbed squirm at that statement. Instead, to her intensifying shock, nothing but warmth inundated her belly and swelled its way up to the corners of her mouth. Ten days ago, she would have vehemently denied this moment would ever happen. Hell, *two* days ago, she would have denounced it.

But her father had made her smile...really smile. No

matter how many times he'd made Rachelle do the same thing, it mattered most that he did it for *her* right now. It mattered that he'd lent her a dose of his Lord Scottney-sized strength when she needed it the most. For that, she silently deemed him her hero for this evening, no matter what happened with the man waiting downstairs to meet her now.

At *that* thought, her stomach began its acrobatics. As Nicholas and she neared the main stairwell, the cartwheels and somersaults increased. *Glide, glide*, she exhorted at herself between measured breaths. *A lady doesn't walk*—she repeated in the same sing-song Aleece had used to instruct her—*a lady glides...glide, glide!*

That litany almost became *slide, slide* as they reached the stairwell in all its meticulously polished glory. The moment Kira stepped onto the wood with her slippers, they provided as much stability as Mama's tea leaves on a pool of oil. Thank the saints Nicholas was in full hero form this evening; he prevented her from taking a full tumble by securing an iron-like grip around her waist, making her near-catastrophe appear merely a slight misstep.

"Well," he declared as he did, chuckling heartily to give her a moment for composure, "here she is at last, everyone."

"Wonderful!" someone answered from the foot of the stairs in a honey-sweet croon—nearly causing Kira to lose her footing again. She blinked in astonishment. Was that exclamation coming from the mouth of the same woman who'd practically drilled her like a military cadet for the last two days?

Surely enough, as Aleece shooshed her way up a few steps, the dulcet tone accompanied her in fine form. "My dear!" she effused, beckoning to Kira with both hands outstretched. "You look absolutely lovely!"

"Thank you," Kira returned, though the second syllable lilted with uncertainty. Should she curtsy now? Salute? She didn't know; Aunt Aleece's face didn't change from its countenance of shining poise. "You're a pretty choice tomato tonight, too, Aunt Aleece," she finally said, and smiled to show much she meant it. Her aunt was a radiant sight this evening, in a royal-blue gown ornamented with glittering violet trims.

The woman didn't lose that luster even as her features *did* flinch, clearly telling Kira "choice tomato" wasn't the best "choice" of words for the situation. Within the next moment, however, a courtly smile again took center stage on her face, and she let out a giggle as thin but valiant as a tin bell. "Oh, Kira," she tittered, "how I am enchanted with the amusing things you say!"

"It's not difficult to see why."

The smooth baritone words hurled an expectant, thick silence across the entire foyer. Kira blatantly understood why. Though the Emperor of China indeed didn't stand waiting in the gaudy, gilt-framed doorway of the Grand Hall, she discerned there'd be no difference between the monarch and this man other than appearance. Standing regal and tall yet comfortable and confident, here was a person who knew exactly what effect his chiseled features and golden blonde hair had on a room. Many liked to say a person like him had "presence." If that were so, then "presence" oozed from him like drippings down a sleek golden candle.

Which isn't a horrid attribute, came a warning voice from inside. *Barnum has presence. Isaac Van Amburgh has presence. Tarnation, even Queen Victoria has it.*

Give him the benefit of a doubt, Kira.

"Mister Pembroke, I assume," she murmured, pleased with the pleasantly level cadence of her tone. Not bad at all, for someone wrestling through her first hour in a fifteen pounds of satin and a coiffure too perfect to be taken in public.

"My Lady Kira," he responded, "you assume correctly."

As he took her hand and leaned over it, she couldn't hold back the impression that she once more touched one of Sheena's snakes, with its scales so smooth...and cold. The sensation found no surcease even in the seamless continuation of his assured tone, as he gazed at her and stated, "It would be my honor and pleasure to escort you into our meal." His next comment, however, he directed solely at her father. "Cook announced the pheasant's readiness just moments before you two came down, Nicholas."

"Splendid," Nicholas returned, all joviality and comradery as he in turn offered his arm to Aleece. "Splendid, Rolf. Lead on!"

And so she was passed off from her hero of the evening to the man allowed to call her father by his first name, to call her aunt everything from "a radiant vision in blue" to "a sublime hostess" and to call *her* nothing at all—choosing instead to send her an unspoken and utterly bizarre message through the evening from where he sat directly opposite her. During the oxtail soup and salmon mousse, Kira compelled at least a cordial smile to her face for Rolf; he returned the courtesy by giving her stares she could only describe as smoldering—and silly. She changed her tactic during the dressed lobsters and orange-potato pudding, giving him coolly neutral glances. He did things with his food that caused more of it to end up on his plate than in his mouth. Silly *and* wasteful.

By the time the raspberry champagne sorbets were

brought out, marking this ordeal as only halfway done, the man found creative ways to bring his *utensils* into his little show. Kira had to admit she found it fascinating that he could lick pink goo off a spoon with so many angles of his tongue, especially when the only encouragement she supplied was a blatantly discomfited grimace.

She never imagined she'd find the explanation for his continuing antics merely by glancing to her right for a moment. For to her right, Aunt Aleece had chosen to seat herself. One fast glance at her aunt's profile—yes, it only took *one* glance—showed her a woman in the throes of enthralled infatuation...perhaps a little more than that. Aleece's enraptured stare provided ample kindling for Rolf's overconfident display, stirring a strange pity for him in Kira's gut. Despite his noticeable expectations otherwise, she would not be concurring with her aunt's inclinations any time tonight. Tongue acrobatics on silverware, with or without the assistance of pink goo, wasn't an interesting *or* sexy spectacle.

As a matter of fact, she began searching her memory for what Aunt Aleece told her about the discreet way to stifle a yawn, when her father came through in heroic style one more time—one more *invaluable* time. As the creamed asparagus and Cornish game hens emerged from the kitchen, he valiantly broke the pervading silence at the table by turning to her with a warm smile. "So, my Lady Kira," he stated with a touch of obvious pleasure, "I understand you've already found the Scottney Menagerie."

Kira gave him a genuine smile in return. Perhaps this meal would have an interesting turn, after all. "It's beautiful," she replied, knowing her tone neared the "unrefined gushing" point but not caring. "It's more than beautiful, really. How long have you had it? Did you design it, my lord?"

Nicholas let out a long, hearty chuckle. "You flatter me, Kira." He pressed a humble hand to the center of his chest. "I'm afraid I cannot lay claim to your praise. I commissioned an architect named Charles Barry to create my flight of fancy. He's got quite a future ahead of him, with that eye for extra flair and detail; wouldn't you say so, Rolf?"

Rolf appeared to contemplate that subject for a long moment—though in truth, Kira knew the man fought to divert his focus away from the erotic possibilities of asparagus spears slathered with white cream sauce. "He's done fine work for me at the Walk," he finally said with his sophisticated smile firmly back in place. "As a matter of fact, the renovations to the ballroom are almost complete." He encompassed Kira and Aleece with his gaze then, as well. "I insist you all come for a visit to see them."

"Mister Pembroke, you are *too* kind," Aleece instantly replied. "We'd *love* to pay you a visit!" The tone definitely crossed the border into gushing. At this point, however, that didn't surprise Kira in the least.

She *was* caught unaware by the next question from the man across the table. "What about you, Lady Kira?" Rolf queried while slowly circling his fork tines in the white sauce. "Are *you* in concurrence with that statement?"

Kira lifted only her gaze at Rolf. A brief connection with his unflinching brandy eyes confirmed her intuition about his inquiry: he'd less questioned her than challenged her, trying to ensnare her now by tempting her with control instead of sex. She dawdled with her own fork in order to stall her reply, trying to decide whether that would consist of thinly-veiled contempt or a gutsier show of outright sarcasm. Tarnation, how she wished the table weren't the width of the Mississippi. A swift kick to the man's shin beneath the table would perfectly resolve everything now.

On the other hand, an enthusiastic assault from a chimpanzee could do the trick equally well—which earned Fred her second "hero of the evening" award at that moment. Kira eagerly welcomed her pet into her lap, voicing approval at how he'd dressed himself up for the occasion in the ribbon remnants from her bedroom floor. He grinned and clapped before turning curious eyes to the food in front of him—and eventually, curious fingers, too.

To his credit, Rolf Pembroke reacted to the arrival of their new dinner guest with distinctly arched brows, but little else out of place on his seamlessly suave face. "An African chimp?" he asked blandly, not surprised by Kira's affirming gape. "A healthy animal," he commented. "You clearly take excellent care of him."

Kira opened her mouth to voice a sincere thanks, but a terse huff filled that pause, instead—the huff Aleece obviously couldn't contain any longer. "But she shouldn't be rendering that excellent care at the *dinner* table," the woman voiced from clenched teeth.

"*Au contraire, Mademoiselle Aleece*," Rolf drawled, curling up a grin at the blush he instantly induced to Aleece's cheeks. "Why, at many Paris dinner parties over the last several years, I've seen seats especially held for the family chimp or pedigree dog. It's quite à la mode now."

Aleece reacted, of course, as if the man had imparted the secrets of the Sphinx—which gave Kira a moment to follow a progression of thought the man instigated in her own head, and issue the question that emerged as a result.

"That sounds like a good bunch of traveling," she commented first. At receiving Rolf's ridiculously feigned shrug of humility, she gained the one extra push of courage she needed to press on: "Tell me, did Damien Sharpe ever go with you to Paris, or did you two just go carousing and wenching in London together?"

Aleece's fork clanged down onto her plate. From the corner of her eye, Kira saw her father imbibe a massive gulp of wine. But she didn't veer her stare away from the man directly opposite her. For a reason she could no more explain than ignore, every nuance of Rolf's reaction mattered to her.

The problem was, his answer had no nuances. No surreptitiously averted glance or uncomfortable mouth twisting. Not even another feigned shrug.

In reaction to her question, Rolf Pembroke cracked first a big smile, then burst out with a charmer's chuckle. "My lady," he said warmly, "your directness is invigorating as India spices." He added with a stare of hooded intent, "And just as delicious, too."

"Well," Aunt Aleece piped with such earnest verve, she instantly betrayed its thorough falseness. "On that note, everyone, I think it's time to adjourn for dessert in the library."

A windy chill pervaded Scottney Hall despite the promise of warmer weather the day had rendered, so the large fire below the library's mahogany mantel was a welcome sight, indeed. Kira found herself actually smiling as she let Fred— and his stomach—lead her to the dessert tray positioned atop a sideboard located between the bookcases housed with "G-H" and "I-J." The sideboard, like most of the room's furniture, was also fashioned in mahogany, adding to the room's warm and comfortable ambiance.

She smiled wider as she perused the large platter of colorful confections. Perhaps, she admitted, this party wasn't the horrid crucible she'd expected it to be. As a matter of fact, she thought while taking a bite of a strawberry filled with a syrupy ambrosia, the only way this moment could be more perfect was if she enjoyed it in her billowy nightrail, curled before the fire with an absorbing book.

And if Rolf Pembroke had finally decided to go home, as well.

It wasn't, she fumed, that his presence unnerved her so much anymore...merely that the man reminded her of it every time she stepped or turned or *moved*. Her conclusion proved itself true the very next moment, when she felt Rolf's touch at her elbow as he sidled smoothly beside her. The man didn't help repair her frazzled patience by eyeing her chest with more anticipation than Cook's sugary pieces of heaven.

"I'd like to thank you, Lady Kira," he said then, as she truly tried to wrestle back mental pictures of the Eden garden's serpent, slithering toward poor Eve.

Despite her failure to do so, she acknowledged the necessity of having to form a reply to the man. "And what, pray tell, would that be for?" she quipped in a light parody of his accent.

To his credit, Rolf accepted the jest in its intended spirit. Though when he issued his own reply, he did so with a serious gaze. "For a delightful evening," he stated. "I can't remember when I've been this enchanted...truly."

"Oh, of course." Kira threw a desirous glance at a chocolate mound with nuts and pink sugar bits. "Truly."

But as she reached for the dessert, Rolf caught her hand in a fervent clasp, instead. He brought her fingers to his lips. His mouth was smooth—and cold. "Kira...please say you'll come and visit me. We'll have so much fun...I promise."

Kira surrendered the dessert in favor of yanking both her hand and her body to a safe distance from the man. Without thinking, she wiped the fingers he'd kissed along her skirt. They felt dirtied from the way Rolf had placed a strange, slinking emphasis on the words *come* and *fun.* The truth be known, her whole body felt sullied now.

The sensation was weird and disconcerting, and she didn't like feeling it at all. Kira gained affirmation for her agitation when Fred discarded a cream puff of his own to come hold her hand again. Her pet chittered loudly at her, his way of voicing his concern. The sound sliced distinctly through the air, needing no interpretation—as Rolf himself verified with his next stinging words.

"Oh, for God's sake!" he sputtered and rolled his eyes in astoundment when realizing he'd just defended himself to a chimpanzee. "My lady, I did not mean—"

"I know you didn't," Kira leveled with a diplomacy she forced to sound sincere. "But now I think it's time you said good night, Mister Pembroke."

Rolf muttered something beneath his breath. That utterance turned into his erupting snarl as he cleared the space to them once more and curled a grip around Fred's wrist. "*I* think it's time we speak without flying fur in our faces!"

Before Kira could think or move, she watched her pet yelp his way through a violently-hurled flight. Fred landed against a divan six feet away—the only impediment that stopped him from crashing into a curio cabinet filled with a deadly cavalcade of china and glass. Kira's own horrified cry sliced through the air, effectively halting the chattering monologue Aleece had been giving Nicholas in front of the fire.

In the ensuing, interminable pause, only the pops of the fire dared to challenge Kira's taut, glaring silence. Perhaps those flying sparks took the risk because they realized they had brethren flaring in the core of Kira's soul; burning hot at the pyre where her composure ignited into unthinking, uncaring rage.

"Mister Pembroke," she at last pronounced, though that fire still seared her senses so completely, the words emerged thick and black as slow-burning coal chunks. "I think it's time *I* said good night."

Aunt Aleece instantly rushed forward. "She—she doesn't mean that!"

"The hell I don't."

"Kira!" came the flabbergasted rasp. "Mister Pembroke, she—she truly, merely just needs some air...er, don't you, Kira?"

"I've had enough air tonight, thank you," Kira retorted. She added with a pointed glance at Rolf, "Yes, more than enough empty substance to last me a while. A *long* while. Now if you'll excuse me—"

"Kira!" The woman frantically followed in her and Fred's wake down the carpeted hall. The woman caught her by the elbow after half a dozen steps. "Kira, you are insulting Rolf"—she flustered her way through an embarrassed pause before correcting herself—"*Mister Pembroke*—beyond the decencies of—of—decency!"

Kira fixed her aunt with a sardonic half-smile. "Then that makes us even."

It was then that they both noticed Nicholas had emerged into the hall, too—and had played witness to their exchange. Kira held her breath in apprehension of her father's reaction.

She didn't have to wait long. Yet just as swiftly, she learned she'd worried in vain. With an unnamable emotion crinkling its way into the corners of his eyes, her father strode forward and smiled gently down at her. He leaned and kissed her on the cheek with equal intent.

"I'm sorry to hear you're not feeling well, my dear," he followed to that. As he pulled away, their gazes met with the mutual understanding of the gift he'd given her in the words: a sanction for her escape that he'd defend to the queen if necessary.

"Thank you, my lord," Kira murmured softly in return. She finished with a smile conveyed from the sincerity of her heart.

She stepped away from Nicholas, then wasted no more time in departing the room. Once out in the massive foyer, she dashed directly for the nearest set of stairs.

★ ★ ★ ★

Just short of an hour later, she slipped into the welcoming white softness of her nightgown. During the same minute, Rolf's coach rumbled out of the courtyard and into the night. The meaning of the coincidence wasn't lost on her; Kira grinned broadly as she let out a sigh mixed of comfort and contentment.

The sound didn't put a nick in Ally's piqued bewilderment. If anything, the maid jerked harder on the counterpane as she pulled it to the foot of the bed, then accordianed it atop the velvet settee there.

"Glad to see him leavin', are ya?" she snipped, clearly craving to say more, but restraining herself from doing so.

The fear of a "reprimand" from Aunt Aleece still lurked in the backs of the maid's eyes.

"Yes," Kira answered her with simple honesty. "Thank you for your concern, Ally." She smiled again.

"Concern," the maid repeated in an incredulous mutter. "Concern."

At that, Ally tossed the bedclothes aside and spun to where Kira now curled up in the window seat. "*Concern* is *right*!" she exclaimed, the force of her ire at last eclipsing her caution. "Beggin' yer profuse pardon, m'lady, but are ya outta yer blazin' mind?"

Strangely, Kira's smile dropped as she responded to that. "I'm beginning to think I'm the only one around here who's *kept* their mind."

"But ya practically gave Rolf Pembroke the cut direct!"

She gave her friend a somber nod. "You're right. He didn't deserve that."

"Bloody straight he didn't."

"He deserved to have his privates kicked in."

"Ohhhhh!" Ally threw up the pillow she'd been carefully plumping. "By all the saints and—"

"You weren't there, Ally," she persisted. "You have no idea how he treated Fred—"

"And perhaps the little stinker needed it?"

"—or the way he looked when he did it."

"I'll wager he looked *devine*."

"He looked like an animal gone rabid."

Without a pillow, the maid now tossed up her hands. "I give up," she exclaimed. "I'm goin' to my room, m'lady, where I'll pray God visits ya in a dream and speaks some sense to that oatmeal in yer head!" She stalked to the door to the right of the closet, which led to the hallway ending at her maid's accommodations. "Good *night!*"

"Good night, Ally."

The words spilled out on a chuckle. Kira couldn't help it. The same way she couldn't help shaking her head in genuine wonderment about the maid's adoration of a man more reptile than human. Yet still, she reminded herself, a reptile who had successfully slithered his way into the regard of all Yorkshire and a good chunk of London, as well.

The realization made her feel a more confused foreigner than the day she'd stepped off the ship from Boston. With that silent confession, her face crunched into a scowl as she pressed her forehead against the window and wrapped her arms around herself. The motion had nothing to do with the chill night gusts now stirring beyond the glass. No, the impetus was more disturbing than that. Just the thoughts of Rolf Pembroke induced a gut-deep yearning to protect herself...and scrub herself. She still couldn't forget how filthy he'd made her feel, from the moment he'd approached her at the dessert cart.

She never felt filthy when she thought about Damien Sharpe.

Oh, no...so many sensations inundated her when she summoned those hewn, hard features to mind, but not a single one made her yearn to scour herself raw. If anything, the man instead stripped her mind clean of all trivialities; his presence burned away all else from her soul except the awarenesses reborn at his command. Then the feelings combined into a rainbow-cloaked Phoenix, rising out of the ashes of the Kira who had once been.

No, he didn't make her feel dirty.

He made her feel desired.

And God help her, Kira conceded, she desired him, too.

She desired him right now. She desired to go to him, finding him in the forest where not even starlight penetrated the darkness, and hold him against the confusion and pain which assailed him like long-fanged night beasts. And kiss him. Oh yes, she would kiss him, too; she would kiss him and in the doing, take some of that pain from him so that he could finally sleep, his face pressed atop the place where her heart would finally beat in peace, as well...

"By the saints and sinners!"

Kira put a more vehement application to Ally's words as she sprang to her feet. Immediately, she banished those heated images out of her mind. "What in the confounded world are you thinking?" she berated herself. "That you'll just gallop into Damien Sharpe's domain and be welcomed with champagne and roses?"

She slumped against the wall next to the north bedroom windows as she uttered the last of that. She did so because her head, followed by the sinking stone of her heart, wasted no time in issuing an answer to the query.

"Damien Sharpe doesn't care whether you live or die, Kira," she told herself in a tremoring whisper. "The sooner you remember that, the better."

CHAPTER ELEVEN

She doesn't care if you live or die, Damien. The sooner you get that through your head, the better.

The trouble was, Damien ruminated, he wasn't thinking with the proper head at the moment. In this hour of the night when even the owls slumbered, he lay wide awake, staring at the beasts carved into the beams high above his head—and he saw a different creature entirely. He saw not leaping stags and growling bears, but a nymph with eyes enticing as candied almonds, lips succulent as glazed strawberries, and a body smooth as fresh-whipped cream, so ready to be appreciated, savored...impassioned.

And he remembered how good fresh cream tasted on the tip of his tongue.

And his erection for Kira Scottney grew harder.

With a snarl and a toss of blankets, he lunged out of bed, landing to the bare wood floor with two violent thunks. As he did, he afforded the sheets one last disbelieving glare. Tonight marked the first time he'd ever bounded so eagerly from them. He loved this bed; he'd loved every foot of its massive mattress and carved oak frame even while paying a king's fortune to have the craftsman hand assemble every board of it right in this room.

He'd only grinned when the man had called him ten kinds of a lunatic for spending so much money on a piece of furniture he'd only see on twice-yearly hunting excursions, though neither of them had a clue there would come a time when he'd call these walls home. When he could call nothing else home.

That thought compounded the fire of his arousal with a conflagration of rage and bitterness. The blaze ignited him into a stomping retreat from the loft and down the lodge's wide stone steps. Damien willingly let the inferno engulf him; in a demented way, he even welcomed it. This blaze was the only force able to burn through his soul's clogging underbrush of emotion and fear, clearing the only necessary path for his life now: the path leading to complete vindication of his name and his honor.

His lips curled in grim satisfaction as he entered the crescent of dim amber light emanating from the arched, ten-foot-high fireplace. As he pulled a tarnished brass candlestick from a chipped side table and used the waning embers of the fire to ignite the wick, the fury settled over him like a comfortable winter cloak. *This* feeling was right, he affirmed. This was the only perspective enabling him to think clearly about that morning two years ago, and the weeks which had preceded it.

This was the only way he could afford to think.

As if his thoughts had been translated into some unknown language then deemed worthy of praise, the source of a baritone bark suddenly decided to head up that particular committee. Another woof followed, replete with enthusiasm only a canine brain could garner at this hour.

"Ham," Damien called to the small mountain of black fur curled up in a faded wingback chair to his right, "come here, you clod-wit." His undertone was gruff but affectionate as the labrador cheerfully complied, rewarded by a dozen vigorous scratches to the area behind his ears.

Clearly in hopes of garnering some more rewards, Hamlet trotted alongside as Damien approached a chopping block which had once supported the fresh trophies of the day's hunting or fishing. Now, the large wood slab was strewn with pages of police reports, many more pages filled with personal notations, and maps displaying the whole of Yorkshire in every conceivable context. Damien leaned over the document labyrinth, and Hamlet propped both front paws to the counter next to him.

"Looks like a bloody hurricane hit, eh, mate?" he muttered. Ham emitted a sympathizing whimper.

Damien braced his elbows to the block and his head in his hands. Yes, it was a hurricane, he confessed. But *nothing* would be tossed. For something, anything, perhaps *all* the paper on this table would turn a necessary lock in a baffling labyrinth he had every intention of deciphering.

For everything on the table contained some detail about Rachelle's last month on earth.

Yes, came the voice from that pit between his heart and his gut, that place where his anger burned most intensely, like the colorless core where a candle's flame met the white wax. *Yes, fill your mind with nothing else but what's on this table, Damien. You will not let any person detract you from this again, let alone a woman!*

Let alone a Scottney woman. Especially not a Scottney woman.

He mustn't think of how that woman never cared about mud in her hair, or donning robes before she raced to see him. He mustn't remember that lilt of softness in her voice...as if she understood the depths of his pain. And he must *not* welcome her to the realms of his dreams, where she helped him forget that pain in sweet, exquisite ways...

"Damn it."

He spun away from the chopping block to drive the point into his brain with the agony of his fist against the wall. Damn it, he had to forget!

He had to forget...by remembering.

He had to remember how her family had destroyed his.

He had to remember how he was going to return the favor, somehow, someday. And the first step to accomplishing that might lie somewhere on this table. Somewhere in this chaos, a single diamond of irrefutable logic was waiting to be found—to help *him* find the bastard who had really murdered Rachelle.

Damien leaned lower over the chopping block. He didn't look up again until the lamp's light was joined by mist-tinted morning beams.

★ ★ ★ ★

"Kira. *Kira!*"

Kira jerked her head up, but didn't pull her sights away from the groomed dirt area in front of the Scottney Hall stables. From the third-floor window, she had a full view of the ring where the trainers worked out a new arrival to her father's prized collection of fine horseflesh.

The stallion was magnificent, she admitted—but her attention centered on the animal holding the opposite end of the lunge rein. The man strode on long, powerfully defined legs, matching the horse's grace move for move, his actions flowing with a hypnotizing, primitive poeticism...

His actions looking so strangely, unforgettably familiar.

She stared harder at the trainer, but a broad-brimmed

hat obscured most of his bearded face. Mentally, she noted his attire—buff shirt and breeches; open black leather vest—so she could seek him out later, and commend his mastery of the horse.

"Young lady," came Aunt Aleece's pinched prompt, "are you quite ready to—"

"Aunt Aleece," she interjected on a sudden surge of inspiration. She wasn't "ready" to concentrate on much of anything on this gloriously crisp Spring day, and perhaps she could distract her aunt into being playing the recalcitrant along with her. "I'm wondering...do you know, perchance, who that man is?"

She held back her smile of triumph as Aleece rose and crossed the sitting room's Aubusson carpet. She'd wagered—successfully—that her primly British enunciation of the question would at least warrant a rewarding glance out the window from her aunt.

"He's one of Tom's new men in the stables," the woman supplied with another pinched sniff. "Nicholas needs more help, since he's insisting on purchasing *more* of those thoroughbred beasts." Aleece's tone descended to the same complaining drone she used when lamenting about Nicholas's cigars. "I think his name is...errmmm...George, or something."

With that, the woman swished back into the room, sat down, and tapped an expectant foot against the floor. "*Now* are you ready to continue, young lady?" *Tap, tap, tap, tap.*

Kira's teeth ground against each other in concurrence with that horrid rhythm. Even after two weeks, the sound wrenched her nerves worse than Fred's snoring.

And today, she decided, was just not a day for snoring. Or foot tapping. Or "continuing" anything at all. Today was meant for taking new chances—even if they were with her prim and pinch-faced aunt.

Perhaps especially if they were.

Kira slammed a satin ribbon bookmark into her forebodingly thick copy of *The Mirror of the Graces* and dared an impudent grin up at the woman across the carpet. "I don't wish to read any more." She rose with a dramatic swish of her own skirts and yanked Aleece to her feet before the woman sputtered a word of protest. "Let's practice more dancing."

Dancing, she'd ruled last week, was her favorite subject. She even tolerated the lectures about proper fan etiquette and seemly ballroom chat topics in order to get to the good part of the lessons: executing the fascinating steps of the reels, the cotillions, and, her most beloved choice of them all, the sweeping beauty of the waltz.

She grabbed her aunt's hands as she lunged into those steps now, orchestrating with a humming version of the tune usually played for them by Marcel, the multi-talented downstairs butler. "Come on, Aunt!" she coaxed. "One, two, three; one, two three!"

"You are one, two, three days behind on your *reading*." Aleece yanked away and stomped back to her discarded book. "And there shall be no dancing until we've come current with it. *Sit*," she charged—but abruptly interrupted herself with a dismayed gasp. "Ohhh, Kira! Look what you've done. The corner of this page is going to be permanently creased!"

"May God strike me dead," Kira muttered while dropping back into her chair. Creasing a book page. Why, certainly that was even worse than the faux pas outlined in the volume in her lap. The book dared to broach "the peculiarities of dressing" and "the importance of temperance," but there was no mention anywhere of what happened when one creased a book page. Yes, she was assuredly going to burn in hell for this. She only hoped waltzing was allowed in hell.

"We shall begin at chapter two," the woman prompted, arching expectant brows across the top of her own book. "Ready?"

With a resigned sigh, Kira began to open her book. But with an equally decisive action, she closed the cover again. In the moment it took for her aunt to discern she still didn't plan on cooperating, she looked at the woman...truly looked at her. She looked and she suddenly saw not Aleece's aversion to having fun, but her *fear* of indulging herself. And as the creases on the woman's face deepened and she raised a frustrated glower to Kira, the furrows in her face no longer belonged to a stern shrew, but a grieving mother.

A *mother.*

"Kira, how are we *ever* to get through all of this, if you won't—"

"Aunt Aleece," she interrupted in a determined murmur, "tell me about Rachelle."

For the first time since she'd stepped foot on Scottney property, including those first days in London, she witnessed her aunt's composure falter on a tightwire of emotion other than anger. "Who—who told you about Rachelle?" she countered in a shaking rasp. With a furious grimace, she fought the sentiment, hiding her face behind the back of her trembling hand.

"It doesn't matter," Kira asserted softly. "Tell me about her...please? What was she like? Am I anything like her?"

"Stop!" the woman hissed. But her tone pleaded as she repeated, "Ohhhh...*stop.*"

"My Lady Kira!"

The appearance of Amy, the downstairs maid with the arms capable of splintering wood but the face capable of tempting a priest, granted Aleece her request by default. Kira didn't invite the maid in to the room as she usually would, but rose and met the servant in the doorway with a friendly smile.

"Hello, Amy," she greeted with a warm smile. "I'm afraid Aunt Aleece isn't...available at the moment. She's suddenly gone a bit under the weather, and I think I'll take her up to her room."

"But...your father has sent me for *you*, my lady."

At that, Aleece's skirts rustled to life. "For Kira?" the woman queried, her voice cracking sharply as it ever had; perhaps with even more clarity. Kira wanted to be surprised at the woman's "recovery"—but wasn't.

Despite that, Amy continued to address Kira. "He'd like to see you in the main sitting room," she stated. "He said he'd like to see you now."

"*Now?*" Again, the reply shot out from behind Kira before her lips parted halfway on any sound.

Amy dared a small, but clearly affronted sniff. "I believe I heard him correctly, Lady Aleece. You can check my hearing against Mister Pembroke's. He was standing there, too."

"Mister Pembroke's!" The woman's "health" had definitely returned. Aleece converged on the doorway with an anticipating gaze and a smile breaking into rosy cheeks. "Well, well! I suppose you're right, Kira. Today is no day to study at all."

Kira, on the other hand, speared the maid with an anxious huff as her aunt disappeared down the hall. "Rolf Pembroke is here? Now?"

Amy planted exasperated hands to her curvaceous hips. "I must be speaking another language today."

How Kira wished that very occurrence were true. How she wished she could confront her father's glower a few hours from now, simply pleading she hadn't understood Amy. How she even wished she could stay here with Aleece now, ingesting the ins and outs of deportment and modesty, instead of trudging downstairs with a head full of dreading wonderings of what on God's green earth Rolf Pembroke wanted with her now.

The trapezes of the man's mind were pitched all backward. Her incensed dismissal of him at that first dinner party had only stimulated him into a flurry of visits over the past fourteen days. Sometimes, he arrived with elaborate excuses; at other times, he showed up merely because he "happened to be in the vicinity," and was interested in everyone's welfare.

Everyone's welfare. Kira snorted as she merely remembered the words. Everyone's welfare. Then let him explain why he never asked about Father or Aleece, and only seemed to endure the latter because somebody had to serve as "proper" chaperon to his calls. Thank God at last for at least one plank making up this corral of English decorum.

Smoothing the apple-green skirt of her afternoon gown as silently as possible, Kira slipped into the main sitting room through the side door while Rolf and her father finished a hearty laugh, apparently about something a now-preening Aleece had said. The trio were clearly content entertaining themselves for the time being, so she decided to take in the beautiful dance of a hummingbird in the main garden, just beyond the cathedral-like windows...

"Kira!"

Clearly, Father had elected another itinerary for this meeting.

That observation was *not* encouraging.

Kira came to a reluctant stop behind a three-sided Turkish couch. "Good afternoon, my lord," she greeted with a halfhearted wave. Dropping her hand and her tone, she added with glum haste, "Hello, Rolf."

The three of them simply stared at her then. Kira raised a hand to her hair, wondering what odd item her curls had managed to ensnare *this* time, but her search gleaned nothing. She looked back at them—

And endured a sudden, queer twist in the pit of her stomach. All three of the faces on the opposite side of the room wore expressions filled with too much mystery. A mystery she wasn't sure she wanted to solve.

"Perhaps we should all sit down," Nicholas stated coolly. Why did his tone remind her of a judge about to issue a life sentence to a prisoner?

Rolf and Aleece murmured their immediate agreements to the suggestion, but she issued herself a stage direction toward the windows from which she'd sighted the hummingbird. "I'll stand, thank you," she returned past the thudding heartbeat in her throat. She peered frantically for the hummingbird. He'd disappeared.

"Well," chimed Aleece then, performing her sing-songy words with more perfect pitch than an Italian diva. "We're all here, aren't we?"

"Indeed," Rolf murmured.

Kira tried to rein in the volume of her impatient sigh.

"Mister Pembroke, has my uncouth brother offered you a libation yet? Cook's cinnamon tea is the finest in all the county, I'm certain of it."

"Thank you, Lady Aleece," Rolf responded, "no. *I'm*

certain Lord Scottney has a plethora of duties to attend before the day is out, and would like to attend to the occasion at hand. There shall be many occasions we can utilize for lingering in the future."

"You are so right, Mister Pembroke."

Kira snapped a questioning stare back upon them. *He is?* her senses railed. *The occasion at hand? Many occasions for lingering in the future?* What in the world was the man talking about?

If her instinct served as the correct answer to that, she needed to prepare herself. She suspected, in an eerie and gripping way, an upset stomach and nervous heartbeat were the first drops of the flood about to strike the ramparts of her composure.

"Yes," came her father's murmur, also delivered with flawlessly lordly inflection. "Pembroke is correct. The sooner we finish this, the better."

Kira's heart thundered up into her ears. Now he sounded like a judge about to sentence a prisoner to *death;* a Pilate anxious to be done with the ordeal of his duties as quickly as possible. That's exactly what this meeting was for him, she confirmed, as her gaze caught Nicholas's for one excruciatingly transparent moment. An ordeal.

Which was why she loathed him for issuing his next pronouncement, anyway.

"Kira...Mister Pembroke has come today to express his growing affection for you. He has asked my permission to court you, and I have agreed."

The words shouldn't have surprised her. Yet she sucked in a fast breath as invisible bonds squeezed her lungs tighter than Zofo, Webber's Hungarian strongman, used to constrict iron bars. Her throat felt like one of Zofo's twisted creations, as well. Everything got bent back upon itself until nothing could get through—except disbelieving pain and the intensifying heat of rage.

She spun back toward the window, attempting to force words past her lips. The syllables stampeded in her head, a herd of sounds and screams as wild and frustrated as the stallion fighting against its tethers outside. Straining against that stranger in the broad-rimmed hat, in the snug breeches around his powerful legs...

Inexplicably, that memory tightened the restraints around her chest. Only a horrid moisture seemed to fight its way past the suffocating ties, stinging her nose, reddening her vision. Father's approaching footsteps only increased the intensity of that sting, causing Kira's reflexive recoil as he grew nearer.

"Kira," he said through clenched teeth as she did, "Blast it, give this a *try*. Rolf is an upstanding citizen. He's a good man."

A sharp laugh accomplished the miracle of slashing through her composure's constraints. Here stood Lord Nicholas Scottney, bold in the decisions of his business, wise in the stewardship of his title, descending to the morass of absurdity. Rolf had duped even him. The whole of Yorkshire actually believed the man only had "upstanding" bones in his body.

On the other hand, this was her father asking this concession of her. Her father, who had made innumerable efforts over the last two weeks to be with her, to know her, whether during the light banter during their sunset walks in the garden, or the peaceful silences they shared late in the evenings by the fire, even after Aleece had ordered her to bed.

This was her father, who had promised her the fulfillment of her dreams in just another eleven months.

"What do I have to do," she ventured cautiously, "for this 'courting' thing?" She veered a glance at Nicholas, whose own gaze warmed like the brandy he sipped during their fireside moments.

"That's the beauty of it," he replied. "*Rolf* must do all the work. He'll call on you in much the same way he has been; however, now you'll receive extra gifts, such as flowers and baubles and trinkets of his admiration."

"Trinkets." She yearned to make the word a question. Heaven only knew what "trinkets" Rolf would deem as appropriate symbols of his "affection"—especially if the unnerving glint at the back of his gaze, piercing at her even now from across the room, sufficed as any advance indication.

As fast as possible, Kira jerked her sights away from the man. "It just seems much ado about nothing," she muttered to Nicholas then, not bothering to hide her punctuating huff.

"Well, it's what Rolf must do," came her father's chuckling answer, "if he wants to win you as his bride."

Immediately, his laughter stopped. As Aleece glared at him. As Rolf stared at *her.* As Kira swept unblinking eyes and pain-creased brows to all three of them.

"Is *that* it?" she finally rasped, though her words felt separate and disjointed in her throat, and sounded even more so as they chopped through the pervading silence. "Is that it, then? Rolf's 'affections'...his 'tokens of admiration'...it's all still the means to the end, isn't it? To get your heir planted in my belly, is that it?"

"Kira," Nicholas grated, "*no.* That's—"

"Were you ever planning to *tell* me about this marriage,

Father? Or were you just going to drag me to the church, hoping I wouldn't notice Ally had dressed me in a wedding gown that morning, then ask me if I minded doing a 'little favor' for you, like marrying a lascivious boor?"

"Kira!" Aleece exploded. "You will apologize for that this instant!"

"Kira, for God's sake," Rolf snarled. "Think about the advantages of our alliance. With Scottney Hall and Hyperion's Walk united as one—"

"Stop it!" She yanked up her skirts until her knees had enough room to move—to run. "Just—stop it, all of you!"

Now she really couldn't breathe. She had to get out of here; out of this place with its unrelenting stone walls and its people pressing her harder against those walls, trying to flatten her into something she wasn't. *Somebody* she wasn't. Mama had purchased her a paper doll in New York once; she'd hated it—now she knew why.

Somehow, she found herself in the hall once more, then the front foyer, the vestibule, and finally the front drive. Still, she didn't stop running. She ran faster, faster still. She turned toward the vibrancy of the gardens, then the wide, wild freedom of the valley beyond that...until raw and pain-filled instinct pushed her toward the thick embrace of a dark-green forest.

CHAPTER TWELVE

Hours passed, but she didn't care. As the forest bathed her in shimmering depths of emerald shade, the heat of her rage was also gradually soothed, like a slow swallow of Mama's comfrey and hyssop cough tea. Kira pulled in great breaths of the clean woodsy air, inhaling life itself, so verdant was the atmosphere with the scents of moss and grass, of pines and willows, of wildflowers and wild things.

Oh, to live here with these contented creatures, she yearned, ripping away her shawl and rolling up her sleeves, reveling in the pine-crisp breeze upon her arms. Traveling further, she came upon a moss-banked stream, its shallow pools emptying over smooth rocks, performing a dance of its own for an appreciative squirrel audience.

Eagerly approaching the water, yet finding the bulk of her crinoline too cumbersome to handle, Kira hurriedly shucked that, too. She didn't even bother with the buttons on her day shoes, opting to pry them off with opposing toes, peeling down stockings at the same time. With a laugh of soft delight, she at last tugged up her hem and waded into the cool eddies.

The water gurgled around her shins as she smiled up into the leaf-filtered sunbeams. As if her expression had summoned them to the boughs overhead, songbirds began to accompany the stream's orchestra, and she quickly decided she'd not heard more beautiful music in her life.

Soon, a contented tune formed in her own throat; an

aimless melody which flowed over her lips in drops of happy, hummed notes. For the first time since she'd left Boston, she let her shoulders sag then her head loll back. She swayed a little to the cadence of her melody, surrendering herself to this perfect moment. A full minute, perhaps two, passed without a thought entering her head of dressing peculiarities, proper fan etiquette, or becoming Rolf Pembroke's wife.

Especially not becoming Rolf Pembroke's wife.

A skittering along the stream's bank thankfully jerked her attention from that direction of thought. She pulled her head upright and her eyes open in time to watch the last member of the squirrel family dash away up a tree, bushy tail swishing as the adorable creature went.

She smiled, and was about to let the expression bubble into a chuckle, when her gaze confronted a sight too beautiful for chuckles. An awed, soft gasp instead left her lips as a pair of perfect almond eyes blinked tentatively at her. Breeze-dappled sunlight fell across those hypnotic eyes, along with the alert, flicking ears, the elegant neck and the graceful body, all covered with fur that defined the creature itself: sleek, soft, and tawny.

Why, hello, she greeted the doe through her gaze instead of her lips. *Are you thirsty, pretty one? Would you like some water?*

The doe, like the shy maid she was, dipped her head and pretended to sniff a patch of daisies while assessing the status of the trespasser in her stream. *Friend or foe?* her stance asked in the language of the wild.

It's all right, Kira assured. *I'm friend, pretty one. I'll share the water if you will.*

The doe came two steps closer.

Just before an equal number of gunshots blasted through the clearing.

A flock of bluebirds burst into the sky as if their sheltering oak was an exploding inkwell. The squirrels squealed in terror, and even at Kira's feet, fish darted out from their rock hiding places, colliding with each other in instinctual terror.

That was, until she jerked those feet out of the stream and marched herself furiously up the bank. She didn't stop there, however. Ignoring the twigs and rocks biting into her soles, she stomped on, her sights set on the wild-haired, black-eyed beast now emerging from the dense foliage. She tried not to notice how much more foreboding he seemed, now that the hard, straight edge of his shoulder supported a rifle and not a cockatoo, but the feat didn't happen easily. She supposed that was why she stopped a full six feet from him, and let a strident shriek do her communicating from there.

"What the damn tarnation do you think you're about! Are your eyes open? For that matter, has your *brain* busted open?"

At first glance, Damien Sharpe appeared calm enough to be merely posing for one of those gentleman-in-the-forest parlor portraits. But then Kira looked into his eyes—dear heavens, *his eyes.* His stare glittered with cobalt malice; his antipathy toward her had clearly been trenched to new levels since the first time they'd confronted each other in this dark wood.

Still, his replying murmur to her was just that: a low, though lethally underscored, murmur. "Well spoken, my lady," he stated. "Though I am chagrined; you stole most of the questions *I* would have posed to *you*."

"*You* would have—" She momentarily forgot her trepidation, pure incredulity sparking her to a burst of laughter, instead. "I see," she drawled. "Your dinner again, I take it?"

Something changed in his stare before he replied to that—a distinct sharpening to the shards in his eyes—making Kira scoot a discreet step back, for all the reassuring good it did.

"*Yes*, damn it," he at last bit at her. "And this time, Princess, I'm not taking promises of pleadings to Papa as recompense."

She should have bitten her lips. And her tongue. And anything else to stay the comeback she flung in reaction to the extra venom he injected to his second sentence. "Good," she snapped, "because I wasn't about to offer such."

"Then what *are* you prepared to offer?"

Napomashch! came the first answer she rendered to that, from the part of her mind that followed pure instinct. *Help!* Oh, dear saints help her, for as the man issued that all-too-quiet rebuttal, he stepped slowly forward, and the glints in his eyes looked exactly like moonlight on the blades of a hundred daggers.

The kind of daggers that could cut a woman's heart out as it still beat in her chest.

Help!

★ ★ ★ ★

Damien knew exactly what state of mind he'd manipulated her into. He watched the pulse throbbing wildly at the base of her neck; he heard the backward scufflings she tried to hide from him, but which he promptly recouped with steady steps of his own.

He imagined her ladyship Kira would leap at a tap on the shoulder from her own shadow at the moment—which was his precise intent since coming upon the clearing and seeing her all but ask his doe to a few rounds of whist. But now that he was at the truth of it, her dread sickened him as much as any of the urges he'd had to go after the deer in the last two weeks. It was true; venison had come to be as appealing to him as castor oil. When he'd come upon the pair of them just now, he'd been searching for rabbits.

Instead, he'd found a hellion looking more damn adorable than she had a right to. Ah God, he'd raged, what was she doing in his stream like that, with her hair half toppled from its pins, her skirts molded so soggy and sexy around her bottom, and her face, *her face*, kissed with dappled sunlight and the sublime beauty of her soft-humming smile. *What*, damn her, was she doing?

To his brain's repeat of the question, his senses gave over the same answer they'd had during that initial, overwhelming moment: gritted jealousy and lashing anger. Jealousy of the happiness she found in the simple act of wading in a stream. Anger because she chose to express it in *his* domain, which he deemed to keep decidedly *un*happy for the time being, thank you.

The thought surged a renewed force of hostility into the retort he growled at her then. "So...what about it, my lady? What *is* going to be the apologetic sacrifice to the forest beast this time?" He pinned her in place with his stare as he closed the final two steps of space between them—and without looking down, wrapped a fold of damp skirt around his fist, then pulled. "An offering of virginal flesh, perhaps?"

A sharp breath escaped her lips, and he watched a tiny bead of perspiration form at the corner of her mouth. Damien clenched his jaw hard, hoping she interpreted it as a sign of his swelling ire, not his swelling arousal. Holy God, how could a woman make him so hard and so incensed at once?

To his grudging respect, she didn't falter her gaze from his as she drew breath to issue her soft, but resolute reply. "I don't think you comprehend me, Mister Sharpe. *I* am not the individual who owes penance in this instance."

For a moment, her words hovered in his brain like a seagull above a wave, waiting for the instinctually right moment to plunge in. When the understanding did descend, it threw his head back on a bellow of laughter. "Penance?" he at last echoed. He tried to emit the statement without chuckling. He *tried.* "Let me see if I comprehend you completely, my lady. *I* owe *you* penance, for doing what I see fit with the resources on *my* land?"

Her reaction began with those ever-present embers in her eyes, which now exploded into fury through her body. In the space of one vehement snap, she reclaimed her clothing from his hold and reestablished her two steps of distance. "Was that creature a resource, Mister Sharpe, or a pawn of revenge?"

The mirth went still on his lips for a full thirty seconds. After another half minute, Damien still didn't know whether to continue laughing or spear her with the blackest of glares.

"What?" he finally snorted, deciding to simply let her see the full extent of his bafflement.

She slammed her hands to the curve of her hips. The action did *not* help his effort to forget she stood there clothed in nearly nothing, so close to him and so far from anyone else. She, however, was oblivious to any awareness other than the spitting force of the wrath she now unfurled at him.

"This may come as the jolt of the season to everyone around here, but that doe doesn't belong to anyone or anything than its Creator! It's only on loan to you, *mate,* along with all the other creatures here. By the disrespect you give that agreement, it doesn't amaze me that you go hungry half the time."

Even the thought of an appropriate reaction eluded him now. "Agreement?" he finally uttered, issuing it from a completely blank stare.

"*Bozhy moj*," she snapped, before firing him a look animated with enough agitation for them both. "You really think this is all yours for the taking, don't you?" She swept a hand at the trees, the stream. "You don't think you'll be held accountable for what you've done with the richness of this land; for the indifference you show to the spirits of the creatures who belong to it?"

"The spirits of the creatures..." *This* time, Damien made an explicit decision about reaction: the ominous glare won the contest. "Lady, what the bloody hell are you about?"

To his further disconcertment, she huffed as if he were missing the very nose on his face. But her reply came on a gentle, sincere tone. "Just because animals can't talk about their souls doesn't mean they don't have them. Those souls are even represented in the heavens by certain saints, the same way ours are. When you dishonor an animal's soul by killing it without honor or thanks, you're also offending its guardian saint." She took half a step forward, into a beam of light which illuminated her growing smile with surreal accuracy. "In retaliation, that saint may send certain events to foul up your plans...or even certain people."

He was glad he hadn't packed away the glare yet. "Let me get this straight—now you're telling me you're a messenger from heaven?"

Her head tilted at that; a pixie's response of genuine

surprise. "I don't know," she murmured. "But that's a nice idea, I suppose."

Damien began his retreat from her with half a dozen slow but steady backsteps. Yes, he affirmed, the retreat. He had to get away from this woman; from this...*creature* with the dark beauty of her face and the blazing spectrum of her spirit, who'd invaded his stream like a half-wild forest nymph, and now threatened to penetrate the thicket of his soul with equal damage.

"My Lady Kira," he finally said into the air which had thickened through an uncomfortable silence, "I think it's time you wandered your wet little arse home."

He flung the profanity with calculated intention, expecting one or both of two reactions: a shocked huff or an affronted withdrawal.

Kira Scottney's aggravated sigh was *not* on the list of options. "*Please* stop calling me that," she said while she was at it. Damien blinked in shock as she concluded the whole thing by dropping onto a boulder with graceful, but guileless pensiveness—again, just like a sprite who'd lived here for centuries.

"What?" he answered, though less in response to her demand than stuttering perplexion at her action.

"That 'Lady Kira' balderdash," she answered while pulling a knee up beneath her chin. "I don't think I'll get used to that." A slight crease formed in her brow. "I'm not sure I want to."

"Of course you do," he rebutted. "A lady of the House of Scottney...it's every girl's dream; surely they've schooled you about that so far."

"*Don't* mention schooling, either." She punctuated that with an I-may-be-sick groan. "How to smile. How to nod.

How to walk. How to talk. *Bozhy moj,* I *know* how to talk. *Sumashehstviye*—it's madness, all of it, concocted by these *durahks* who don't know their *yahgaditsas* from their *mosks. Khvahtit!*"

Astoundingly, Damien found himself battling to suppress a chuckle then. A smile, however, he could not defer from his lips as he murmured, "Er...you tossed me out of the carriage back there...somewhere around *durr-awks*?"

"*Durahks,*" she repeated with the bite of familiar usage. "Fools," she clarified. "I was tempted to say something else, but Mama taught me my manners, despite what my dear aunty is inclined to believe."

Damien dipped his head as the chuckle spilled out, anyway. Odd...from all the boulders of derision he'd heaped in his soul over the last six months, he couldn't find a single chunk of the stuff to hack off now. "Thank you for the consideration," he instead replied with sincere congeniality, "but I don't believe you mean all that. Scottney Hall isn't Newgate Prison, after all."

"It's not home, either."

Her retort came so swiftly, so adamantly, that her ensuing look of surprise came as an equal revelation. Yet as Damien looked on, another emotion assaulted her features, explaining the force which had caused that surprise.

Pain.

She didn't cringe with a twitch of mere physical discomfort, nor even a wistful wash of faint longing. No, sheer agony inundated this woman's gaze like a February downpour: a consuming wash of grief, of lost love, of lost life. Of a home she longed for in more than words...because that home no longer existed.

Ah, God. He knew exactly how she felt.

The recognition froze Damien there, letting his stare intertwine with hers for too long; *too long.* And still, he didn't run. *Too long!* He didn't command *her* to run. *You've let her stay too damn long!*

He wanted to know more about her.

On legs suddenly feeling more flimsy than the wind-fluttered leaves overhead, he found his way to a fallen log near her boulder. As he lowered himself to the rough wood, he took in the sight of her again: damp and small and beautiful, even in the sorrow which so clearly enveloped her now.

"Tell me about home," he at last asked of her, drawing in a full breath as conclusion. When was the last time he'd spoken to anyone so gently? The tone felt as different in his throat as an attempt at her foreign ramblings.

At first, her answer consisted of a solitary tear down her smooth cheek. "The answer doesn't matter," she snapped, swiping the droplet into her impossibly tangled hairline. But the next moment, she erupted into an irony-filled laugh, her emotions helpless prisoners to their jailor of grief. "It's not as if that wagon wasn't about to fall apart, anyway. The fire just accomplished the job quicker."

"The fire," he repeated, his tone questioning, but empathizing. That she'd lived in a wagon was strangely effortless to accept; a vision easily bloomed of her in satin gypsy garb, her hair bound back with a tasseled scarf. But the image was torture to maintain when picturing her standing in the charred remains of a once-colorful wagon, alone and lost and truly homeless.

"Fires are a fact of life in the circus," she explained then, her gaze directed down the stream bank with a faraway softness...and sadness. "Unfortunately, with a little help from a panicked crowd and a strong wind, they can be a murderer, too."

"I'm sorry," Damien murmured, and meant it.

Her sigh conveyed the obligatory thanks—and somehow, Damien sensed, they both knew it was enough. Another minute of silence passed before she spoke again. "I just wish I'd been able to get Mama's things out. Her embroidered shawl, her *nauzy* necklaces, her books of herbs and potions... her treasures, she called them. She'd brought them with her from the old country."

Curiosity sparked his query this time. "The old country?"

"Russia," she supplied. "Mama left when she was only fourteen, but she remained true to the Orthodox saints and the spirits of nature her whole life."

"The saints *and* the spirits?" He quirked a genuine scowl. "A paradox of a woman, was she?"

"To the people of your world, yes." Surprisingly, the answer came tinged with mild disdain. "But the Creator Mama taught *me* about is not so small."

To his amazement once more, Damien felt himself reacting to her utterly unconventional talk with a concurring nod passable in any standard tea salon chit-chat. He didn't feign an inch of the action, either. He conceded the strange, startling rightness of her words...the strange, startling rightness of *her.*

The revelation prompted him to an unignorable restlessness. He rose from the log and moved to stand directly in front of her. He said nothing as she rose, as well, her head reaching the level where his heart beat out a rhythm surely filling the clearing with its deafening cadence. Perhaps not the whole clearing, Damien rectified—but he knew *she* heard the cacophony, as she turned her face up to him, adorned by a soft, knowing smile. A soft, soul-inundating smile.

"You are the oddest woman I have ever met," he growled in retaliation to that smile—to the alarming havoc it unleashed through his senses. That was why he wondered where the hand came from, looking terrifyingly like *his*, which raised to the corner of her rose-hued lips, then traced the crease there with a reverent sibilance of a touch.

Funny...that hand even felt like his, as she turned her head and breathed across the fingers suddenly trembling with the yearning to explore the rest of her face. Hell. Bloody *hell*. She *was* a forest fairy, he ruled, and now he was caught in her bewitching spell. And the hex felt wonderful. Beautiful...

Until her smile tilted a little higher, and she issued her whispering reply to his statement.

"And you, Mister Sharpe, are the first outlaw *I* have met."

You had it coming. His head resounded with the censure before Damien jerked from her by two hard steps. *You had it coming even before you snarled at her; you knew it was coming, yet you dawdled here with her, trying to believe otherwise. You damn fool!*

He dropped his hand, fingers now turned to icicles. His heart pounded with the chill of a hibernating grizzly's, a beast forced into darkness until Spring's salvation.

His mistake was in confusing this hoyden for Spring.

"Wh-what's wrong?" came her voice, faltering with confusion and hurt. Oh, she was good, this little performer from the colonies. He almost believed she felt those emotions.

He glared directly at her as he leveled a demand of his own in return. "Where did you hear that?" he asked her in a lethally soft murmur.

"Where did I hear what?"

"You *know* what. You don't call a man an outlaw without bloody good reason, Princess." The words seethed from the same gut that prompted his determined advance back upon her. "You know, don't you? You know all of it."

He stopped short as comprehension smacked him like a sopping wet rug against a cleaning paddle. "Ally," he sneered. "I should have known. The little prattle-hen. Ally's your maid, isn't she?"

Her downcast gaze told him the answer to that. But as Damien spun on his heel, muttering an oath, she pulled him back by the elbow, meeting his glare with a stare brimming of her own resolve.

"I commanded her to tell me," she pleaded on behalf of the maid. "So if you're going to gnash your jaws at anyone, gnash them *this* way, all right?"

Damien ran his regard down the rigid line of her arm, coming at last to the white-knuckled fist still clamped around his elbow. From beneath hooded lids, he finally asked, "Why?"

She rendered her reply with surprising softness. "I wanted to know why you were so...why you were hurting so much."

She could have landed an arrow into his chest and given him less shocking agony. The *hell* with her, he raged. He didn't need her pity, so thinly disguised as "concern." He didn't need the exhilaration of her touch, the warmness of her gaze, and most of all, the truthful blades of her words, slicing much too close to certain places inside him. Places he'd vowed nobody would ever see again.

"That's none of your bloody business," he retorted to those words now, spinning from her once again.

"Perhaps I'd like to make it my business."

"Perhaps you aren't invited."

"Perhaps I don't care."

"Then you're a bigger fool than I thought, because you're wasting your time."

"Damn it!" she at last erupted. By the brevity of her ensuing sigh, he wagered she'd slammed her arms across her chest once more. "No wonder nobody cares about you anymore," she muttered. "You won't let them."

In reply, Damien just dropped his head and stiffened his shoulders. She was right, he conceded. She was so bloody right, he sucked in a painful breath from the force of the realization. She was the first human being he'd stepped within three feet of in the last half year—and holy God, just the wisps of her warmth and life had felt magnificent. So magnificent, he almost forgot his anger, his resentment, his weariness of this world and all the wonder it had stolen from him.

He was *not* going to forget. Not now. Not for a long time.

Forgetting meant surrendering.

"Go home, *Lady Scottney*," he willed his lips to drawl then, despite the screaming protest otherwise from every drop of blood in his veins. "Go back to your papa's castle, and don't trespass in my forest again."

To underline the lethal import of what he said, he scooped up the dagger and slammed it back into the sheath at his waist with a loud *thwick* of steel against leather.

Then, without so much as a parting glance, he turned and left her.

That's better, he told himself, escaping urgently down a path back into the thicker trees, where night now dripped its chilled darkness already. *Yes, much better.* His blood flowed more tepid already. It would soon slow to its usual safe frigidity...as soon as she got out of here. *As soon as she got out of here.*

As far as her repeating the mistake...Damien didn't give that dread more than a passing shrug. After Ally and her cohorts pumped her with a few more tales of "Damien the Forest Beast," Lady Kira of the great Scottney Hall would not come venturing within a mile of this wood again.

So she was truly out of his life now. She was completely gone.

Yes, he felt much better about things already.

He only wondered why his soul didn't seem to hear that overture, as well.

CHAPTER THIRTEEN

Men, Kira resolved, had "evolved" backward. As Fred eagerly greeted her in the garden, she resoundingly sealed the conclusion, for surely her pet's tender kisses were the most civilized behavior she'd received from a male primate today.

"You sneaked away from Ally again," she murmured to the chimp, only partly attempting an accusing tone, and failing even at that. Fred himself was fractionally to blame, playing lightly with her hair, making her giggle from the ensuing tickles.

"Frederick..." she warned, but dissolved into harder chuckles. "Oh, Fred," she finally sighed, a resigned lilt permeating the sound, "perhaps you *are* the only man around here who doesn't belong in a cave."

The chimp echoed her wistful tone with a soft, sad whimper of his own before resting his head back against her shoulder. "Why don't we run away and join the circus?" she asked him then, and again, as if understanding not only her tone but her words, he flashed a toothy chimp grin.

Her mind, however, rendered another reply. *And why don't you jump over the sun and the moon while you're at it, Kira? Attempting that would be easier than convincing yourself to leave...breaking your promise to your father...and abandoning the dream he's now placed within your reach.*

You've got another eleven months to spend with this tribe of lunatics, Kira. Get used to it now.

"Get *used* to it?" she muttered while trudging up the stone garden steps, onto the south verandah. Get used to batting her lashes in time to her fan; to pretending hemlines and bodice styles actually meant something to her? Get used to having no choice about her clothing, her books, the time she spent and who she spent it with? Worst of all, get used to complimenting those companions on their wit and charm, when they really (and easily) should be stuffed and mounted on the walls of the smoking room?

She began to wonder if she could pull this act off. Especially when she imagined being trapped in a ballroom with those half-rigomortised idiots, and yearning only to run for the depths of a dark emerald forest, instead.

A forest she'd been banned from, as of an hour ago.

She dropped onto a stone bench as the remembrance of Damien Sharpe's dismissal assaulted her again. Her mind's eye watched his retreating back, his anger-tautened muscles visible even through his thick, buff-colored shirt, his strides so long and determined, they definitely qualified as stomps. The stomps of a bitter, frightened man.

A blind man.

He was the worst kind of a blind man at that, she concluded with a resolute sigh, because his infirmity had nothing to do with his eyes. The man had sealed shut his *heart*. And he had shut himself so thoroughly in that darkness, he mistook an extended hand of friendship as an attacking sword of enmity... he treated words of kindness as if they were chunks of diseased meat: sniffing them, grimacing at them, then dismissing them as vehemently as he could. *She* might as well have been a lice-infested whore, for all the respect of the parting glare he flung at her.

Kira reacted to the memory of that moment with the same

actions she'd presented to Damien's departing backside. First, she jerked her head up, then back, ordering the distinct sting behind her eyes back into the stupidly vulnerable pit she'd opened in her heart. "*Idikchyortu,*" she softly spat after that.

Go to hell, Damien Sharpe.

She sighed again, and dropped her head. The oath didn't carry half its strengthening impact of an hour ago. All too swiftly, she identified the reason why.

Even if Damien went to hell, she'd willingly accompany him.

Oh yes, she'd offer her hand to him again without hesitation—showing him he was not alone; showing him she understood the pain of being prejudged and cast out. She'd show him she wasn't afraid of him...

She was only afraid of *her* reaction to him. She was only terrified of what her body did, directly against any orders her *mind* railed at it, whenever she even looked at the man, standing on his impossibly powerful legs, glaring with his impossibly fathomless eyes. Even now, like molten silver, the heat puddled in her belly, then brimmed over into her limbs, thick and hot and consuming...and dangerous. Dear God, and *dangerous.*

They're positive it was murder, m'lady...she was stabbed ten times...he was covered in her blood...but there wasn't a scratch on him...

"Kira!"

On one hand, she could count the number of times she welcomed Aunt Aleece's summons. This moment counted as one more of those occasions. Kira rose from the bench, gratefully leaving behind all broodings of blood, knives, and murder trials along with the cold stone they belonged with, and plastered a reasonably serene expression on her face as the woman approached on a thunderous step.

The situation, she realized, raced past ironic and into absurd. The growing dread on Aleece's face confirmed her theory. Oh yes, she was quite certain *The Mirror of the Graces* didn't address proper behavior in the instance of coming across one's niece with Cleopatra's smile on her face and Cinderella's tatters on her body.

"God's sweet mercy," the woman gasped, each word requiring a renewed intake of breath to huff out. Aleece's gaze, easily wide enough to accommodate both her shock and horror, assaulted Kira from disheveled head to bare toes, then again, then once more. "Your—your shoes," she at last stammered. "Your stockings...your *crinolines;* oh, for the love of heaven, Kira; not your crinolines, too!"

"And good afternoon to you, too, Lady Trevor." Kira added a courtly nod to her sardonic tone. "I am quite fine, thank you for your concern. No lasting damage, as far as I can tell. And how do *you* fare?"

"It's evening, not afternoon, young lady. Tea was served well over an hour ago. Now we shall clearly have to delay dinner because of you, though I am sorely tempted to simply send a tray to your room, instead."

While Kira concentrated on cloaking her joy at *that* prospect, another head-to-toe glance from her aunt resulted in more outraged gasps. Apparently, Aleece's first three scrutinies hadn't revealed half the atrocities she found this time. "Oh, *Kira,*" she harrumphed again. "You have chagrined your father and I to incomprehensible fathoms—and now this. Oh, *what* unearthly beasts did you find to take you to hell and back?"

Though she admitted the news of her father's disappointment made her chest cringe in a strange way, Kira's lips quirked with bittersweet humor at her aunt's unwitting accuracy. What kind of beast, indeed, she ruminated...and what kind of hell. *I'd like to know those answers myself, Aunt Aleece*, her heart added with sad wistfulness. *But I never shall. Nobody shall.*

The admission sank deeper and deeper into her soul, finally lodging itself at the bottom like an anchor stuck in a drift of dark mud. Yet as she felt her heart descending into that morass, too, Kira jerked back on that line with her mind. She jerked back swiftly—and furiously. *If you want to keep on wallowing in a pond of your anger and resentment, you'll do it alone, Damien Sharpe*, she silently proclaimed. *I said I'd go to hell with you, and I meant it, but I refuse to live there!*

"...sometimes I wonder if you even like living here!"

The uncanny overlay of Aleece's words to her thoughts effectively drew Kira back to the confrontation at hand. Irony hadn't finished playing with the situation, however; the moment she returned her attention to her aunt, Aleece paused to take a formidable breath, letting an intimidating silence follow.

"I...enjoy quite a few aspects of living here," Kira finally said in her defense, though she hoped Aleece wouldn't ask for supporting details. She doubted the woman had ever noticed the balustrades of the north wing were the perfect height and width for practicing tightwire maneuvers, nor would her aunt appreciate the value of having a chamber maid who didn't mind colorful cursings in the morning.

"Well, young lady," came the reprieve of a mutter, "you choose to show your enjoyment in utterly obtuse ways." A cluck shot off the woman's tongue, sharper than the kitchen maids' children tossing their marbles on the courtyard cobblestones. "Really, Kira. Surely you were *not* raised to think debacles like this afternoon are acceptable. Regardless of what you think of the man, Rolf Pembroke is still a neighbor. He didn't deserve—"

"You're right." The words spilled off Kira's lips before she acknowledged their presence in her mind.

Aleece clearly shared her disbelief. The woman blinked hard at her. Several times. Finally, she forced her own mouth around some stammering syllables. "I—I'm—"

"You're right, Aunt Aleece," Kira repeated, and even nodded an affirmation this time. Beyond knowing she didn't feign the conviction behind the action, she still didn't think about she was doing. Nor did she want to. She was tired of thinking. By the saints, she was tired of *caring*. What good was caring when all it gleaned was an incinerated past, a charred present, and a future best looked at through the thick gray haze of uncertainty?

"Rolf may be a bit of an arrogant bird," she continued with an attempt at a congenial smile, "but he didn't deserve to be screeched at by a harpy dodo, either." The smile broadened, but it did *not* make her next statement any easier to articulate. "Perhaps...we can see about making it up to him in a special way."

Amazement grappled with vindication for possession of Aleece's features. Yet the moment the woman reclaimed her composure from both, and prepared to issue an appropriately gracious, yet gloating response, her face tautened into silence once more.

Kira turned to see the reason why. She looked up just as her father moved to wrap a hand around her shoulder, his own eyes sparkling with amber and bronze shards of delight, his mouth curved with a mysterious sort of pleasure...

A pleasure, Kira admitted, she *liked* bringing to his face. The smile warmed even the color of his skin, luring her to burrow closer to him as the first of the night winds sneaked around the west tower's parapets, flattened her damp skirt to her legs, and sent a chilled shiver through her.

"You heard?" she asked him then, though merely as a formality. Her father's response to the affirmative read as plainly across his face as a child's alphabet letters. And again, she inwardly conceded her happiness at making *him* happy.

Clouds closed in swiftly over that satisfaction, however, as Nicholas pulled back and fixed her with a suddenly solemn stare. "Kira, your offer is generous—as well as unnecessary. A letter of apology by your hand will be a fair enough token to Rolf. You needn't propose doing more."

"I know I needn't." Her face scrunched for a moment at the disconcerting ease with which she emulated the ornate wording. "But...I want to. Rolf has been a good neighbor to you, and everyone thinks so well of him. He...should have proper recompense."

Though she hesitated several times over the words, she battled to believe what she said. But her jaw only clenched tighter when the effort didn't work. To this minute, the only "recompense" she wished she'd given the self-sure churl was her palm print across his jaw.

Confound it, Kira! she argued with herself. *Not everyone in Yorkshire can be wrong about the man! There's something you're missing about Rolf Pembroke. Something you're just not seeing.*

Something you're just not *seeing...*

Why did those words only tighten the mangle which squeezed her heart in a seemingly permanent grip? Why did they not summon Rolf's smooth, handsome, *safe* features, but a face of completely different structure, eyes shrouded in shadow, jaw set in hatred, full lips hidden beneath a slash of compressed bitterness? Why did they make her think if she only looked long enough and doggedly enough, she'd find the man behind that forest monster...the innocence beyond the accusations?

Why did they make her gaze to that forest now, as if she could begin the miracle from where she stood? And *what* in the world made her believe her endeavor would be successful, when she hadn't wrested even a smile from the man when sitting but three feet from him? Unless, of course, she counted the times he had cracked those caustic smirks at her.

Kira bit hard on the inside of her cheek and forced her soul to accept the ruthlessly inevitable conclusion of her mind. Damien Sharpe didn't *want* anyone to know his truths. Damien Sharpe didn't *want* to smile with anything other than cynicism, or live in a world other than his dismal forest.

Damien Sharpe wanted her to leave him alone.

"Fine," she retorted to that, wresting her sights away from the forest now transformed by the encroaching night into a clump of jagged-lined blackness on the horizon. "Fine, Mister Sharpe. If that's the way you want it, that's the way it shall be. I only hope you're perfectly miserable with your decision."

Helping divert her attention further was her father's reassuring touch, both of his hands alighting on the backs of her shoulders as he said, "I'm sorry, daughter; your aunt briefly distracted me. What were you saying?"

With a smile filled with more gratitude than Nicholas

would probably ever know of, Kira pulled on one of his hands, bringing his arm around her in a comforting embrace. "Nothing, my lord," she replied softly. "Nothing at all."

She felt her father smile. "Rolf and I are scheduled for a ride tomorrow morning. Would that be too soon to deliver your invitation to him?"

Suppressing a wince, Kira swiftly replied, "No, my lord. As a matter of fact, it won't be soon enough."

CHAPTER FOURTEEN

She should have tried this cooperation routine a long time ago. As a matter of fact, Kira almost dealt herself a long chastisement for not thinking of it sooner, but tossed away the urge along with her hairpins as she chose to enjoy the dramatic cloudscapes and bracing wind which greeted her and Fred on their free afternoon together.

Though he hadn't told her so directly, the "time gift" was Father's way of saying thanks for her agreement, however halfheartedly rendered, to give Rolf another chance. The man's cheerful departure from the breakfast table gave him away this morning, though he'd allowed Aunt Aleece the pleasure of telling her about the reprieve in his stead.

Though "pleasure," Kira surmised, probably wasn't the word the woman herself would select to describe the task. Perhaps her aunt's pinch-nosed delivery came from the discomfort Kira had sensed as they'd discussed gown selections for the upcoming sojourn to Hyperion's Walk. It did seem that since Rolf's disastrous dinner visit, Aunt Aleece got flustered as a loose tent tie at any mention of the man or his estate.

Kira tossed the musing out of her head with the same swiftness she motioned permission to Fred to trot on ahead of her. This time was too precious to waste considering anything but the invigoration of being part of this land. After Aleece had released her from the last of the morning lessons, she hadn't even had the patience to wait for Ally to change her into simpler clothes. She'd simply grabbed a light velvet afternoon cloak then absconded through the herb garden, her voluminous skirts swishing every which way as she went.

Now, those layers of poplin and crinoline swirled more wildly around her than a mop wielded by a blind woman. Kira only grinned every time they did, reveling in the powerful wind sweeping her along without direction, without care; without any manners to mind or steps to watch. Above her, the clouds danced a billowing waltz across the sky; at her feet, fragrant grass brushed her ankles. The verdant stuff flowed on endlessly, the way Mama's hair used to cascade along her pillow. Just as she did when she used to run her fingers through those silken strands, Kira began to hum a little tune, letting the wind compose the soft melody just as it guided her feet...

Oh, Mama, her heart cried as her lips sang, *Mama, I miss you.*

A loud snap of underbrush to her left sharpened the ache of her heartbeat into a whetted blade of alarm. Kira jerked her sights that direction to discover the wind had steered her and Fred to an interesting locale, all right. A flower-strewn meadow was lined on two sides by towering, fragrant pines. Dark pines. Forbidden pines.

The pines of the forest Damien Sharpe had banished her from.

And right now, from the edge of that forest, a prettily spotted doe stared at them in unmoving vigilance. Only the tips of the animal's ears moved, tiny twitches showing the doe's piqued assessment of them, sending out a frightened deer's rendition of the proclamation snarled at her yesterday...

Get out! Get away from here now, and don't come back!

Though the command stung nearly as sharply as it had the first time, Kira only grudgingly respected it. Slowly, she began to step back.

Fred, however, did *not* receive the same message.

Kira realized that fact as her pet, instead of following her, cracked a friendly grin at the doe. "Fred!" she rasped as loud as she dared, "No! No friend, Fred. No friend!"

Fred answered her edict with a mutinous grimace. He turned that into a series of affectionate grunts as he decided to greet his new playmate in a more effusive manner. In horror, Kira watched her pet throw open his arms to the doe and run toward the animal with affable abandon.

"Fred!" The predicament called for a full shout this time. "No, confound it! *Stay!*"

But like a dog who recognized the "let's-give-you-a-bath" tone of its master, her pet intensified his rebellious flight. The doe bolted. Fred shrieked excitedly and ran faster. As the pair sprinted into the densest section of the woods, Fred's cackles were punctuated by smashing underbrush and the whipperings of birds taking frantic flight at their approach.

"Fred! Fred, blast it, get your sorry little rump back here now!" *At which point, I'll kick it all the way back to Scottney Hall.*

Yet while her mind hurled the spears of angered authority, the devil's own pitchfork gashed her heart to terrified shreds. One barb dug in and twisted with the realization that if she wasn't wanted here, her hell-raiser of a chimpanzee certainly wasn't, either. The second blade inflicted even deeper injury: the horrified contemplation of what Damien Sharpe would do if he came across Fred frolicking after *his* doe, through *his* forest.

Two seconds of pondering the possibilities were all the influence she needed to make a decision. Hoisting her skirts to her knees, Kira lurched into a full run down the path her pet had "kindly" forged. Sharpe's ultimatum could burn in Hades.

And if he so much as twinged a strand of Fred's fur before she found him, much more than the man's injunction would burn in Hades, too.

★ ★ ★ ★

"You should be darn grateful I'm not pining for a chimpanzee fur coat."

She snarled the words nearly thirty minutes later, past a scowl so peeved, it hurt. Dripping in sweat, pine needles, fern fronds, and mud clots, Kira had finally burst into an open space in the forest, only to promptly trip over herself because of the sudden dearth of underbrush to tromp through. Though the clearing was drenched in shadow, enough thin shafts of light broke through to illuminate her pet hunkered comfortably on a fallen log, as if merely waiting for her to catch up during their leisurely afternoon stroll. The doe, of course, was nowhere to be seen.

"Are you happy with yourself?" she huffed while pushing up onto her elbows, then her knees. "Are you *happy?* I'm filthy, Frederick, and we'll soon add *late* to that, too, if we don't find our way out of here."

She emphasized the last of that with a disparaging glance around the clearing, which appeared to be just that: a small hollow carved out of the pith of this forest, almost like a secret wizard's cave formed in the depths of a vast mountain. There seemed no discernible way in to the clearing, and *no* simple way out. The walls of dense, dark foliage rising all around her might as well have been boundaries of stone.

If stone walls also had numerous pairs of little yellow eyes.

Stifling an unsettled gasp, Kira scooted closer to Fred. So he was only a four-foot-high simian who preferred snuggling instead of fighting, but she'd lost her "lucky" stuffed horse seven years ago, during the Menagerie's run in Cincinnati, and furthermore, those eyes did *not* belong to the "Bugbear" or "Bluebeard's Ghost." *Real* paws scuffled the leaves in those thick shadows; *real* teeth made mealy gnashings at each other in that impenetrable murk.

A real shiver sluiced down her spine, then back up again.

Perhaps the portent in Sharpe's intimidations was founded in truth, after all.

"For the Lord's own sake," she chastised herself, heartened upon discovering she could summon a chuckle as punctuation. "You let Sheena tell you too many stories of the *skvoz zemliu*, Kira."

"*Holes to hell*," came the woman's voice now in her memory, so easily and clearly, along with an image of Sheena in all her dark-eyed glory, baubles jingling from the hem of her shawl as she'd twirled her arms in dramatic reenactment for Kira. "*I only saw one* skvoz zemliu *once...and yet, once was enough, Kira. I found it quite by accident, in the midst of a forest darker than the night...*"

"Stop," Kira dictated to the vision—as well as her thundering heart. "Fred, put that stick down. We're getting out of here *now*."

She held her hand out to her pet as she determinedly shoved up from the ground.

She went nowhere. A hand slammed her back down to the ground. A hand dark and stiff and corroded with wet earth—as if it had just emerged from the pith of hell itself.

CHAPTER FIFTEEN

She screamed. Loudly. But then she continued to scream, and Damien almost relented his hold, wondering if he'd seriously hurt her.

What the hell do you care if she's hurt or not? came a savage bellow from his senses, joining the tortured ringing in his ears. *The reckless fool deserves whatever penalty she has coming. She has violated* you—*again!*

That thought detonated the outrage in his gut into a ferocious sound on his lips, an outburst mixed of a snarl and a roar. He punctuated it by hauling the hoyden to her feet, then spinning her around to face him.

Her scream immediately gave way to a stunned gawk. But the bronze defiance in her eyes didn't wane by a spark; an observation Damien should have allotted more importance. *Much* more. At least if he'd wanted to elude the sudden whip of her palm across his jaw.

"What the—"

He managed to sputter the two words before her physical backlash exploded to verbal form. "You conniving, sneaking, skulking—" She paused, breathing hard, mouth working to find the right word. "—bully!" she finally blurted. "For God's sake, you scared the living ghost out of me! Probably the dead ghost, too."

The last line, muttered as half an attempt at humor, effected the opposite reaction from Damien's thread-thin temper. He shook her hard, no longer caring how she interpreted his burning glare or harsh, animalistic breaths.

"Do you think this is a game?" he leveled at her in a guttural growl. "This *isn't* a game, damn it. Papa's riches can't rescue you here, you little fool!"

Her chin jerked at him in reflexive reaction, and her eyes glistened even brighter—but at least now, shards of fear began to show amidst the brazen gold audacity of before. The sight pumped him full of satisfaction so exhilarating, it panicked him. He yearned to grab her other arm and agitate her anxiety into true terror. But the other half of him overruled that rashness, thank God. Damien wrenched away his hand, making sure to insert a flick of vehement disgust to the movement.

He only wished she had the decency to return his aversion. But no, damn her, Lady Kira Scottney had to stand there rubbing her shoulder as if he'd truly hurt her arm. She stared at him as if he'd truly offended her heart.

She didn't stop her torment at that, either. "You really think I came traipsing back here on purpose, don't you?" she murmured, leaving Damien to assume poisoned dart juice would render a less agonizing impact on his chest.

Nevertheless, he returned on a convincing sneer, "The court does find the evidence overwhelmingly convincing."

"Well, the evidence is wrong!" As she jerked backward herself, leaves and mud clumps flew from her dress and hair. He wondered if he'd ever get the chance to see her coifed and clean. Or if he wanted to. "I trespassed again only because I was retrieving Fred," she went on. "Because he went on a tear after *your* stupid doe, and—"

"Fred," he stopped her then, incredulity carving new furrows into his forehead. "Fred...your *chimpanzee*? Are you telling me you violated my express request in order to—"

"That wasn't a request. It was a royal decree."

"Stop digressing from the subject."

"That *is* the subject. Your ridiculous edict *is* the subject, and the fact that you think I 'violated' it, for whatever small-minded reason you've concocted." She slammed both hands to dirt-smudged hips. "Let me make you aware of something, Mister Sharpe. I don't give a fig about your stupid decree, or whatever it is you're hiding because of it. I *do* care about my pet, who has more compassion in his toenails than you have in your entire body."

By her concluding look of smug vindication, Damien saw she believed her final sentence as the worst damage of her diatribe. But he'd been called a compassionless bastard, and much worse, before.

He attached his attention instead on the accusation she rendered before that. "Whatever it is I'm hiding," he reiterated, each syllable gaining clearer pronunciation through his clenched teeth. "Is that what you think, lady? Is that what *they* think, up at that goddamn castle of yours?" The words came from lower and lower in his throat, yet shot seething pain higher and higher into his head. "They think I'm *hiding* something?"

The hoyden didn't say anything. But she didn't have to. No matter what she told him, Damien observed her answer in the frantic rubbing of her lips, in the hasty diversion of her gaze from his face to his boots.

"They—they don't tell me much of anything around that place," she finally blurted, and Damien conceded a grudging respect for her protection of the servants who'd clearly become her friends, as well.

"But you listen," he asserted softly. "You listen well, don't you, Princess?"

"No. *No.* Stop—stop staring at me like that. I don't know anything!"

He cocked a casual shrug. "I believe you. You don't know anything. But..." He took a step toward her with *un*casual precision, making sure she heard every last crunch of every last leaf beneath his boot. "You've formed some opinions, haven't you?"

"I told you, I haven't 'formed' anything. Look, I'd just like to take myself and my chimpanzee out of here, all right? Come on, Fred." A nervous huff spilled off her lips. "Fred, *come!*"

She sidestepped him to motion more urgently to her pet. Against reason's protesting screams in his head, Damien smoothly made the steps with her. He wasn't done with her yet, he decided belligerently. He wasn't done with this insolent Scottney who had walked herself into the lion's den he more than clearly warned her away from. *His* lion's den. Meaning he had the right to bare *his* teeth at her.

Teeth he'd wanted to sink into the Scottneys for six long, damn months.

"The possibilities *are* endless, wouldn't you say, princess?" he drawled with all-too-feigned gallantry. "After all, I live here alone, without a soul to bother me or police me, as it were. But you didn't know that, did you?"

"No," she retorted, lying as clearly as she stood there, still frantically darting her gaze for her chimp.

"No matter. You have, after all, been warned of my need for privacy in a firsthand manner." A stroke of twisted sardonicism inspired the sensual purr of his next words. "Perhaps you've even wondered what I've done about the people who didn't respect that need."

He didn't expect her, of all women, to swoon at that. But nor did he anticipate the eruption of unhesitating anger in her mien and her voice, as her chimp reappeared and she snapped a commanding finger at the animal. "Fred, get over here. We're leaving Mister Sharpe and his forest of delusions. *Now.*"

But Fred, it seemed, had other plans, for which Damien suddenly found himself glad. The moment she began to stomp toward the chimp, who had decided a fallen log needed investigating before they departed, Damien caught her soundly around the waist. He used the momentum of her determined stride to swing her around and pin her against a broad oak tree.

"What on—" came her spitting, seething reaction. "Let me go!"

Damien retaliated with a slow, feral smile. "I don't think so. No, not yet. Not until we discuss just who's got the delusions around here."

A raging snarl erupted from her throat. Damien's smile spread wider. *God,* this felt good; so damn good to have the upper hand over a Scottney once more. The exultant joy coursed through his veins, leading him to press his advantage— literally. He leaned his whole body into the purpose of holding her against that tree, halting only when his face loomed but inches over hers.

"You—damnable—barbarian," she bit out then.

"Well," he murmured back, "at least we're in agreement about something."

"What the hell does *that* mean?"

"Because that's just what I am, my lady. A damnable, dangerous barbarian..." He leaned and smiled against her temple then. "Who's now got you trapped in my lair."

"Let—me—go." She jerked away from him while firing the last syllable. But the movement was strong from defiance, not desperate from fear.

The effect on *his* body struck as another force entirely. Damien swallowed against the terrifying mix of frustration and stimulation...dear God, and stimulation. The rush of sensation was intense and primal, battle triumph now heated with sexual awakening, the yearning to bolt away from her, yet the craving to thoroughly conquer her.

His vacillation made him more vulnerable by the minute. He had to commandeer another offensive on this cunning, beautiful opponent. *Now.*

"The Indians of your great plains are private people, too, aren't they?" Before his lips finished the query, they curved in a predatory smile. He lifted his hand to her hair as he delivered the final stroke of the assault. "They scalp their violators, don't they?"

She stiffened, but didn't surrender an inch of her stance. "Let me go."

"And the ancient Celts..." he went on with ruthless ease, working his fingers to her nape, "their invaders were drawn and quartered. Interesting, don't you think?"

"Let me *go.*"

"But the conversation is getting so interesting, Princess." His voice descended into a husky sibilance, for while he spoke to her of violence, he moved against her in suggestion of just the opposite; of creating life. "I'd like to know *your* thoughts on this matter..."

"Let me *go!*"

This time, unbelievably, Damien complied with her. Perhaps it was due to her pitched cry of tearful desperation;

most likely, it was because of her frantic, scrambling shove.

The only shove she needed.

That one push not only caught him sound on the jaw, thoroughly jarring what little perspective he maintained on the situation, but propelled her completely free from him and the tree. With careening sights, Damien watched her stumble back, legs working to regain her balance, but instead, she transformed her skirts from a wrinkled mess into a hopeless tangle.

Too late, he cleared his mind enough to be capable of catching her. And too late, he saw the twined tree roots which jutted through the soil straight behind her—

Waiting to snag her foot, just as they did now.

Waiting for her to fall hard against them, just as she did now.

Breath held, he awaited her ensuing oath—for once she gave him that blatant provocation, he could start his own swearing at her stupidity. And damn it, would he give her an earful. The little idiot! The meddling, intrusive little idiot!

The little idiot who now also remained ominously quiet. Much too quiet.

And still lay heaped on the ground, much too motionless.

★ ★ ★ ★

"Christ. Ah, *Christ*."

Kira's brow furrowed of its own accord in response to the rasped words, emitted somewhere to her right, and sounding like they came from Sharpe himself. But obviously, her ears had been as damaged by the fall as the ankle which now throbbed at the end of her left leg. Damien did *not* say those words. Too much urgency seized the tone. Too much concern turned the last syllable more into a broken breath. Too much fevered swiftness marked the leaf rustlings and dirt churnings that followed, bringing the oath-maker to her side before she took two more ragged breaths.

Kira wondered who that person was. Damien Sharpe would race to rob a grave before he raced to be by *her* side.

Yet when she opened her eyes, he filled her vision; his own eyes, still endlessly black as the depths of this forest, bore into her without a blink. His hand, big and rough, engulfed hers, but she didn't remember him taking hold of her in the first place.

She wondered if she'd taken a harder fall than she thought, and she was imagining all this. Yes, that had to be the explanation, she thought with a rush of satisfaction. She was dreaming, and he really wasn't here, kneeling next to her, staring at her as if she actually mattered to him—

"What the bloody *hell* did you think you were doing!"

Now that was more like it.

Oh yes, Kira confirmed, she'd definitely been hallucinating. The man himself gave her the credence for the conclusion, following his snarl with a glare so intense, she almost laughed at the distorted absurdity of his features.

"Good heavens," she blurted, instead. "You'd better be careful, Mr. Sharpe. Fred may confuse you with one of his cousins and decide to follow you home."

A long moment passed before she realized the quip was worth giggling at. Sharpe did *not* share her mirth. His lips screwing into an agitated grimace, he instead shot to his feet—though he didn't let go of her. While she scrambled to accommodate to being jerked up like a rag doll, she attempted to step down on her left foot, and found she couldn't. Her options in the next instant were clear: cling to Sharpe for balance, or tumble to the rocks and gnarled tree roots again. Despite the bruises on her thighs and the pain now shooting up from her ankle, Kira almost opted for the latter.

The instant after that, Sharpe helped render the decision. He clasped one hand firmly around her waist, while the other steadied her balance at the most logical point of contact—the top of her hip.

Kira went utterly still the moment he touched her there. Just the sight of the man's hand on her body—*there* on her body—brought a strangely weak, yet wonderful feeling to her limbs. The sensation was a more intense version of what she'd experienced the first moment he'd loomed over her... an awareness of her smallness next to him, her womanliness next to him. Yes, this racing, reeling feeling was just the way he'd affected her then, only today, she endured thousands of torturous, marvelous tremors because of it.

If only the man himself would notice those quiverings, too. "Damn it to bloody hell," he muttered while jerking aside her skirt and giving her ankle a closer inspection. The problem was, he gave her leg all the dispassion he'd give the forecannon of a lame horse. A lame, *ugly* horse. "You're swelling like a rising soufflé."

"Then make it apple," she sallied to that, preparing to punctuate with a disgusted snort before a shriek got the better of her. "*Ow!* Damn it!" She swatted viciously at his shoulders, as well as the hand he'd slid down and now prodded against her tender injury. "What the hell do you think *you're* doing?"

As he rose, his features revealed nothing of the answer to that. His brows still slanted low over the gaze he kept directed at her foot; his mouth remained a hard-set slash against his firm-angled jaw. "It doesn't feel broken, but it's one devil of a sprain."

"Thank you, doc," she drawled. "I wouldn't have been able to figure out the answer on my own."

He grumbled something else; an unintelligible curse of some sort, Kira guessed, though not prompted by or directed at her retort. He finished the line with a quick, "Hang on," and before she could question what he meant by the command, she found herself swung off her feet, tightly yet gently supported by both his arms. Without another word, he set off through the trees down a path it seemed he alone discerned.

Kira's mouth popped open, yet she swiftly slammed it shut. She dared not speak out now, when she could see his beard stubble more clearly than his state of mind. Subsequently, the silence of her lips intensified the barrage of questions in her head.

Where was he taking her? And what was his purpose once they got there? When would he let her leave? Or would he let her leave at all?

Dear saints help her. It seemed she'd gotten herself into a world of trouble this time.

She just wondered why that realization didn't make her heart slam in terror against her ribs, or her stomach churn with terrified nausea.

As a matter of fact, Kira conceded the next moment, she felt quite secure here, ensconced between Sharpe's sturdy embrace and broad chest. From where her forehead nearly touched his jaw, she could smell the forest on his skin, the leather of the vest he wore against a simple lawn shirt, the damp collection of sweat between his hair and his nape. Male smells. Working smells. Everyday smells to her at one time, when she'd join the Menagerie crew for their midday breaks.

And yet...the essence was different now. It was different in this wild, ancient wood...it was different on the body of this large, commanding man.

This man, she suddenly comprehended, whom she trusted.

A smile exploded on her lips. *That* was the clarification to her confusion! She *trusted* Damien Sharpe. Yes; yes!

No!

The scream came from an inner part of herself—a primal, instinctual part that would *not* let itself be ignored. *No! He's been hiding in this forest for a reason, Kira! They found him standing over the dead body of his wife, Kira! They took him to court and put him on trial for that, Kira! If not for the lack of evidence, he'd been in prison right now, not carting you off to God-knows-where.*

It seemed God truly *was* the only one in on the secret of where Sharpe marched with such steady intent. Into the thickest part of the forest the man continued, emitting only deep breaths of exertion as conversation—meaning Kira had to contend with Sheena's ghost as a discussion partner.

Skvoz zemlius...holes to hell...watch out for them, Kira. They exist only in the darkest parts of the forest...

Never in her wildest imaginings could she have assumed Sheena would be so wrong. But never did she realize Sharpe had such an incredible destination in mind. Not ever would she have dreamed he'd step forth from the trees onto a plane of flat, moss-covered rock, then stop because even he had to take in a breath at the grandeur of the scene before them.

The rock ledge jutted out over a swath of green grass as thick as a bolt of new velvet, only much more luxurious.

Edging that miniature meadow were the entwined roots of several trees, which Kira took cautious note of before raising her sights to their boughs, leafy and abundant, spilling over the iridescent layers of a dancing stream. The stream was fed by a pool more stunning than any decorative reservoir she'd seen in London, its satin-like waters swirling in patterns dictated by a silver wand of a waterfall, cascading down from rocks as intricately created by nature as any man-formed pillars.

Kira took in the scene with equal parts of awe and joy. It had been a long time since her heart had halted from the force of sheer beauty. But it had been longer since her heart felt as if it had come home.

The impressions grew stronger as Sharpe made his way down a narrow dirt path to their right. Fred romped ahead, and had nearly finished his exploration of the grass patch by the time they arrived. Kira smiled at her pet's antics, and issued a soft, "Go ahead," at the chimp's questioning glance. Fred took the words and literally ran with them, scrambling up the trunk of one of the waterside trees, happy grunts indicating his progress into the boughs. A truly contented smile bloomed on her own lips, as well.

Until Sharpe set her down.

Kira winced once more as he bent to settle her on a boulder near the water, but lost an inch of his footing on some moss, and ended up plopping her on the rock, instead. Her ankle bumped against the stone in the process.

"Sorry," he emitted on his own wince. "Hell. I'm sorry."

"Oh," Kira quipped in return, her smile returning, "you should be flogged at the least."

Sharpe didn't react to that, instead returning his cobalt gaze back to her leg. "There's no other way to do this," he stated then, with a similar dose of efficient coldness. "I shall try to have a lighter hand this time."

Before Kira could query what the stars he was about, he cupped her ankle with one hand while gingerly pulling free her boot buttons with the other. After he slid the shoe off, he turned his attention to her stocking...after, of course, he moved his hands up to her knee with as much gentlemanly decorum as possible.

But nothing inside Kira felt decorous during those moments. Nothing at all. His fingers barely touched her skin, yet those unintended grazings were the exact cause of her involuntary tinglings, racing their way up her leg...and collecting in the private depths between her legs. Before she could contain it, a shuddering breath escaped her in response, releasing a rush of heat across her face, as well.

"I'm *sorry*," Sharpe roughly answered her exhalation. "There's no way to divert some of the pain."

Kira suppressed the urge to let out more demented laughter. Instead, she said on another wobbling breath, "You're not hurting me."

If she'd told him the waters had turned to wine, his hands wouldn't have halted against her flesh with such sudden stiffness. The gaze he raised back to her wouldn't be permeated with half the unblinking intensity he focused on her now. And he'd be breathing, Kira affirmed, not as statue-still as he was now, making it maddeningly easy to fill her own gaze with his hewn, bold features and his untamed waves of black, black hair.

Breathing...yes, perhaps *she'd* be breathing now, too.

Perhaps that was why the sound of her own voice sent her stomach into a somersault of surprise. "I...can see why you're such a monster about protecting this place." She even managed to circle an admiring gaze around the verdant borders of the glen. "It's beautiful here."

She was too late with the second half of her comment. Or perhaps the praise wouldn't have made a difference in the words she received as reply to the former. "I'm a monster for many reasons."

If not for his guttural delivery and lowered eyes, the man might as well have been affirming he was a chimney sweep. For one instant, the contradiction jerked Kira's sights back to him with the swiftness caused only by unguarded shock.

But only for an instant. Kira hadn't survived to see her nineteenth birthday without learning to keep her head when a beast challenged her with the unexpected. So what if *this* brute had hands which felt wondrous as they laved water over her ankle...and a torso she easily imagined touching, now that a breeze tugged his shirt away from his body, allowing her glimpses of his dark-haired chest...

"Sharpe," she heard herself say, dragging out the name's beginning, turning its end more into a puff of air than a note of punctuation.

"Hmmm?" came his answering murmur, equally soft... and as gentle as the continuing ministrations of his fingers. The man was turning her attempt at composure into a hopeless fiasco. Between his fingers and his voice, he tempted words up her throat faster than a plantain bribed Fred out of any hiding place. Unbelievable, unconscionable words.

Yet out those words came, uncaring of what he'd think of her or do to her for so baldly hurling them at him. "Did you... kill her?"

A pulse beat in his temple once. Only once. "No."

"Did you...love her?"

This time, the pulse beat twice. "No."

He'd barely moved his lips or raised his voice, but Kira heard the answer as if a choir had helped him issue it, and she swayed slightly with her answering shock to it. But this blow was more deep and disturbing than the other jolts he'd dealt her already. For what reeled her senses this time hadn't been his admission—

But her heart's rush of joyed relief as he made it.

At *that* admission, she squeezed her eyes shut against a consuming wash of dizziness.

Oh, by God and all the angels, *what* was happening to her?

★ ★ ★ ★

By Satan and all His hounds, what was this hoyden doing to him now?

The demand whirled through Damien's brain like a tempest of leaves in a March wind—much like the gust that invaded the glen then, bringing a chaos of tree cast-offs in its wake. Pine needles, acorns, and dried husks of foliage sprinkled the air behind Kira Scottney's head...behind the eyes which seared his soul with every whimsical, wonderful glance. And behind her lips, too—those lips with their questions so egregious, he should hurl her into the stream like the slick little carp she was.

Instead, he *answered* her damnable queries. Good Christ, he'd answered her *honestly*.

Oh, Nicky, came the inward snarl, mingling effortlessly with his frantic confusion. *You've trained this one well. She's taking careful notes for you somewhere behind that entrancing almond gaze, and I don't give a bloody damn. I don't give a damn about anything except how right she looks on this rock, next to me now...about how good her skin feels beneath my fingers... about how good it feels to touch* anybody *again.*

God...God, when was the last time he'd just talked to a woman like this? When was the last time someone had just let him be a gentleman?

When was the last time someone believed he could be?

A sensation assaulted his lungs then, slicing his breath in half. The sensation was so foreign, it took him half a minute to recognize the intruder, and another half minute to repress his responding laughter to it.

Holy hell. He was nervous.

The revelation returned his heartbeat to him, but didn't prevent an awkward gulp from thudding down his throat as prelude to his next clumsy mumble. "How—how does it feel now?" He gently prodded her foot.

"Fine," came Kira's quick answer—sounding as if her nerves danced at the mercy of the same fiddler as his.

Certainly enough, Damien kicked a glance up at her face, to see she already fixed *him* with a stare so open, so unschooled, he saw clear through to the thoughts inciting it. And he detected not a trace of terror in those thoughts. She was afraid, yes, but not terrified. He also noticed that the anxious sheen sparked brighter each time his fingers trailed along her foot. When he lingered an extra moment during one caress, a consuming shiver also claimed her.

He almost stopped then. He should have stopped then. But the triumphant tremors which claimed his own senses waged their attack on his self-control with equal greed. Good Christ, he couldn't remember when he had last induced a woman to shivers with his touch. Long before conceding to the logic which had guided his pursuit of Rachelle. Long before any of the dalliances before that, the entanglements full of skillful sex with practiced duchesses and cunning courtesans who all only bothered to shiver during appropriate crescendos in their playacts of love.

But when *this* woman trembled for him…this unmannered, unpretentious, and thoroughly unpredictable woman…

It made him wonder what would happen if he lingered again.

So halfway down the bridge of her foot, he slowed his fingers once more.

Kira Scottney didn't bite her lip.

She was too busy releasing an unsteady sigh.

The sound impacted Damien like a sibilance of intoxicating Greek summer wind. Only he needed no ouzo to help the breeze's influence on his body. He had but to watch this woman's eyes blink slowly, drugging him with their hooded, dark brandy pools…

Those eyes that gave him the courage to press not only his fingers, but his whole hand around her foot.

In response, Kira sucked in a breath as raggedly as she'd expelled the former. Yet her gasp was still so intense that he slackened his hold until only the tips of his fingers still touched her. "Am I…hurting you again?" True concern underlined his query.

"N-no."

Only as she issued the reply did he realize how deeply he'd hoped for it—or how heady the affirmation would be at hearing it. Dear *God*, this was insanity, thinking he could play the tender suitor again; thinking Kira Scottney would be his willing leading lady; thinking her suddenly bashful murmur and her suddenly averted eyes meant *his* nearness made *her* senses career confusedly, too.

Yes, he was courting madness. Because he was courting nothing. A reckless dervish. A chimpanzee's mother. The side-slip spawn of the man who had led the cause to ruin his life. A dream. Not even a very comfortable dream, at that.

Nonetheless, he didn't want to wake up yet.

"Then am I...tickling you?" He heard the humor sneaking into his tone with this query, but managed to prevent his lips from surrendering to the mien.

Flickerings of a smile played at her own lips. "No," she finally said, drawing the word out as she tilted her head back. "No, it feels...nice."

It was Damien's turn to fumble for breath. He returned the pads of his fingers to her skin. "Nice?"

"Mmmmhmmm..."

Another breeze rippled the branches overhead. Another current of awareness crackled between them. Leaves rained down. His heartbeat thundered louder. In the distance of his brain, alarmed screams sounded.

Listen to them, some desperate voice implored him. *Listen to them before it's too late!*

For an instant, he did. In that instant, he summoned all the strength of his lungs to force words past his reluctant, rebelling lips. "Do you want me to stop?" he asked her in the barest of murmurs.

Her first reaction came with miniature explosions in her eyes: hot gold sparks screaming at him *no*! But her lips moved a moment later, stammering, "Y-yes. Yes, I think...thank you; I think perhaps you'd better."

Damien lowered his sights and nodded hesitant

agreement. He shifted his hand to cup the heel of her foot again, taking care to slide his fingers as gently as possible along the way…

In direct contrast to the ruthless spray of water she kicked into his chest with her opposite foot.

"What the bloody—" His stunned choke severed his conclusion, as he gaped at her serenely smug expression.

Not a trace of surprise tinged the hoyden's features, however. Nor remorse. As a matter of fact, she stated with the peace of a damnable angel, "*That* tickled."

Damien stared at her. Hard. She gazed back. Innocently.

"That tickled," he finally repeated. He finished with an expectant upturn of brows, leading her toward the rest of her explanation.

"Yes," she said. And nothing more.

"And do you do this to everyone who tickles you?" His pitch contained equal parts amusement and sarcasm—and truth be known, it was an accurate embodiment of the sensations doing battle in his brain.

"Not everyone," she qualified while diverting her gaze to study the length of the waterfall. "Only grouches who need to have their scowls rearranged a bit."

So blithely did she issue the impugnment that Damien didn't recognize it as such for thirty confused seconds. Then a rankled growl rumbled up his throat. "Who the devil are you calling—"

Another wet blast cut him short, though she didn't even veer her gaze to hit her mark this time. "You're scowling again."

Damien truly found himself wishing Nicholas had been a good little libertine, and sired a male bastard. He couldn't give this wench her true comeuppance, even if she used that talented foot on his face. There was simply no way to gain vengeance upon the self-sure little Scottney, yet retain the few tatters of decency to *his* name.

No way except one.

Not hesitating another second, Damien scooped a hand into the stream, gathered enough water to properly douse her ladyship's all-too-tranquil face—then did just that.

Her stunned outcry filled him with more delicious satisfaction than he expected. But he hadn't expected the gleaming droplets on her eyelashes to make her appear even more a dew-kissed wood sprite, nor the flecks of fire in those eyes to spark with such unfettered defiance. Such mesmerizing defiance.

Such mischievous glee.

He detected the ensuing upturn to her lips a moment too late—the moment she used to turn her own hand into a substitute paddle, and jab a thick spray of water across everything from his waist down.

But Damien hardly felt the soaked chill in his legs. Not when he had the music of her ensuing giggle to distract him— and to warm him. Oh yes, to warm him as he hadn't been warmed in so many years...from the inside out.

The effect on his body made him wonder when tiny miners had decided to camp out in his limbs and explode new shafts along them. He felt like bellowing into the trees. He felt like *climbing* into the trees, swinging giddily along the branches with that impudent chimp of hers.

Instead, he forced himself to arch but one brow, slowly sneering out that side of his mouth, as well. "You've declared war, madam."

Appearing every inch *opposite* the genteel new lady of

Scottney Hall, the woman next to him angled up her own dark auburn brow. "Perhaps I have."

Before she was finished, Damien bent again to the water. But Kira Scottney, he rapidly discovered, was thoroughly capable of maintaining an angel's countenance while devising a devil's scheme. She waited until he reached his lowest point over the water before sweeping another small squall into his chest and face.

He waited for rage to flood him with equal alacrity. The wrath never ignited. Instead, another kind of heat formed behind the curling ends of his lips—the same inner warmth she'd introduced him to moments ago—only this time, he wasn't gifted with just a brief flash of the stuff...

This time, dear Christ, the heat remained.

This time, dear Christ, the heat grew. It swelled into a tidal wave that cascaded down the excavated tunnels of his body and filled them; flooded them as his retaliating splash instigated the start of a no-holds-barred water skirmish that, had the great painter Joseph Turner been witness to, would surely have been immortalized on canvas to preserve its glory. It seemed an impossible phenomenon, but it was true: the more this woman soaked him with her zealous kicks and splashes, the higher she stoked the flames rampaging his arms and his legs, his senses and his mind.

She made him smile with her tempest of giggles. She made him start with her unabashed baring of knees as she yanked up her skirts to better attack him. She made him think—really think—in order to counter the astute strategy she utilized to completely soak him.

Then, in one flash of a precious moment, she made him forget.

She made him forget who he was. Who *she* was.

In that moment, Damien laughed for the first time in six months.

CHAPTER SIXTEEN

The man's smiles didn't near the brilliance of his laugh. Kira's own laughter halted in her throat as that observation crashed through her senses with resounding surety—as she sat and watched the beauty of his mirth illuminate this shade-shrouded glen to the radiance of a sun-dappled meadow.

A meadow that darkened again all too rapidly.

As spontaneous as his laughter had come, it was eclipsed by a stare of hard and potent anger. He directed the look at her but somehow, she knew, Sharpe intended it more toward himself. As if he'd again broken some law applicable only to the kingdom of his soul—that land hidden away beyond ramparts of interminable heights.

Kira dropped her own gaze then, as a sudden downpour of hopelessness inundated her. The feeling instigated a chill to the marrow of her bones, and she trembled from the intensity of the illogical but inescapable grief.

Just yesterday, she'd raved at this man about trusting someone; if not her, than *someone*. Her anger had been ignited by the assumption he simply wouldn't do that.

Now, she realized he *couldn't* do that. Dear God...this man had lost more than his lands and his honor six months ago.

So much more.

"I—I think I should go now," she blurted then, trying to steady the rasp of her voice while sliding slowly from the boulder. "My ankle feels much better, and—"

"And you're shivering like an icicle in a morning wind." Sharpe cut her off in a tone sounding more command than observation; an impression confirmed as accurate when he swung cleanly around her, halting her path with his firm-footed stance. "You look like one, too," he appended to his statement, curving one finger beneath her chin, raising her sights back to him, whether she liked it or not.

The sight of his face, now realigned into its usual veneer of untouchable composure, deepened the chill of her sadness... and the intensity of her shiverings. To *that*, the man responded with one cluck of his tongue, then a softly drawled, "Princess... you're a real mess."

"Thanks," Kira snapped, yanking her chin away with equal pique. "I'll be sure to invite you to my show when I'm looking for a son of a bitch to help generate bad reviews." She ignored the confused frown she generated on his face then—as well as her own confused senses, merely from the impact of his touch—to shout into the trees in a tone reflecting her rising aggravation. "Fred! Fred, get down now. It's time to—"

But as if the man in front of her had dominion over the heavens, as well, an ominous rumble of thunder effectively doused the rest of her words. Tilting sights upward, Kira beheld great bundles of dark gray clouds, the promise of a literal deluge evident in their increasing girths.

A frustrated oath formed in her throat yet never reached her lips, replaced instead by Sharpe's tautly muttered directive: "That's it, Princess. It's going to dump like Noah's flood any second now, and you've got the beginnings of a cold at best. I'll not have Papa Nicky blaming me for pneumonia, as well."

Before she could wonder about, let alone question what the tarnation he was getting at, she found herself hoisted off her feet once more, pressed even closer to the man's chest as his prediction indeed came to pass; fat raindrops began to plop around them with increasingly steady fervor. Sharpe moved forward with confident strides, expertly crossing the water about ten yards downstream, where a row of slick stones formed a natural bridge of sorts.

At the other side, it occurred to Kira that she should protest their progress until he informed her where he was headed. In the next moment, she confessed she didn't care. Whatever destination Sharpe had in mind, she knew she would be safe there.

Again, she confessed the strange, but sure conviction that she trusted this man.

Sharpe himself confirmed her belief wasn't so wide off the mark when he abruptly halted, even though the rain shower threatened to become a full downpour any moment. To Kira's questioning glance, he explained, "Just making sure Fred gets across in one piece, too."

"Thank you," she replied softly to that, truly meaning the words, yet unable to escape the feeling they were shillings representing a fortune's worth of gratitude. That was why she repeated more boldly, lifting her hand to his face this time, "Damien...thank you."

Though Fred now rolled delightedly in the mud at his feet, the man didn't move on. "You're welcome," he murmured back as he lingered there, responding to her gaze as well as her words...replying to her with a stare of his own, his eyes black as they ever had been, yet emanating a message from their depths, all the same.

A message telling her he was just as grateful as she was.

Dear God, Kira thought, absorbing the impact of that look

into the depths of her heart, *has it been so long since somebody last touched you, Damien Sharpe?*

Whatever biblical scribe made the assertion that thoughts could be as detrimental as deeds certainly knew of what he spoke, for the next instant, Sharpe flinched back from her hand as if it had become a red-hot branding iron proclaiming her pitying contemplation. On hard, silent stomps, he now raced the rain through the trees, proceeding on a path only he seemed to know, for Kira certainly didn't discern any visible trail herself. She only identified that the blanket of trees got thicker and thicker, the depths of the forest got colder and colder, and the rain kept falling harder and harder.

Between one blink of her eyes and the next, the lodge seemed to appear. But perhaps the dwelling had been visible for a while and she hadn't recognized it as such. Its angled roof and dark wood construction had been so clearly designed to complement, rather than stand out from, its lush natural surroundings that the lodge indeed looked like a diminutive cousin of the pines closing in on the dozen stones serving as a front walk.

But, as some other biblical author had said, *look not on the outward appearance.* The credo was certainly true of this building, Kira discovered as soon as Sharpe carried her through the front portal. Nothing "diminutive" existed about the beauty of the room she found herself in. Its high, vaulted ceilings rose over a room populated by six overstuffed sofas, ten equally comfortable chairs and two sturdy tables, all arranged with artful abandon around a massive stone fireplace that was surely built with the intention of roasting an elephant. If the elephant escaped the fate, he could easily run to hiding places up the broad staircase flanking the wall opposite the fireplace, its banister carved with geometric designs proclaiming its purpose as function more than decoration.

"What—" Kira stammered, interrupting herself to take in the fascinating smaller details of the room: the rugged bookcase full of well-used tomes, the spirits cart stocked with mismatched colored bottles, the international patchwork of rugs across the floor that gave way to an enticing bed of furs in front of the fireplace. "*Where* are we?" she queried with a laugh as she turned around on the sofa Sharpe had settled her on.

"Home," he answered with the same pragmatic economy he employed to stack a sheaf of loose papers on one of the tables, then hastily tuck them into a wooden box stuffed with the same. "Or at least what I call such these days."

"It looks as if half of Yorkshire helped decorate it."

"They did, I suppose." In any other conversation, the statement would have been delivered with a finishing chuckle, a conversational stance. Sharpe looked and sounded more like he revealed military secrets under torture. "My father built the place after he returned from his battles in France. He called it the Hunting Lodge, though it was more his excuse to invite thirty or so friends out for a weekend of rustic cooking, home-stilled spirits, and all the cigars they could puff away before my mum detected the smoke haze on the horizon."

"And all of this is the collected result of those weekends."

"Right."

Kira spent the next moment just watching him; she intently took in the rugged lines of his profile, now cast into shades of gold and black by the flames he stirred to life. She looked at the shadows of memory in the fathoms of his eyes... she recognized the battle for self-control as he slowly blinked back those memories, and inhaled a long, uneven breath. A droplet of rain fell from his hair and trailed down the bridge of his nose.

The yearning to hold him rose in her heart, and radiated through her whole being.

She knew how he felt. Saints, did she know how he felt.

"So," she began again, pulling in a deep breath of her own and praying for its calming effect through the tumult of her limbs, "I take it you continued your father's tradition."

She reaped the tiniest of smiles on the man's full lips. "Of course."

Another moment passed. Kira couldn't drag her stare away from his lips. Curved in that mysteriously sublime expression, the sight of the man's mouth had more a maddening effect on her senses than any of his snarls did. A racing, yet weakening effect, all at the same time...

An effect that brought a giddy smile to her face, too.

As that feeling blossomed fully inside, she felt the barriers to her innermost feelings fading in its radiance. The next moment, without hesitation, she confessed to the man next to her, "I love it here."

Sharpe's humorless laugh didn't come as a surprising reaction. "That's heartening to know, Princess," he followed with an equally sardonic slant.

Kira didn't let either of the actions hinder the mischievous smirk she threw at him then. "So...do you have any cigars around here now?"

Sharpe shot her only a cursory glance in return—until he observed how serious she really was about the suggestion. Once that comprehension struck, his smile grew into a full grin, and Kira triumphed at the laugh it seemed she'd coaxed from him, as well—

The laugh he yanked back at the last moment. Instead, he bemusedly shook his head as he crossed to a closet built into the underside of the stairway. "I have *this*," he told her, producing a maroon satin smoking jacket that had to be one of the most luxurious garments Kira had ever beheld. "It shall benefit you infinitely more than a cigar."

"I'm not going to argue with that," she replied in awe as he handed her the ornate garment.

"Well. There really is a first time for everything."

"Hmmm?" Already anticipating the decadent pleasure of immersion in the robe's warmth, she only faintly heeded his murmured remark.

"Nothing," Sharpe answered, and Kira *did* look up then, for the hint of a laugh had again sneaked into his tone. "I've got to fetch more fire wood," he asserted. "While I'm gone, get out of your wet things and put it on."

"Aye aye, captain." She gave him a zealous flourish of a salute and a wide beam of a smile.

Sharpe didn't salute back. But he did smile once more, before disappearing out into the thickening rain. He took no lamp with him. But if he wielded the full power of that smile, Kira mused, it stood to reason he didn't need another light source.

That thought kept her own lips fixed in an upward bend throughout the shucking of her cloak and fan-front bodice. Yet as she worked at the back hooks of her skirt, a long sigh gave voice to the renewed onslaught of bewilderment in her head.

How is it possible for one man to possess such a spectrum of personality?

Ally had called Sharpe trouble. Tom glared at him like

Satan incarnate. The rest of Yorkshire county knew him as wife killer, conviction or not. The man himself hardly helped to negate the images, growling his way through his warnings about her explorations in his wood, then following through on that menace with terrifying enthusiasm this afternoon. He was unbending and impenetrable, a secret with legs, an uncharted territory who posted the same sign on his soul that he did on his forest: *No Trespassers Allowed.*

And yet...Kira had never seen anyone calm a skittish cockatoo with such instinctual gentleness.

Nobody she'd ever known had stopped in the middle of an encroaching rain storm to check on the safety of her chimpanzee.

And *nobody* had warmed her whole body by dipping her ankle in an icy stream. Or glided his fingers up her leg with such deliberating, hesitating grace...

Touching her as a man touched a woman.

Kira's arms slackened to her sides as she remembered those time-frozen moments next to the stream. Remembered the thunder of the waterfall in her ears...the thunder of her blood in her veins...the thunder of awakening sensation in parts of her body she'd never imagined...

Thunder crashed suddenly over the forest.

She jolted out of her reverie with a stunned gasp. No, she thought, the clouds had descended to earth and collided *in* the forest, so thoroughly did the booms fill the air for a very long minute.

But then the thunder came accompanied by a damp, cool wind.

And she realized the storm sounded so loud because the door of the lodge had been opened again. She looked and realized a figure now dominated that portal, large and rugged and dark against the wet emerald world beyond. And silent. He stood there so tense and silent, and just stared at her...

That was when the last realization struck her—like a stampeding *herd* of elephants.

She stood here before Damien Sharpe with a smoking robe clasped in her hands—and nothing but her drawers and corset clinging to her damp body.

★ ★ ★ ★

Damien felt rain droplets fall from his hair and trickle down his back, but he couldn't shake his stare, let alone his whole head. The weight of the ten logs began to burn the muscles of his upper arms and shoulders, but he gripped the wood like an armful of diamonds...or a makeshift battle shield.

God, yes, he decided, a battle shield; for war *was* what he waged here—between the sight before him and what his body wanted him to do about it. Between the half-nude nearness of Kira Scottney, and his craving to turn that proximity into intimacy.

Between his craving to satisfy his first surge of desire in well over a year...

And the look on her face that said she'd let him.

CHAPTER SEVENTEEN

"I'm—sorry," he blurted at last, and clenched his jaw against a surge of fury at the damnable, beautiful chit for making him search for form like an untouched whelp. "I should have knocked—"

"Hogwash," she cut him off, though the blade of her tone sounded as if she sliced through butter instead of the thickness they now tried to call air.

Indeed continuing the illusion she'd donned a kitchen apron to protect her gown instead of a smoking jacket to shield her nakedness, she went on, "It *is* your home, Mister Sharpe, and I was dallying instead of dressing."

Damien's eyebrows bunched together as he considered that. Were all American women as frustratingly logical, he wondered, in the midst of being so tempting?

After a minute of rumination, the answer came no clearer, and was now eclipsed by the growing aches in his arms. Deferring to the call of instinct, he no longer hesitated about proceeding to the fireplace then depositing the logs in the wood box.

The intuition, he admitted, hadn't been so difficult to obey. The unassuming manner with which *she'd* slipped back into propriety—as if her former state of dress had been more natural than iniquitous—had pulled him free from the shell of the untried lad and back into a man in control of his urges.

At least as controlled as he could be when standing alone

with a wood nymph sheathed in his smoking jacket and not much else.

"So…" he ventured, congratulating himself on the steady stretch of his hands toward the flames, "is dilly dallying a regular habit for you, Lady Kira?"

The first half of her answer consisted of a soft chuckle. "My mama preferred to call it day dreaming."

"Ah." He drew the syllable out, neither confirming his agreement or dispute of that supposition, but speculating the beauty who'd raised this creature knew well of which she spoke. "And what were you dreaming of just now?"

To his startlement, the question changed her mien like a cloud transformed a sunny meadow into a murky glen. "Nothing," she replied with shadows in her eyes. "Nothing of great importance."

To his further surprise, Damien confessed her reaction wasn't the response he'd anticipated—or wanted. So he pressed on with a question he'd not expected to pose, either. "Were you dreaming about your show?"

She fired him a stunned stare. "How did you know about that?"

"Directly from the source, my dear." Though threads of sarcasm laced his tone and small smile, Damien attempted to share his mirth with her, rather than fling it at her. "Or don't you remember? I think your exact words were, 'I'll be sure to invite you to my show when I'm looking for a son of a bitch to help generate bad reviews.'"

At that, her mouth pursed in mortification. "I did say that, didn't I?"

"Rather well."

She gave him an adorable version of an apologetic smile.

"My mouth doesn't always mind my head, Mister Sharpe."

"Thank God," Damien returned to that, granting permission to a small breeze of warmth to enter his chest as reward for the smile he kindled into a genuine laugh.

After a moment of easy silence, he offered, "I'll be bold enough to conjecture your tongue is connected more closely to your *heart*, Lady Kira."

Now, she slanted him a twinkling glance. "I suppose it is."

"And is that where your heart indeed lies? With this 'show'?"

Solemnity straightened her posture again, but this time, the stance was born of pride, not apprehension. "Yes," she answered him after a lengthy pause. Then with gathering conviction, "*Yes*. It—It's not that I don't think your country is beautiful, Mister Sharpe; it *is*—"

"Yes," he interjected with quiet conviction, "it is."

"—but I've got members of a family scattered all over the place in *my* country. Now, my father has given me a way to gather them and keep them together again. In exchange for a year of my life here, Father will give me the backing to form the most stupendous circus in the world. We'll not just rival the best. We'll *be* the best."

For a small explosion of a moment, her enthusiasm became a living force in the room, sparking excitement even in Damien's gut, before she aimed her happy gaze back toward the flames dancing in the fireplace. "Most importantly," she finished in a satisfied murmur, "we'll be together again."

She barely took a breath after that, so deeply did she plunge into the haven of her dreams. It came as little wonder that she didn't notice Damien indulging a long stare of her before he spoke again.

"Together again," he reiterated. "Just as you all were before, eh?"

Again, he wasn't surprised at her oblivion to the fact he'd delivered the question as a piece of rhetorical irony. "Yes," she answered him, completely serious. "Yes. Exactly as we were!"

"And you'll be happy then?"

"I'll be very happy then."

So emphatically did she issue the rejoinder, Damien almost felt reprimanded rather than reaffirmed. *That* was when astonishment struck him—and a surge of anger. The woman truly couldn't be so daft. No; despite all the antics he'd seen Kira Scottney instigate, not once during those adventures had he thought her a half-wit who surrendered a grip on reality so easily; who sincerely believed if she surrounded herself once more with the façades of her old life, those false fronts would transform from canvas, paint and nails into happiness, joy, and satisfaction.

She was dreaming, he concluded on a deep scowl. Dreaming dangerously. The past *was* one of those scenery flats, burned to its foundations like a Caribbean funeral effigy. The past could *not* be reconstructed again.

Nobody knew that better than him.

Damien clenched his jaw as the fury raged hotter inside him, as it always did when he forced himself to eye the bitter truth of his fate head on. But he managed to gain containment over the conflagration within a handful of deep breaths, telling himself he might as well turn her ladyship back out into the forest if he was only going to sit here and smolder at her.

No, that wouldn't do at all. He had to say *something* to her. He had to save her from the silliness of her fantasies.

Just as he wished someone would have saved him from his.

"So," he said. Just that. *Superb, Montague,* came the inward jeer, as he shifted on his feet and admitted to the strange sensation of...nervousness. *Simply, bloody superb. You've saved her now, Sir Lancelot.*

If only she wasn't so close. And so damnably unaware of how lovely the crimson of the robe looked against the cream of her skin.

"So," she repeated, not helping his dilemma by slanting a look at him full of the same curiosity in her tone...only infinitely more entrancing. The depths of her eyes pulled in the hues of the firelight, and were filled with more golden magic than he thought possible in a woman who wasn't some artist's fabrication.

For a moment, Damien gave his senses permission to swim in those deep amber depths; to experience their radiance inside of himself as well as outside. At the conclusion of that moment, he almost released an amazed laugh, for the moment at last presented him with *words.*

"So," he began again, bracing an elbow to the mantel with confrontational confidence. "Absolutely nothing can persuade you to stay in Yorkshire, then?"

"No," she replied, though a slight breath wobbled the word. "No. Nothing."

"And...no*body* either, I suppose?"

"Nobody, either."

Damien would have dismissed the soft snag in her final assertion to the bumblings of his own senses—had he not witnessed the vacillation in her gaze at that moment. Oh yes, he verified, she vacillated, all right; just as her sights urgently swerved around him now, searching for an object, *any* object, to yank her free from the heavy haze of awareness settling between them. The air grew more potent by the moment... more heated by the moment...

Nobody, either. Nobody can persuade me to stay here.

Nobody?

Nobody.

Then why, Princess, do you quiver quietly as I step nearer to you? Why do you frantically nibble the insides of your lips, making your mouth so red and irresistible? Why do your eyes flutter shut, as if expecting me to say something...to do something...

"Perhaps," he heard himself say, the sound emanating from his gut more than the lips hovering a breath over hers, "that's for the best."

"Y—Yes...for the..."

She said no more. Damien robbed the remaining sound off her lips with the passionate downsweep of his own.

She tasted like rain and wind, like wetness and wildness, her mouth a more delicious maelstrom than he ever imagined or dreamed. And yes, he *had* dreamed of this moment; he released the confession now without compunction as he kissed her deeper still. Because now, he knew what miniscule drops his midnight visions had been compared to the rain shower of awakening he truly received from this woman...and gave to her, as well.

Oh *yes*, his whole being confirmed as he at last pulled away and gazed into her face, what *he* gave to *her*, too. He raised an exploring hand to her face as he took in the lights now glimmering in her gaze, almost painful in their intensity; as he explored the damp but warm smoothness of her skin; as he watched her release a ragged sigh when his fingers traveled down the column of her neck, over the vein pulsing out the evidence of what her own body experienced in this unbelievable moment. This moment, he now saw, she'd been dreaming about, too...perhaps, like him, since those first sleepless hours after she'd careened into his world.

Damien curved a bewildered smile at that thought; at remembering the "accident" responsible for forcing her life's path across his. Yet now, the incident didn't seem an accident at all. It didn't *feel* an accident.

It felt right. So right. As right as she felt, so warm and soft and smooth beneath his touch, as he slid his fingers beneath the collar of the robe, yearning to pull the damn thing away completely, wanting to unwrap her. Hell, simply *wanting* her in a way he never remembered wanting Rachelle...

In a way he never remembered wanting anyone.

His own breath came raggedly now, terror fusing with need in his veins, rendering him motionless. He hadn't been this awkward even when tumbling his first countess behind a strategic Vauxhall hedgerow! But then, Charisse hadn't been an intrepid, inquisitive little American without a pretentious bone in her body or a status-seeking fiber in her fingernails; who could madden him with one dauntless quip of her tongue, yet then enflame him with one glance full of her spirit and fearlessness.

Who could press closer to him, just as she did now, and not appear at all calculating or coy about the action. On the contrary, Kira only brought to life the fulfillment of his deeper fantasies, emitting a needing cry in her throat born out of an instinct she didn't understand yet, let alone control. An instinct he yearned to teach her about...

An instinct now flooding *his* body with undeniable demand. With hard demand.

On a groan replete with that exquisite agony, Damien sealed his lips over hers once more as he curled his hands around her shoulders, wordlessly approving her advance, silently showing her his growing need.

His hoyden responded with an explosion of passion, echoing his moan from a place so deep within her, she trembled all over with the force of the sound. Damien was confident of that conclusion because every inch of their bodies now touched, her form molded to his, her damp warmth driving the last of the chill from his skin, her fervor and her fire setting a blaze to life in parts of himself he'd thought forever blackened and dead.

"God," Damien grated as the flames of that conflagration raged higher, burned hotter. "Ah, *God.*"

Her concurrence with that came as another head-to-toe cry, as she slid her mouth up to his again. With the kiss, she began to move against him with unconscious sensuality, fitting herself around his hardness with a need woven into the very blood and sinew that made her woman. With every writhing stroke, she stirred primal hungers into a frenzy he imagined a starved man endured when a king's feast was suddenly his for the taking. Only this woman was much more delicious than such a repast...much more creamy, much more sweet; the milk of her skin and the honey of her mouth like no other delicacy he'd savored before. As his hands raked down her back and cupped around her bottom, fitting her more snugly against him, Damien only thought of tasting more of her, having more of her, letting more of her inside his bleak and lonely soul.

And being inside her, as well.

Another epithet left his lips as *that* inferno of a thought ignited his body. Madness, he concluded; surely this was what madness felt like, this feeling of being so aware of his body, yet not *part* of his body at all. This feeling of knowing who he was, yet knowing that person only in terms of facts and dates and figures, a distant stranger who couldn't be the same person engulfed by this fire, breathing in the heat of this woman, shuddering from the texture of her skin as he pulled her down with him to the furs at their feet, and at last peeled the satin jacket away from the silken beauty of her body.

"Ohhh..." she sighed, repeating the syllable on a lower octave as he pressed to her again, suckling the hollow of her throat, nipping his way up the damp column of her neck, rocking against her as his erection throbbed more painfully against the scant fabric barriers between them. He quivered violently again—yet upon feeling a corresponding shiver claim her own frame, slowed to the point of nearly stopping.

You've got to douse the blaze now, *idiot!* he forced his brain to bellow at his body. *She's frightened and shaking, and you're half a minute away from adding* 'convicted rapist' *to your record at the York courthouse!*

But then she whispered his name. Breathlessly. Imploringly.

She slid her hands from his back to his buttocks. Urgently. Unthinkingly.

She repeated his name again. Directly into his ear. And this time, added one word that incinerated his endeavor at self-suppression in a bonfire of pure desire.

"Damien," she rasped to him. "*Please.*"

He was lost. Lost to that fevered flood she made of his blood, racing hot and torrid and uncontrolled through him; lost to the amazed realization that she didn't shake in fear, but in passion; lost to the ecstatic comprehension which swiftly came after that: that this woman trusted him. That this woman *wanted* him to take her; here, now; with the same drenching intensity as the storm now pummeling the world around them. Flowing with unstoppable demand. Thrashing with nature's mindless impulse. Crashing together with the magic of lightning, with the force of thunder. Crashing; *God, yes*, crashing...

Crashing.

Something was crashing outside. Loudly.

A dog's frantic barks interspersed with the sound. *His* dog's barks.

"What the bloody—" Damien managed to mutter in the two seconds between comprehending the disruption—

And becoming *part* of the disruption.

He had a chance to discern the door didn't burst open by itself. Two wet-furred forms took credit for figuring out how to flip up the portal's simple bar closure, then celebrating their achievement by erupting into the room with all the cackling, barking glee of ancient savages. Only these invaders rendered twice the damage.

"Good Christ!" Damien bellowed as the forms bounded straight over an arm of the sofa, refurbishing the thing in "fresh mud puddle" before discovering where their *real* conquests lie. Down to the floor they bounded, still chasing each other as they attempted to greet Kira and him with as much slobber and snot as possible.

"Hamlet!" he shouted, with no effectiveness. The labrador had gotten in three hearty licks to his face and now moved on to the greater challenge of bestowing the same to the chimp, who insisted the two of them play a rowdy version of "peek-a-boo" first—using Kira as their peeking shield. Damien wished he could admit shock as a reaction upon witnessing the woman not only oblige them the game, but join the pair of mud balls in their sport; in truth, the surprise would have come if she'd done anything *else*.

Even so, in under a minute, he found himself working to hold back his own grin at viewing the three of them there, tussling in undomesticated abandon, cooings and pantings and giggles blending into a din that filled this room with more warmth ever garnered from thirty sweaty men. The heat took just another thirty seconds to permeate his chest, as well. The sensation spread so swiftly across his heart, Damien lifted a hand to the area, pressing it in confused irritation.

Hell. If any region of his body deserved to be buggered about this sudden change of the afternoon's plans, his sympathies lay with valleys far more southward than his chest. What the blazes was *this* attack, that it rendered him struggling for air as if a humid tropical storm surrounded them, not a chilled front from the Cheviots?

Almost as stunning as the answer to that was the fact he found it only due to his dog's clumsiness. So immersed in counter-intelligence against the strange invaders to his chest, Damien doubted he would have ever caught the moment Kira's indulgent giggles turned into whole laughs—the instant Ham made another enthusiastic lunge for the chimp, but crossed his front paws too fast and ended up sprawled in her lap, instead. Deciding to make the best of his predicament, the labrador gave his new friend an affectionate swipe of muddied paw, then made up for the damage by ardently licking the dirt away. Kira's laughter came instantly and thoroughly, igniting her whole face.

Damien's comprehension followed instantly and

thoroughly, clamping hard around his whole brain.

He didn't just want this woman with his body.

He hungered for her with his soul.

God, yes; it wasn't just her skin he still tasted in his mouth, but her vitality he still savored in his blood; the joy she took in life because she lived for something other than vengeance... because she was driven to create and to build, not demean and destroy.

The goals he'd once strived for, too. The ideals Father had imbued him with. *I've begun the dream, Damien, and now I pass it to you. I pass this land to you, and all the pride I take in it. I know* you *dream the dream now, too, Damien...and I know you'll honor it. I know you'll honor* me.

But Damien hadn't honored Kenrick Sharpe.

He'd killed him.

And the Scottneys had all but helped him load the bullets to accomplish the crime. No, those chambers hadn't been filled with lead and powder, but their effect had been just as lethal to Father's heart. They were bullets called Scandal. Shame. Distrust. And eventually, Dishonor.

As if an invisible assassin aimed a rifle barrel at *his* chest and pulled the trigger, Damien jerked backward in a series of violent starts. Yet his eyes never left the woman he thrust away from—this woman he shouldn't have even invited into his home, let alone his soul.

Or, bloody blazes, considered taking with his body.

For one instant, he let his gaze fall to the mud tracks across the sofa again—only now, he beheld the mushy paw prints like heaven-sent stigmata. Silently, he promised Ham a place of honor on the bed for the next month. His dog had been the only one to save him from his own reckless stupidity.

Moments after that recognition slammed its full force into his brain, Damien made a second vow: Ham would not be called on to rescue his sorry arse again.

And the mission to honor that pledge began now. No matter how thoroughly he likened Kira's continuing laughs to the sound of angels from the same heavens he'd just thanked for warning him from her. No matter how much she appeared one of those celestial beauties right now, her hair tumbled around her face in a riot of dewy curls, her eyes twinkling with sienna glory as she settled against the sofa, one pet ensconced beneath each arm.

No matter how inviting her twinkling gaze, as she looked up to him once more. "Damien Sharpe," she queried, though bemusement tinted her voice more than real puzzlement, "you're not turning into a moping gargoyle again, are you?" A smile teased at one side of her face. "Come here, Mister Gargoyle. I think your dark and handsome friend wishes a proper introduction."

So much for nominating Ham for knighthood. *Dog*, Damien decided, would serve just fine to describe the traitor who now reveled in the woman's scratches behind his right ear, exactly where he liked his affections. At the same time, the chimp enjoyed some gentle rufflings of his nape fur. The three of them formed a portrait if a perfectly cozy, if perfectly bizarre, little family.

The fire of conflict sucked the air from his lungs once more. He was *not* a family man, Damien told himself. He hadn't been for six months. He never would be again.

Her family had made sure of that.

"No," he at last said to her, glad of the fact he hadn't even made an effort to sound so dead and cold. "No, I don't think that's wise, my lady."

"My lady," she repeated in the kind of murmur a person used before they got ill. Yet she didn't surprise him when yanking her chin aloft the next moment. "My name is *Kira*, and I'll thank you to call me that unless I really *am* your lady."

Damien gave no comeback to that. In her own idiosyncratic way, the woman had a bloody rational point.

"I'll also thank you to tell me what the blazing tarnation is wrong, Damien."

That demand, he truly had no intention of satisfying. Pivoting to her clothes, which she'd draped between two chairs, he scooped up the pieces of soiled but warmed fabric with brisk concentration.

"It's...late," he said to her instead, thrusting the garments at her. The sooner the temptingly feminine things were out of his hands, the better. The sooner this entrancing angel was covered with them again and out of his life, the better. "Yes," he repeated, making it a demand this time, "late. You should be going. Now."

★ ★ ★ ★

She didn't agree with him. As a matter of fact, had he and she been opposing Lords of Parliament, she would have forced the entire chamber to keep hours until midnight due to her silent, stiff protest to his assertion. She didn't break the unspeaking affront until Damien carried her across the crest of the high knoll overlooking Scottney Hall—just steps from where he and Dante had wondered about her mere weeks ago. He looked to the spot where he'd pondered her boldness, her recklessness, her quirkiness...where he'd tried to envision how all the facets of a creature named Kira appeared when more intimate demands were rendered upon her senses…

Dear God, Damien inwardly groaned. Now those days seemed but a minute ago. And at the same time, a lifetime ago.

Because now he knew. Now, his wonderings no longer went answered by frustrated curiosity. Now he knew exactly what kind of a diamond a man held when he stirred this woman to desire.

A radiant, fiery treasure of a diamond…

For a splinter of a moment, Damien hesitated his pace. Retightened his hold around Kira. And clenched his way through the urge to whirl back around, return to the lodge, and hoard his discovered jewel forever. Yes, damn it, *his* jewel. The prize *he'd* unearthed beneath the recalcitrant hoyden.

A journey he never should have begun in the first place.

That thought effectively helped him bring *this* hike to an end. He crouched to set Kira down as gently as possible, but needn't have bothered with the courtesy. As soon as she was able, she pushed against him with determined ferocity, tumbling her way out of his arms like a cat frantically escaping a trip to the bath. She landed hard on the mushy ground—and her left leg.

"Damn it," Damien growled, the words inflected with more savagery because he really meant them for himself, not her, "have a care for what you're doing!"

To the arm he offered as seemingly ironic aid after the disparaging remark, she flung an equally searing glare. "As if *you* 'have a care,' Mister Sharpe?"

Touché, he yearned to chuckle darkly in response. *I deserved that, little hoyden.*

And yes, damn you, I do care. No matter how hard I tried to fight you off and order you away, Kira, you made me really care again...

That's why I'm doing this, hoyden. That's why I'm doing this now...before I bruise much more than your ankle and your ego.

"I really shouldn't accompany you further," he muttered, feeling more like he confessed he'd have to cut her leg off. "And it looks as if the clouds are clearing off. Can you make it from here?"

"Would you care if I couldn't?"

When he gave her nothing but silence as reply, she raised her gaze from his arm to his face, using that one unguarded moment to make certain he beheld the intensity of the pain-kindled blaze in her eyes. Indeed, Damien's senses raged at the confines of his skeleton, but he forced himself to meet her stare moment for moment. Perhaps, he hoped, perhaps for a shard of a second she'd peer through the flames and the façade of his own stare, and glimpse once more the man she'd reignited in the lodge, during that storm when even time and reason had been washed away.

If she did see anything during that confrontation, Kira didn't notify him of her observation now. Instead, she bid her chimp to her side with a stiff snap of fingers, then turned from him as she gave him one last statement, spoken with cold calm.

"Don't waste another of your precious thoughts on me, Mister Sharpe. I've vaulted off speeding horses on worse sprains than this."

As she took her pet's paw and began limping away, he willed his jaw to open, even forced air up from his lungs—only to find his brain a mutinous participant in the endeavor for words, any right words, to say to her.

It's better this way.

He didn't know what part of him produced that announcement, but he knew his gut recognized it as truth, however bitter the dose. At best, her ladyship Kira was pure danger to the ramparts of his control, with her arrows of adorable Russian tirades, uninhibited readiness to laugh, and intoxicating passions. At worst, she was the gust which would start the hurricane once more, whipping the winds of Yorkshire into a tempest involving the heavens themselves. And this time, he was certain Nicholas Scottney wouldn't rest until the tatters of his honor had become dust in the wind.

Yes, it was all better this way. Better that he had found the strength to turn her away with his cad's mask firmly in place, rather than a torment of tender explanations and agonizing kisses. Better that she thoroughly hated him for that charade, giving her a reason to glare at him as she did, instead of leaving him with one of her stares bordering on magical mesmerization.

It was better, Damien commanded himself, that she didn't look back at him once as she neared her home, even though *he* watched *her* until she became an imperceptible dot against Scottney Hall's back garden wall.

Odd, he thought then. If his whole body wasn't clenched so tightly, he might just chuckle at the scene: the grandeur of the Scottney empire swallowing even the identity of its heir apparent.

Though he was certain the effect was only temporary. Once Kira Scottney bestowed a person with her cocky little smile, she climbed under their skin to stay. The first moment she tossed that mane of auburn curls and released a string of syllables sounding more an exotic sex practice than Russian oath-taking, her prey was forced to not only acknowledge her identity, but be smitten by it.

And as for the man who experienced the sweetness of her kiss...

There would be no forgetting her at all. Even if that kiss had been a mistake. A very bad, very dangerous mistake.

CHAPTER EIGHTEEN

A mistake.

He'd considered her a mistake.

The surety of the conclusion blurred Kira's vision as she hobbled toward the back garden's gate, though she swiped angrily at her face several times with the hand she didn't use to pull a weary Fred along. Still, the stinging drops insisted on assaulting her eyes then welling over and sliding down her cold cheeks. And every time one of those wet warriors declared its triumph over her self-control, the tormenting impugnment came, too:

A mistake.

Every syllable of the comprehension constricted her chest as if Damien had gone ahead and stated it with his lips as well as his eyes. Oh God, his *eyes*! Why the *blazes* had she believed it possible to stir embers of warmth or light in those piths of black ice? Why had she even taken the time to look for such, especially after he'd all but dictated her departure from his robe and his home? What the devil had she thought she'd find when she did, other than a churl who truly fooled her for the devil, with his taut forehead, clenched jaw, set mouth, and *those damn eyes*. They'd been agonizingly clear in their message, though their depths remained the color of one of the abandoned Swaledale lead mines.

My Lady Kira, touching you was a huge mistake. And kissing you...well, I must have been out of my mind.

She cleared the gate by slamming it back with a hard whoosh. Nothing like pain and fury to lend a body some strength when they needed it, she mused grimly. Past the rain-kissed peonies, daisies, and even her beloved pansies she rushed without a second glance. Neither did she give half an ear to the rise of twilight wind through the willows, along with the night birds' awakening harmonies. It was an after-storm symphony she'd normally give one arm to savor, but tonight, she'd never hear it past the stinging throb dominating her head and the thrumming ache resounding in her soul.

She sought out a place of uninterrupted solitude, of dark aloneness; some forgotten nook or closet in the castle's labyrinth where her ankle and her heart could scream in pain together without anyone telling her to sit properly while she fell apart inside. She didn't want to daintily dab her tears as she battled to forget Damien's hands trailing the water over her foot at the stream...then those same hands running up her leg, so gently, so gracefully...and, dear God, those hands later on, gliding on her body in front of his fire, holding her like her skin was more precious than silk and her body more miraculous than fire.

Making her feel like fire, too. Stirring flames within her that had been but unsure smolders until today...the flames celebrating her womanhood in passionate splendor...

The flames he'd extinguished with such a violent turn of spirit, she'd almost laughed at the "ruse" he played on her. But that look into his eyes had given her the truth, instead. The truth leaving her to sweep up the charred remains of her heart in confused, frustrated silence.

Just as she'd had to do two months ago. Two months ago, when she'd stood kicking at the dead, burned rubble that had, but twelve hours prior, been the color and glory of the Webber's Magnificent Menagerie and Circus. Two months ago, when she'd entombed a part of herself with Mama and Sheena and the others; when she'd promised her heart it would never have to know such a pit of betrayed pain again.

To hell with her precious promise now, she seethed. The *diavol* himself seemed to have stolen it. For who else but the devil could be responsible for this heartache which made her ankle's injury feel little more than a bothersome throb? What else but a black-gazed demon with the authority of the Underworld could have made her forget herself so completely today...made her treasure the amazing magic of life again...

Made her *feel* again.

"*Damn* you," she rasped, stumbling harder and faster down the path. "Damn you back to the abyss you came from, Damien Sharpe!"

"Kira."

The syllables reverberated across the garden at her with such ominous portent, she considered whether her profanity had indeed summoned a member of the Underworld. But upon identifying the voice up on the veranda, she swallowed a laugh at her presumption. She doubted her three-times-a-week-to-chapel aunt would ever come within shouting distance of hell's gates.

She supposed she'd have to stop sometime, so she did. But she didn't look up. "Good evening, Aunt Aleece." She was proud of the pleasant enough tone she managed to feign.

"Kira, you are late."

"I am also tired." Her pride was premature. The act became quickly tiresome. "So if you'll please excuse me—"

"You are also filthy." That came as soon as Aleece

descended but half the stone steps; close enough to observe the extent of the ordeal her poor ensemble had endured today. "Where are your gloves? And your hat? And all your hair pins?"

Another urge to laugh mingled with bitter tears as she contemplated simply blurting the truth to that. *If you must know, auntie, I was playing in a stream with Damien Sharpe. Then the rain came, so he took me home with no escort but Fred, and I took off my clothes and draped them in front of his fire. And then...*

Then he confused me more than all of you combined.

"I've got the hair pins in my pocket," she stated past a throat constricting once again. "Aunt Aleece, I am going to bed."

"I hardly see why. It looks as if you've just come from there." A grimacing sniff contorted the woman's face. "And lying there with swine, I'd wager, as well."

"Lying with swine," she muttered, no longer able to hold in an exhausting, huffing laugh as punctuation. Her exhausted senses didn't help, using the words as permission to broadside her memory with visions of Damien's legs intertwining with hers, sleek and muscular and powerful, as he'd lowered her to his rug in the dancing firelight...

Lying with swine. For once, Aunt Aleece, you have gathered a perfect selection of words to describe a situation.

"Fred decided he wished to go on an adventure," she continued instead, the mere act of producing the words seeming a feat akin to crossing the Rockies in bare feet. "In retrieving him, I discovered some new parts of the countryside."

The wan smile she used to emphasize the humor, not to mention the sarcasm itself, received only a tighter pinch of her aunt's features. "Well," Aleece finally stated, "we attempted to hold dinner for you, but your rudeness met its limit at thirty minutes."

"I understand." She also understood her aunt's "we" as a paraphrase for "your father." At Aleece's table, delaying dinner for Victoria herself might require a decree from Parliament.

"Cook prepared a lovely meal." The woman was determined to wring every drop of reprimand from the reservoir she'd obviously gathered, even if that meant disguising the censure in "casual" conversation. "Honeyed game hens and herb pie comprised the top of the menu."

"Yes," Kira agreed absently, concentrating more on cloaking a pained wince while she passed by Aleece during her ascent up the steps. "It sounds lovely."

"It was, though the best was assuredly saved for last. Cinnamon baked apples. Your favorite, I believe?"

"That sounds delightful as well, Aunt." She finished the response at the same time she concluded the grueling climb, rewarding herself with a heavy, fatigued sigh.

For another half minute after that, her brain occupied itself with ordering the throbbing in her ankle to let her breathe again. When it did and she opened her eyes, she grew aware of the odd silence now permeating the veranda...the silence, she realized, because not another twit emanated from her aunt.

She dared a curious glance at Aleece—to see the woman had indeed abandoned her twitting disposition in favor of a halfway puzzled look. Perhaps that was because the other portion of her expression looked like...compassion.

"You really *are* exhausted," Aleece murmured, prefacing a deeper softening to her features. Kira nodded a reply slowed by true weariness, yet also fixed fascination. For the first time, she beheld the Aleece whom Rachelle must have known as Mother...the Aleece who felt something other than grief and anger, who cared for something other than her brother's cold castle. Right now, Kira admitted, it felt nice to be that something.

"I'll go speak with Cook," the woman said then, some edges returning to her tone as "Lady Aleece" once more stepped in to help handle the situation. "I'm positive some sort of a tray can be warmed and sent to your room. As you're waiting, I'll have Ally prepare a bath." She angled a knowing glance toward Kira's hem. "And I'll take a look at that ankle personally."

It took several seconds for the relief to flood Kira—succeeded swiftly by a wash of gratitude. That single look might as well have served as symbolism for a padlock, for in volunteering to tend the injury herself, Aleece also declared her intention to keep the disastrous results of Kira's afternoon shenanigans "just between us girls." Nobody at Scottney Hall would know what a mess the American had made of herself today. Not that Kira cared much what anyone here thought; in a year, everyone from Ally to the courtyard chickens would be only fond memories, anyway. The *meaning* of Aleece's goodwill was what mattered the most.

"Thank you," she replied to her aunt then, sincerity thickly underlining the words. Still, they seemed but a petal of the grateful bouquet in her heart. "Thank you, Aunt. I—" But she stopped and sighed in resignation, conceding she'd have to *show* her appreciation to Aleece in some way.

"I know," the woman filled in, her eyes showing the briefest flicker of a smile as she brushed tangled curls off Kira's forehead. "I know. Get going, now. This wind isn't helping you avoid a chill, and you've got quite a full day ahead of you tomorrow."

Kira obliged, but not without a baffled frown. A full day? Whatever did Aleece mean? She'd assumed today's afternoon reprieve was a special occasion, and that they'd be back to lessons again after breakfast tom—

"Oh, no."

The words might as well have been oaths, so vehemently did she emit them while coming to a fierce stop halfway up the servants' stairwell. Aleece would *not* have her back at lessons tomorrow morning, came the scathing reminder.

Her aunt would be hand selecting the gown she'd wear to suffer an afternoon in the clutches of Rolf Pembroke's "hospitality."

"Damnation!" Kira muttered, feeling at least a degree better as the true curse left her lips. But not "better" enough. She drummed a fist against the stone wall and wondered if this queasy sensation in her belly and this acidic burn in her throat could be forged into a true bout of something, *anything* to render her bed-bound for the next few days.

No, she concluded, that was no good. After those few days, she'd still have to face the ordeal—only it would be worse, because she'd have spent all that time in dreading anticipation of her fate. She'd have all those hours to *try* to concentrate on anything except the smooth-as-oil letch she'd have to be cordial to for a whole afternoon.

Not to mention the rough-as-stone letch she'd rather be spending that time with.

An even saltier oath escaped her as that realization clutched her heart. The words comprised a fitting accompaniment to the salty sting welling again behind her eyes. She now pounded her fist on the wall, inwardly wishing Damien Sharpe into a *skvoz zemliu* for all eternity. Wishing him there for making her feel what nobody had before—certainly none of the boys she'd endured selfish gropes from before; definitely none of the men she'd known, mostly the Webber's crew, who had all been too consumed with protecting her like a daughter or sister to notice she'd grown fully into a woman.

A woman awakened today by a forest demon with midnight in his eyes and starfire in his touch.

A woman cast aside by that demon like nothing better than yesterday's ashes.

And yet, even now, a woman whose body warmed all over from the memories of his caresses...whose nipples hardened, whose throat convulsed, whose legs threatened to fold beneath her because of the sweet heat pooling between them...

A fool.

A fool who had better cast Damien Sharpe out of her mind now!

For once, Kira conceded her complete agreement with that messenger from her brain. She compelled her body to show that compliance as well, immediately straightening her spine and ascending the rest of the stairs with a new attack of energy. Yes, she resolved, she'd banish the devil's bastard from her thoughts just as he'd evicted her from his damnable forest. Swiftly. Efficiently. Heartlessly.

And she could think of no better aid to the task than Rolf Pembroke. Who, after all, would remind her more that men were just conscienceless beasts in thin disguises?

It would be a boring, banal, absolutely perfect day.

★ ★ ★ ★

She had never made such a wrong presupposition in her life.

Her heart didn't hesitate in concurring with that admission in her mind, mainly because it was so irrevocably true. *Oh yes, Kira,* that heart followed by admonishing her in a tone oddly reminiscent of Mama's gentle reproofs, *you were wrong. So wrong, wrong, wrong!*

Thus went her inner litany, intensifying with each minute, as the Scottney carriage cleared the arched gateway bidding them welcome to Hyperion's Walk, and rumbled down the extensive drive leading to the main estate buildings. *Hyperion's Walk.* She hadn't ever paused to think about the reason for the appellation, but during their journey, Kira observed the sense beyond the poeticism of the title—in vivid, glorious detail. Oh yes; surely the father of the sun had deemed this valley would bear his name, for what other explanation existed for the caress of golden light upon seemingly every tree, flower and shrub they passed?

And what trees and flowers! Kira marveled with more amazement at each new vista they encountered. Around the first bend, a copse of evergreens cradled a rabbit family's meadow picnic ground. Around the next, a butterfly *corps de ballet* pirouetted along a wall overgrown with clover and thistles. Further up the road, ancient oaks climbed to the sky in tangled grandeur, almost as if attempting an escape from the chaos of bluebells, dandelions, and wild pink tulips grappling at their toes. The banquet of beauty went on for at least a mile, but she devoured each new course with enraptured anticipation.

Hyperion's Walk, she repeated in her mind, but her senses gave the name new and exhilarated meaning. *Hyperion's Walk.* Everywhere she gazed, nature existed so bold. Splendor dwelled so honestly.

Everywhere she gazed, she saw Damien.

A wince flashed across Kira's face. She felt like fifty kinds of a fool. Why hadn't she realized? Why had she thought just because this place no longer called the man its leader, it would no longer bear the evidence of his administration? Why had she assumed Hyperion's Walk would look more like—

The manicured grounds they entered now.

Like a bank of fog giving way to a blast of sunshine, the wilderness suddenly deferred to an expanse of precisely cut grass bracketed by pristine stone walls. The carriage wheels clattered on symmetrically laid tile stones as Tom steered them closer to a soaring, but somehow inviting, structure. The Tudor-inspired gables and windows imparted the feeling of arriving not at a castle or hall, but a home.

If only the master of the mansion really wasn't at home.

Surely enough, however, there stood Pembroke himself before the front steps, a portrait of suave grace even in his casual afternoon attire of loose stock, brocade waistcoat, and jacketless white shirt. Nicholas stood next to him, having ridden ahead of the carriage during their journey from Scottney Hall. Kira didn't understand why her nerves calmed by several beats when seeing her father, but she was grateful for the sensation, whatever its source.

All too soon, the coach slowed then stopped. Tom swung open the door, yet Rolf superseded the servant when it came time to help her down the stepping box. As she slipped her hand into his, Kira wondered if the day would ever come that she'd not think of a python when coming into contact with this man. She doubted it, especially if he planned on continuing to wear his hair as he did now, forced into fashionable waves with half a jar's worth of oily styling fixative. Kira managed to bite back the dozen gibes that instantly rose to mind at the expense of the fancy coiffure, a feat she applauded herself for as Rolf turned and aided Aunt Aleece from the coach, and *she* began a steady stream of gushing approval for the look.

"There's no explaining some people's taste," she muttered to her father, who offered his arm to escort her behind the still-chattering Aleece and the patiently nodding Rolf.

"Or the whims of fashion," Nicholas replied, also speaking beneath his breath.

"I guess the world needs a few remaining mysteries." She couldn't help a tiny giggle as punctuation then, but was validated by the crinkles deepening around her father's eyes, as well.

She was taken by surprise, however, when the next moment, he slanted that expression at *her*. And this time, Kira noticed, he really *looked*, not just glanced. "You have, however, seemed to have unraveled that mystery today," he told her as they emerged from the porte cochere into the sunlight flooding an expansive back lawn. With a proud smile, Nicholas explained, "You are the loveliest of visions, Kira."

She endured her second jolt of astonishment at the man's hands as a blush suffused her cheeks. Though Aleece had, as usual, selected an ensemble for her to wear today, Kira had defiantly ordered that pink confection—which had reminded her of a puff pastry even when they'd purchased it back in London—back into the depths of the closet. Instead, she'd chosen this simpler dress, fashioned of peach-colored muslin and trimmed in copper velvet piping, with a faux copper rose connecting the ivory lace fichu along the V-shaped neckline.

Running a hand along that lace now, she murmured in a teasing imitation of a beguiled London debutante, "Why, thank you, my lord. You speak the prettiest flattery."

"I thought that was *my* job."

Her spirit swiftly deflated at the voice emitting that assertion—the voice belonging to the lips now pulling her hand down and brushing gracefully over her knuckles. Funny, Kira thought sarcastically as she watched, she didn't think snakes possessed lips.

On the other hand, Rolf seemed intent on proving her wrong, curving his mouth into a smile displaying those lips to what some women would term "sensual perfection." Kira preferred the words "lascivious" and "leering."

If the man himself discerned that turn of her thoughts, he didn't betray that knowledge beyond his steady smile. Just like Eve's beguiling serpent, Kira added to her musings with an upturned brow.

"My lady," Rolf bade, dipping another cultivated bow, "welcome to Hyperion's Walk." As he rose, he swept a hand toward the stretch of lawn before them, its trimmed perfection only interrupted by a collection of white lawn furniture islands in the center. "My home is your home."

Thank God Aleece decided that declaration worth a bout of enchanted laughter. For while her aunt reattached herself to Rolf's arm and once more tittered away about Rolf's charm and wit, Kira had a moment to swallow against the instant, instinctual acid that had twisted through her belly at Rolf's little innuendo. *My home is your home.*

"My *arse*," she spat, narrowing eyes at the glare of sunshine on the snake's brocade-covered back.

Her right ear resounded with a series of subtle *tsks*. After that, her father whispered, "He's just being nice. You could try to do the same, daughter."

Kira dropped her sights to the grass, which she subjected to a trio of contrite skuffs. The remorse deepened as Nicholas wrapped an arm around her shoulder, reminding her once more of the hundred ways *he'd* been trying to make *her* happier since he'd arrived. "You're right," she admitted softly, and compelled herself to offer a sincere smile up at him. "I can't really get mad at a clod who has no idea he's a clod."

"*Kira.*" A heavy huff helped dispense the chastisement. "So Rolf is a touch cocky around the edges—"

"He's a clod."

"But a clod with a beautiful home...yes?"

Kira obliged him on at least that prompt. Circling her gaze around the area, she imbibed of the breathtaking view of the peaks protecting Reeth, Fremington, and Grinton beyond, their heights adorned in mosaics of gleaming snow. The mountains descended into foothills which became the lush valley occupied by a good portion of this estate, its air redolent with fresh-cut grass, sprouting acorns and the savory tang of the luncheon Rolf's kitchen staff now prepared *al fresco.*

"Yes," she finally, though reluctantly, concurred with her father. "It *is* wonderful here."

An approving sound resonated from Nicholas's throat. "I knew you'd think so."

Despite her staunchest efforts, however, she exhaled her next breath on a suddenly melancholy sigh. "It must have been horribly hard for Damien Sharpe to give it up."

One moment passed, then two, before the horror at last struck—the horror, Kira realized, that her thoughts had once more overrun her tongue; this time in a disastrous way. Her father jerked his hand away from her, joining it with his opposite hand to form a hard fist at the bottom of his spine.

As he did so, she flashed a glance at his profile, now recast in equally harsh angles. She opened her mouth three times yet slammed it shut with more rapid haste, the proper words and tones eluding her like forgotten dance steps in the middle of an opening show.

"Kira." Nicholas's low inflection told her he understood her dilemma, but he was speaking to save him, not her, from it. "Rolf Pembroke may be a clod, but he's not a murderer."

"*Accused* murderer." Hell, if her composure was surrendering the reins to raw emotion this afternoon, defiant anger might as well have a turn at the driver's box. "He was accused, Father, never convicted."

"I don't care if the Archbishop of Canterbury gave him pardon. I won't tolerate that bastard's name spoken in my presence, Kira. Please remember that, beginning *now*."

Those were the last words between them for the next grueling hour, for just then, Rolf called them over for luncheon service. Aunt Aleece fawned over the gelatin mold, fashioned for the occasion in a lime and lemon version of the Scottney family crest; she went on to praise the grilled salmon, spiced potatoes, corn salad, goose pâté, and fresh dark bread as if she'd not eaten in over a week. Rolf responded to her patter with drollery that increased in exuberance with each glass of wine he emptied—which Kira tolerated by stealing more looks at the mountains and imagining herself ensconced in some cool glade there.

But when the man picked up an extra fish filet and made it "swim" its way toward Aleece like a voracious shark, Kira knew even the mountains would provide no further patience. She jerked her skirts and herself up in one emphatic motion. "Air," she explained, ignoring Aleece's raised brows of reprimand at eschewing "proper" phrasing in favor of an exit that didn't take six hours. "I need air. Lots of it. Now."

She already had a perfect route in mind, and it was that course she set herself on with no wasted steps. The untamed foliage through which they'd first driven lay so close now, beckoning like a mischievous best friend, and Kira fought the temptation to bunch her dress up to her knees and break into a run for the wilderness. Her abrupt exit from lunch had already earned her a sizable lecture come tomorrow, she was certain, so she moderated her pace to a steady but swift stride, finally indulging an anticipatory smile when her feet left the spongy grass and crunched on pine needles.

"I promise I come bearing no talking fish."

Her smile plummeted as she came to a halt. "Mister Pembroke," she replied to the bearer of that verbal olive branch, "I would very much like to be alone right now. Besides, my aunt was taking a real liking to your talking fish." *And your vintage wine.*

She could practically hear the ropes and pulleys in his brain whizzing, trying to weigh in her remark as compliment or insult. In the end, not amazing her a bit, he did neither. Instead, he converted the comment into an assertive opportunity of his own. "And you've 'taken a real liking' to Hyperion's Walk, haven't you?"

Kira discharged a soft laugh as she took several paces from him. She had to give the man credit for one thing; his uncanny ability to identify a prey's most tender spot. And yet as if Rolf willed her to abet in his quest, she heard herself confessing, "It *is* beautiful here."

A short chuckle came from the man now leaning back against a towering pine. "Ahhhh. Gotcha," he quipped, and unbelievably, Kira found herself seconding his laugh.

She pressed her back to a tree about eight feet away. "It reminds me of Virginia, back home," she told him in a wistful murmur.

When Rolf answered with nothing but a longer-than-needed pause, she smiled, interpreting the silence as a request for more details. All too easily, she summoned up mental images of the resplendent mountains and valleys she'd traveled and loved so well, preparing to relate them to the natural splendor surrounding her now.

"Just wait until you see what I've got planned for all this, Kira."

If a polar bear's roar had broken the silence, she wouldn't have shot a stare across that clearing steeped in deeper disorientation. Though perhaps, Kira contemplated, a detachment from the Arctic was indeed bearing on them. The tree at her back now felt more like an uprooted glacier spire.

"What?" she finally got out as response to the words still not finding their way to her comprehension. "What do you mean...what you've got planned?"

"For the development of the land, of course," Rolf supplied. The well-tutored baritone still modulated his voice, but his body now resembled a tiger eager to take center stage in an opening performance, pacing back and forth across the clearing, biding his time until his ferocity could be vented. "Damien, in all his rustic charm, was also a bloody stubborn savage, if you'll forgive my vernacular. He saw some kind of wild poeticism to all this. He'd get rather wild himself, defending it to me when I suggested that a reflecting pond and sculpture garden—"

"A *what?*" Kira bolted from her tree now, blood igniting

with a wild indignation of her own. Forgive his vernacular? She had a feeling that on the list of things she'd pray to forgive him for tonight, his language would soon relegate to the end of the conversation.

"Surely Aleece took you to a garden or two before you left London," the man continued, practically chastising her, hearing her question as a true request for information and not a cry of astonishment. "Well, think of the grandeur of such a place, aided by these mountains and a collection of the finest sculptured works, commissioned from the top artisans of the world today. The reflecting pool will be fashioned of Italian marble, of course—"

"Brought here on an army of imported pack mules, as well?"

"Of course not," Rolf rebuked again, leaving Kira to wonder if she could have gotten away with suggesting message pigeons for the marble-toting employment.

He didn't give her much of a moment to enjoy her sarcasm, however. Not when he triumphantly stated, "It shall all be brought in by train."

"Train," she repeated, drawing out the word so that it made two syllables. Two syllables weighted hard by apprehension. "You mean...to the station in York, then—"

"No. I mean brought by train *here*."

"Oh, God," she groaned. "That's what I thought you meant." Frantically, she peered around, overcome by a bizarre urgency to gather all these woods into her arms, load them into the carriage, and take them back to Scottney Hall with her like protected treasures from a shopping spree. "But—" she managed to stammer, "but how—"

"A few pounds go a long way toward building friendships

in London government, Kira." The dog before her rocked back on his heels, actually proud of his corruption. "My *friends* have been all too happy to necessitate the grants and permits for a private rail line from York to Hyperion's Walk. The first spike on the line will be driven before summer."

She couldn't repress a stunned grimace any longer. "I don't believe it."

"I don't, either." Rolf's words, on the other hand, found themselves set against a bemused chuckle. The sound quickly turned into another sound, a growl reminding her of a tiger once more, only now in a state of delicious conquest.

A sound making her want to throw up.

"The best part about this is that I'm *making* money on the whole project. Half a dozen buyers have already committed to shipments of the lumber from these trees. A small mill will have to be built, of course. We'll position it right next to the switchback on the line."

"A small mill," Kira echoed, the words tasting like sour milk in her mouth. "Next to the switchback."

"Precisely."

No, she thought, *not* precisely. Not at all. Something still wasn't right. Something still didn't work correctly into Rolf's grand plan.

On a surge of glaring realization, she recognized what that something was.

"What about your tenants, Mister Pembroke?" she asked him then, her voice no longer hesitant, her stance straightening and stiffening. "What about the land they've farmed and the animals they've raised for generations? The last time I checked, sheep couldn't graze on switchbacks."

"And the last time *I* checked, time didn't stand still for

anyone." Changing his weight from his heels to an even-footed bearing, he nevertheless didn't attempt to confront her eye-to-eye. Instead, looking out to some point on the distant horizon, he finished, "People will simply be taught new skills, Kira. They'll have to change as Hyperion's Walk changes."

"And what if some people are too old to fell trees or cut lumber? What if they're not *people* at all? What are you going to do with the creatures who have found refuge in these woods, Rolf—the wildlife that depends on you for its sanctuary?"

He dropped his head then, erupting a huff sounding strangely like the beginnings of a...laugh. "That's really not my concern."

At that, Kira's lips formed the beginnings of a dozen choice "concerns" *she* had, and none of them started nor ended with laughter. But she ended up shredding each curse between her furiously grinding teeth. The effort would be wasted on any man who possessed half Rolf's callousness.

Instead, now feeling like a dangerously provoked wildcat herself, she whirled from the ass, hoping the leaves and pine needles she scattered also rained a coat of dust on his precious shined boots. Still without another word, she continued in the direction she'd set before—even though her steps were now savage stomps, thanks to Rolf's interference. Lord, what an earful she'd have for Ally tonight! She wouldn't cease, she decided, until every girlish illusion the maid harbored for the bastard was annihilated like the forest *he* planned on razing for the sake of some marble statues.

In the great name of "civilization."

The civilization in which she'd yearned to prove herself an accepted member.

Revulsion roared through her, clawing free on an

anguished cry, pumping her pace faster and faster through the trees until her legs threatened to tangle in her petticoats and topple her to the ground. As if she'd care. Let the dirt cake on her precious satin dress. Let the pine cones tangle in her hair. At least she'd be part of something *real*.

But her skirts never got the chance to trip her. After rounding a thick copse of trees, she was halted by another impediment altogether.

A building. She stopped to take in the sight of a good-sized building. A structure once created then maintained in beautiful detail, too, she surmised from the elegantly carved eaves and the masterful detail to the stained glass windows. Those panes all depicted different kinds of flowers—at least the ones that weren't broken or boarded shut. The paint accenting the carved mountain scene in the door now peeled and flaked from the wood, and a strip of curved windows down the center of the roof were also in need of extensive repair.

And yet, a definite pathway cut across the dust of the broad stone serving as a front stoop, indicating this place was still used for *some* purpose. "An abandoned hothouse," she muttered. "The perfect venue for pulling wings off butterflies, eh, Mister Pembroke?"

She was answered by a low, tormented moan. A sound that gripped her belly with dread and her heart with anguish.

Because a human hadn't produced it.

Kira cocked her head to one side, physically enacting the baffled keeling of her thoughts. The deep mewl came again, confirming to her its source: from inside the building.

"What in the world...?" she whispered, though the last of the query trembled as a more intense anxiety gripped her instincts. The last time her whole body had been gripped by such trepidation was the moment during that last show with Webber's in which she'd smelled acrid smoke, then seen the beginnings of the fatal fire...

She battled to shake her head loose from the terror which came so easily after that. Though her vision cleared, the weight of apprehension remained in her stomach, heavy as a cannon ball lodged there.

Yet when the creature's outcry came once more, ten times more plaintive than its first call, an equally urgent distress transcended her fear, inexorably dragging her forward. The movement helped alleviate the anxiety, though. As she moved across the stone and reached for the door handle, she even chastised herself for her ominous portentions. *Tarnation, Kira. A trapped kitten in a hothouse is not a tent full of perishing animals.*

But then, her mind could form no more words. For that matter, neither could her lips. The shock overwhelming her heart nearly rendered it impossible to *breathe.*

Indeed, an inhalation got tangled with a sob as she proceeded forward by scuffling steps, forcing her throat to go to fisticuffs with a violent choke. But Kira barely comprehended the pain of her body beyond the agony of her soul. She hardly cared about the tears now brimming from her eyes, outside the screams echoing in her senses.

She'd found a baby cat, all right. A baby *wild*cat. A scruffy little tiger cub she'd guess at six months old, give or take a few weeks, romped around an area dictated by a cage no bigger than ten feet square—or at least the poor thing attempted to. While swatting at a brown bug scuttling through the hay, the little one had no understanding that the chain secured to its back leg wouldn't allow it more than a six-foot radius of movement.

With each lunge it took at the bug, the chain went taut, and the iron dug into the cub's flesh. The cub's exclamations of frustration and pain gnashed into Kira's heart like the teeth he had yet to grow.

If he'd ever get a chance to grow them.

Kira wrenched her gaze away from the tiger and slowly assessed the rest of the enclosure and its tenants. *Tenants?* her heart spat. *Prisoners* was the more accurate designation, though she was certain some penitentiaries would show these creatures greater compassion. More of those brown bugs boldly zipped across her path as she passed cages containing a large and lethargic bear (held by *four* leg shackles), a llama with chewed-off sections of wool, several nasty-eyed mongooses, and a gorilla who appraised her with a hooded, defeated gaze.

She nearly threw up her lunch when coming to the enclosure next to the ape's. Lying there on the dirty hay were three African chimpanzees. Two of them picked hordes of fleas from each other's fur. The third looked asleep.

No, Kira thought as she pressed a quivering hand to her lips, the third looked dead.

This morning, she'd reluctantly left Fred behind, not wanting to wrest him from enjoying a tart-making session with his bevy of admirers from the Scottney Hall kitchen staff. Now, she realized that coincidence as heaven's abundant intervention.

For now, she also fathomed how much hell could make itself known on earth, too.

"Ahhhh. So here's where you've gotten off to."

Kira spun around, though less surprised by the voice than by the relaxed ease of its tone. Her stomach turned again while watching Rolf stroll up the aisle to her, one hand in a pocket, the other swinging casually at his side. He reeked of the same attitude Aunt Aleece had adopted during their sojourns through Picadilly Square in London, when they'd pass the begging waifs and cripples like so much mud beneath their heels.

"So it seems," she replied past a throat still struggling back oceans of bile. Her expression, more a grimace than a smile, did *not* go lost on him this time. She saw that much in the twitches of his own eyes, before he flashed her a false plastering of a smile once more.

"Forgive me if I say I'm not surprised," he stated smoothly then. "Somehow I knew you'd sniff this place out."

"It's a miracle *everyone* hasn't," Kira retorted. She sucked in her lips and clamped them between her teeth in order to stay the sting behind her eyes—a burn caused not only by anguish, but the practically visible stench of animal sweat and feces.

"Well, that's the beauty of selecting this site in which to keep our acquisitions." The second hand slipped into a pocket as the back-on-heels stance returned. "It's downwind from the main buildings; far enough away so the noises don't keep the whole household awake at night, but close enough that—"

"Acquisitions." It had taken Kira a half minute to wrangle her voice up her throat again, but now that was back, she used it with vehement force. "Acquisitions? Is that your name for these creatures?"

Why did the man's answering gape actually clutch her gut with shock? "That's what they *are*, Kira," Rolf returned in an equally ingenuous murmur. "Do you think I've got hunters and agents scouring the globe because I enjoy having smelly, snorting, dangerous beasts lurking about my home?"

"They're *not* beasts. They're living creatures, damn you,

with minds and souls and—"

"They're profit-making commodities." He severed her off with a quiet but lethal tone, like parents at Webber's used to do when ordering their children away from Sheena's tent. "You may not like that truth, Kira, but you won't change it. Look out your own *boudoir* window. Haven't you noticed your papa is one of my best clients?"

She coiled her fists to keep them from lurching for the man's neck. "You have no right to even whisper about my father's compound," she retorted from equally tight teeth. "My father has invested thought and care into the treatment of his animals. My father—"

"Is an eccentric, just like many others of his kind during these colorful times we live in. And as long as those eccentrics find it *de rigeur* to have a llama or a bear to show off during dinner parties, these animals are money in my pocket. The orders are placed and I fill them, that's all."

"My, my, my." Kira batted her eyes in mocking punctuation of each exclamation. "Mister Pembroke, I had no idea. So you're the Great White Hunter now, too, in addition to the Princely Patron of the Artists. Indeed, what a man you are!"

"And what a flippant, disrespectful girl *you* are." The man's nostrils flared and his lips twitched, as he battled to repress his ire like no more than a scandalous burp or sneeze. "I have fully explained my inculpable position in this matter, my lady. Ergo, your hostility is very wrongly placed."

"My hostility," Kira seethed, "lies right where it should be. When was the last time these cages were swept and scrubbed? And the hay changed?"

An eye twitch joined the spasms of Rolf's lips. "I have an extensive and experienced staff on hand for the maintenance of the acquisitions and their needs. I'm certain my men know—"

"Do they know one of those chimps is close to dying? Think of how many pounds *that* will cost, Mister Pembroke. And these creatures are exotic animals, not convicted murderers. You have them in iron shackles like—"

"Only the dangerous ones," Rolf qualified, raising a righteous finger.

"The dangerous ones—like a four-month old tiger cub? Don't bother to tell me he'll grow into something more fierce, because you've assured he won't see his first birthday, anyhow. Whatever you're feeding him won't equal the nutrition and attention he should be receiving from his mother."

The last word of that faltered on a frustrated sob. Still, she expected no other reaction than the response she received: a taut crease across Rolf's forehead; his fingers raising to pinch the bridge of his nose. "Kira," he said with that same parental impatience, "I think you may be overreacting a bit."

"And *I* think," she swiftly returned, "you just may be a bigger bastard than I imagined."

The insult hardly assuaged an iota of her rage, but she accepted it as enough vengeance. She'd just have to. That conclusion reluctantly reached, she spun and raced out the door, restless to be as far away from this monster as possible.

Until, just as she stumbled off the stone step, the monster's lethally soft voice cut into her senses. "Tsk, tsk. Such nasty words to hurl at me, your ladyship, when I was about to propose a mutually satisfying solution to our little problem."

Our little problem. Rolf's purposeful selection of words, in addition to his actor-perfect delivery, should have spurred Kira to a more frantic escape. Instead, she allowed herself to be snagged by a tendril of his well-woven web, and surrendered to it like a helplessly hypnotized fly.

She attempted to justify her vacillation by cocking a hands-to-hips pose and rebutting on a wary sneer, "Well, I've got to hear *this*."

Both Rolf's hands returned to his pockets. Uh-oh. Back he went onto his heels. *Uh-oh.*

"The answer is terribly simple," he stated past a mouth curled in urbane ease. "*You* should be in charge of this place, Kira. And...you can be."

Her brows slammed low over her eyes. He was right about the first assertion, of course. But there was a hidden trap door to the second, she was certain of it. "What are you talking about?" she queried, maintaining her stance.

Rolf's smile kicked up by a fraction of an inch. A fraction that carried a mile of meaning. "You can do anything you want with any part of these grounds...as soon as you've become Mrs. Pembroke."

CHAPTER NINETEEN

"I'll marry a lizard first."

The words, however harshly she ground them out, had not been Kira's first choice of reaction to this bastard's outrageous combination of proposal and insult. Her first inclination had been to break out in laughter, until she gaped harder at Rolf, and realized he'd issued his "solution" as seriously as he would an offer to a business associate. (Though more passion certainly would have been furnished for the business bargain.)

Indeed, as the briefest of dignified scowls rushed its way across Rolf's forehead, she wondered if the man realized he'd just experienced defeat at a marriage proposal, not a horse auction. Yet when he spoke again, his all-too-clear intonation gave away his all-too-clear understanding of the situation.

"My Lady Kira," he stated with aplomb befitting the stuffiest of administrative offices, "I must again caution you against speaking in such haste. I *do* possess your father's sanction on this endeavor."

"Then my father can go sop in the same swamp you crawled out of." The retort ended on a pained lilt she didn't anticipate—an aberration she experienced upon mentioning Nicholas. Fighting against that strange feeling, as well as the vulnerability it seemed to strip bare in her soul, she rushed on, "Furthermore, I don't care if Saint Peter himself arrives with your precious 'sanctions'. The answer, if your outlandish proposition warrants one, would still be *no*."

Releasing that declaration helped ease the chest cramp somewhat, though the pain played an encore in her belly as Rolf merely *tsk*ed at her again, shadings of a smile playing at his face. "You're making this much harder than it has to be," he said with sing-song inflections.

"No, Rolf," she snapped, "*you're* making this harder." She cocked a glare at him crossed of curiosity and incredulity. "Are you really so daft? I am not at all fond of you, Mister Pembroke. I don't even *like* you."

Equal surprise flashed through the glance she received in return. "What does that have to do with anything?"

At that, Kira did laugh. As she expected, Rolf didn't. The absurdity of this whole scene suddenly struck her. How many times had she dreamed, as all girls did, of the moment a man would ask her to marry him? Her fantasies had come complete with bowers of roses and stacks of candles, and were usually accompanied by the nighttime sounds of Chico's soulful violin melodies and Mama's sentimental singing. Even her most creative variations of the scene had never included a fetid stand-in for a barn and a putrid excuse for a suitor.

She shook her head while she lifted her skirt once more and murmured as pleasantly as possible, "Good bye, Mister Pembroke. I think we're finished."

"Mmmm," came the alarmingly easy agreement, even for Rolf. "Yes, I suppose we are.

"For now."

Once more, Kira stopped. Though once more, she sensed she'd regret the decision. She slowly pivoted a taut glare back at Rolf, not saying a word—knowing she didn't need to. Indeed appearing the cobra who'd just mesmerized a mouse into submission, he returned her look in smug, anticipating silence.

"I assume your father has told you about the Hyperion's Walk May Day Ball next week," he finally stated.

"He mentioned it." Kira doled out her response with quiet caution, her face equally wary, her hands remaining posed to grab up her skirt again.

"It's quite a grand tradition." Again, seemingly guileless as a boy bragging about his marble collection, he grinned, giving Kira a glimpse of the façade which had won the man devotees like Ally. "The season gets to be a bit wearisome by now, and the ball affords many an ideal opportunity to get away. We always have quite a crush, but this year the affair should be extra well attended, as it marks the grand opening of the Pavilion Ballroom, my pet project for the last four months."

"That's...er, nice." What on earth was the man up to?

"More than nice, I'd say. I'm sure you saw it when arriving. The new building with the golden shingles...it's been patterned on the grandest palaces of Persia and India."

"I'm certain you'll have a very nice time, then."

"Yes. I should, at that—especially as I am looking forward to having your father, your aunt and yourself as honored names on my guest list this year."

An obligatory thanks poised ready for release on her tongue—but the sentiment, Kira recognized, would be a boldfaced lie. She didn't care to be on the man's *market* list.

Summoning up an extra surge of nerve, she instead decided to call the sneaky serpent out from beneath his own grass. "Rolf," she fired, scattering leaves as she advanced two steps upon him, "what the *tarnation* are you about with this?"

Maddeningly cryptic serenity continued to shroud the answer she received. "Not a thing, my lady," he practically crooned at her. "Not a thing. I look forward to receiving you next week, that's all." He bowed low over her hand, sweeping his dry lips over it. "I bid you *adieu* until then."

He disappeared with more stealth than he'd used in his approach. Kira had barely tugged back her hand and steeled herself for the sneak's next ambush of manipulation when she realized he was truly gone this time. Between one eye's blink and the next. Just like that.

No, charged the combined chorus of her heart and head. *Not "just like that." Not at all.* A plaintive mewl from the toddler tiger inside seemed to cry out an ardent second to the motion.

She quickly reassessed what had just transpired here—concentrating particularly on Rolf's behavior after he called her back for the second time. Why had he halted her once more just to throw in an easy mention of his ball? Why had he given her all that easy banter about the whole thing—and then, departed so easily, as well?

Rolf Pembroke didn't make anything that easy.

And somehow, Kira now knew, the man was preparing to make the May Day Ball his *pièce de résistance* of difficulty.

★ ★ ★ ★

Several hours later, she was finally able to dismiss that foreboding premonition for at least a few minutes at a time—though the feat entailed locking herself inside the Menagerie for an hour, then an equal period of walking the Scottney gardens with Fred. As late afternoon shadows made their way around the Main Hall ramparts, she spent a majority of her time soaking up the beauty of the lovingly-tended wildflowers, liking the way the grounds staff let this section of the garden be governed by nothing more elaborate than dirt paths with stone borders.

There were certainly no marble reflecting pools. Nor was there an ounce of commissioned statuary.

The flowers weren't complaining, and neither was she.

"I had a feeling I'd find you out here, Lady Kira."

The greeting made its way down the path on undertones of friendly levity. The problem was, Kira didn't care to be on "friendly" terms—or *any* kind of terms, for that matter—with the voice's source.

Nevertheless, she replied with perfunctory deference, "My Lord Scottney."

Her father's boots made soft but steady thuds on the walkway. "How are you?" he queried in a similar cadence. He'd used the same tone when they'd arrived back from Hyperion's Walk this afternoon, the words quiet and controlled, but his eyes full of concern about her tangible silence.

She presented him with an identical response now, as she turned her sights to the mountains rising in the distance. The setting sun made the peaks appear dipped in a huge vat of Cook's honey apple glaze. "It's a lovely evening, isn't it?" she finally murmured, almost to herself—and purposely so.

She endured a start of surprise the next moment. Without conscious thought, she'd just utilized one of Aunt Aleece's silly "etiquette tactics." But before she could properly condemn herself for the lapse, her father gave her a bigger shock: proof that the maneuvering worked.

"Bloody hell, Kira," Nicholas pronounced. "You're going to unpack your goods right here and now, no matter what they are, or we'll stand here all night until you do!"

For a fraction of a second, a handful of flippant quips sprang to mind as response to her father's idiom. She might even have used one of them, if Nicholas and she stood here twenty-four hours ago. If this was yesterday, before her "England Experience" had been enhanced by a royal-sized dose of disillusionment.

But this was today. Today, her father commanded honesty, not frivolity. And today, she was ideally prepared to give that to him.

With no other preamble than an efficient pivot back toward her father, she "unpacked her goods" with clear, clipped pronunciation. "Is it true you gave Rolf Pembroke consent to propose marriage to me?"

Within the next instant, she observed why her father was wanted the country over as a business partner. Not a muscle on his face gave away what he'd answer to her. If he answered at all.

"So," Nicholas did state the next moment, "he did speak with you."

"Because he did have your permission." The words rasped in her throat, astounding in how much they stung—because, she realized only now, of much doggedly she'd hoped she *wouldn't* have to say them.

"Yes," came her father's even-toned agreement. "I gave him my approval...in broad generalities."

"In broad general—" She sliced herself short with a burst of breath ignited by sheer exasperation and rising anger. "What the hell is that supposed to mean?" she finally fired when her voice returned, fighting the dual urges to simply run from here, or wallop her father where he stood. Anything to destroy the man's obvious illusion that nothing he'd said or done had betrayed her in any way, or made her anything more than a commodity traded between two businessmen.

"It means that Rolf asked my views on the matter, Kira,"

her father replied with that same remorseless calm, "and I gladly shared those views, which are certainly no secret to you. A union between our families would be a highly advantageous match."

"Advantageous!" The outcry came on a frantic laugh, verbalizing the battle her head waged to understand what her ears heard. "I can't stand the wretch!"

Equally insane was her father's insistence on continuing his placating gentleness with her. "Compatibility in a marriage is a blessing in that comes with time."

"And *you're* the authority on the subject?" This time, true hilarity inspired her high, harsh laugh. "I think you've got your contracts crossed, my lord. A marriage bed isn't the House of Commons!"

"And *I* think you should give the matter a second consideration."

"Then maybe you should also think about going to—"

"Damn it, Kira!" He captured her attention *now*, though the swearing carried tiny impact compared to the relief of hearing him address her as a grown person, not a gullible maid. He clutched both her shoulders as he continued, nearly beseeching her: "You're not a mindless gull, daughter. You've traveled; seen the colonies and the territories, too. You've seen enough and experienced enough to know the world runs right over those who get in its way."

Reluctantly, Kira nodded. She couldn't dispute a word of his statement. Her father closed his eyes while releasing a small, relieved sigh.

"All right," he went on determinedly, "then all I'm asking is that you place all of that on the scales of your consideration, as well." One of his hands lifted to brush some stray curls off her cheek. "Kira...my beautiful Kira," he murmured. "Rolf can give you a happy, easy life. You'll never have to work hard again. And you'll see the entire world—"

"Without my circus."

She should have taken her father's replying silence as clear enough confirmation of that. But she didn't want mere agreement. She wanted explanation. She wanted to know what made Nicholas, Lord Scottney think she'd simply abandon her dream—the aspiration that had kept her from boarding the next train for London at least twelve times over the last month—or if he'd ever truly recognized her goal at all.

"Kira," he said softly at last, "everybody must grow up at some time..."

"*Bozhy moj*," she gasped. "So that *is* the way of it. You really did think you'd convince me to—" She choked on a sob of shock as she jerked back from him. "You thought my circus some silly girlish whim, didn't you?"

"Bloody *hell*." The retort began as a growl but swiftly exploded into a maddened burst of his own. "It *is* a silly girlish whim! Damn it all, Kira, you're a woman now—"

"Yes, I am." She emphasized that by marching directly to him again; by securing her feet in the same obstinate stance as his, her toes two inches in front of his. "Yes, I *am*, Father. Look at me, and see that! Look at me, and look at the dreams I cherish in my heart. *Look* at them, damn you, instead of throwing some of your fancy, worthless words at them!"

"Wait a minute." At last he did snap his head up, and his eyes burned with more burnished intensity than the sun's last departing rays upon the horizon. "Our agreement is binding," he snarled. "My word is *not* worthless."

"Neither are my dreams," Kira quietly reciprocated. "So if

you thought all it would take to turn my head from them was a handsome face and a mountain of money, then you have much to learn about your daughter, my lord."

At that, it was her father who stepped back then turned away. But he didn't relinquish an inch of his stone-hard stance, his shoulders more undeviatingly straight than the parapets of the castle he faced. In an equally rigid tone, he murmured, "I'm sorry to hear that, Kira."

"So am I, my lord," she replied—and meant it. "So am I."

★ ★ ★ ★

"Damn!"

If he'd been able to glean a pound for each time he'd gritted the word in the last five minutes, Damien surmised he'd have a small fortune puddled at his feet—the feet now fast losing their hold in the slick mud as he waged a losing battle with a stable latch that refused to slide shut.

The entire structure, though barely a tenth of the size of Hyperion's stone-walled stable, needed to be razed and rebuilt. Not that it had been assembled right in the first place, if Damien remembered the occasion halfway correctly. In honor of his sixteenth birthday—and ergo, the first time Father had included him in on a weekend jaunt to the lodge—twenty of Yorkshire's most upstanding gentlemen were also invited to help usher in his manhood. Of course, the lot of them did so with enough brandy and vodka to float the back teeth of an army.

Sometime shortly after two in the morning, Father proposed they added to the festivities with a groundbreaking ceremony for the lodge's new stable. The trouble was, nobody wanted to stop at simply breaking ground. The bigger trouble was, everybody had their own ideas about the ideal design of a good stable. The foundations were laid for what Damien beheld—and battled—now.

He'd let the whole sotted lot of them have at it again, if they stood here once more.

If he were only sixteen again. Hell, if he were only twenty-seven again. One year ago...was that too much to wish for? Yes; he needed but one year from time's relentless clock, so that he could stand here with these memories and only have to reply to them, *I miss you, Father*, instead of, *I'm sorry, Father...God, I'm so sorry I've let it come to this!*

A vehement oath, worth at least three pounds, growled up his throat to claim anger's dominion back over the grief's uninvited intrusion. But the curse wasn't enough. It barely faded the vision of Kenrick Sharpe, giddy and grogged as a seaman, swaying in this very spot as he christened his half-built stable with an empty brandy decanter.

A horrifying sting surging behind his eyes, Damien attacked the memory. He threw himself against the bar as his throat erupted with a sound between a snarl and a sob. The bar didn't slide an inch. His feet, however, made up for that. In an instant, the slick ground gave up its tenuous support. In the next instant, he went down into the muck with one swift *thwop*.

The first thought to penetrate the equally thick, yet infinitely darker, mire of his senses was the conclusion that mud tasted as nasty as it looked. Hamlet, however, took it upon himself to differ with that inclination. Just as Damien finished grimacing and began spitting, the labrador halted him with an attack of wide, wet, rhapsodic licks.

"Christ's sake, Ham," he snarled. "You're shoving this swill up my nose. Bugger *off*!"

Ham forced him to emphasize the command with a vigorous shove; behavior he immediately hated himself for, since it usually resulted in a good three-hour sulk on his pet's part. But in scowling astonishment, Damien watched the dog not only acquiesce to his rebuke, but accept it. Ham fell back into the sludge and rolled over three times before bounding back to his paws, ready for more rough play, grinning like an idiot while dripping mud, spit, and God knew what else from his lolling tongue.

The crazy beast's predisposition had Damien wishing for a three-hour sulk, instead. He didn't feel right about this abnormality. He sure as bloody hell didn't trust it.

The next moment, he knew why. And wished he didn't.

Hamlet cut loose an ecstatic bark as greeting to the chimpanzee who became as dirty as his mate after two seconds of affectionate tussling. The pair departed the mud slick quickly, however, their antics taking them to points unknown around the other side of the stables—but not before they managed to send a hearty spray of gook Damien's way.

He felt Kira's gaze upon him as he attempted to backhand some of the slime off his face.

In shock, he noticed his hand trembled at the effort. The tremors corresponded to the sudden, painful thudding in the center of his chest.

Her voice, more rich and vibrant than he remembered, did not help his torture. "Can I...give you a hand?" she offered, the intent resonating with sincerity.

Damien squeezed shut his eyes, gritted his teeth, and told his mind to command his body she really wasn't here. She was merely the 100th mirage he'd created of her in the last two days; the 100th fabrication born of regretting touching her in the first place, and regretting he'd stopped when he did.

Regretting he'd ever given the woman more than a disdainful glance when she and her carriage had first invaded his world.

"What are you doing here?" he finally replied to her by way of a lethally low murmur. When he opened his eyes again, he steeled them on the hopelessly askew stable latch. He commanded himself to hold the position until Michaelmas, if it took her that long to leave.

"Well," she replied with equally soft volume, her feet nervously scuffling some leaves, "I have to admit, I asked myself the same question a dozen times while walking here."

"Sounds like your instinct knows what its doing."

"This...isn't easy for me, you know."

"And you think it's a stroll in the garden for me?"

"At least I'm trying to be civil."

"And *I'm* trying to tell you the effort is wasted here."

She expelled a long sigh before delivering her next comeback. Damien didn't trust the sound at all. The lilt she imbued to it was too pretty, too carefree...too calculated.

"Well," she at last lilted at him, "if you want it *that* way, Mister Gargoyle—"

"Don't."

"Don't what?" He could only imagine the wide, innocent, adorable stare she joined to that. God, could he imagine.

"Don't call me that!" he returned, attacking her in the heat of his frustration, verbally and physically. "I'm not a building fixture," he growled, shoving to his feet again. "I have a name, damn it. I have a *name.*"

He didn't expect her to understand. Christ, of anyone

he had to go and unwittingly afford a peek of his soul to, he wouldn't have picked her. Not after her last visit here. Not if he expected that patch of soul to be given any more consideration than what *he'd* given *hers*.

Yes; he would have deemed Marie Antoinette a more likely candidate to generate the words he heard now, especially in the way he heard them now.

"I know you have a name," Kira stated—though every shred of sardonicism was now replaced by steady solemnity. "It's Damien Sharpe. Damien Sharpe, the owner and leader of Hyperion's Walk."

So much for self commands. Damien's inner arsenal hadn't girded itself for a force like those words...for the power she not only wielded on him because of them, but the strength she *gave* him, too. He submitted his surrender immediately, spinning and throwing a stare at her mixed of astonishment and dread, joy and sorrow, condemnation...and gratitude.

His turmoil only had its beginning there. If her voice incited eddies in his senses, the actual sight of her stimulated a hurricane. She wore no fancy walking gown or multiple layers of crinolines today; instead, her Napoleonic-style jacket and matching dark-blue skirt helped promote the captivating complexity of her features: alert eyes, imp's nose, slightly lopsided lips parted on a half-smile with the same alluring irregularity.

Despite all that, with a monumental effort, he might have still been able to look upon her with a platonic eye—

If he observed her hat on her head, instead of swinging by its ribbons from her right hand. If the hair that was supposed to be piled and pinned beneath the bonnet didn't fall around her face and shoulders in a curly, careening cacophony that somehow still looked exquisite enough for the court at Versailles itself. Luxurious enough for his tunneling, caressing hands.

God help him.

Damien cleared his throat, which suddenly felt as if he'd sucked up, instead of fallen into, the mud slick. "What the hell's blazes are you getting at?" he demanded of her in a voice that nevertheless sounded caked with dirt clods.

"Precisely what I said." Kira neither rose nor shirked from his surliness. She didn't need to. She stood there appearing confident as one of the pagan demigods she was always calling upon, absolutely assured of the honesty with which she stated her facts.

"We...visited at Hyperion's Walk yesterday," she at last went on in explanation. Damien visibly stiffened; she mercifully averted her gaze—though the next moment, he saw that mercy might have been for her sake as much as his. When she looked up again, a light silver sheen glittered against the copper of her eyes. "It was beautiful, Damien," she confessed softly. "Everywhere I looked...everything I saw..." Unbelievably, a bashful laugh stumbled across her lips. "Well, let's just say I thought about you a great deal."

He coughed again. To her mind, she'd merely expressed a fact, forthright and frank, but he didn't think he'd feel more warmly satisfied if Victoria marched up and conferred him a knighthood. He hadn't felt this way in a long time. A terrifyingly long time. "Which is why you're here?" he managed to grate in answer.

"Which is exactly why I'm here." Her smile broadened.

Damien found himself unable to return that look with anything except furrowed perplexion. "Because you visited

Hyperion's Walk, and you thought about me, and...?"

She filled in that pause with an agitated huff. "They were more than thoughts, all right?" she snapped. Then, before he could anticipate it, she tromped right through the mud to grab up both his hands into hers, squeezing them with fevered energy. "Damien, *you're* the rightful master of that land!" she professed. "You understand its magic, its beauty—"

"And its *tenants* understand that I'm a murderer." The word never failed to burn bitter bile up his throat; only with clenched effort did he swallow the sickness down now. "Or did you forget that crumb of information, Princess?"

"I didn't overlook anything." She didn't relent her grip on him. As a matter of fact, her hold tightened with her next words. "Especially the fact that *I* don't think you're a murderer."

He should have yanked away then. Good Christ, he should have gotten away while he still could, treating every syllable from her mouth as a potential lie sanctioned by the house of Scottney. Hell, perhaps even scripted by Nicky boy himself.

But at the moment, he didn't care if it *was* a script. At the moment, Damien felt only the pressure of her hands in his... he felt another human being, unafraid to touch him. At the moment, he watched only the steady fire of her gaze...another human being, unafraid to look at him. Equally intense fires raged against each other inside him. Ah God, how he wanted to believe her. How he yearned to consider even one person now dared to believe in him again.

But why the hell did that person have to be her?

The subject of his deliberations prevented them from becoming broodings by a few merciful seconds, as she returned her hands to her hips and angled a look at him replete with efficient cheer once more. "So," Kira piped, "*now* do you want to hear my offer?"

It took Damien ten seconds to concentrate on her words, not the lucky pine needle that fell and tenaciously lodged in her hair. "Your offer?" he repeated hazily, but then suddenly straightened. "Your *offer*?" He punched the word out this time.

"Yes." She rocked up on her toes, face animated like a child about to include a friend in on great mischief. "An offer that will yield advantageous results to us both."

Instinct kindled his first reply to that: a suspicious growl. "Do you realize you're talking like your father?" he said next. It was the truth, but only partly so. On *her* lips, words like "advantageous" became bright, fun opportunities. Sexy opportunities.

The irony of *that* thought was she now snapped him a glare filled with anything but brightness or fun. "My father can go freeze on the iceberg which obviously spawned him."

Well. If Nicky was thinking of submitting the script for London production, Damien pledged his place in the queue for a ticket now. "I think I may be interested in this, after all," he murmured.

"Good." She smiled again, though the look was fleeting. Still, Damien reveled in his small triumph at giving her the reason for it.

He allowed the feeling to linger as she paced a wide circle in front of him, nibbling on the insides of her lips while her forehead creased hard over the gaze she leveled at the ground.

Finally, however, her agitation eclipsed even his satisfaction. "Princess," he ventured, trying to inject some levity into the moment, "either you're plotting to assassinate the queen, or your boots are laced too tight. Which instance deals with your 'offer'?"

She didn't return even a shadow of a smile now, but she did stop pacing. Damien wasn't sure what that exactly boded, so he realigned his own mien with careful, cross-armed insouciance.

"I...have been forced into a dilemma, Mister Sharpe," she stated at last. "And I'd like you to help me...contend with it."

Now his instinct sent him specific warnings about her intent. The feelings *weren't* comforting. "And if I do?" he queried. "What's the 'advantageous opportunity' for me?"

In answer, Kira slowly slid her hands behind her back... and started pacing in that circle again. Damien bit back another growl—born of the suspicion this "opportunity" was gaining new strings by the second.

The imp who'd proposed merry mischief in the last minute now turned toward him like a pouting wood fairy caught under glass. "All right," she conceded, coiling her own arms together, "I'll just come out with it."

"What a unique idea."

His sardonicism went muffled by her despondent sigh. "I've been ordered to attend the Hyperion's Walk May Day Ball next week."

A blank stare required no effort to maintain through the next long minute. Finally, between hard blinks, he countered, "*This* is why you've wished Nick Scottney to Antarctica?" When her scowling silence provided ample enough answer, he found himself on the losing side of a skirmish with a bemused chuckle. "Pray forgive my impudence, your ladyship, but perhaps you haven't been informed that invitations to the Hyperion's soirée bring out only the sharpest claws in London's parlor kittens. Your special entrée to the event assures you'll be the subject of at least a hundred additional eyeball scratching fantasies for the next week."

He consummated that with a look dipped in blatant blitheness, though he wondered if she was cognizant of just how truthfully he'd described the deepest fantasy of half England's population. But he only needed to look once at Kira for the answer to that. Of course she didn't fathom his meaning. The only scratching or back-biting this hoyden cared about was when her chimp's misdeeds involved such.

He mentally kicked himself for arriving at that conclusion. For in doing so, he separated the two parts of her yet further: she became more "Kira" and less "Scottney." She became more the woman he'd kissed to life two days ago, not the daughter of the man he'd vowed to gain vindication from.

And, dear God, she became much more dangerous to him.

In the agitation she expressed the next moment via a string of heated Russian syllables, she also became an even more dynamic creature for him to behold, lips full and rosy from her bitings, eyes big and defiant and beautiful. The alluring spell didn't lose meaning when she switched into English, either.

"I've been informed of just how 'lucky' I am, all right?" she snapped. "The point is, I feel as lucky as a jailbird about to swing from Deadman's Tree. But his mighty lordship Scottney has issued me a damnable ultimatum about the whole thing."

"No Kira at the ball, no Kira in the ring of her own circus," Damien supplied, discernment dawning.

"Give the man a prize," she rejoined. "Bull's-eye answer."

A nearby crackling of underbrush and panting of animals denoted Fred and Hamlet's continuing enjoyment of their let's-get-reacquainted romp—not to mention filling the silence Damien had as sole response to the story just presented him. It wasn't that he didn't understand—only heaven knew how explicitly he *did* know what frustrated helplessness felt like—it was simply that he hadn't received all the facts, either. She was an American and a hoyden, yes, but she was also a woman, and no woman usually compared the opportunity to dress in satins and dance on marble to the dread of facing a hangman's noose.

Ohhhh, yes. She'd deliberately pulled out some important pages of this proposal.

"Damien," she cut into his thoughts at just that moment, soft and yet cautious, as if knowing precisely what course his deliberations had proceeded. "Damien...I can't do this by myself."

She'd pulled out some *very* important pages.

He leveled a stare at her he'd last utilized three years ago in a York tavern, when Rolf and he had taken advantage of Rachelle's absence on a London shopping trip. He'd downed entirely too much ale, then challenged the biggest brute in the place to an arm wrestling match.

"You are *not* suggesting what I think you're suggesting," he alleged, hands coiling.

He'd gotten his elbow dislocated that night, he recalled. Yet that pain didn't near what he endured now, grappling against the pull of a consuming, imploring sienna gaze.

"Please, Damien," she murmured, her voice more melodic and entrancing than he ever remembered, "please. I—I know you aren't particularly fond of me, but in this case, that doesn't have to matter."

He couldn't contain an acerbic laugh from breaking free. "It doesn't, now? Princess, I've been cut out of society for six months, not six years. Mountains erode faster than the morés of the Mayfair crowd."

"True," she conceded. "But I really need an escort for this ordeal, and you really need to get back inside Hyperion's Walk."

His incredulity about the second assertion instantly overshadowed his curiosity about the first. "I've got to know how you arrived at this apparition of thought."

She actually rolled her eyes at that. But the look wasn't as interesting as her muttered prologue to her reply; a frustrated plea to Saint George, if he got half the Russian words and intonations right.

"The scene of the crime," she said when deciding to address him again. "That's the best place to go for the most telling clues, right? Well, until now, you've had no access to that...or at least you haven't taken that access. Now, I'm giving you the chance to honorably achieve that access. Who knows? Perhaps you'll find the key piece of evidence for your case."

"My case?" He floundered through a deeper pool of astoundment. "What the bloody hell are you talking about?"

In contrast, an assured smile again spread across Kira's lips. She was back on more certain footing, even if he'd forcibly hauled her there. "You're working on proving your innocence in Rachelle's murder," she stated. "Don't gawk in such surprise; I've suspected for a week, and I've known for certain for the last two days." She actually winked at him then. "When we first got here during the storm, you put away those papers on the table like you were harboring Queen Victoria's corset size."

Damien shifted away from her, rolling his shoulders, making his body put up the defenses he felt toppling inside. "Maybe that's what I *was* harboring."

"Right. And maybe you really don't want to claim back your name, your honor, and your home. Maybe you just want to mope in this forest forever and watch Rolf turn Hyperion's grounds into a bunch of reflecting pools and statue gardens and—"

"Into *what?*"

He erupted that while spinning back toward her, the action nearly a leonine pounce. Yet Kira met his vehemence with equal conviction, eyes aglitter with gold flecks of challenge, shoulders set, feet braced in a preparatory stance.

That was why he supposed her lioness-smooth tone came as no surprise to his mind—despite the ambush of temptation it struck upon other parts of his body.

"*Now* do you understand why this can be an advantageous evening to us both?"

Damien halted an inch more than an arm's reach from her. He selected the distance on purpose, since he didn't know which yearning took priority: kissing her or strangling her.

Damn it, he let his senses rail. Damn it all, the worse thing was, he *did* understand what she meant. He knew that this woman had just issued him more than an invitation to a ball. The offer even went beyond the golden opportunity of searching out clues in the morning room he hadn't seen since they'd dragged him from it six months ago—in chains.

This offer surpassed all that. This offer represented the chance to let his tenants see him at home again. They'd all be there, too, on this most special of all nights at Hyperion's Walk. His people would see him in frock coat and white gloves; not in a courtroom defendant's box; not in a prisoner's shackles.

They'd all see him at *home.* Where he belonged.

Or would they see that at all?

He cursed viciously at himself for the thoughts; for the doubts that pelted him like a hive of enfuried bees. God, had it come to this? Was Kira right? Was he really perfectly happy "moping about" in a forest where he was called nothing, rather than confronting a society where he was called murderer? Was he going to sacrifice the prize of his honor on the pyre of his pride?

But damn it, pride was all he had left.

He glared that conviction at the woman with the pine needles in her hair and the determination in her face, as she approached him once more. In her outstretched fingers was a pristine white envelope. The missive was sealed with a tormentingly familiar wax crest: the Greek-style sun, Hyperion, shining down on a scene of pastoral perfection.

As she took his fingers and curled them around the invitation, a message emanated from her eyes, too. *Please come, Damien. I know it'll hurt...and I know it'll be hard...but I'll be there, too. I'll be there to help you.*

I'll be there waiting for you.

Then her gaze fell silent. And she let her lips do the rest of her speaking, though no words passed between them.

Softly yet deliberately, she leaned up and pressed a kiss to the corner of his left jaw.

Long after she pulled away, summoned her chimp then departed, Damien remained standing there. He felt the cold mud caking on his skin; he watched the afternoon shadows begin to lengthen into twilight. He still didn't move. For inside, he fought tremors of heat that wouldn't stop radiating down his limbs. He fought the way this insolent American had somehow tunneled her way to his soul, and brought along the blinding light of her spirit while she was at it. He fought the way she had touched him merely by believing in him.

Ah, God...by believing in him!

He fought all the things that realization made him feel. He shuddered in terror at this bonfire of sensation, erupting against the icy midnight he'd wandered for so long. The exhilaration, the anticipation, the uncertainty, the fear, the desperation...the hope. *The hope.*

All represented by one square of vellum, clutched in his hand.

"Damn," he rasped at that beautiful, horrible missive now. He slowly shook his head. "*Damn.*"

She was offering him so much.

She was asking him for so much.

CHAPTER TWENTY

What did it feel like to be on the verge of suffocation?

Over the last six weeks, Kira thought she was well familiar with the answer to that. Not a day went by when at least one memory didn't assault her with ruthless force, taking her back to that night when flames had roared to the heavens and animals had screamed in fear; when she'd battled frantically to save all her beloved beasts, yet had come far, far short of her purpose. Her throat had closed as the smoke closed in around her—

But at least smoke allowed a body to *move*. Smoke was also finicky, favoring certain places to hoard itself, grimacing in black disgust at those who chose not to play in its domain, but never daring more retaliation than that.

Not like rosewater perfume.

Gallons of rosewater perfume.

Rosewater perfume, Kira decided, was the undiscriminating spinster of the scent clan. The poor thing clung to everything and everyone in hopes of sticking *somewhere*, and instead, gave new meaning to the word *suffocation*.

Rolf's glorious Pavilion Ballroom nearly floated on a cloud of the flowery aroma, as the stuff wafted with increasing potency from the dewy shoulders and necks of "London's most influential *dames de société*," as Aunt Aleece had glowingly phrased it two hours ago. *Two hours*, Kira groaned inwardly, the words blending perfectly with the throb of her rose-scented headache. Somehow, one hundred twenty minutes sounded much more appropriate. A torturous term to match a torturous ordeal.

The worse realization was: it wasn't over yet. One hundred twenty *more* minutes stretched between here and midnight—a persecution, Kira suspected, of which she'd feel every agonizing second, if all those minutes had to be spent like this one.

She was alone, she was discouraged, and she was trapped.

She stood pinned between Miss Marietta Traybrow of Hightower Grange and Lady Lucille, future Baroness of Fitzwater (of *those* Fitzwaters, Aleece had also pointed out during her crowd appraisal), both young women of ages near hers, donned in gowns similar to the ensemble she wore. Respectively, they preened in off-the-shoulder coral-pink taffeta and dark-blue silk brocade, both their bodices then tapering to tight-corseted waists. Crinolines—unbearable layers of them—then took over, creating skirts that rivaled the bells of Notre Dame for gaudy size.

Yes, from her coil curl-topped head to her silk slipper-covered feet, Kira looked like she'd grown up behind the walls of some fashionable London address down the street from these two.

She might as well have been positioned between a pair of exotic flamingoes.

The scariest rejoinder to that thought came in observing how accurate the comparison really was. Marietta and Lucille wrested their necks in all kinds of contortions as they perused the crowd, at the same time flouncing their skirts and spreading their fans; displaying their "feathers" to best advantage, so to speak. Their antics would be kind of entertaining, Kira mused—if she didn't realize *her* purpose in the scene was being their "advantage."

"Now, Kira—" said Lucille then, "*may* I call you Kira? Well, of course; we're going to be such good friends; how silly of me! Kira, you simply must tell us all about yourself. We're fairly bursting to know about you."

"Oh, yes!" echoed Marietta, punctuating with at least the fiftieth scrunch of her elfin nose. "We're bursting! Bursting!"

Kira, personally engrossed in wondering how the girl had managed not to permanently affix her face in that expression, didn't respond. Lucille obviously interpreted the silence as permission to sidle as close as their skirts would allow, and slide a gloved hand to her shoulder.

"You're quite the mystery lady, you know," she murmured conspiratorially. "All we've heard in town is that you're from the colonies, and that you brought an adorable monkey with you."

"A monkey!" Marietta chimed. "Adorable! Adorable!"

"A *chimpanzee*." As Kira leveled the tight words, she pointedly stepped away from her new "friend's" hold. "He's *not* a monkey. I'm also afraid you've received other erroneous information, Lady Lucille. I'm from America, not 'the colonies.'"

"Well, of course," came the indulgent answer. The hand realighted on her elbow. "Now you must tell us where you had this gown made. It's exquisite, Kira; really."

"Oh yes, really! Exquisite! Exquisite!"

Another inner groan reverberated twice as loud as the first. No, Kira affirmed to herself then, perhaps she truly didn't know the meaning of death by suffocation; at least the slow, steady, wrap-its-claws-around-you-even-in-a-crowded-ballroom kind. She yielded, however, to the fact that she was about to find out.

Especially because no new arrivals to the ball had been announced in the last twenty minutes.

No long-legged figure dominated the Pavilion's silk-draped main portal, appearing a dark and exotic foreign prince himself. No black waves of hair cascaded about a face of ruggedly arresting features, the eyes there raking every corner of the room, their fathomless depths possessing more than enough room to accommodate whatever information he gleaned.

Nobody remotely different from the peacocks in this palace who called themselves men.

No Damien.

He truly didn't want anything to do with her, then.

The realization struck her solidly enough to sway her on her feet. Not that Lucille and Marietta noticed, the two now immersed in a consultation about gown fabrics which would make a war council appear a tea party. Not that anyone could see the shards of her heart as it splintered from the admission that she'd tamped down her pride and found her way back to Damien with the invitation because she yearned for much more than commiserating companionship this evening.

She yearned for *his* companionship this evening.

She'd been a childish fool.

The man was clear as Venetian glass to you, Kira, a voice resounded inside, worsening her headache tenfold, though she welcomed the pain if it eclipsed her heart's agony at all. *You were a momentary dalliance to him, and nothing more. He'll never see you as anything beyond the bizarre little appendage of the family who accused him of murder.*

She forced a deep breath down while struggling to assure herself this was all for the best, anyway. In ten more months, she'd almost be done with this cold island full of cold people. She'd be preparing her journey back home, and she certainly needed no boulders to worry about cutting loose before she left. Especially no boulders which also had the gentleness of rain in their touch, and the power of thunder in their kisses...

"Kira! Kira, aren't you coming along?" Lucille, like the reality she came with, refused to be disregarded. "This is the most delightful part of the evening!"

"Delightful!" Marietta crooned, right on schedule. "Oh, indeed; delightful!"

Kira surprised herself by managing a wan smile. Dare she entertain curiosity about what these two considered "delightful?"

It didn't appear she'd have a choice about the answer to that, anyway. Her new companions hooked an elbow through each of hers, and pulled her toward the expansive dance floor, its shiny black marble fashioned into an onion shape. The fast swishings of their skirts joined with the rising hum of excitement through the room. The twelve-member orchestra had ceased playing, and only one figure now occupied the dance floor: an impeccably attired, casually smiling Rolf.

At the sight of him, Kira unhooked herself and shifted backward. Between the throngs in the room and the man's responsibility to their needs, she'd successfully managed to avoid contact with her host beyond a brief nicety per hour. She had no intention of changing that status now, no matter how incredulous or accusing the gape Lucille spun and wielded on her.

"Kira! Have you mice in your blazing attic?"

"No," she countered tersely, her gaze still watchful of the dance floor. "Just a rat. A very large one."

"This is no time for teasing, love. Come on; this is when the fun begins!"

She couldn't help the sardonic angle with which she raised one eyebrow. "The fun?"

"Indeed!" Marietta collaborated.

"You see," Lucille responded with gentle patience to Kira's deeper puzzlement, "it's the midpoint of the ball." Her eyes, however, sparkled with excitement as she swept her open fan toward the dance floor. "Now is when we get to leave those silly cotillions and quadrilles behind, and begin the waltzing."

"The waltzing!" Marietta clapped her gloved hands.

"The *waltzing*?" Immediately, Kira's piqued interest shoved the scowl off her face. Perhaps she would liken the next two hours to merely being imprisoned instead of tortured. "There's going to be waltzing?"

Lucille's black sausage curls bobbed on either side of her nodding head. "And could there be anything more romantic than waltzing with that man?"

"That man?" Kira's frown returned. "What man? Where?"

"*There*, silly! Right in front of you. That man...Rolf Pembroke."

"Ooooo, yes," Marietta said as Lucille sighed. "That *man*."

Kira didn't know what expression to select then, having narrowed her choices to a grimace of either nausea or dread. "What...what do you mean?" she managed in a discomfited mutter.

"As host of the ball, Rolf gets to dance the first waltz of the evening." Thank heaven Lucille was a walking encyclopedia about all this pomp. "Normally, he'd select his wife, but we all know *that* isn't possible!" She shared a giggle with Marietta that stretched to lengths Kira didn't even wish to understand.

"Anyway," the girl at last continued, "he shall select a partner for this first dance...and then that lucky bird gets to be his partner for every third dance, for the remainder of the evening." In merely speaking the words, Lucille induced herself to a bout of frantic fan flitterings. "What a divine, *divine* dream!"

"Simply divine," Marietta sighed with her friend.

Kira closed her eyes and shook her head. Many words entered her mind at contemplating the fate of spinning around a giant, flat marble onion with an insensitive, self-important ass. *Divine* wasn't one of those words. *Punishment* was, perhaps. *Impossible* came even closer to the mark.

That last thought gave her the fortitude to open her eyes. She could have used an infusion of common sense, instead.

God, no, Kira raged as she looked directly out across the dance floor, to where Rolf's stare awaited with all the smoothness—and coldness—of latent lamp oil. Oil, that unblinking gaze told her, he intended to ignite in a waltz with *her.* By all the saints and even the sinners, *nyet, nyet*! No!

"No!" Lucille suddenly gasped.

"No!" Marietta swiftly seconded.

It took an instant to fathom the pair couldn't possibly be commiserating with her unspoken thoughts.

It only took half an instant more to discern Lucille and Marietta weren't the only ones in the room voicing such sentiments.

The other half of that instant resonated with the thunder of Kira's heart in her ears...a thunder echoing the thrum of power suddenly filling the ballroom to its grand-arched rafters. A presence had entered the room, she realized...a presence imposing enough and commanding enough and dramatic enough to freeze this throng of hundreds right in their patent-booted, dance-slippered feet.

In that half moment of shimmering comprehension, she smiled.

For in that moment, she knew he was here.

CHAPTER TWENTY-ONE

"I can't believe he's here," Lucille muttered, finishing with a sniff so exaggerated, the half-blind Lady Rothschild, standing next to them, reacted as if a blob of pond muck had walked itself into the room. Marietta, in a moment of shock too profound even for echoed words, made up for her muteness by sniffing longer and louder than her friend.

"Damien Sharpe," came a concurring whisper from behind them. "I never thought I'd see him in *this* ballroom again."

"What a positively delicious turn of things," someone responded. "And just think, we were about to leave."

"I don't think anyone's going anywhere now."

"True, darling, true."

"He's a savage," Lucille hissed. "Just *look* at him. His ensemble is medieval, it's so old. Did he think this was a costume ball? And his hair—ecchh! He's fooling nobody with that pomade."

"Nobody!" Marietta agreed with swift vehemence.

"How did he get in?" Lucille sniffed. "Who invited him?"

"I did."

Immediately after issuing her declaration, Kira concluded her ordeal of the last two hours had been worth every minute, after all. She even would have endured the torment with a smile if she'd known this moment would be her reward; if she'd been told she'd have the satisfaction of watching horror completely blanket Lucille's face, as the priss realized she no longer appeared best girlfriends with "the mystery woman of London," but "the scandal maker of Yorkshire."

The moment had its ideal conclusion when she turned her back before Lucille recovered enough to do so first, eliciting a round of titillated murmurs in her wake. The sound induced Kira's lips into a sublime smile, thrilling her more than a storm of applause. It was well past time a few ripples livened up Rolf's little pond.

Ripples, she conjectured, that were going to spread much wider within the next minute.

"Mister Sharpe," she said softly, arriving at Damien's side after traversing the neat path the crowd had cleared for her.

But while the journey had been easy, the going from *here* presented a clear complication. Damien's attire, though not truly fulfilling Lucille's "medieval" depiction, was still a good ten to fifteen years beyond the modes of the men surrounding them. And by Saint Nicholas, that made him into the most captivating sight in the room. His cream-colored stock was wrapped tightly around his neck, a perfect aid to show off the bold angle of his clean-shaven jaw. A regal blue, tight-buttoned jacket molded alluringly to the strong lines of his torso, and matching breeches fitted even more snugly around the defined muscles of his legs, until black Hessian boots took over from the bottom of his knees. With his hair pomaded and pulled back into a black-ribboned queue, he looked like a gentleman pirate from one of Sheena's fantasy tales...or perhaps a rogue prince from one of Mama's equally romantic stories.

He looked more beautiful than she'd ever fantasized.

How was she going to form coherent sentences with him looking like that?

Again, choices were pulled from her control; she forced composure to return to her nerves as Rolf appeared before them, flared nostrils and blazing gaze contradicting his otherwise cool mien. "Damien," he ground out. "What the devil—"

"Good evening to you, too, my lady," Damien cut him off, selecting that moment to respond to her greeting. Kira grinned, enjoying herself more by the second as he took his time kissing her hand.

"My, my, my," she managed to quip as he did. "Don't you clean up nicely."

"I believe you purloined *my* line, Princess," he murmured back, finishing with a fast wink that did *not* help the butterflies deciding they wanted to invade her arms and legs as well as her belly.

At last, he rose and turned back to Rolf. The black velvet of his eyes hardened to cobalt during the coldly decorous moves. "Mister Pembroke," he said with tight decorum.

"Sharpe." *That* low growl came from the space next to Rolf's left shoulder, now occupied by a glowering Nicholas and a gaping Aleece. "Get your hands off my daughter," Nicholas commanded.

Indignation surged Kira forward, where she curled an arm beneath Damien's elbow. "*My* hands were on *him* first." Surprise flooded her at the calm of her tone, though she knew she owed Damien thanks for the feat. Her strength was merely a loan of his amazing serenity.

"Move away from him, Kira," Aleece intoned. "He's dangerous."

The advantage clearly mounting in his favor, Rolf curled a confident smile. "Don't despair, Aleece. He's about to leave."

The man held his features in that expression of sickening self-assurance. The crowd held its collective breath. Kira held her stance next to the man who held his; who didn't move except to quietly pull out a mud-smudged envelope from his jacket, place it on a silver tray he absconded from a nearby waiter, and hold the offering out with smoothness that made a pulse in Rolf's forehead leap in irked envy.

"Even if he's an invited guest?" Damien queried with the same combination of knowingness and guilelessness.

Two veins jumped at Rolf's temples now. He snatched the tray, but glared at the envelope as if he'd just been presented with a platter of raw animal entrails. Still, when he lifted his sights again, one of his beloved statues couldn't manage a more impressively regal façade.

"Where did you get this?" he inquired in a tone that didn't require an answer, as it already provided one in its accusing inflection.

Kira felt Damien's frame clench in reaction—though she knew he prepared more to hold her back, not himself. He didn't take the precaution in vain. Every muscle in her body yearned to lunge at the letch who'd once called himself Damien's friend, but now stood here linking his "mate" to insinuations of murder and thievery.

Yes, she longed to assault Rolf—but she wouldn't. Instead, she swallowed deeply, and fought to borrow another dose of composure from the one occupant of this room who shouldn't have any. Yet a glance at Damien's steady profile proved he had self-control to spare.

A soft laugh echoed inside her heart. He'd welcomed her to Yorkshire with a demon's snarl, yet now helped her deceive all Yorkshire with a pirate's smirk. The man was out to either show her the way to the asylum, or show her he'd at last separated the identity of her first name from the stigma of her last.

She was willing to take a chance on the latter, Kira decided. God, how she wanted to believe the latter!

As proof of that pledge, she looked up again at the glaring trio opposite she and Damien, yet refused to surrender to the enticement of marching forward, grabbing the invitation off the platter and exultantly informing them *she* was the traitor behind this scandalous imbroglio. No, this time she would play the game as Damien would...and have twice the fun.

"Mister Pembroke," she pronounced then, stepping forward with a graceful sweep of her fan and an elegant swish of skirts, "I believe you were about to begin the waltzing." Without waiting for an answer, she spun back toward Damien. "How fortuitous the timing of your arrival this evening, Mister Sharpe. We were about to begin the waltzes—my favorites."

She bit the inside of her cheek to avoid giggling at Aleece's horrified gasp. Rolf wasn't the only sneak around here who could imply things with his tone, as she proved with the expectant emphasis on her final two words—an emphasis not only understood, but appreciated by the man who now met her gaze with eyes twinkling like a night sky packed full of stars.

"Shall we, my lady?" Damien asked then, proffering his arm. His tone resonated with a secondary meaning all his own...a meaning spurring Kira's smile yet higher.

Because that meaning was meant for her ears alone. Her heart alone.

Because that meaning vibrated with the warmth of how proud he was to have her on his arm.

Because that meaning couldn't possibly equal how happy

she was to be there.

"Mister Sharpe," she declared with the full, clear force of that joy, "I *knew* there was a good reason I invited you."

Aunt Aleece actually released a whimper then, and the loud crumple of her skirts denoted she'd sagged against Nicholas. She didn't grieve in solitude, though. A cloud of shocked gasps and ruminating whispers formed over the room, thickest around the dance floor, where Damien and she took their beginning pose then waited for Rolf and his own partner to do the same. The orchestra conductor, seeing the master of Hyperion's Walk had returned to the dance floor, would begin the musical strains to set them all in spinning motion.

But while they waited, something happened.

The music began, anyway. It was a thick, exotic kind of melody, seemingly written to be played in this similarly-appointed room. Perfect for waltzing.

Confused, Kira looked at Damien. But his stare was fixed on the conductor, who in turn gave him an I-know-what-I'm-doing glance—and an encouraging nod.

"Damien?" she queried. "What's going on? What is this?"

As prelude to his response, he actually let out a soft laugh. "It's my favorite waltzing music," he told her, shaking his head, clearly moved by the strains now flowing around them, inspiring a listener to contemplate mysteries...and memories.

"But why is he—"

Sheer emotion helped her interrupt herself. Sheer emotion—and the advent of lifting her gaze to the perimeter of the room, beyond the murk of rosewater perfume and appalled whispers, to where another contingent of May Day Ball attendees had gathered to watch the stunning goings-on.

They were party attendees, Kira realized, because they

were also party servants.

And right now, they stood there as a united whole for one purpose: to confirm their agreement to the message just sent by the conductor to all of London and Yorkshire's elite.

Listen, that message said. *Listen and look. The master of Hyperion's Walk has indeed returned to his dance floor.*

★ ★ ★ ★

"Damien? Damien, are you in here?"

Damien entertained a full half minute's worth of reluctance about answering the fervid whisper. Here in the darkness of the drawing room, he'd gotten his first reprieve of the last hour: a blessed few minutes of escape from the bombardment of feeling that hadn't relented since he'd stepped foot into the Pavilion sixty minutes ago. Sixty minutes, he ruminated, that felt sixty years. Awkwardness and anger, exhilaration and indignation, pride and humility; *what the hell is a homecoming without them all,* his heart and mind had gleefully proclaimed to his nerves and his gut.

Then there were all the sensations he'd endured when *she'd* approached.

"Damien? Now where in the world do you think he got off to, Fred?"

They were the same sensations making themselves known now, merely with the sound of her voice. The bittersweet catch of his heartbeat. The anticipating tugs at the corners of his lips. The complete interruption of his anger, his bitterness, his—

The complete interruption of everything in his world. Just the way she'd done things since the beginning.

"Dam—"

"I'm here," he called, finishing by giving in to that smile. He may have just taken advantage of his only chance to interrupt *her*.

All too quickly, however, he set his jaw again. He needed all the support he could get from any controllable parts of his body, for he certainly wasn't getting it from the *un*controllable parts tonight.

Not when she walked around looking like that.

She was illuminated only by flickering slivers of light from the torches lining the garden paths outside, but she turned him into an unblinking imbecile as swiftly as she had beneath the full chandeliers of the ballroom. She'd chosen to clothe herself in the colors of the forest, the lush green velvet of her bodice and skirt accented by gold and copper "leaves" fashioned out of gold-threaded silk, then bunched into strategic arrangements on her waist, between her breasts, in her coiffure.

God, to turn his fingers into fabric leaves. To turn his whole body into deep-green velvet. He rendered the appeal to heaven more ardently than he had back in the ballroom, before dancing with her had turned his body into a perfect waltzing partner with his agonized mind. Before he'd endured the experience of holding her again, of guiding her body across the dance floor with his...and as he had, remembering what it had been like to guide her body in other ways. Remembering what it had felt like to watch her passion for life become passion for *him*.

"Fred got conveniently 'hungry,'" she told him with a light laugh as she and the chimp stopped in front of his sanctuary: a high-backed Queen Anne chair. Chuckling again, she murmured to her pet, "As if you're not always hungry, eh?"

Fred cooed contentedly as she ruffled his fur, shameless

and silly primate sounds gurgling up his hairy throat. *A raised cup to your health, mate,* Damien nonetheless expressed to the animal. *If her hands were all over me like that, I'd be babbling incoherently, too.*

Hell. He didn't even want to think about the implications of her touch when at the moment, being the object of her dark copper stare presented an excruciating enough challenge to the distance they maintained. "I—er—" Kira stammered herself, her fidgeting lips belying her own cognizance that they weren't on a dance floor anymore, with a thousand eyes watching their every movement. "I really just wanted to make sure you're all right."

"I'm all right," he returned so swiftly, he doubted Mother would believe him—if she were here. Bloody *hell*, he seethed, not for the first time this evening, *she should be here.* Honora Sharpe should be sitting in this nook with him, contemplating the silliness of the couples outside as they sneaked away for their trysts in the gardens, chuckling gently as she needlepointed another of the pillows still scattered across so many sofas and chairs around here.

Except for one chair in the room across the hall. The pillow Rolf had thrown into the fire that fateful night.

The pillow with Rachelle's blood all over it.

The stiff cracklings of fast-moving crinolines shattered the stillness in the room as if they were made of glass, not horsehair, definitely arresting Damien's attention once more. He looked up to watch Kira walk along the large fireplace, her fingers skimming the equally lengthy mantel as she went.

At last, she stopped. And without turning, she posed the question he'd been expecting from her—in the hesitant rasp he'd expected it in. "So...is...is this the room where—"

"No." He cut her words off with the haste he'd anticipated from *himself*...closing his eyes against a surge of remembered horror, which he'd also foreseen. "I didn't find Rachelle in here. It was the morning room, across the hall."

At that, she pivoted and directed a steady gaze at him. "Have you...been in there yet?"

Damien couched his chin in the L he formed with his thumb and forefinger, and returned her stare. "Yes."

She hurried back across the room, her features animatedly studying him as she did. When she got to his side, she dropped down so that she clutched one of the chair's padded arms with one hand, and his forearm with the other. "Did you find anything?" Intense interest underlined each of her words.

He waited through one beat of time, simply drinking in the lovely life of this woman's face...wishing they sat here in the dark talking about anything, dear God, *anything* else besides evidence and clues and murdered bodies.

"No," he finally told her—instantly hating himself for the lie, but instantly exonerating himself for it, as well. The truth was, he really had discovered nothing in the morning room besides the pristine conditions of the redecorations Rolf had ordered—nothing, that was, that he could physically take with him. Yet the anomalies he'd sensed while walking the new Chinese carpet on the floor, while gazing at the new flocked wallpaper and feeling the craftsmanship of the reupholstered furniture...something had *not* been right, he'd concluded. A detail somewhere—a detail continuing to elude his mind, even to this moment—chopped a serious chink in the chain of events he damn near knew by heart now, so often had he heard the story ranted by detectives and barristers in that freezing York courtroom. The story they'd tried to fashion into a shackle of conviction around *his* ankle.

"I'm sorry, Damien." Kira's voice moved into his conscious with the gentleness of one of her silk leaves. Yet sans her tone, Damien still knew she meant it. He was sure of it before she moved her hand from his forearm to his jaw, pressing warm and tenderly there.

In response, he cocked her a brief but weary smile. "Not as sorry as I am, Princess." Galileo he wasn't, but he knew that even if he could clarify the anomaly this moment, the clue would very likely link to little in the way of concrete evidence—the only kind of evidence a magistrate accepted.

He gave her hand a quick squeeze before rising and crossing to the window seat, where he looked out upon the horizon, the tree-covered hills appearing marbeled beneath a sky where the moon was engaged in its own waltz with regal clouds.

His land. *His* land, he repeated inwardly. Land as much a part of him as the heart beating in his chest, as the legs he now braced against the window seat's edge. He smiled as he did the latter; as his body of the present connected with such a meaningful piece of his past, and he eagerly pilfered some gypsy superstition from the woman behind him to believe that contact let his heart cross that bridge, too.

All it took was that moment. All it took was that sliver of belief in magic—and magic indeed visited him, smiling at him from a vision which suddenly materialized on the seat before him, shaking her silvered head as she laid down her embroidery in order to hug him...

"She loved to sit at this window," he heard himself murmur then. He watched his hand reach out to touch the vision back, but instead, he sent the image back to the thin air from whence it had been created.

"Who?" Kira asked softly.

"My mother." Slowly, he pulled his hand back to his side, battling against forming it into a fist. "I...miss her."

In that black moment, in that dark room, he dropped his head as he dropped his voice...as he let his spirit plummet, too. One last warrior of hope marched valiantly into his psyche, and Damien snarled at the foe while brandishing a broadsword of fury. *I'm tired*, his soul bellowed. *Can't you see I'm tired, damn you? This is useless and I'm tired and I'm giving up. I'm giving up.*

But just as despair snapped open its jaws and gleefully bade him welcome into its blackness, an amazing force intervened. A pair of arms caught him, tenderly wrapping around him from behind, saving him from his fall even as they lifted him back up to a plane where peace negotiations with hope might become an option.

Those arms belonged to the gypsy princess who now held him even tighter, imparting to him not only the warmth of her body, but the strength of her voice. "I can see why she loved it here," she said to him in a tone barely above a murmur, but vibrating along his spine with firmness and conviction. "I'll bet the sunrise looks beautiful on the hills and the trees."

Unbelievably, Damien felt himself smile. "It does."

She sighed, the sound lilted with a musical quality, which made his spine now feel incredible as a rainbow woven into his back. "I would have liked to have known your mother. Many people spoke kindly of her earlier this evening."

That statement produced a conflicting reaction from his gut. Pleasure filled him at hearing Mother was remembered as a saint. But wrath stepped onto the scene upon remembering those same people still called him Satan.

"The May Day Ball tradition was begun by her, you know," he said.

"No...I *didn't* know." Pleasant surprise inundated her voice, but quickly gave over to heavy sardonicism. "But lucky me; I got invited by Rolf Pembroke. The man only has enough time for *necessary* information between talking about himself, himself, and himself."

She started snickering at her crack, but Damien used that moment to turn around in her embrace. He slipped his arms around her waist as he did. Her giggles faded swiftly as he let her behold the full, solemn intent of his stare.

"*I* was invited by the most beautiful woman in the ballroom tonight," he told her in a whisper worthy of the midnight fast approaching them. "And now...I'd like to properly thank her for that."

Her breath caught, Damien noticed—just as his did. She swallowed deeply as he urged her closer, and his attention descended to the hollow of her throat, where a green velvet choker bestowed an amber amethyst onto the deep cream of her skin. Ah God, he didn't think it possible, but she surpassed his every fantasy of how lovely she'd be in his arms, in this dress, in the beginning tremors of her sensual awakening... tremors he yearned to turn into shivers...and then shudders...

As that thought flared red-hot flames through his mind, Damien dropped his lips to that creamy nip in her neck, enduring a long shudder through his own being when Kira not only gasped in reaction, but fervently grabbed the back of his head.

"Yes," she beseeched him in a hoarse rasp. "Oh, yes, please...Damien, please don't stop this time..."

Not if your papa's whole bloody cattle herd stampedes through here, Princess, he returned as he suckled higher up her neck, higher. At last, he crested the curve of her chin, and greedily eyed the open, pleading fullness of her lips.

"M'lady! Oh my heavens, Lady Kira, you've got to stop *now!*"

They opened their eyes together, dazed at first, as if yanked out of a wonderful shared dream. Their stares swiftly widened in shock as they recognized the urgent cry had indeed emanated from a real person: Kira's maid, the never-at-a-loss-for-lots-of-words Ally.

This time, however, Damien had an ominous suspicion he'd be thanking Ally for her loquaciousness in a few short minutes.

"Oh my heavens," the servant fretted again, slapping a cheek so deeply steeped in chagrin, Damien discerned its dark rose hue even through the dimness. "Oh my heavens, m'lady, we've got to set ye aright, and we've got to do it fast!"

"For God's sake, Ally, *breathe,*" Kira rejoined, walking to the maid, but pulling Damien along by an unrelenting handclasp. "Unless I'm about to be sold into white slavery or Fred's about to be offered as a May Day Ball midnight snack, I don't understand why you're about to swoon."

She even laughed then, concentrating so much effort on calming her maid that Damien was certain she didn't discern the precise opposite effect had been accomplished. Oh yes, he observed Ally thoroughly now, and took inventory of all the changes in the servant's mien as soon as the words "white slavery" had left Kira's lips. Ally's eyebrows sprang skyward in alarm while suddenly, amazingly, the blush blanched clear off her cheeks.

When the maid spoke again, she addressed Kira in a cautious but calculated tone, reminding Damien of how graziers spoke to cows when leading them to slaughter. "M'lady, I only know that both yer father and Rolf Pembroke are demanding ye be found and brought back to the Pavilion. They say they've got an announcement to make, and they're commanding yer presence for it."

★ ★ ★ ★

The Pavilion Ballroom was nearly a separate structure from the rest of Hyperion's Walk, accessible only by traversing one hundred feet of vine-covered walkway between the Carriage Courtyard and the Pavilion's foyer. But even after traveling that walkway through the chilled night, Kira didn't truly shiver until she arrived at the ballroom's entrance and was bustled a full dozen steps inside—before realizing the stodgy footmen there had actually blocked Damien's way with a militaristic crossing of their pennant standards.

By then, it was too late. A series of strange hands attached to bodies with strangers' faces jerked and pulled her to the dance floor again—where she was thrust face-to-face with Rolf again.

An all-too-relaxed, all-too-confident Rolf.

She decimated the insides of her lips as she released a frantic prayer to whatever saint was minding the store upstairs tonight. *I want the other Rolf back*, she implored. The other Rolf; the Rolf who'd been so thoroughly incensed an hour ago that both words and actions had eluded him. Realizing that fuming at the side of the dance floor was equally unseemly as any fury-driven spectacle, the man had retreated to a private seating alcove with Nicholas and Aleece, and started to lick his wounds with a vodka-soaked tongue. Assured he wouldn't be wanting for company after she observed Lucille making her way to the alcove, Kira hadn't given him another thought, instead joyfully surrendering herself to Damien's masterful lead in the next ten dances.

It didn't look like he was going to let her ignore him now.

The alcohol had extolled its price on his face with swift and savage thoroughness, turning the "Pembroke charm" into pathetic ugliness. From his hooded, bloodshot gaze to the unnaturally ruddy flush of his cheeks, Rolf had aged ten years in the last sixty minutes. And then there was the grin. That insolent, disturbing grin.

"Your ladyship," he proclaimed, hoisting a glass aloft as two smiling strangers urged her out on the dance floor. "Thank you ever so much for joining me!"

The caustic bite to the words couldn't be ignored any more than the flute of champagne he clumsily thrust into her face. In his own hand a similar flute teetered, though half its contents had already been depleted.

Kira gritted her teeth past a discomfited grimace as she forced herself to lean closer to Rolf. If he listened to her now, perhaps he'd even thank her tomorrow for being his sober salvation tonight. Perhaps he'd even agree to stop bothering her altogether.

"Rolf," she uttered urgently, "you're drunk as a French Quarter cat. You don't know what the tarnation you're saying, or—"

"I know exactly what I'm saying!" he shouted, snatching her around the waist and shoving his leering features so close, her stomach turned from the smell of his breath. Vodka, champagne and cod with egg sauce. By the saints, where was a gallon of rosewater perfume when she needed it?

"Rolf—" she attempted again.

"I know exactly what I'm saying, and I'd like all of our friends to hear it as well, Kira darling!" he bellowed. "Does everyone have their champagne now? Good; good!"

As a tangible buzz of expectancy sizzled through the crowd, a painful thudding of dread grew louder in Kira's chest. She glanced behind her right shoulder to selfishly soak up a strengthening look from Damien, but at the edge of the dance floor now, she only saw her father in his normal lordly stance and her aunt in an *ab*normally emotional state. Neither one of them met her gaze. Nicholas steadily scanned the crowd, and Aleece's eyes followed every step Rolf took. The woman's expression tightened to tearful intensity when he actually spoke again, addressing the crowd with Caesar-like drama.

"My friends! My thanks to you for joining us for the ball this year. Hyperion's Walk has undergone quite a few changes in the last months, and I've been proud and elated to hear so many of you approve of them."

The man paused to let the reacting murmurs, as well as some spatterings of applause, fade down. He coordinated his next words with a grand, outstretched motion of his arms. "I am also pleased to say we shall soon break ground on even more renovations to the estate. I invite you all to return for personal tours, of course."

A slightly louder hum of murmurs voiced approval at that, yet Rolf didn't wait so long to go on, craftily letting that tide of energy bolster his continuance. "But despite all of this, Hyperion's Walk is missing one important addition," he stated with calculated mystery, carefully scanning the borders of the dance floor. "And I have gathered you all here to announce the plans to rectify that vacuity."

At that, he turned to *her*, his stare as carefully orchestrated as the scripted swill preceding it. But pre-fashioned or not, Kira took that stare seriously. *Very* seriously. She forced her eyes to meet that stare even as her whole being resonated with agonized thunder because of it.

Bozhy moj, she knew exactly what that stare meant.

Because she knew exactly what his next words would be.

"Lords and ladies, friends and family, I am pleased to announce to you my betrothal to Kira, Lady Scottney, of Scottney Hall!"

CHAPTER TWENTY-TWO

Applause exploded through the room. Horror exploded in Kira's senses. She shook with the force of the shock, her eyes riveted to the amber bubbles in the liquid that fizzed and popped in a flute held by quavering, cold fingers.

This isn't happening, her brain screamed, and the sound reverberated to the depths of her heart. *This isn't happening! How can this be happening?! How can this bastard, no matter how drunk he is, possibly think I'll consent to marry him after—*

She snapped her head up as a second fire storm burst through her faculties. A fire storm ignited by heart-searing comprehension.

Rolf thinks I'll consent because that sanction has already been given to him.

Her epiphany concluded with the appearance of the very monster who was its subject. Oh, yes; Papa dear strolled up as if right on cue, acknowledging the well-wishing shouts from the crowd as he held out both arms toward her, his face the epitome of paternal pride and affection. *Isn't it wonderful?* she could practically hear the matrons coo and croon behind their fans and gloves. *Nicholas's long-lost daughter is found again— and now betrothed to Rolf Pembroke! Such a lucky girl, loved by two such splendid men!*

"Don't—touch—me," she ordered the older member of that "splendid" pair. "You, neither," she spat at Rolf as he approached, too. "Dear God, especially not you!"

She wouldn't have thought it possible, but Rolf's face deepened by another shade as he lunged for her, instead. Fury darkened his eyes, as well; they burned to demonic intensity above his flaring nostrils and snarling lips. Yet he was the most pathetic sight she'd ever seen, Kira decided. His rage was born of nothing but fear.

Her father unwittingly transferred that conjecture into the realm of fact with his actions of the next moment, as he rushed to Rolf's side and threw a restraining arm in front of the rampaging moron. Though the crimson hue of Rolf's face didn't lighten one degree, he nevertheless halted as if a burning bush had appeared in front of him.

"Your frustration is acknowledged, Pembroke," Nicholas asserted lowly. "But I think this is a situation best left to me."

Kira fired a sardonic chuckle at that. "Oh yes, Rolf. Leave the *situation* to him." As she narrowed her glare more specifically at her father, she wrapped her tone more tightly around the bitter end of that sardonicism. "Because the *situation* is about to inform him what a lying, betraying flesh peddler he really is."

"Kira! Dear *God*!"

"Stay out of this, Aunt Aleece."

"She's right, Aleece; stay away," Nicholas pronounced with such low inflection, his tone nearly sounded a whisper. "It's time I speak with my daughter directly about things like lies and betrayals."

Kira blinked for a moment, not believing she actually battled the sting of tears at the undertone of accusation just scythed at *her*. "Then—then you're not denying you're behind this," she rasped, some part of her still praying for it not to be true...still praying the nobleman's calm defining her father's face would break by just a wrenched eyebrow or a quirk of lips.

Instead, he moved those lips just enough to level, "Are you denying you invited Damien Sharpe tonight, without my knowledge or consent?"

"Did you care about *my* knowledge or consent when blackmailing me to come in the first place?" When Nicholas didn't look as if he even contemplated an answer to that, she pressed on, "So you're telling me yes. You're telling me you gave Rolf your blessing to make that announcement to half of Yorkshire."

Her father only drew in a steady breath straight from the etiquette manuals. "I did what I had to, Kira—to save you from yourself."

"To save me—" She laughed then, pure incredulity sparking the outburst. "To save me from *what*?"

"You heard him." Apparently the burning bush had waned, for Rolf stomped himself back over in all his hellish obnoxiousness. "To save you from yourself—and the damn enthrallment Sharpe was casting over you!"

"The *what*?" she repeated. "Oh, for God's sake, Rolf; that's—"

"That's the truth, my lady." He issued the words with more solemnity than a priest. The disparity of that analogy with his Satanic appearance forced to Kira to bite back a renewed slew of giggles. "I'm sorry," he went on, "but you need to know. You have only to look as far as Rachelle Sharpe's grave to behold the depraved killer beneath the man's fripperies and flirtations."

She found her mirthful urge as fleeting as her patience with this flea who called himself a person. "That 'depraved killer' was your best friend, Rolf," she charged with seething amazement, instead. "Your *best friend*. Nobody ever proved he was a depraved *anything,* yet you stand here flinging accusations about him like facts, and—"

"And attempting to save your life in the process!" The gritted vehemence of his retort came with the bruising grip of his hand around her upper arm, spilling half her champagne down the front of her skirt. At last, her father's face furrowed in concern. But Kira lifted her other hand to Nicholas in a reassuring motion; the next moment, she wrenched free with equal ferocity.

"Don't do me any favors," she ordered as she did, making certain she drove a similarly deliberate stare into Rolf as punctuation. "And don't *ever* try anything like that stunt again."

She spun and started back toward the door. She was definitely done with this ball. Especially its host.

If only somebody would inform the host of that.

She'd taken two and a half steps before a hand clamped around her elbow and yanked her back around with less care given a rag doll. Though Kira had half expected such retaliation, the savagery with which Rolf delivered it dunked her in a momentary vat of shock.

That was all the moment the *zyver* needed to unleash a feral fury that pitched his voice to a raw, screeching intensity. "You will *not* turn your back on me!" he ordered her in front of a crowd that suddenly fell silent as a Quaker congregation. "And damn it, we *shall* be married!"

A hundred enfuried responses, each excruciatingly tempting and most involving severe pain to this man, barraged Kira's mind at once. Yet in the end, profound simplicity won her choice. She broke the room's stillness with a single sluice of sound: the sharp slice of the champagne she liberated from her glass and into Rolf's face.

The crowd released reacting gasps, but she effectively shut them up, too, getting rid of the empty flute by breezily tossing it onto the marble floor. Just before she sent the shards flying further with a spinning swipe of her skirts, she muttered with fully intended disdain, "I think it's time you cool off, Mister Pembroke."

★ ★ ★ ★

The woman was either the most bold and brilliant creature Damien had ever known, or the most reckless and dangerous nutcake running free in Yorkshire.

Either way, every instinct in his body told him her flight from the Pavilion wasn't the nonchalant show she wanted everyone to believe, and shouldn't go unsupervised—even if the job was taken on by the only guest at the ball who'd witnessed her horn-locking with Rolf from the ballroom's foyer.

Then again, he pondered, who else was better for the task? He certainly had nothing better to do, at that. Returning to the scene of Rachelle's murder had convinced him even more it *wasn't* the scene of Rachelle's murder.

Despite the erupting buzz of scandalized conversation, matched in urgency only by the strain of craning necks across the ballroom, he found it easy to slip out of the foyer unobserved. He almost chuckled as he did so. For once, he didn't harbor a shred of envy toward Rolf for usurping him— not when the title was "Man Most Likely to be Gossiped About for the Next Three Weeks." Therefore, his erstwhile mate was now the sudden object of *everyone's* attention.

Fate dealt him a fortunate hand once more, as he located a certain retreating hoyden, chimpanzee in tow, with minimal effort. The occurrence was indeed an intercession from the universe, too, for Damien had prepared to make his way to the carriage waiting lot, where he assumed Kira would charm Tom Montgomery into letting her expel some tension by guiding the horses home again.

He should have remembered this woman smelled assumptions on the air like foxes detected hounds. Through sheer luck and an inexplicable instinct, he spied Kira stalking off down the path leading to the hothouse, instead. Damien cut through the unoccupied pantry, then used his boyhood "secret path" through the trees in order to beat her there.

He didn't have long to wait. On rapid, incensed strides, she broke into the clearing in front of the building where Mother had once tended the prized Hyperion's Walk orchids and hothouse roses. Kira looked at the hothouse and her face crunched into a grieved frown, as if she shared Damien's own concertation about the decrepitude now creeping around the walls and roof along with a slew of untrimmed vines and weeds.

"*Idiot chyerf!*" she spat then, imparting the impression to Damien that the sight of the hothouse had served as the last releasing shove on the slide lock of her civility. "He's an idiot worm, Fred, and I should have kicked in his kneecaps when I first had the chance!" Fuming, she paced the clearing. "Now that I think about it, I should have kicked in much more. Perhaps those balls that have a constant royal audience with his brain. No, that wouldn't hurt him so much. To *hurt* him, I'd have to start with his face..."

She continued the tirade, adding flourishes of more profanities Damien hadn't heard for a year. It had been about that long, he estimated, since his last visit to the Whetted Wick ale house on the Thames.

Yet the venting did let him indulge a moment's satisfaction. His instinct back in the ballroom was a bull's-eye hit. The well-heeled disdain she'd given Rolf was a mere hair on the harpy of wrath she truly yearned to unleash on the man.

That realization led Damien's confidence down a sudden curve of perplexion. Yes, the woman before him had journeyed a good way down the path of fury—which meant she'd been traveling it well before tonight. Which meant Rolf's trespasses encompassed much more than proposing marriage to her more in the manner of announcing a cock fight.

Damien found himself enjoining his own anger to hers now. The protective edge to his feelings didn't surprise him, but definitely seared a new curiosity into his brain: what the *hell* had Rolf done to hurt her so?

The question burned so intensely for an answer that he almost gave up his anonymity in order to beseech her for it—and then ask her how she wanted him to exact retribution from Rolf for it. But Damien had taken just a step from behind the two pines that provided his camouflage when she lifted her face into the moonlight, releasing an expression to the heavens clamped in pure, merciless anguish. The cry she let out with it, a sound delivered straight from some raw, aching core inside her, compelled Damien to take back his step. She clearly intended this moment for no eyes but those of the angels... though her face conveyed her doubt even in their attentions.

Christ, he wanted to hold her. To tell her he knew exactly how it felt to wonder if even heaven didn't want to help anymore.

On the other hand, maybe she didn't have heaven in mind at all. The oath she erupted into next invoked just the opposite realm, as she resumed her pacing with doubled vigor. No,

Damien amended himself the next moment, no more pacing; she had a destination in mind now: the hothouse's door. Yet she spun for the entrance with such impassioned deliberation, she nearly tripped herself, tangling her feet and legs up in the layers of her crinolines.

A rapid string of Russian curses later, Damien was presented with the undeniable evidence that the crowd in the ballroom had been privy to a mere spark of the firestorm known as Kira Scottney. For while she spat and sputtered those exotic epithets, she hiked every layer of overskirting on her body all the way to her leaf-endowed waist, so that nothing covered her legs except her drawers, her dancing slippers and half a dozen crinolines.

Within the next half minute, the crinolines had been sent the way of the dirt clods in the path.

A dry gulp slammed down his throat as she reveled in a brief moment of freedom from the undergarments she so obviously dreaded. A brief moment in which her adorable, silk-clad bottom was guilelessly exposed to his stare...the bottom encased in *his* robe last week...the body he could have had beneath him, around him, offered so freely to him...

Damien clamped his teeth and gripped a pine branch to battle the arousal that rose fast and hard beneath his breeches; the worst of the hundreds this American had already given him. It was therefore the most ironic of snorts he released, upon realizing this was also the erection he'd have to tamp the fastest—at least if he wished to move at all within the next minute. That was precisely the deadline Kira unknowingly gave him, as she proceeded into the hothouse with a determined shove at the door.

She had definitely *not* ventured out here on an arbitrary

whim for a carefree respite, he concluded. Something—or someone—awaited her inside that building, and Damien had to command his body to move *now* if he wanted to fill in that mystery.

Clamping his teeth against an initial groan of discomfort, he edged closer to the hothouse's entrance. As he moved nearer, his heart sank a notch; the damage to the structure was worse from this proximity.

But his nostalgic broodings didn't have an iota of right to share the same vicinity with the desperate sob emanating from inside. Conflicted between invading the moments she thought her most private, yet yearning to help turn that crying into laughter again, Damien stepped up onto the stone before the entrance, but only pushed in the door by a fraction.

What he saw shattered his senses in shock and shattered his soul in awe.

She only needed the proper attire—furs and leathers instead of velvet and satin—to appear every inch the jungle princess gathering with her denizens. From the hopeful lights in the eyes of the exotic creatures beholding her, it seemed this tiny kingdom had found their own sovereign to adore, as well. Of course, those were the eyes of the animals that raised their heads. Some of the beasts tried, he noticed, but they gave up the effort with weak swiftness.

But while he noticed the creatures' enfeeblement, Kira breathed in their agony—and choked on it. She sobbed on it. While it surprised him little that his entrepreneur friend had taken an abandoned hothouse and turned it into an *en vogue* profit producer, Kira's hands curled into fists as if a heinous desecration had been dealt to the whole universe.

Hell, how he wanted to go to her.

She stopped when a beseeching mewl sliced the air, louder than the other creatures' grunts and snorts. Damien had to prod the door open a few inches more to watch where she went in responding to the sound, but the door's squeak went unnoticed beneath the frantic swoosh of her skirts—and an instant later, by the filthiest curse he'd heard from her yet.

He watched her fall to her knees beside a scraggly tiger cub, who cried at her again and attempted to climb into her lap. The cat succeeded, but only after tripping twice over its back leg chains.

"Oh, God," she rasped. Her hand quivered as it gently stroked the cub's head. "Oh...God."

Under his breath, Damien emitted a curse of his own then. The naked anguish in her voice and the pure grief riding her shoulders would liquefy the heart of Satan himself.

She shouldn't have to suffer that misery alone.

After a half dozen steps, he was beside her then kneeling next to her, ensconcing her in the brace of his thighs, enfolding her shoulders in his arms. He had no idea what she'd say or how she'd react, but when she instantly sagged against him, he knew he'd accomplished the most "right" thing in his life in a year. Such a tragic irony, he ruminated, that in this world her sadness should result in his strength, but that increased his resolve to pour that strength back out in the security of his embrace, in the kiss he pressed to her temple.

"He's...he's a monster," she rasped, voice shaking with tears and rage. She didn't clarify to whom she referred. Nor did she have to, Damien conceded.

She gave further evidence to support her claim, however. Horrifying evidence. Leaning deeper into him so he could see the tiger more fully, she gently turned the cub over onto its back—to expose a belly infested with dirt and fleas, and back leg wounds saturated with blood and puss. The wounds were the exact width of leg chains.

"You're right," Damien told her in a voice now as taut as hers. Silently, he thanked God for Rolf's absence at this moment. If the bastard was present, perhaps he'd give the courts real reason to call him a murderer. Cruelty like this broke the bounds of wanting to turn a fashionable profit.

Cruelty like this broke the bounds of the man he'd once called friend.

"The rest are just as bad," she continued, a bitter hardness suddenly fortifying her voice. "None of them have been fed or watered in days. There were an ape and another chimp in here before. Now I think they're both...oh God, they're both—" A soft but gritted sob sucked away the rest of the sentence.

"*Damn* him!" she burst then, and her shoulders convulsed when the tiger batted her chin, offering comfort in its innocent animal way. "God damn him! He says he has a whole crew hired. He says they're trained and experienced. Well, where the damn hell are they!"

"Kira," he murmured, though hardly knowing why. He definitely didn't know what came next. "Princess—"

"Stop it!" she snapped. She gathered the cub to her breast and wrenched from him. "Don't placate me, Damien! Don't try to calm me or soothe me or tell me it's all right. I'm not calm! I'm outraged!"

"And I'm not the enemy," he returned with as much force but composure as possible. Though he stared at her as he did so, he stole fast glances at the bear, who restlessly paced his enclosure now. Like a dutiful centurion, the creature felt his queen's agitation, and prepared to defend her from the black-furred creature who apparently agitated her.

"I know you're not," Kira answered, breaking his heart yet again with her face, torn between giving in to hopeless defeat or hopeless wrath. "The enemy is that—that barbarian and his friends, hiding behind their sickening waistcoats and top hats and fans and feathers..." She sighed and shook her head as the tiger spied an interesting dust ball to roll over and play with. "*They* aren't rolling around in filthy hay tonight," she muttered. "*They* aren't fighting leg chains, or trying to sleep on empty bellies. They have plenty to eat, don't they, up there in their fancy ball—"

While a door seemed to slam on her words, a window opened upon her face. Damien, on his way to help her up, stopped in the captivation of watching her brows suddenly jump, her eyes suddenly sparkle and her mouth pop open in amazed delight.

He only wondered why that look made *his* pulse skip a beat in trepidation. "Kira..." he said again, though this time he tinted the word with warning, not consolation.

"They have plenty to eat in the ballroom," she repeated, fixing him with a disconcertingly intent stare. "They have plenty to eat in the ballroom!"

Despite his continuing flounderings through befuddlement, her impish grin was impossible to ignore. Past his own quirking lips, he decided to take a try at hitting her mark of meaning. "So...you're proposing we bring them platters from the buffet?"

His pulse omitted *two* beats as she popped to her feet, the imp's grin growing into a mischief's smile. She held off her answer to him until she opened the cupboard Mother had used for gardening tool storage. After a moment of tentative searching, she pulled out not pruning shears, but a ring of jailer's keys. Swinging the thing from her finger so it jingled with dementedly melodic triumph, she then looked at him with waggling eyebrows and dancing eyes.

"I'm proposing we bring them to the buffet."

★ ★ ★ ★

A laugh bubbled up Kira's throat as Damien gaped like she'd just proposed they steal the queen's jewels. She'd anticipated the response, but the actual occurrence of it surpassed her expectations. Heavens, the man's handsomeness became devastating when she stunned him beyond words.

But words he eventually did find...sort of. "Bring them—you want to—of all the—Kira!"

By the time he finished his stammerings, however, she'd already successfully found the key to the chimpanzees' cage. The creatures cackled their enthusiastic thanks then milled around her legs as she freed the mongeese, the llamas, and the tiger cub. She scooped up the little thing, who still had a hard time walking with his impaired back legs, and took him over to the man who stood looking thoroughly dazed and wonderfully adorable.

"You'll have to carry Rico," she said, gingerly handing the cub over. "He won't be able to make it all the way. I'll tear some of the table linens up for bandages when we get there," she finished with a sly wink.

"Rico?" Damien queried, fumbling with the cub like a father holding his newborn for the first time.

Kira shrugged and smiled. "An old friend who was also a fighter," she explained. "Now take him and the others outside while I let this big guy go. Their noses will take over from there."

Her words proved to be prediction before she'd even finished them. What she didn't foresee was the depth of joy *she'd* feel in the next fifteen minutes, returning up the path at an ever-increasing pace behind creatures who hurried to eat again...to live again. She smiled at the bear's suddenly alert eyes and twitching nose; she laughed aloud while watching Fred personally take his two new chimp friends into care, chattering at them about the wonders awaiting ahead. The mongeese, of course, had disappeared, but she'd assumed that. After a few hours of necessary shut-eye, they'd be happier with kitchen rats than pâté molds.

What made this elation complete, however, came with another unexpected advent: the eruption of Damien's own laughter. She joined him when she looked to see him give Rico one last affectionate pat, as the cub settled itself more comfortably atop the bear's upper back. That feat accomplished, the bigger beast let out a bawl as if saying to Damien, "Three's a crowd, mate," before lumbering on ahead.

Damien actually lifted a hand at them in farewell, before lowering that hand and curling it into her own. As he added a smile to the gesture, leaning close to do so, it suddenly hurt Kira to breathe—though she hardly could blame her lungs. How could they concern themselves with breathing when a feeling broke out inside her with more force than a tumbler bursting through a fire ring? How would she feel *anything* normally again, after this intensity of sensation that had her pleading the universe to simply stop everything so she could aright her mind again? Just for a moment, she begged.

No...just for an eternity. An eternity she'd gladly spend by this man's side.

An eternity that was shattered by a scream from inside the Pavilion Ballroom. Then another. Then hundreds more.

To her shock, Damien reacted with a devilish jump of eyebrows and a gleaming flash of a grin. "Come on," he urged, running around the last curve in the path, still grasping her hand. Willingly, Kira followed.

When they reached the back lawn, she moved into the forward position, leading the way back to the Pavilion foyer—though they combated a throng of epic proportions to at last arrive there. Through the rosewater perfume, the hysterical keenings and the drunken panic they struggled, both of them mercifully unrecognized and unnoticed in the frantic chaos.

Despite the mass exodus, they still found a large contingent of the crowd gathered inside the ballroom. Men comprised the majority of the group, most of them armed with chairs, rapiers or, in the case of one gleaming-eyed orchestra member, a violin bow. The women who remained clung dutifully to their escorts' sides, gasping and shrieking at appropriately dramatic moments.

While taking in the scene, Kira couldn't contain a long giggle. Those "dramatic moments" were defined by any move made by the llama or the bear, who greedily chomped at the dessert tray and the spiced whole salmons, respectively. They were so enraptured with their culinary discoveries, their audience could have turned into pine trees for all they cared. A short distance away, camped out on the edge of the dance floor, Fred and his crew munched happily on the spilled contents of a gigantic fresh fruit bowl. The trio was equally oblivious to the gaping stares upon their every move.

She let her laugh dwindle into a contented sigh. "*Now*

we're having fun," she murmured, a sense of true contentedness washing over her for the first time this evening.

Damien, approaching and handing Rico back over to her, didn't echo her chuckle this time. But a broad smile did define his lips as he professed, "My Lady Kira, you certainly know how to liven up a party."

"*Moi?*" She pressed a hand to the base of her neck, putting a sarcastically coy interpretation on the action favored by the females opposite them. "Why, Mister Sharpe, it was *you* who set off the firecrackers first tonight, with your dramatically late entrance and your devastating charm."

At that, he threw back his head on a deep laugh. "Princess, they didn't call me charming even *before* they called me a murderer."

"Well," she said, huffing, "it's about time someone—Rico!"

Her concerned outcry came three seconds too late. Three seconds that provided the tiger cub with all the time he needed to push free from her grasp, romp down her skirt, and skid his way to the base of the buffet.

"Leave him be," Damien assured as the cub took only another three seconds to claw his way to the table's surface, making the best use of the flounced silk overlays Kira had observed all evening. "He just wants to join the fun."

The explanation looked the truth down to the detail. Rico seemed to underline Damien's words with a sliding entrance into the orange truffle the llama was enjoying, yet the cub didn't eat the dessert as much he swatted paw-sized gobs of it up into the llama's snout. Next, he rolled over across the plate, as if following his own recipe for a new confection, *Tiger Cub A l'Orange.* The disconcerting factor was, the little thing indeed looked like a colorfully delicious treat.

But when the llama responded to his antics with a harsh snort and a "get lost, you weanling" bray, the cub dejectedly rose to his feet and shook out as much cake and cream as he could. He glanced at the throng still jostling and arguing in their semicirle around the table, and appeared perplexed by the unruly scene before him. Kira smiled then, shaking her head, realizing she appeared every inch the cub's odd, but proud mother—yet rather welcoming the image. *Go ahead, Rico,* she cheered her messy little buffet warrior. *You show them what you think of their shrieks and their swoons and their struttings. You show them what a spectacle they are. You show them—*

But her alarmed outcry sliced short her thoughts, as Rico decided to indeed show them what he could do.

Spurned by the llama, the cub had turned his attentions toward winning the favor of the bear. In order to do that, Rico had to make his way past an eight-pronged candelabra three times his height. But the cub, after impatiently attempting a few paths around the fixture, concluded success lay in no other tactic but to proceed *through* the candelabra.

Poor Rico had no idea he couldn't leap through a forest of solid brass.

He had no idea his valiant jump would send the eight tapers toppling aside, instead.

He had no idea those eight flames would turn that buffet into a feast *en flambé* inside of a minute. Or any idea *he'd* be the delicacy doomed to be cooked alive as a result, if she didn't do something. Dear saints in all the heavens, she had to do something!

"Rico!" she yelled, but only knew she'd voiced the plea because of the instant burn of smoke she inhaled for the effort.

She didn't hear herself above the instant eruption of panic inside the Pavilion, escalated by the bursts of shrieks and bellows outside, as well.

Pandemonium fell far short of an apt depiction for what ensued then. Kira lunged for the buffet and snatched Rico into her arms just before the whole table collapsed in an angry roar of silver, wood, china, and fire—fire that now declared *itself* the voracious beast of the evening. The flames stalked across the Pavilion's flocked walls like a dragon on a killing spree, celebrating in spirals of blinding orange destruction when they reached the seams of the walls, where flowing draperies and towering flower arrangements provided perfect sustenance to continue the journey.

So hot and rapidly did the rampage happen that Kira barely blinked before realizing she was no longer part of a spectacle, but a disaster. Now the flames hacked their hot blades at the Pavilion's roof, and the arched buttresses creaked with the effort of resistance. Screams and wails filled what little silence the inferno didn't dominate, turning the ballroom fantasyland into a living reproduction of hell.

"Come on!" she heard someone bellow, and blinked back ash-filled tears to bring Damien's face into view. She responded with an odd laugh; he still looked pristine and collected enough to join her in a few quadrilles, while hair feathers, tie pins, fans and canes rained from the throng now racing past them in a frantically sloppy surge.

Yet she and Rico found themselves part of that horde the next instant, with or without her permission. As a chunk of the roof plummeted into the alcove in which Rolf had sulked earlier, the crowd became a panicked mob. Fear dominated minds and bodies, turning everyone into a mass of unthinking instinct with only their own survival at concern. Kira had no idea if she was finally pushed forward by Damien or pulled forward by the throng's frenzy, but she clung to an equally frantic tiger cub through what felt like interminable minutes, until at last finding herself gulping in reasonably fresh air again.

The debris-littered lawn stretched around her, peopled by the crowd who preferred to celebrate their safety by watching the blaze claim its last few feet of victory over the structure. Some of them even smiled and laughed in morbid fascination, their faces cast in an eerie orange glow, adding to Kira's sudden sense that somewhere tonight, she'd fallen asleep and dreamed all this—for she couldn't share their serendipity. At least not until Rico bolted from her hold, and guided her gaze to the exact sight her subconscious had been exhorting her to seek. She watched as the cub dashed to a large, dark form virtually camouflaged by the darkness of the trees where the Hyperion's Walk wilderness began; a lump which would appear a huge rock to the casual passerby's eye—unless that passerby watched long enough to see the lump move.

Kira smiled as she indeed saw the hulk move. First, it flinched as Rico leapt aboard; then it settled into its distinct bear's lope, retreating into the darkness with its distinct bear's taciturnity. Bringing up a loyal rear on a regal gait, the llama rounded out the oddest threesome that wilderness would probably ever see.

The little gang would take care of each other, Kira assured herself, and they'd sure as blazes fare better with their own devices against the foes of the wild than they would have in the grip of Rolf's "civilization." As for Fred's two new primate friends, she had no doubt the Scottney Hall kitchen girls wouldn't mind a few more helpers for—

A jolt of pure and horrifying dread seized her whole body.

She'd been so busy verifying the welfare of the other animals, she'd forgotten to assure Fred's presence at her side.

He wasn't there.

"Fred," she rasped. Then in a shout she tried, and failed, to keep from breaking in panic: "Fred!"

He didn't answer. He didn't come.

The last time she'd seen him was on the Pavilion's dance floor, happily munching on fruit.

She looked at the fire-engulfed shell of the ballroom now. And screamed.

CHAPTER TWENTY-THREE

Damien had pushed Kira and the tiger into the frenzied exodus from the ballroom, but had deferred his own departure to help the dowager countess Raincroft, who had tangled herself thoroughly between her walking cane and her crinolines. Realizing *her* escape from the structure would be under more tragic circumstances if she wasn't assisted, he'd extricated her despite the glare of agitated shock he'd gotten for the effort.

After handing the shrew over to her sister, who rendered an even more affronted look his way, his sights instantly sought Kira. He'd just confirm she was safely clear of the Pavilion, he told himself, then he'd cut back to the stables for Dante, and leave with no further delays. At least no further delays like saying some sort of official farewell to her. After their disrupted passion in the drawing room, combined with the exhilaration of working together against Rolf's maltreatment of her beloved animals, he didn't possess a single extra nerve of "official" feeling toward Kira Scottney.

Everything he felt for her now was very *un*official. And indecent. Heatedly, excruciatingly indecent.

Bloody hell. He needed to douse himself in some ice water. Lots of it. Soon. He just needed to locate her in this chaos of orange and black shadows, assure himself she'd gotten out of the Pavilion in one piece, then be safely on his way home, with a required detour by way of the stream and the waterfall. Their currents would be wonderfully frigid at this time of night, he mused gratefully.

If he could only find where the *devil* that hoyden had gotten off to.

His dilemma was resolved the next instant—though he immediately wished for an hour of futile searchings instead of Fate's selected solution. For he knew exactly where to find Kira as soon as her horrified scream rent the air.

Barreling over or through the sputtering idiots who chose to get in his way, Damien sprinted to her side as if he'd departed the Pavilion with his shoes on fire. He grabbed both her hands and peered into her eyes—and for the first time since meeting her, saw not an ember of defiance or spirit in those dark amber depths. Only the glitter of raw fear stared back at him now.

"Princess," he demanded, "what is it?"

She sucked in a quivering breath before emitting her explanation in a distraught rush. "Fred—Fred—it's Fred—no, it's not Fred, because I can't—I can't—he's not—Damien, he's not—"

"Sssshhh," he soothed, stroking her cheek. "*Think*, Kira," he prompted. "Where do you remember seeing him last?"

Her face contorted harder as she drew in breath for her reply to that—a reply stolen from her during that faltered moment. The thief wielded a dagger of laughter as his weapon; coupled with the ironically suave sneer he curled at one side of his upper lip, Kira's last shred of strength leapt off her cliff of composure and into a pith of trembling dread.

"Lost our little monkey, did we?" Rolf crooned at them then. Damien no more believed his lilting sweetness than the man himself did.

Kira, however, jerked herself around, and took a painfully

polite step toward Rolf. She even bowed her head slightly in respect. Damien swallowed, moved by the mettle it took her to simply do that, yet half surprised she didn't fall at the man's feet, too. She was ready to relinquish even the precious possession of her pride on the altar that would bring her pet back.

"Rolf," she pleaded from gritted teeth, though maintaining that deferential stance, "please...have—have you seen him?"

"Not since he helped you destroy my home," came the snide snarl. "Not since I watched him infest my fruit with his filthy fleas."

"Rolf!" Damien told his best-not-to-intervene resolution to go to hell. Who was he duping, anyway? He qualified as "intervened" in this crisis the moment he'd stepped foot into the hothouse in the woods. "For Christ's sake, did you see the chimp or not?"

They were interrupted again by an ominous *whoosh* of sound from the building now engulfed in flames. The eruption corresponded to a rush of heat, caused by the roof panel suddenly sacrificed to the fire by its weakened support beams. At that, a frightened, shrill howl joined the din, as well.

"*Bozhy moj*," Kira immediately gasped. "Dear God, I knew it! That's him. That's *him*. Fred!"

With the same swift panic, she abandoned her humble position toward Rolf, but Damien almost wished she'd remained where she was in favor of where she now lunged. He arrested her from breaking into a full run at the Pavilion only by grabbing her with both shoulders, grunting greatly in the effort.

"Let me go, damn it!" she sobbed, beating at his chest. "You don't understand! We've got to do something!"

"Looks like your brat's done it already," the man behind them taunted from that same curled lip. "Went back for more from the buffet one too many times. Perhaps he should have had a little snack before coming tonight."

Damien didn't bother wasting even a glare on the bastard, but he wondered if Rolf realized how lucky he was that a chimp needed rescuing more than he needed his face turned inside out. Yes, right now rage had to serve as support force to firm command as he ordered Kira—and her ten extra pounds of very combustible skirts—to not dare a step closer to the Pavilion. He did so just before wheeling around himself, and sprinting toward what used to be the ballroom's foyer.

Insanity, he castigated himself while loosening his stock and pulling it over his mouth and nose, as the heat became a suffocating force around him. *This is insanity, Sharpe! Are you insane? You're risking your life for a hoyden who's not playing with balanced dice herself. Actually, you're risking your life for something more ridiculous than that. For a bloody chimpanzee who—*

A chimpanzee who now locked his arms around Damien's right knee, and clung with the tenacity of a five year-old welcoming his father home.

His chest, first to respond to the animal's ebullience with a leap of strange, soaring sensation, was also the source of the incredulous chuckle he gave in return. "Hello there, mate," he greeted, looking to observe the chimp had taken shelter beneath a glass-top table that looked astonishingly ready to report for duty again in some other vestibule.

"Hell," he muttered, scooping up the animal who trembled violently nevertheless. "You're one lucky bounder, Fred. Let's hope your providence follows us now."

Fortune indeed chose to look upon them with benevolence, waiting until Damien had cleared the foyer to send three more overhead beams to their demise. When his feet hit the relative safety of the night-dampened lawn, that entire section of the building collapsed in on itself. As it did, a huge rush of relieved air left his lungs.

He never got the chance to inhale with relief, as well.

Fred's burst of excited cackling prompted him to set down the animal and raise his own sights toward Kira. He expected to smile at her tear-filled face and her outstretched arms, ready to wrap around her pet once more.

But he couldn't see her face. And her arms—well, they were stretched out, surely enough—though an embrace appeared the farthest purpose she deemed for them as Rolf grabbed them both by the wrist and shook her violently, shouting something savagely. As Damien ran nearer, he discerned the contents of the man's diatribe.

"You're *sorry*?" Rolf seethed at her. "You're *sorry*, are you, Kira? Well, why don't I believe that? Why don't I believe you're not an ant's piss sorry about any of this?"

"Rolf," came her strained plea, "Rolf, you're hurting me—let me go!"

He only answered her with a laughing bark. "You're not sorry, Kira. *I'll* give you a reason to be sorry!"

Damien was close enough now to hear her attempt at a reply to that—

A reply turned into a sharp outcry by the loud smack of Rolf's palm across her face.

★ ★ ★ ★

Kira's sight swam in dizzying specks of light as pain suffused

314

the whole left side of her face. She'd been thrown and even kicked by many a recalcitrant horse, but never struck by a man before, so she had no idea if Rolf had just tapped her or belted her. She had *no* desire to further study the matter, but also harbored no doubts Rolf wouldn't give her a choice about that, either.

Yet at the moment she expected the monster to bestow her the second half of his matching palm prints on her face, her world went careening again. She was grabbed and spun around, then thrust behind a stone pillar that seemed to erupt out of the lawn from God-knew-where.

But then the pillar let out an enraged roar. And she realized the pillar wasn't a pillar at all.

She opened her eyes to confront Damien's taut, braced spine, bracketed by one arm ending in a coiled, hard fist and another arm ending in a spread-eagled hand. That hand conveyed one resolute message to her: *step back and stay back.*

"*You're* the one who's the sorriest bastard here tonight, Rolf," he emitted in a voice that momentarily stopped her, wondering if it was Damien who'd freed her, not a wild beast dressed up in his clothes. But a fast glance at his profile, with teeth bared and eyes intense, didn't assuage her fears a drop. This feral, wrathful being looked like Damien, but there the likeness halted.

Especially because of what happened next.

Saying nothing further, giving Rolf no quarter to spew even a syllable of what looked like a derisive comeback, the Damien-animal swung high his white-knuckled fist, and drove it hard into Rolf's jaw.

Semiconsciousness struck Rolf before he hit the ground. Even so, a groan swiftly gurgled off his lips, and he battled to push up onto his elbows. Damien vanquished his campaign with one boot strategically-placed boot between his ribs.

With Rolf secured in that position, Damien paused only for one brief moment, to arrow a glare down at his prisoner that, surprisingly, glittered not just with raw rancor, but sad disillusionment, too. Then he leveled from tight lips, "You're going to be even sorrier if you lay a finger on her or the chimp again. That's my solemn promise, Mister Pembroke. You have my word as a fellow gentleman on it."

The drawling sarcasm with which he concluded didn't allude at all to the brusque force of his turn back to Kira. He secured a hand around her elbow, but in the long moment after that, he didn't move further. Neither did she. For in that moment, their gazes intertwined with each other, and Kira found herself seared to the spot more assuredly than if a flame from the Pavilion had burrowed beneath the grass and melted the soles of her shoes there. But in truth, she knew, the fire came from inside her...just as it came from inside Damien, too.

She knew that because in the depths of his black, black eyes, she beheld two flames of pure blue light.

She held her breath as those dual flares grew yet brighter, showing her just how much of this man's soul had been torn open tonight...showing her how deeply he'd had to excavate that soul to find the courage to confront Rolf...Rolf, who'd probably been one of the few shown those flames at some time, as well; Rolf, who'd seen the vulnerability of this man, and repaid him with rejection.

Then with a fast self-conscious blink, the flames were extinguished. The hard-hewn, ash-darkened features assumed the guise of animalistic fury once more. But Damien's voice came incongruously soft as he slid his hand down to hook his fingers through hers and pull her toward the stables. "You're coming with me," he said. "*Now.*"

CHAPTER TWENTY-FOUR

Now. Kira thanked him for that word as she let its simple beauty pervade her every sense, and dictate the only concern of her mind for the next indiscernible stretch of time...for all that mattered, she told herself, was *now*. The swiftness of *now* was exhilarating, as Damien thanked a groomsman who had his massive stallion at the ready, then swung her and Fred into the saddle ahead of him. The darkness of *now* was welcome, as the night wrapped around them the moment they left Hyperion's Walk via a narrow lane behind the stables, into the forest.

But most of all, the man of *now* was perfect, with his warm breath upon her neck, his powerful torso at her back, his commanding hand upon the reins. In the vortex of Damien's hold, she felt the strength she needed to trust, at last; to surrender, at last...to release the agonized clench her body had become since stepping onto the dance floor and facing Rolf's drunken leer. She entrusted her weight against him just as she entrusted the midnight shadows with her streams of releasing tears.

Now, she decided in that complete and warm and safe moment, was a wonderful place to be.

She didn't know where Damien was guiding them, but when they at last halted, she wasn't surprised when she heard no other sound but the sough of wind through pines and Hamlet's gentle whimper of greeting. Damien didn't answer his pet, his silence thick with the same tangible tension that had defined his mien since they'd left Rolf moaning among the ashes on the lawn.

Still without a word, he dismounted with economical grace, but didn't help her and Fred down until he guided the stallion to the barn and turned up the lamp. Though the flame's potency was diffused by the lamp's dingy glass, the light was powerful enough to highlight the ravages of the fire on his face: the dirt-encrusted scrapes and nicks, the all-over coat of gray grime, the strain around his eyes from squinting against the smoke.

As she gazed at him, Kira pulled in her lips and bit them hard, struggling against another surge of tears. He'd never formed a more beautiful sight to her eyes.

Fred and Hamlet romped away somewhere outside, chattering and panting enthusiastically at each other. Giving their departure barely a glance, Damien led the stallion to his stall, secured the reins, and removed the saddle. All the while, Kira didn't wrest her gaze from him. She *couldn't*. When he finished slinging the saddle over the stall wall, she knew he realized that, too. He stood with both arms braced on either side of the saddle, his stare affixed to the leather as if his death sentence was emblazoned in it.

Kira didn't begrudge him the ominous intuition. Not if his blood thrummed the way hers did; so deafening, her ears hurt because of it. Not if he heard each of her heartbeats the way she suddenly heard his...aware of each breath he took, too... sentient of every move he made...

Wondering if he thought of all the insane events which had conspired to bring them together this night, and if he questioned to Fate and its extraordinary hand: *why?*

Wondering if the only answer his heart rendered made

him shake from inside with desire and need...

And love.

She drew air in on an audible gasp as the revelation rang through her senses with astounding clarity—and undeniable truth. *Most holy Mother of God and the saints help me,* those senses cried out. *Help me, I've fallen in love with this man. I've fallen in love with his depthless gaze and his surly scowl; with his hands on my ankle and his face in my dreams. I love his majestic forest and his doting dog; I love the boy who speaks of his mother, and the hero who braved a fire to rescue my pet.*

I love him as the woman I've become because of him.

She now battled the tears in vain. Kira blinked to clear her vision, but before she had the chance to wipe the salty tracks off her cheeks, Damien looked back up. Straight at her.

Her heart pounded once. Twice. Before she watched him shove away from the wall and march out of the stall. Straight toward her.

Not a sound left her lips or a breath left her body as instinctively, eagerly, she opened her arms to him. She received the crush of his body as she surrendered to the domination of his kiss, her own body reveling in the heat of him, the power of him, the hardness of him. In turn, she gave back her own passion, her own heat, her own need.

Oh God, she thought, more tears welling to her eyes, that was exactly what this sensation was...a raw, blinding need to not only feel her love for this man, but *show* him. It was the name for the yearning which had encouraged her to wrap her arms around him in the drawing room, which had given her succoring words for his grief, and welcoming words for his kisses.

It was the name for the force she let enflame her now.

With a succumbing sob, she let the flames fill her being as Damien parted the folds of her mouth. His tongue swept against hers with a hungry ferocity; his hands raked her body with fevered intensity. He was everywhere; around her, against her; pulsing with hard strength and with a yearning finally allowed to flare into desire.

And still, she wanted more. More, as she delved her own tongue into the hot recesses of his mouth. More, as she licked his lips, savoring their taste of smoke and midnight and man. More, as she let her hands explore him, too, seeking the places she had lain awake dreaming of on so many nights: the curve where his neck met his shoulder, the muscled vale down the center of his back, the dusky circles surrounding his male nipples.

"*God,*" he grated as she touched him there, tautening the nubs to erect attention. "Oh, God, yes, Kira...my Kira."

At that, her lips released a smile of trembling joy. "Say it again," she commanded as that bliss shimmered its way to the tips of her toes and fingertips. Then again, against the underside of his powerful jaw, "Say it again."

She felt Damien's smile before it reached his face, erupting from a rumble of pleasured laughter deep in his throat. "As many times as you want, my Kira," he concurred in a whisper. "*My Kira.*"

Then his lips were on hers again, and with a whimper of enkindled desire, she opened to him as she never had before. She opened to him because in that moment, with the final urgent and hoarse utterance of those words, she knew Damien comprehended what overjoyed her so much about them, too.

Rolf Pembroke and his arrogance and his violence had no jurisdiction over her any more...nor could they threaten so, either. *My Kira.* Oh yes, from now on, her skin would know the imprint of one man's touch, her body would know the feel of one man's possession...just as her heart, for the last four weeks, had known the sweet ecstasy and fear of dreaming for one man's loving.

If she in fact dreamed now, she'd send a prayer to God to never end this night. She never wanted to wake up from the magic of the masterful hands that entwined their fingers as they descended into the hay, bodies instantly pressing, heartbeats instantly merging into one.

One. Oh yes, *one.* Sweet *Bokh,* how she yearned to be one with this man. How she yearned for it *now;* no more hesitations, no more fears, no more regrets about the scars of yesterday or the pains of tomorrow. For now, she lived only for the incredible, beautiful fire of tonight...

"Damien," she gasped as his lips captured the sensitive corner where her jaw met her neck, causing the night to explode into even more intense beauty. "Oh, Damien...we're not going to stop this time, are we?"

She felt him swallow deeply. And his body tighten perceptibly. "No, Princess," he answered while sliding his lips to her forehead. "No, we're not going to stop."

"Thank God!"

Damien's reacting chortle spread warmth through her heart, as his corresponding kiss sent heat through her body. The effect on Kira's senses reminded her of how she'd felt once before a summer dust storm in Kansas: restless, breathless, and full of wild, inexplicable animal impulses.

She moaned from the potency of those instincts now... from the undeniable need to act on them. Damien answered with a similar sound, though his utterance emerged as more a guttural masculine growl. She knew that because she felt the vibrations of the sound as he dipped his mouth to her bodice... and pushed aside the velvet there.

"Damien!" she cried, and repeated the outcry as he freed her other nipple in the same way.

"Heavens," she rasped between short, shallow breaths. "Heavens!" And that was certainly what this was, she determined, her whole body arching and perspiring as Damien reached beneath her to loosen her corset, giving him even fuller access to the stiff, aching peaks. *Oh, heaven*, her senses sighed. *Dear God, this is a wondrous taste of heaven.*

While he did so, she made short work of dislodging his queue and restoring his hair to the tangled black waves she knew and loved. But removing just his hair ribbon wasn't enough, Kira swiftly decided. Not nearly enough.

Now, she wanted to see his nipples, too.

No...she wanted to see all of him.

Perhaps, she concluded the next moment, the best way to show him that was to let him see all of *her.*

A deliciously powerful tingling took over her belly as she gently scooted back from him, and rose to her feet. Though Damien frowned his protest at first, a fine sheen of arousal quickly formed again over his features as she curled her hands around to the half dozen hooks securing her bodice. When her skirts, chemise, and drawers joined the puddle at her feet, a dark and mysterious force transformed his face into a vision that turned Kira's breaths into an even more rare commodity.

She waited through a tormenting stillness for him to say something. Damien emitted nothing except one half-strangled sound that followed a deep swallow. A sting of tears threatened to brim over in her eyes. Perhaps Aunt Aleece had been right all this time, she thought. Perhaps a man did appreciate a coy coquette instead of a forthright gypsy. Or perhaps her body didn't please him. Her skin wasn't ethereally translucent, as so many of the women she'd seen tonight, and her limbs weren't soft and rounded, but lean and defined by years of tumbling, riding, and performing. She was an American wildflower, not an English rose. And now, oh God, he was remembering he preferred roses!

But then Damien stood.

In the process of doing only that, he tore his shirt away from his torso. Yet Kira barely had a moment to behold the muscled magnificence of the sight, let alone ride out her body's reaction to it, before he'd tugged and tossed aside both his boots, and had swiftly started to work on the buttons of his breeches.

In under half a minute, her breath eluded her completely as he freed his erection.

In contrast to her agog silence, Damien unleashed a moan sounding strangely of relief and pain at once. The sound escaped him again as he took his hard length into one hand.

"Look, Kira," he said to her then, low and huskily. "Look what you do to me...what you've been doing to me since the day you crashed your gorgeous arse in my forest."

"Damien," she whispered, smiling, and the tears at last did break free—only this time, in happiness.

"Come here," he entreated, now raising both arms to her. "Come here, darling, and feel what you do to me. Come here and touch me."

As she joyously obliged him, he lunged toward her, too, and they collided in an ecstatic explosion of an embrace. Arms and hands, thighs and legs, tongues and lips all pressed and writhed, ignited and enflamed, conquered and consumed. A beautiful, primal need began to pulse in Kira's blood as she reveled in the feel of this man's nakedness against her; as she savored his sculpted chest, his ridged stomach...his swollen desire. She moaned as heat throbbed between her own thighs in response to his arousal; she delighted in the similar sound from Damien's throat when she slid herself tighter against him, wanting to feel more of him. Wanting...*wanting.*

"Damien," she pleaded, trying to express that scorching yearning, but finding her voice an abysmal intercessor for these exquisite, liquid heat sensations. "Oh Damien, I—"

"I know," he assured, and somehow, she knew he did. "I know...I know..."

He repeated the words while he pulled her down into the hay again, making them an increasingly urgent litany against the skin where his mouth roamed: first along her neck and shoulder, then over the rise of her breast, down the plain of her stomach, teasing against the line of her hip bone, at last dipping to softly lick the inside of her thigh. The excruciating gentleness of his action sent a vibration of trembling pleasure throughout her whole body.

His mouth...dear sweet *svitojs*, what this man could do to her with his mouth! Kira arched and gasped with the sweet torment he induced, hardly believing *she* had been selected to feel this erotic, this ecstatic...this astounded. For eighteen years, she'd been trained to consider her body an instrument; only a prop for a show, year after year. Nobody, not even Sheena, had told her about *this.* Nobody had told her the mere flick of a man's tongue could transform her leg into a magical ribbon of sensation, or turn her breasts into starpoints of enlivened awareness. Nobody had told her she could be a burst of fire, bold and bright, aroused and alive and ready to—

"Damien!" she cried out, suddenly not knowing what she was ready for at all—but certain it had something to do with the press of his mouth to the most intimate part of her being. "Oh, *Damien.*" The last of it came as but a breath, as he parted her feminine folds, and kissed the tender nub he unveiled.

"Kira," he answered, murmuring the word against her, bringing her tears anew as he cherished the most womanly part of her. "You taste so good...so damn good..."

He proved it to her the next moment. As tears seeped down her cheeks, Damien slid up her body and joined his mouth to hers once more. He brought sweet warmth and delicious tanginess with him, delivered with the passionate sweep of his tongue and the masterful sucklings of his lips. Kira mewled from deep in her throat as she buried her hands in his hair and took him in yet deeper, craving the ambrosia of him like a starving woman.

When they broke apart, their heavy breaths mingled together while their slick bodies writhed together. Kira felt his heartbeat between her breasts, thundering like a plummeting anvil, and her hands clutched the quivering tension of his shoulders. He was ready, more than ready to take her; he valiantly fought the building forces in his body that pounded and throbbed and ached for release. He was waiting for her, she realized, and the knowledge of that filled her heart with joy anew—for now she comprehended the enormity of such a feat.

For now she battled the same clamoring forces in her own body.

The confession, even made inwardly, exploded the dam on an entirely new flood of the maddening pressure. It crashed over her and through her, resulting in a head-to-toe quiver she seriously doubted had an end...and completely toppling any restraints she had left. Direct proof of that came from the hand she descended down Damien's side, around his hip...then around his beautiful erection.

"Ah...*God*," he grated, his own tremor joining with hers now. "Kira...my God, Kira, what—"

"You invited me to feel you. Don't you remember?"

He emitted a tight sound that attempted to be a laugh. "Yes. Yes; vaguely, I do. Oh Princess, your fingers..."

"Are they all right? Is—is this all right with you?"

Now he *did* laugh. "Oh yes, Kira. Oh...*yes*." He kissed her to emphasize his point, sliding his tongue against hers in correspondence to the same motion of his erection between her fingers. Soon, however, they both breathed too fast and intensely for that, the heat and tension and friction exploding more rapidly than the table that had gone afire beneath poor Rico.

"And...how *do* I feel, darling?" he managed to ask in a rough grate against her lips, while his body rocked against hers ever faster, ever harder.

Kira wondered how he got the words out. All she achieved was a half-strangled "Dayyy..." before reason waved a surrendering flag to instinct, and she rendered her answer by way of movement, instead.

Sliding hesitantly at first, but with increasing surety, she opened her legs for him.

Damien breathed passion-filled nonsensities and half-words into her ear as he fit perfectly into the wet, warm valley she created for him. The essence of him pulsed madly against the entrance of her, hardness stroking impatiently against softness, man pulsing to become one with woman. Yet still he tarried, his body awash in the sweating strain of holding back. Oh God, *why* was he holding back?

"Damien," she got out in a harsh rasp, as an unnamable maelstrom swirled higher and hotter through her body. She writhed unthinkingly beneath him, seeking surcease from the tempest, while at the same time, craving more of the storm. Oh, sweet saints, *yes*, she wanted—

"More," she implored aloud. "Please...Damien...*please.*"

"I know, darling," came his strained-to-the-limits grate. "I know what you want, but—"

"Damien!"

"But I don't want to—"

"*Damien!*"

She arched as he plunged. She moaned as he groaned. Her outcry swiftly became a gasping shriek, though, as she soared into heaven, her body convulsing in rapturous spasms of pleasure all around his pulsing erection. Sheena had told her there would be pain and Kira supposed somehow there was, but her senses barely acknowledged the physical consequences of what she'd done; at least not now. Not through her haze of such exploding bliss; such sublime completion; such sheer fulfillment.

Damien gave her even deeper pleasure as he moved inside her with increasingly urgent abandon, his breath coming with faster and harsher frequency, his face awash in mindless, reckless passion. "Kira," he rasped, gripping her hips, "Kira, it's been so long for me...God, you feel so good..."

"Don't stop," she begged, combing her hands up and down his flexing, thrusting body. He was a magnificent creature, as sculpted and sinewy as the most graceful panther, as powerful and strong as the most commanding lion. She reveled in his increasingly untamed domination of her body, telling him so in the intense feline sounds vibrating up her throat and singing from her lips. Faster she urged him on; faster and hotter and harder until—

"God...Kira!"

His body shuddered in overlapping spasms as he drove into her with a final, beautiful motion, his head thrown back, his chest gleaming with sweat. And again Kira's tears came, as she watched him and moved with him through the gentle rockings that evened his heartbeat and cooled his skin.

And she loved him.

In this sweet, wonderful *now*, she loved him.

And in this sweet, wonderful *now*, she told herself that would have to be enough. For it was perhaps all she'd ever have.

Tomorrow—and the uncertain reality it would bring— would come soon enough.

★ ★ ★ ★

Tomorrow lay just a few minutes away.

Damien accepted that fact with grim reluctance as he watched the sky laboring to shed its last few stars in favor of a lavender and peach dawn. Tomorrow would officially begin when sun threads wove their way past the pines, and fell into scattered stitches along the foot of the bed in which Kira and he lay. The bed he never thought he'd share with anyone but Hamlet.

But this woman felt right here. Very right.

And at the moment, he refused to acknowledge the danger of thinking that. He only wanted this moment...and then he'd allow tomorrow to come.

He slowly turned to his side and propped his head on a bent elbow. After gathering her up in a blanket and bringing her up here from the stable last night, he'd let the darkness woo him into an exhausted sleep. So he indulged himself a long, lingering stare of her beauty now—though "beauty," he mused, was hardly the sufficient term for the sight which filled his gaze.

Even in slumber, Kira Scottney was more a firebrand the angels decided to turn into a woman. Her hair spread across the pillow like curling smoke tendrils from a gypsy incense burner...bayberry scented, he decided, observing the mahogany tints in the strand he fingered. Centered in that cacophony of dark curls was the flame of her face, her brows set in expressive dashes even now, her lips slightly parted and promising lush warmth, her skin the color of candle glow on ivory roses. Oh God yes, her skin...

Three seconds of recalling how the golden silk of that skin extended to her toenails—and the manner in which he'd discovered that fact—was enough to make his groin jump to life with arousal again. *You're not making things easier on yourself,* he commanded while watching the knuckles of his free hand brush a savoring trail around the curve of her shoulder, down her arm, to the slender hand that rested against the counterpane. He swallowed, berating himself for starting the action, for he wished to finish it by moving his hand beneath that cover, to embrace the warm, soft mound waiting there. He imagined how her nipple would feel as it tautened to life beneath his touch; he clenched his teeth against allowing the fantasy to continue further.

Until the woman beside him brought that fantasy to life.

With her eyes still closed but her lips curving into a

sublime smile, Kira guided his hand to the very curve of flesh for which he'd been yearning. Their breaths caught together as his hand closed over her breast, awakening its perfect, dusky bud to taut attention. The rest of her body came alive with swift succession, and she writhed her way next to him with impatient abandon. The texture of her skin and the feel of her body were all the prompting he needed for what he did next: sliding his mouth to hers, he explored the sweet heat of her like a child discovering the deliciousness of his first candied apple...with one important exception. Candied apples didn't emit such sexy, trembling mewls while being ravished.

When they pulled apart, many minutes later, he still kept her burrowed close to him. "Good morning," he murmured, brushing another kiss to her forehead.

She didn't respond in kind—not a surprising occurrence, since he was beginning to expect anything but the expected from this woman—though the furrows that formed beneath his lips were definitely not on his roster of anticipations. She explained the frown by way of a soft-moaning protest. "No. No; make it go away. Make it night again."

She needed to expound no further. The night had been their reprieve; their black forest of time where names meant nothing and passion ruled everything. The morning razed that forest and built manicured gardens in its place; gardens filled with stone formations that called themselves people.

People like the man who'd once been closer to him than anyone else in the world.

Squeezing his eyes against the sickening remembrance of having to punch Rolf, as well as the reason why, Damien succumbed to a grimace of his own. "Ah, Princess," he said, brushing tendrils of hair off her cheek, "I wish I *could* make it go away. I wish I could make many things go away."

This time, it was she who shifted to bestow a soft kiss against his temple. When he felt her linger afterward, he opened his eyes, and let himself be filled with the intent, compassionate glow of her sienna stare.

"I know you do," she whispered then, caressing his face in return. "I know what you wish for every time I look into your eyes."

His reaction to that took him by greater surprise than her first frown. The fear jolted up from his gut like a geyser, pummeling the backs of his eyes and slamming them shut again. "Really, now?" he retorted, concealing his uneasiness behind a gruff chuckle. "I'm just a bloody open book, is that it?"

"Only to those who wish to read." Her voice was smooth with the same steady warmth of her gaze—only heating *his* agitation higher. Still, she persisted: "I read it in every stare you took of the drawing room last night. I read it in the way you spoke toward those servants, who weren't just servants but friends. You love Hyperion's Walk like a part of your soul."

"Yes," he answered, swallowing tightly. "I do."

She lay down against his chest again, and he instantly acknowledged how perfectly she fit there, in the place atop his heart—though with her next words, she did manage to stop the beat of that heart altogether.

"Your mother would have been so proud of you last night, Damien. And your father."

The ache in his chest erupted into a dark laugh off his lips. "Well, that shows how much of my book you have yet to read, my lady."

She tensed at his deliberate use of her formal title, but he assured her the barb of his bitterness was aimed elsewhere by running a caressing hand over her head and down her back. He just wondered if she knew his target was the very heart beneath her ear. Of course not, he debated. Until this moment, *he* hadn't had the courage to admit what his soul now bellowed at him in resounding fury...he hadn't had the courage that Kira Scottney now gave to him.

He hadn't had the courage to concede that his hatred wasn't reserved for the Scottneys alone.

The realization exploded inside him as if a dozen Pavilions had been built there then put to flames at once. He breathed in and out once, putting his body through rigorous torture as he did so, though barely throwing a drop of water on the blaze igniting him deeper.

The only way to cool the torment, he realized, was to get help doing it.

Bloody hell.

"Damien? What is it?"

Both questions came gently, almost politely, verbal versions of help given generously. Still, he only took harsh breaths as answer. Damn. *Damn.* So intent had he been on remembering the morning he'd found Rachelle that he'd almost been able to forget about the years before that...almost. He'd almost succeeded at forgetting the crimes he was truly guilty of, yet for which he'd never find redemption.

Now he knew he'd only forgotten them in mind and body. Souls never let a man forget.

In the uncanny way she had of discerning the timbre of his thoughts, Kira repeated her questions by way of holding him tighter. Then for a long while, no sound passed between them.

As the first birds rose to trill in the trees outside, he took another deep breath, and spoke at last.

"Your father and your aunt have good justification to believe I killed Rachelle."

It came out all wrong, of course. The instant the words left his lips, he felt like going after them with a grappling hook, but instead spent the energy preparing for Kira's terrified flight from the bed.

To his shock, she only glanced up at him, her face scrunched in a piqued frown. "What the tarnation does *that* mean?"

He almost precluded his reply by bellowing out a laugh. She might as well be stomping her way up a stream bank at him again, raving at him about shooting at deer, frightening squirrels and crushing flowers. She had no idea he'd crushed much worse.

That though sobered his laugh to an indulgent smile. "It means I haven't always been this charming and debonair, Darling."

"Stop cutting up."

"The hell I'm cutting up." He apologized for his irritated growl by running a gentle hand over her mussed curls. "Kira..." Christ, this wasn't easy. "Kira...you didn't know me ten years ago."

"I didn't know you ten months ago. What does that have to do with anything?"

He stared at her again and was unsuccessful in restraining another soft smile. There was much he'd learned from this woman with gypsy in her blood and America in her spirit. So much about trusting the moment at hand, not the specters of the past. So much about visiting that past, but not living in it.

Ah God, what all of Yorkshire could learn from her. But they hadn't yet, and that was why he compelled himself to go on.

"I wasn't what you call a dutiful son." He let out a self-deprecating grunt. "Hell, I wasn't what you call a dutiful anything. I suppose I had too much time on my hands and too much money in my pockets. The crux of the whole thing was, my father even encouraged my rebellion at first; I used to hear him calming Mother, telling her I was going through the 'rites of manhood,' and other babble such as that. But his casual attitude only made me angrier, and by the time I was sixteen, he and I were strangers. My 'happiness' lie in whoring and gambling with all the wrong kinds of friends, in all the wrong kinds of places."

A strange shadow fell over her gaze then, as she looked at a place on his chin with deep concentration. The cast of her thoughts was thoroughly eclipsed from him—until she asked one simple but exposing question. "Was Rolf one of those friends?"

"Yes." He answered her honestly—but also knew the honesty wasn't complete until he expounded further. "But he was also the friend who pulled me off the bricks of a London alley after a gang of cutpurses had beat me, robbed me, and left me there for dead."

At that, she jerked up her head, her expression giving over to incredulity. "He saved your life?"

He nodded. "In more ways than one, I think."

She gave him a brusque huff. "Let me get used to the one first, please."

At that, he swatted her shoulder in play. "Easy, Princess; the pea in your mattress is beginning to take its toll. And believe it or not, Rolf wasn't always such a monkey's ass."

She relinquished no response save one skeptically arched brow, prior to leveling with determined firmness, "You were saying...about the cutpurses?"

"Yes," he emphasized, "the cutpurses who almost killed me."

She winced. "*Prasti minyah, pazhahlusta.* I'm sorry, Damien, that you had to go through that."

"I'm not," he returned—and meant it with every muscle and bone of his being. He massaged her upper arm as he looked to the ceiling, the memories now too numerous to battle... memories of those exhilarating, terrifying days in which more than his body had fought to live wholly again. "I'm not," he stressed again, "because that attack not only brought me back to Hyperion's Walk for my recovery, but brought me back to reality itself."

"What happened?" she prompted gently, her own embrace tightening, again as if she felt the shadows of his thoughts, if not their complete content.

He concentrated on pulling in a deep breath before answering. "I looked into my father's eyes for the first time in three years, that's what happened," he stated. "And what I saw there made me wish as if those thugs *had* killed me."

"Damien!" came her reacting blurt, full of shock and concern. The tone brought all his own feelings of that damnable day back like a ship full of shame and remorse unloaded onto the rickety dock of his soul.

"He was so...saddened by me," he heard himself grate, though the sound was muffled by the interminable stacks of those shipping crates. "I kept wishing he'd just explode; just find some rage and swing a good fist at me. But...I'd hurt him much deeper than that." He finished in a fading mutter, "*Much deeper.*"

"What did you do then?" She didn't raise her own voice

above a silk-soft touch of sound, though she joined it with a compassionate caress to his chest.

"First, I gained my strength back as rapidly as I could." He filled a pause with a fast snort of mirth. "I think Father was of the impression I was craving a swift return to my London hedonism. Instead, one day I marched myself into his office and demanded he begin to teach me about my responsibilities; about the land and the tenants I'd inherit from him one day. I also told him it was my intention to start courting Rachelle Scottney, with the goal of marrying her and expediting the creation of his grandchildren.

"While he smiled and poured celebratory brandy for us both, I silently gave him one more promise. I vowed I would never be the cause of such sadness in his eyes again."

He stopped there, on a long and difficult swallow. Then he squeezed shut his own eyes, struggling to push back the forward rush of his thoughts...the inevitable surge toward that day—*ah God, that day*—when his life had been doused in a pool of bright red blood...

"Damien," came her whisper through that nightmare haze of memory. "Oh, Damien...but you did see that sorrow in his eyes again, didn't you?"

He felt himself nod. He raised his hand to the bridge of his nose and clamped two fingers there with the force of a vise, yearning for the pain between his eyes to eclipse the sting behind them.

And still, he forced himself to speak. He ordered himself to finish the story, so he could lock it away again and get this torture the hell over with.

"The trial sucked away his spirit," he said gruffly. "And the scandal sucked away his life." His breath escaped him on a shaking sigh. "The afternoon after I was released from prison, a letter arrived from one of his biggest buyers, stating they'd decided to purchase their wool elsewhere that season. In the middle of that night, we were awakened by Mother's scream. He'd had a seizure of some sort. He...never woke up from it."

An odd sense of relief filled him as he emitted the last agonizing syllable—at least as much as he could define relief, when the woman against him dampened his chest with her tear-spiked lashes. "Damien," she rasped, "it must have been so difficult for you."

He didn't respond for a long moment. When he did, the hardness of his tone came as a shock—yet a reassurance. "I didn't stop to think about that, Princess. I couldn't. I had an estate to run and a murder to solve."

Kira moved her soft strokings to his shoulder blade, wordlessly telling him she knew he had more to say. The dilemma he faced was: what would that "more" be? Ally had no doubt supplied her with every disgusting detail of the financial ruin that had led to Rolf saving him once more by purchasing Hyperion's...

Which only left him with one thing to talk about. A killing—and what he'd found out about it. The theory he hadn't disclosed to anyone...

The theory he shouldn't divulge to her, of all people.

But at that moment, she moved by a slight inch, and he felt her shoulder beneath his hand...her heartbeat against his ribs... her tears drying on his skin...

And he once more remembered the tears she'd cried last night. Once more, he witnessed every second of her anguish as she'd held Rico in her arms, and wept for that hothouse full of abused creatures. He remembered how she'd trusted him with those tears...how she'd trusted him with herself.

And for a moment, he told his mind to go sit at the edge of the dock, while he trusted her with the instinct of his own heart.

"Believe it or not," he began then, very quietly, "there's a funny side to all of this."

A pause preceded her reply; a long enough space to accommodate the formation of her perplexed moue. "However do you mean *that*, Mister Sharpe?"

Damien meted out another pause before summoning his resolve again, and answering her. "Because if all the information I've gathered already is even half correct, then the key to discovering Rachelle's real killer doesn't lay at Hyperion's Walk.

"It's at Scottney Hall."

CHAPTER TWENTY-FIVE

"Scottney Hall?"

Kira pushed up sharply as the words spilled from her mouth. The syllables sounded foreign and unattached, as if they spoke of the Tower of Pisa or the Globe Theatre, not the place she'd called home for nearly the last month. "Why..." she at last stammered, unable to invoke anything more coherent through the muck of her confusion, "but how..."

"I wish I had those answers for you, Princess," Damien replied, and she watched a thick cloud of frustration settle over his own features. "I only know that right now, it's the only explanation that makes sense." He finished with low conviction, "A great deal of sense."

Yes, his words and tone were filled with certitude, but as he spoke, he kept his gaze fixed on the painted designs in the ceiling beams. His eyes glittered with the apprehension of not only revealing what he had so far, but wondering if he could or should continue.

Kira's heart swelled as she looked at him, and she knew she had the ability to fill in the answer to that for him. She did so by pressing her hand to the side of his face, urging him to gaze once more at her. When he did, she smiled softly in encouragement. "Go on," she requested with her lips. *It's all right*, she told him with her eyes.

Damien didn't say anything as he pulled her hand off his face, then fit his lips into the center of her palm. For a long minute he remained like that, his eyes closed, breathing in slowly, as if drawing in her strength directly through that contact with her hand. Kira watched him through every precious second of that time, not blinking, wordlessly heartening him to take all he wanted, all he needed...for in seeing his renewed strength, she was wondrously replenished, too.

When he spoke again, he still didn't open his eyes or overtly shift his position. Without preamble, he simply began: "The night Rachelle was murdered, I was summoned out of dinner by a message from Scottney Hall. My presence was requested at once. Naturally, I complied."

Kira's brows lifted in curiosity. "Did my father send it?"

"No. Your father was in London. The request came through the stables. During my courtship with Rachelle, I'd gotten to know the lads there well. There was a beautiful bay mare I'd been keeping my eye on, especially when I heard she had a foal on the way. I'd made some offers to Nicholas, was even considering giving the foal to Rachelle as a surprise...in any case, the boys knew I'd enjoy being present for the birth."

"And that was the reason for the message?" At his confirming nod, she gave him an opposing move, shaking her head. "So...shouldn't that have supplied you with a locked-up alibi for the night? If all those people saw you at the Scottney Hall stables—"

"I never showed up at the Scottney Hall stables."

As her brows shot higher, Damien opened his eyes. In the ink-dark depths of his gaze, she instantly saw he was telling the truth, but she also saw he explored her stare in return.

He searched for the safe harbor where he could continue telling her the truth.

"Damien," she murmured, compressing her palm again to

his stubbled jaw. She wished she could touch him deeper, in the soul which had lived so long in spurned solitude, it had to be retaught how to trust. *Oh Damien, I wish I could take away all that pain for you.*

Instead, she could only tilt him a small smile, and say with gentle sarcasm, "You certainly know how to make things interesting, don't you?"

He compensated her effort with a genuine, if sardonically so, laugh. "I received a hearty share of help that particular evening. Just as I'd crossed over onto Scottney land, I was stopped at the Two Rivers' Bridge."

Kira nodded at that, albeit with a puzzled frown. She knew the location; had marveled at its beauty during her first footbound entrance onto Scottney Hall lands. A heavy wood bridge spanned twin rivers plus the fifty feet of wetlands created between them. For that reason, the area possessed a wild, remote ambiance—an odd selection, she ruminated, for any kind of a security stop.

Her expression must have disclosed her thoughts well, for Damien explained then, "The crew was checking the bridge itself, not travelers on the road." But then he qualified, "Or so these fellows told me. To this day, I have no idea who they were or what they were doing 'repairing' a bridge in the dark of a winter's night, but at that time, their Scottney liveries seemed enough. I obliged with their detour instructions without another question. Hell, who was I to argue with representatives of the uncle-in-law who was about to practically give me a prize foal?"

Kira nodded again. The reasoning made sunlight-clear sense to her. She didn't, however, understand where the account went from there. "So you're saying...the detour wasn't a detour at all?"

Damien's reply first came in the form of a trenchant grunt. "Let's put it this way," he sneered, "by the time I realized I'd been directed to the middle of nowhere, then found my way back home through the sheer luck of a clear night sky, it was well past midnight. The whole house was asleep."

Kira voiced the obvious following to that. "Including Rachelle."

"Of course. So I thought."

"So you thought?" she rejoined. "You didn't *know*?"

Surprisingly, Damien glanced at her and chuckled then. He gave her upper arm an indulgent squeeze. "My little hoyden, we do things a fraction differently in English estates than you do in circus camps. Rachelle's bedroom had an adjoining door to mine, of course, but I would never think of barging in on her in the middle of the—"

"Her bedroom!" Kira exclaimed. She jerked from his hold as she closely examined his eyes for the gleam of a jest. "Adjoined to yours? You mean you two were married, but you had completely separate—"

"Everything," he filled in, and she indeed saw that no teasing mirth sparkled in his gaze...only the haze of an unusual, but apathetic kind of loneliness. "We had separate everything. Separate lives."

He attempted to make that addition into nothing more than a casual quip by accenting it with a flippant tone and a fast shrug. But the disparity rang as false as Aunt Aleece hiking up her skirts for an Irish jig...and Damien could do nothing about the truth, stalking through its own lonely dance in the shadows of his eyes. A loneliness, Kira now suspected, with beginnings long before the scandal that merely gave it physical form.

Almost a month ago she'd stood before a window, looking out on a forest, wondering how a man could so easily seclude himself from the world. Now, she realized that man had already been doing it for years.

She stared at that man now, and ordered away the heavy, hot sting behind her eyes. The tears were not hers to shed. Instead, she poured her compassion into her voice, softly asking him, "When...did you finally find her?"

"In the morning," Damien answered after a tense, tight-muscled delay. "I'd dressed quickly, because Rolf and I were scheduled for a ride." Another pause was created by a quirk of a smile, his memory clearly turning up an unexpected image. "We never worried about being pretty when we rode, Rolf and I."

She mirrored his smile for a moment. "I imagined you looked every inch the incorrigible rogue."

"I imagine I did." As he issued that, the corners of his mouth fell again, a dark and quiet tone curling back around his voice.

"She...wasn't in her room when I entered," he at last continued. "But even that occurrence wasn't so extraordinary. I wagered she'd just fallen asleep in the library, where she ended up many evenings. I went down, but she wasn't there, either." His next words came from even deeper in his throat, as his body tensed tighter. "That was when I went to the drawing room...then the morning room."

The last of that fell raggedly from his lips, like an ancient Roman messenger just finished with a hundred mile delivery. He could say no more, and via the splints of tension he kept secured around his limbs, he begged her not to ask such, either.

The request was fine with Kira. More than fine. She

remembered the next events of the story in gruesome detail from Ally's accounting of that day...details that now made her face grimace, her heart ache, and her arms wrap closer around this man who had been forced to live the nightmare. She laid her head back against his chest and eventually, slowly, she listened to his heartbeat thump at a more regular rhythm—though she yearned to help render the same effect to his body. But his returning embrace was wooden at best; his limbs remained the captives of an unseen apprehension...as if now, the person he entreated silence from was *himself*.

If indeed the battle he waged was an inner conflict, then one party claimed a startling victory then—for the "last tidbit" of information his lips now reluctantly surrendered sent Kira's own senses leaping fast from startlement to astoundment.

"I knew bloody well I wasn't supposed to go near her, let alone touch her. But do you know what made me do both those things, Kira? It was the knife—the knife that monster used to first cut out her throat so she wouldn't scream, and then—"

As his voice faltered, Kira pressed a gentle hand to his chest, telling him her imagination could amply fill out fill out the rest of *that* thought. "I'll *never* forget that knife," he went on in a vehement growl. "I'll never forget how I wanted drive it through somebody's heart myself, seeing her blood all over it...

"Seeing her family's crest carved into its ivory handle."

★ ★ ★ ★

There was so much more to say. There was nothing left to say. The incongruity formed a tangled wad in Damien's throat just as all the remembered horror and confusion twisted together in his gut, forcing him into a silence he both welcomed and dreaded.

A thick lull fell, filled with nothing but the twittering birds outside and his thudding heart inside...as he waited and watched for this woman's reaction to the fact he'd just dragged her family into an ignominy called murder and scandal.

"It...was a dagger from Scottney Hall?" Kira finally asked, though the pause in her query seemed induced by nothing more than intrigued curiosity. She might as well have been consulting a maid about the appropriate silver pattern for a dinner party.

"Yes," Damien replied, trying to similarly school his voice until he discerned where she was taking this exchange.

"You're sure?"

He fought the urge to bellow his exasperated response. Nicholas, just like any other bored nobleman on holiday in Yorkshire, had loved spending many an evening demonstrating the might of his lineage by way of the accumulated "treasures" which had once taken God knew how many lives. The Scottney arsenal was as plentiful as it was gaudy—both factors working to the favor of Damien's memory.

He determined, however, she probably didn't need to know all *that* about dear papa. Instead, in a tight-reined growl, he told her, "I held the thing in my hand. *Yes*, I'm sure."

She contemplated that for a moment, her features again divulging nothing except deep concentration. Finally, she asked evenly, "Well, what happened to it?"

He should have foreseen her path to that question. On the other hand, he qualified, how could he have seen it, when he'd been searching for her thoughts on a separate path? He'd been looking for, and expecting, her shock and bewilderment and outrage...and eventually, her departure back to Papa dear. Instead, *she* ambushed *his* course with bizarre wonderments like trust and acceptance and belief.

Belief.

Dear God. Could it be she really believed he didn't kill Rachelle? Could it be she really wanted to know all this so she could *help* him?

The mere consideration of the miracle slammed open the floodgates of his mind and soul, releasing the torrent of enraged frustration he had held in for so long; *so long;* ever since that day when the magistrate had ordered him hauled from the court for "unruly conduct" and "disruptive disobedience." Hauled out before he could ever tell the rest of his story. Before anyone could hear his truth.

"I don't know," he said then, the crest of that flood sweeping the words from taut agitation into snarled stress. "I don't know what happened to the damn knife, *that's* the pissing irony of everything." He stopped and concentrated on taking in a breath. Even that ability had been sacrificed to the flood. "I remember holding the thing in my hand, then Rolf came in, and...everything becomes a blur in my mind then; that's when the nightmare began. I didn't know they'd never recovered the knife until the next day, when Rolf came to see me in prison."

The flood seeped its way into the marrow of his bones then, making him shiver from the inside out. He'd shivered the same way in that grimy cell, in that gray void of a world interrupted only by the brief flicker of Rolf's visit that day—and the news his mate had brought of the mysteriously-vanished murder weapon.

Just as he had done then, Damien emitted a dark grunt of a laugh. "The loss, believe it or not, turned out to be my salvation. Without the knife, they couldn't convict me."

Kira's reply came after a pause he'd expected from

her—a pause weighted with the silence of careful, thoughtful contemplation. "But without the knife," she stated at last, "you couldn't prove your innocence, either."

"Right on target, Princess. Just as I said; it's a—"

"Pissing irony." She supplied the finish for him with three times the vehemence *he'd* planned on throwing into the words—at first taking him by such surprise, he found himself coughing back a laugh erupting clear from the depths of his belly.

But swiftly, another reaction seeped its way into him like an outpouring of warm honey into the crevices of a bread loaf. Only that chunk of parched dough was now his heart, and the honey was *Kira's* heart...the heart she offered him so freely, so fervently, that he could no more resist her than empty bread canyons could shun a gift of precious, delicious sweetness.

Just like the sweetness of the kiss she openly lowered to his lips now.

He didn't know why she decided to direct her passion away from her rage and onto him, but Damien now knew what to do with heated honey when he tasted it: get as much as he can, and thoroughly savor the experience of doing so. And so he not only accepted her mouth, but drew it tighter against his, steadily sucking her in, gently playing with her tongue and lips in a dance of moist nips and caresses.

When she pulled up from him, he didn't let her go very far—though now he admitted the instinct of his body, not the counsel of his mind, as the instigating culprit.

He knew a moment of contrition for his primal tendencies, however, when looking into her eyes, and seeing the earnest, urgent force of her heart staring unblinkingly back at him. "Damien," she whispered, "you took a great risk in telling me this."

He drew her words in for a long moment before answering. "Yes," he replied at last, but battled frustration as he did. It was too short a word to adequately convey his gratitude...his thanks to her for seeing that he'd given her not just a massive block of information.

He'd given her his trust.

"I'll keep it all safe for you, Damien."

A tender smile came to life on his lips. With one finger, he stroked the sweet, full contours of her own mouth. "I know you will, Princess."

"Do you know why?"

"Why, Princess?"

"Because I love you."

His smile dropped. Yet not a muscle in Kira's own body tensed, not even after the interminable silence that was clearly the only answer he'd be able to give her declaration right now. Perhaps the only answer he'd ever be able to give.

You took a great risk in telling me this. Ah, God...the woman didn't level such words lightly. When Kira Scottney talked of taking risks, she didn't speak as a casual observer on the pastime. She committed to her emotions as completely as she embraced life itself, whether the experience be the joy of wading in a cool forest stream, the anguish of petting an abused tiger cub, or the unsurety of professing her love for a man who had nothing to offer except an isolated hunting lodge, a slobbering labrador and a soul full of grief.

She deserved more. And yet he bluntly admitted that if he stood on the Hyperion's Walk lawn once more with the choice to take her or leave her, he'd not change his actions of last night by a step. A life as Mrs. Rolf Pembroke was *not* the "more" she had due. Just thinking of her standing before an altar with that bastard spurred his pulse again with furious speed.

He diffused part of the rage by releasing a rough cough. The other part, he funneled into the clipped statement he gave her as he threw back the counterpane. "We'd best be hying our naked arses out of here, my lady. They'll have the Scottney hounds out after you soon."

But before he'd finished the sentence, he shoved the blankets back into place and pulled her close again. "I want to keep you here all day, damn it."

She eagerly burrowed herself back against him and quipped, "And all night?"

"Yes," he chuckled indulgently, "and all night." The mirth, however, fast gave way to a heavy sigh. "But I can't."

He finished that by pushing the curls at her temple aside with his chin and brushing a kiss to the skin there, while waiting for the disheartened exhalation she'd issue in return.

He should have remembered he lay here with a creature who'd undoubtedly been named *Walks with Wild Step* by her American Indian friends. For with the agility yet unpredictability of one of their untamed Pinto ponies, Kira instead reared away from him with eyes afire and features ablaze.

"Well, of course you can't keep me here." As she punctuated the assertion with a huff, she sorely tested his concentration by letting one breast fall loose from its blanketed confines, uncaring that its nipple tempted him in pert, dark copper perfection. "We both have work to do."

If her actions jerked him down one unexpected path, her pragmatically-delivered statement hauled him down another with twice the speed. "Work?" Damien heard himself echo through the spinning upheaval of his thoughts. "What are you—what do you mean, work?"

The woman actually rolled her eyes at him. "Finding evidence of who really killed Rachelle," she said as if reminding him the sky was blue. She gave the bedclothes a brisk snap of her own. "And the sooner we get going at the task, the—"

But Damien jerked short her retreat with one hand, deftly ensnaring her wrist. "Hold on, Wild Thing." He lowered his tone to convey his seriousness. "There's nothing *we* are getting to, all right? I'm going to get you home, then I expect you to—"

"What?" Kira fired, for once giving him a reaction for which he'd more than steeled himself: her indignant fury. "What exactly do you expect me to do, Damien? Go back to my embroidery lessons and my gown fittings and my Latin readings, and pretend I don't hear anything or see anything that may prove the key to exonerate the man I love?"

When he rendered nothing in reply but a taut and silent glare, an incensed breath hissed from between her teeth. But her voice quivered when she went on: "That's exactly what you expected me to do, wasn't it? You were going to shut me out again, weren't you?"

"*No.*" He emphasized the protest by hauling her fingers to his lips and crushing them there. "No. For God's sake, Kira, that's not it."

"That's precisely *it*," she retorted. "That's precisely what you mean, if you've trusted me enough this far, telling me the evidence to prove your innocence may lie beneath a cushion I sit on or a desk drawer I open, but with your next breath, commanding me to move through those actions like a mindless figurine—" The word lilted as if leading to a conclusion, but her harsh sigh accomplished the feat, instead. Accomplished it, Damien ruled from the cramping pit of his gut, with gloriously discomfiting success.

The cramps were worsened when the fury struck him a moment later, familiar in its agonizing heat but foreign in its consuming intensity. *Why?* his mind raged in frustration. *Why can't everything be different? Why can't I simply return this woman's declaration of love then spend the rest of my life proving it to her, instead of having to prove I didn't commit a murder? Why can't I hold her here, safe in my arms, instead of letting her go...possibly into the path of the bastard who really drove that knife into Rachelle?*

Not making the torment an iota easier was the interjection of her voice once more, reflecting her struggle through a mire of her own angered confusion. "I don't understand," she told him. "I don't understand. Damien, I can really help you this time!"

"No," he returned evenly, "you can't."

"I can be your eyes—"

"No."

"I can be your ears—"

"*No*," he persisted, "you can't."

"*Why?*" She pushed at him hard, the American hoyden version of a tavern drunk itching to start a brawl. "Why, for heaven's sake?"

Unbelievably, Damien cocked a small smile then. He'd compiled the wrong metaphor. Nobody would ever place this gorgeous, golden-skinned beauty on the same continent with a drunken dock rat. That conclusion helped bring a fast but gentle reply to his lips. "Because it's too dangerous, that's why." He ran a gentle finger down her arm. "Because you're too valuable to me."

"That's a pigwashed excuse and you know it," she rebutted.

"Damien, you need some help!"

"I don't need help."

"You need someone to be watching for things at Scottney Hall!"

"I have someone watching for things at Scottney Hall, thank y—"

The word died in the middle of his throat. The sound was stabbed silent more swiftly than Rachelle probably had been—though this time, things had happened in reverse. While he could only imagine the terror she'd known before her assailant struck, *his* dread began with the slaying, and deepened as he witnessed the transforming hues of reaction across Kira's face. Her blank confusion quickly became a puzzled frown...but then, very fast, exploded into a wide and comprehending stare.

"You have someone," she reiterated softly. "You have... you have *you*, don't you?" An excited giggle skittered off her lips. "*Ehta Prahvda!* It's true! You're the mysterious one from the stables...the trainer with the wonderful legs!"

For a fast moment, Damien forgot he'd just surrendered the secret known only by two other people in the world; the two mates from the Scottney stables who'd not only risked everything to give him his "job" as "George," but who routinely repeated that risk to bring him information at times when it wasn't safe for "George" to be "at work."

"So...you think George has wonderful legs?" he asked with a carefully neutral expression and a distinctly jealous tone.

Clearly not fooled by him for a moment, she nodded zealously. "The most wonderful legs I've ever seen, I think," she quipped with exaggerated coyness.

"Really, now?" He accompanied the words with a purposeful swing of one leg from beneath the covers, extending it in front of her then subtly flexing. He qualified his intention for the action as completely noble, of course. By making her forget her mission to help him, he'd assure her safety a degree further—perhaps the degree that would matter.

Yes, he commended himself, that was certainly the most honorable of incentives. His motion had nothing to do with the appreciative surprise he sparked in the captivating shards of her eyes, nor the ascending admiration of her brows, nor the audible gasp she let slip as she was now face-to-knee, as it were, with one of the very limbs for which she'd just been swooning.

"George...is a very nicely formed man," she murmured after a long, swallowing pause. "I wouldn't know firsthand, of course..."

"Of course," Damien echoed, holding his tone at the texture of oriental silk...holding his leg hard and tight and close to her.

Too close.

The realization blared through his senses like the warning sirens of the Great London Fire: it was too little, too late. Too little because the moment she lowered her hand to his thigh, flames of awakening licked up and down the entire length of his leg. Too late because those flames also leaped into the juncture *between* his legs, powering an undeniable reaction there. A reaction he could no more cover than he could control. A reaction Kira didn't miss...nor overlook.

A shrewd confidence curled its way up one side of her mouth, *not* aiding Damien's effort at composure; the expression took on sensuously adorable meaning when joined to her face. He compelled his own features to as suave a demeanor as possible—a fairly *im*possible feat. In the space of a few tiny seconds, his hoyden had switched the tracks of this journey entirely. Now *he* was the hapless locomotive, at the mercy of *her* guiding levers, though he had no idea where their destination lie.

The sensation was alarming. And exhilarating.

"Oh, yes," she said then, calculated both in her guileless tone, and her not-so-guileless caress down the outside edge of his leg, "I've heard George is an exceptionally fine man."

"But...?" Damien hedged, supplying the word implied by her tone but not uttered by her lips.

"But he doesn't have the sense to ask for help when he needs it." That, she issued as she brought her hand back up to his hip—while pinning his other leg with the naked, warm weight of her own thighs. "Can you imagine that?" she queried in the most cotton-light of whispers. "Can you imagine he has to be actually trapped and tormented before he'll admit he can't do it all by himself?"

Damien first only inhaled ragged air through his teeth as response. When he exhaled, he vowed, a litany of oaths would be riding past his lips, too; all bound for one conniving, calculating, irresistible hoyden-woman.

But the curses didn't sound like such. When he did breathe out, his lips only stuttered out something resembling, "T-Torment? Wh-what do you mean?"

"Mmmmm," she replied blithely, lips moving against his neck, hand trailing closer to where the force of his body flowed and pulsed in ever-increasing readiness, "you know, the usual torment; the kind where pressure is mercilessly applied until appropriate surrender is given."

"P-pressure?" He rasped more than voiced the query, dreading for her to show him her answer; praying for her to show him.

Kira showed him.

"*God,*" he grated, as her hand slid up each inch of his arousal. She emulated the stroke he'd given himself last night before making love to her, closing her fingers around his turgid head, and squeezing gently.

Damien groaned.

Just before she did it again.

"Kira..."

"Hmmm?"

"Ohhh...*Kira...*" Holy God, how thoroughly her touch torched his whole body, astounding in how freely she gave it, exciting in how innocently she administered it. He was certain she had no idea where her fingers would foray next, and that made the experience thrice as thrilling and precious for him.

"Yes," he heard himself rasp, hoping she still heard the depth of his pleasure through the sparsity of his tone. "Yes, darling...touch that...touch *those*..." *God, what you do to me, Kira.* "Touch me...hold me."

She pressed a finger again to the moistened tip of his erection as she slipped her tongue slowly back between his; shyly at first, but intensifying the kiss when Damien stimulated her with a welcoming moan. A shudder claimed him, moving through her, too, as he slid a hand around one sphere of her bottom and squeezed appreciatively. He heard her breath catch and felt her heart pound, and he clenched back the surging explosion in his groin in preparation to turn the tables on his little minx; to roll her over and enter her in a thundering rush, knowing his completion inside her sweet, hot—

In the moment he took to indulge that fantasy, the crafty hoyden reminded him just who was in control of this causerie.

Before he even opened his eyes following the mating of

their tongues, Damien found himself the conquered prey of the woman who clearly yearned to emulate that action with the lengths of their bodies. His eyes sprang open to behold her creamy beauty straddled atop him...and wrapped around him. An aroused half-smile tilted the edges of her mouth just before she bit on her lower lip and glided the folds of her femininity around his ever-hardening penis.

They gasped together.

And still, the damnable woman summoned the presence of mind to form coherent words to him. "So, Mister Sharpe," she murmured while repeating that intimate action—as well as the shuddering repercussions through both their bodies, "do you now admit that a number of life's circumstances require the efforts of a cohesive ensemble, working together for a common aspiration?"

At first, Damien could only moan in response. Christ above! Of all the women on the face of this earth, Fate had crashed one into his life who spouted not pillow talk on the brink of her climax, but half the bloody dictionary. Someone like her could have only happened to someone like him.

And damn, was he grateful.

"Y-yes," he finally managed to reply, albeit after four heavy swallows. "Y-yes; all right, Princess; we'll find the bloody killer together!"

The endeavor was worth it. She showed him her gratitude by crushing her mouth to his again, now vanquishing him with the delicious assault of her lips, tongue, and teeth. Greater satisfaction came as she broke away on an impassioned gasp, as Damien clasped her hips and began to drive their bodies against each other at a fevered rhythm.

She looked at him then, conveying the love she'd confessed

in a manner more potent than any words she could ever speak: through the incredible fire of her eyes. And though Damien was the one wielding the controlling grip, he'd never felt more forcefully held by anything or anyone before. He couldn't blink. He couldn't *think*. Looking away was an option long cast into the realm of impossibility.

He could only grit his teeth and subject himself to the torturous splendor of this woman's gaze, of this woman's body, of this woman's love as she lifted a joyous smile at him, and repeated in sexy, out-of-breath intensity, "Together...oh, *yes*."

"Yes," Damien echoed her, as the conflagration in her gaze licked its way up the length of his arousal. "*Yes*." He was so hard. So hot. So ready to burst simply from the feel of her skin and the caress of her eyes. He tightened his grip and pumped her faster against him. This woman was going to make him come with the sheer force of her gaze!

"Together," Kira whispered again. "Say it again, Damien."

"To...gether..."

"Again!"

But his lips couldn't summon the word. His ecstasy-filled groan filled the air, instead, and for a moment, the birds fell silent outside, and the wind stilled in the trees.

For a moment, the world stopped...and he knew the bliss of simply being alive again.

Of simply hoping again.

CHAPTER TWENTY-SIX

Together.

Kira had never realized the word could have so many wondrous shadings, so many brilliant meanings...but during the next ten weeks, she discovered them all. She created a few new definitions for the list, as well.

Every one of those definitions came accompanied by the precious memory that had inspired it. The memory of the man to whom she'd completely, deliriously given her heart.

Now knowing it was Damien beneath the hat and beard of the mysterious "George" from the stables, her afternoons were no longer filled with merely Latin conjugations and needlepoint sessions, but the elation of watching his body at work, striving to move as one with an animal...anticipating the moments when the sun would set and he'd move as one with *her*. Sometimes, she simply knew it would be impossible to wait. Proclaiming a headache or fatigue to Aunt Aleece, she'd beg for the ease of fresh air, then conveniently start out her "walk" in the vicinity of the stables. He'd come to her there, in some dark corner of the extensive complex, where they used care to refrain from words or cries, pouring their silent frustration into their passions, instead.

The words would come later, after the world tucked itself once more under darkness, and lights were slowly dimmed through the corridors and courtyards of Scottney Hall. Using the sea captain's eye glass Damien had given her, Kira instead sought out one bright light, beaming solitary against the black trees on the horizon, signaling he'd come for her. Down to the kitchens she and Fred would tiptoe as fast as they could, knowing that soon, *together* would be a moonlit, star-bright reality once more.

Together. Many times, it meant merely lying in his arms through the night...awakening to see him by her side; witnessing the transformation of his features as sleep enfolded him; giggling at his disgruntled scowl when Fred and Hamlet decided they wished to "join the party," and inevitably ended up with the better share of the bed in their enthusiasm.

Together. As the nights warmed with summer's magical caress, it also meant midnight adventures such as she'd never known...a journey north to Ilton Temple, where William Danby had constructed his charmingly accurate reproduction of Stonehenge; a night spent in exploration of Aysgarth Falls, turned into a collection of spectral silver streamers by the moon; another trip to Swinnergill Kirk, during which her grinning rake of a lover showed off his knowledge of the secret cave beneath the waterfall there—as well as the interesting uses one could glean from such a place...

But her favorite sojourn was their visit to Linton Village. The little town, in existence since the days when Norman invaders had tromped these lands, imparted a life of its own despite that its occupants had banked fires and climbed into bed hours ago. As she and Damien crossed an ancient packhorse bridge then a thick, dewy green, it took no effort for Kira to hear folk songs of old in the breeze through the trees; she saw children playing on the lawn in medieval dresses and doublets. Then, when they traveled further and stopped at the village's thirteenth-century chapel, she saw those children growing up, falling in love, and coming here to have their love recognized and blessed before God and Eternity.

That was when the best part of the trip had occurred. As they'd entered the chapel hand-in-hand, she'd taken a quick moment to glance at Damien's profile—and in that single instant, she knew he saw those lovers of centuries past, as well. Yet then he'd returned her gaze...and she realized he envisioned much more than just what history had given them.

She realized he wanted to be part of that history, as well.

He wanted to be part of it with her.

They'd walked wordlessly to the altar together, moonbeams and confessional candles lighting their way. The pew had creaked as they'd lowered before the solemn, silent crucifix, just before they'd pressed their foreheads to each other's and bowed their heads. She didn't know much time passed then, nor had she cared; she only remembered feeling as close to Damien as if they were back at the lodge and his body was intimately fused with hers...perhaps closer.

When he brought her head up again by coaxing her face upward with a soft, suckling kiss, she gazed back at him through a haze of tears welling straight from the completely fulfilled space of her heart. That haze thickened with the next syllables he uttered to her past a tender, intent smile.

"Together," he'd said to her.

An angel could have alighted on the altar that moment, conferring them a prophecy straight from the Upper Realms, and Kira swore the message would not have been more precious to her.

Together, he'd said...and yet, there was something more in Damien's utterance that night, too...

Together, he'd *promised.*

Her new meanings for the word had burst to life with that comprehension. Indeed, her new meanings for the *world* had sparkled into existence. Now, the days weren't so frightening to face, and the nights were a starlit synonym for heaven. *Today* was now just as perfect a place to be as *tomorrow* and *forever.* Even etiquette books became interesting when she looked forward to sardonically recounting their contents to Damien, which earned her a stiff acceptance of sorts with Aunt Aleece again. Though things with Father didn't progress so smoothly, her sudden knowledge of Yorkshire landmarks and folklore garnered his subdued approval, and he even excused her from lessons one day to treat her to a trip into York, where they shopped and dined in quiet compatibility.

During the trip, neither Rolf nor Damien's name were mentioned once.

Even so, Kira admitted herself taken aback during a handful of moments in the day; moments in which Nicholas would laugh or smile in reaction to her or something in the world at large—

And she was reminded exactly of Damien's laughter and smiles.

At first, that acknowledgment prompted her to a vast collection of disconcerted scowls. That she saw the most minute similarity, let alone these blatant parallels, between the man who'd let her grow up on a separate continent and the man who now lived in her heart was unsettling as starting a handstand on a galloping horse who suddenly threw a shoe.

But during the return journey to Scottney Hall, she again pondered the phenomenon...and this time, she began to smile. She did so as she raised her face into a pine-scented twilight breeze; as she looked to the kiss of amber light on the grass fanning out from the road; as she listened to the bleats of sheep and the rush of a creek and the inexplicable "sound" of Yorkshire magic...

And she realized none of her observations were so bizarre at all. Her perceptions had changed because *she* had changed. Because somehow, sometime within the last three months, she had, indeed, given her father's land—*her* land—a chance.

And in the process, she'd fallen in love.

She'd grown to see the beauty not just in a lonely man named Damien Sharpe, but in mist across the moors and storms across the mountains; in soaring emerald hills and sheets of purple heather; in ancient waterfalls and Norman castles and medieval churches. She also heard it in the voices of the past harmonizing in the songs of the present, and in the whisper of a dream which began to grow tentatively in her heart...a dream that perhaps Yorkshire would like a circus troupe to make its magic that much more special.

Simply because of one wonderful, all-powerful word.

Together.

They would make that word a full, glorious reality, Kira vowed. All she and Damien had to do was find a killer first.

No matter how hard the task was turning out to be.

Though she soared to new heights of elation each night because of Damien's loving, Kira nevertheless found herself battling equivalent waves of disappointment during the course of each day. No matter how many desks she'd sneaked through, conversations she'd eavesdropped on, and even volumes in the library she'd shaken out, she brought back no new information to her love each night. Concurrently, Damien relayed that his progress among Scottney Hall's servant ranks fared no better.

The only night his gaze did narrow with interest was

when she expressed confusion about a letter that arrived one afternoon for Aunt Aleece. The messenger wore no livery, but Kira swore she'd seen the boy the night of the fire at Hyperion's Walk, in the stables when they'd gone to mount Dante. Damien had nodded, claiming he knew the lad of whom she spoke, but his faraway tone and even more distant stare prompted Kira's suspicion that his mind had traversed much farther back than the night of the Pavilion blaze. When she followed up the statement by asking if he was hungry, then received an answer of, "Yes, give Ham another bone if he wants it," she moved her conjecture to the status of certitude.

Days, then weeks blurred that moment like raindrops filling in the depression of a footprint in the mud. But the exchange clung to Kira's mind just like a thick slap of the gooey muck—though it eventually dried, she knew it wouldn't come off until she gave it a good, hard scrape.

She obliged herself that scrape during her and Fred's walk back to Scottney Hall from the forest ridge early one Sunday morning in August. Carefully, she took out and examined the memories of both her confession and Damien's reaction, especially attempting to decipher the meaning to the latter.

The day promised to be exceptionally warm and Ally wouldn't venture near her bed chamber for hours yet (now that she'd developed the liking for sleeping in like a "proper lady" should), so she took her time strolling through the gardens and down the foot path to the kitchen, indulging her senses with sniffs of the pollen-heavy blossoms and the summer-heavy air while wrapping her mind in theories about Hyperion's Walk stable boys and the purposes of letters they carried to her aunt, of all people. Of course, she reasoned, perhaps the missive had been for Father, and Aleece had merely accepted it for him—

"Kira."

She yelped out a cry and jumped back by three feet as the utterance soughed through the kitchen with ghostly implication. By the looks of the long-haired, white-robed figure standing in the dimness made possible only by a hand-carried candle lamp, Kira didn't immediately dismiss that notion as fiction, either. After all, she'd been thinking about secret plots and possible murder suspects as she'd entered the kitchen, a mind-set that formed an ideal invitation for a visit from an ominous *kikimora* or *shishimora* spirit.

Only after her heart settled back between her ribs and she looked again at the figure did she remember the household spirits would have only worn traditional Russian costumes... and they definitely wouldn't stare like *she* was the intruding specter, with a look of intent curiosity; even confusion.

"Aunt Aleece," she at last murmured, trying to hide the fact it had taken her another ten seconds to fully recognize her aunt in such an informal state. "Heavens, you gave me a fright." She flashed a self-chiding smile as she pulled her shawl back up from her elbows to her shoulders. "I actually thought you were a—"

"You've been out all night." Again, the words sounded more spectral than substantial, more inquisitive than accusative, like a mirage of her aunt stood here in place of the real woman.

Nonplussed at the transformation, Kira didn't know how to respond. "I—" she stammered, "I was—well, I was—"

"You're not wearing a chemise, let alone a corset. Your lips are swollen, your skirts are a tangle and your hair looks like you rode to Scotland and back." Each observation came as fast and succinct as the Latin verbs the woman fired at her in the third-floor sitting room each afternoon, but like those conjugations, they were all simply pieces of information, not allegations.

Baffled deeper still, Kira said nothing. She raised one hand and pressed those fingers to her lips. Erotic warmth rush to her face at the remembrance of how her mouth got to look this way—

And she instantly realized she'd "said" entirely too much.

"You were with him, weren't you?" Aleece grated then. This time, incrimination did taint her voice—when the word *him* emerged from her throat powered by raw hatred.

Kira leveled her chin at a regal angle, refusing to lower her unblinking sights; refusing to convey shame and contrition she didn't feel. "Aunt Aleece," she asserted then, "I—"

"You were with *him*!"

"Aunt Aleece, if you'll only—"

"He's a murderer, Kira!"

"He's the man I love, Aunt Aleece."

An interminable length of thick silence followed. The warmth of the approaching day now felt more like suffocating humidity. Perspiration trailed between Kira's shoulder blades and breasts like Nature's sly form of water torture. Still, she didn't move a muscle. She didn't yield her stance by even a lowered eyelash—though as Aleece's wordless glare persisted, she resigned herself to facing the terrifying ramifications of her impetuous courage. Worse, she contemplated the price *Damien* would be forced to pay for her recklessness.

I'm sorry, my love. So sorry.

The last situation for which she expected to form a reaction was her aunt's nearly despondent sigh, followed by an equally hopeless upsweep of a hand. If the actions possessed a degree less despair, Kira would swear the woman practiced for one of those opportune ballroom moments during which one matron threw up exasperated hands, encouraged by a dozen surrounding matron clucks, exclaiming, "Nieces these days! What is a body to *do* with them?"

If her actions didn't resonate with such despair.

If Aleece didn't avert her tear-gleamed gaze then, shaking her head slowly as she rasped, "So...you love him. That's the way of it, then."

Kira swallowed hard, her eyes filling with a sweet, hot sting of their own. "That's the way of it," she whispered back. By the saints, could it be that this softened, vulnerable incarnation of her aunt actually understood what she felt... actually understood the incredible, terrible irony of being in love with her family's enemy?

She didn't know the answer to that for certain yet. But she knew she wanted to find out.

"Aunt Aleece," she stated, trying to sound humble instead of apologetic, "it...just happened. Please believe that. Please believe I didn't do this on purpose, or to hurt you or Father."

"Of course you didn't," the woman rejoined, though the words were tight and quiet—much too quiet.

On the other hand, Kira debated, perhaps she should be grateful for even this modicum of sensitivity from the woman who stood before her clearly waging an inner battle of her own. Aleece had set the candle lamp on the cutting board and now fixed her eyes to the flame glowing through the frosted glass. The reflection of that intense gold orb in her unblinking stare also illuminated the conflict of her thoughts: her niece had just confessed a love affair with her daughter's supposed murderer. *Ehta prosta nivazmozhna,* that stare screamed. *This is impossible.*

But it *was* possible. Dear God, how she did love him. Just thinking of Damien now snapped a torturous band around Kira's heart—a longing not only for him, but for his name; for the honor he so vehemently fought to regain; the honor that was rightfully his. Her love turned the dream into her aspiration, too, she now realized...which meant she also shared the pain of battling for its reality.

And the pain of keeping that campaign a secret.

"It's...been so hard," she said past her own taut throat then, venturing a step closer to her aunt. "It's been so hard not to tell anyone."

"I know," her aunt replied, still staring at the lamp.

"You *do* know," Kira murmured, "don't you?" She moved to Aleece's side, not looking away from her. "You do understand what this feels like, don't you?"

"Oh, yes." The reply came swiftly, positively; almost ferociously. But her aunt's voice gentled as she reached and settled her hand atop Kira's. "Yes," she repeated, now comforting with the syllable, "I do."

Kira burned to ask the reasons behind this spurt of such absolute assurance from her aunt—the reasons why the woman empathized so completely with her frustration and pained silence. But she also realized she'd just been given the consummate moment to pose her unavoidable question—her all-important supplication. She had to seize that opportunity *now.*

"Then...will you keep our secret, Aunt Aleece?" she asked. "At least for a while longer?"

At that, the woman finally looked up. But her expression affixed to Kira with unguarded perplexion. "Why *are* you keeping it a secret?" she queried, truly without a clue to the answer. "If it's your father you're worried about, I can assure you he won't be happy, but—"

"Damien didn't kill Rachelle, Aunt Aleece." She let out a huge breath after blurting the interjection; a breath having nothing to do with staying alive but everything to do with her capability to make the proclamation with complete conviction. She truly *did* believe in Damien's innocence, her senses joyously told her. Her certainty was truly based on the honor of his heart and the integrity of his soul, not the way his gaze mesmerized her or the heat his kisses scorched into her.

"I know you probably don't believe me," she followed to the declaration with swift surety, "but for the last two months, I've been helping him gather evidence to prove it. We've been secretive because—"

"You think you can find the evidence *here*." On that final word, the woman jerked away from the chopping block. Once more she stared at Kira as if she beheld a *kikimora* wraith, and she'd just been forced to listen to the specter's message of portending doom. "That's why *you're* helping him...because he thinks he can find—" Aleece's gape sprang open yet wider in comprehension. "*He's* that strange trainer from the stables, isn't he? George...that's his name. He doesn't live here with the rest of the stablemen..."

Kira rushed forward until she stood squarely opposite her aunt by three feet. She neither lied to Aleece nor confirmed her the truth, but instead leveled, "Aunt Aleece, we are on the way to discovering who really killed Rachelle. I am beseeching you now to let us continue—if only for your own personal gratification of seeing the monster hang at last!"

Her aunt's face contorted as she flung the last of that. After Aleece had entrusted her with this rare glimpse of her "other" side, Kira loathed herself for having to cause the woman even deeper pain; yet she freely admitted she'd wield that blade again, if that was the only method available to slice open the most violent ends of Aleece's own grief, fury, and frustration.

She watched her aunt endure the brunt of those emotions now. With her heart panging in sympathy, she watched the grimace of anguish, the tears of sorrow, the clenched jaw of rage, and wished she could close those three steps between them, taking Aunt Aleece into an embrace of comfort. But a wordless instinct told her the woman would condemn her the action more than thank her, and that Aleece had to fight her way back to composure on her own.

That was exactly what the woman did, too. And when she at last straightened, scooped up her lamp and regally smoothed her hair, she issued an answer to Kira clearly proving that though the crinolines and starch weren't back in place yet, the primly commanding Aleece certainly *was*.

"I don't know about this, Kira," she stated with a chilled evenness that directly defied the morning's gloppy humidity. "I simply...don't know."

She pivoted then, leaving Kira standing in the dimness of the kitchen—and the terror of her thoughts.

The terror that she'd just made an elephant-sized mistake.

★ ★ ★ ★

For the next two days, she didn't breathe. She could sleep barely more than that and ate in equal rarity, her largest meal consumed at Damien's concerned bidding when she saw him on the second night.

"George" had participated in a Scottney Hall stud-buying

trip to East Ilsley the night before, keeping them apart for the longest period since they'd formed their alliance, so the first hours of the evening had been consumed with ample demonstrations of how much they'd "missed" each other. When they'd at last curled up before the fire for a repast of dark bread, spiced potatoes, and roast beef, Kira had fumbled for ways to tell him about her confession to Aleece, but a giant clog in her throat had only grown larger through the ensuing hours. It formed as she'd watched Damien smile more than he ever had, the gleam of hope now transforming his eyes from cloudless midnights to star-strewn summer skies. The clog thickened while she watched him talk with animation about the invaluable information he'd gleaned during the Ilsley excursion.

The danger of posing as "George" for such an extended period had been worth it, he'd told her. The tedium of their journey had loosened the tongues of his traveling companions enough for him to discover life was not so peacefully "normal" as it seemed around Scottney Hall. Carriages were sometimes ordered for strange hours of the evening, but drivers were never requested with them. Every hand in the stable was in turn ordered not to ask questions about the matter, nor did anyone have cause to, as the vehicles were always returned by morning in pristine condition.

The information, Damien believed, was a boon; possibly a large boon, depending on the details they'd glean together to complete it. He'd spoken on about the matter with such gusto, Kira could only shake her head with answering amazement at times. So this was what the man looked like when he had a satiated belly, a well-loved body and a mind full of purposeful excitement. *This* side of Damien, she decided, she could absolutely get used to loving...loving it so much, as a matter of fact, that she also decided she could hold her own tongue for one more day.

When that day dawned, however, she admitted the difficulty of finding that tongue, let alone holding it. Maddeningly lost, it now seemed to be, in the pasty, bile-tinged interior of her mouth; horrifyingly incapable of forming a protest as Ally nearly skipped into her bed chamber at the stroke of ten that day.

She rolled over and groaned when the maid pulled back the curtains, letting in hazy sun and lazy warmth—a day she should have been happy to greet. She'd been well-loved and well-fed last night, and forty-eight whole hours had passed with little more drama happening at the Hall than Cleo once more disappearing from the Menagerie. Aleece had apparently decided silence was prudent at this time. Their secret was safe.

Life, it seemed, was reasonably well.

Kira was not.

"A bright good mornin' to ya, m'lady!" The maid's cheerful cadence, normally one of the best things about Kira's days, was today put into the sound category with over-rusted gate hinges and fingernails on chalk slates. "Up, up, now! Cook tells me there's berries along with breakfast," she crooned temptingly.

Kira groaned again, tugging Fred comfortingly into the crook of her arm. "No," she protested, the word drawn out with guttural emphasis. "Oh, no. No berries. No anything."

"Fine. Ya'll starve 'til tea, then, but at be early to lessons. Lady Aleece will pop out of her corset with pleasure."

"*No*," Kira stressed again, sighing frustratedly. "No lessons. Please tell her I'm ill."

"Right," came the sardonic snort directly over her head.

"And I'll also tell her you've received the calling and are taking vows tomorrow." With one efficient grab and one snapping *fwoop*, she jerked the counterpane and covers away from Kira's curled-up body. "I'm simply afraid ya've tried to get away with that one a few too many—" Her banter ceased on a startled gasp. "Heavens above." A hand pressed coolness into Kira's forehead and exposed cheek. "Ya *are* sick, m'lady, aren't ya?"

Within the next hour, Cook and Aunt Aleece were summoned to confirm Ally's conclusion. While Cook and Ally ruled out a simple ague or quinsy in favor of more dramatic diagnoses like cholera or consumption, Aunt Aleece gazed at her knowingly and attributed her condition to "a little bug" that would "take care of itself by tomorrow." Kira managed to give her aunt a meaningful, grateful look as she was ordered to stay calm for the day...which included, the woman strictly added, no afternoon walks to the stables, either.

To her mild startlement, Kira all too happily complied. After sleeping the morning away, she rose and took a glimpse of herself in the dressing closet looking glass—and promptly decided it best that Damien not see her wan, tired features until darkness arrived to lend her some useful shadows.

That decision didn't stop her from greedily gazing her fill at him, however. She looked down from the third-floor window of the conservatory as the late afternoon sun acted like a huge candle over the world, casting alluring amber light over the varied aspects of the Hall. The stable yards were no exception, and the "candle" perfectly illuminated her lover's beauty and grace as he rode in on a spirited dapple gray stallion. The mount was one of their East Ilsley purchases; a prize selection at that, Kira observed via the horse's eager gait and alert ears.

Damien's own confident spirit was evident in the powerful

fluidity of his dismount, every leg muscle deliciously defined and flexed, and in the smile so broad she noticed its gleam even from this distance. She watched him lavish some strokes to the stallion's neck before passing the reins to a stable boy; she also observed the uncomfortable scratches he gave to his "beard," clearly indicating his discomfort with the stage glue and wig he'd been under for several hours now.

With amiable haste, he bid Tom and the others a good day, then departed via the courtyard and the Hall's main porticullis. His next destination, Kira had no doubt, was the forest waterfall—accompanied, no doubt, by Hamlet and a big cake of Pears' soap.

The thought marked her body's turning point toward recovery. Though she'd indeed been feeling progressively better all afternoon, Kira's senses now came alive with seemingly supernal strength, expanding and tingling to life within the first three seconds of imagining Damien beneath that cascade of water. As she envisioned his wet hair plastered to the muscled valley between his shoulders, her heart pumped color back to her cheeks. As she envisioned the soapy bubbles sliding down the ripples of his torso, the aches in her joints were replaced with expectant tension. And as she envisioned the splendor of his manhood nestled between the wet planes of his thighs, she grew wet without the aid of *any* waterfall.

By God and all His angels, she couldn't wait to see him again.

The giddy warmth of that thought lasted only half a second longer than the words took to traverse her brain. Immediately, an icy reality moved in and vanquished her anticipation. *He* couldn't see *her* like *this!*

Kira jolted up from the window seat, scattering the

needlepoint she'd been laboring over. She left the project on the floor; her stitched "roses" appeared more like blood splotches anyway, and Fred seemed more fascinated with the piece than she'd ever be. She returned to her room swiftly as possible without giving away her sudden spurt of "health," deciding she'd use her extra time to create herself into an especially lovely sight for Damien's eyes tonight.

Occupied thus, the next few hours turned the afternoon into twilight before she realized it. The sun had just dipped beyond the parapets of Castle Bolton when she slipped into one of her favorite items in her closet: a short-sleeved, off-the-shoulder dress with a simple, fitted bodice and an even simpler skirt. What made the ensemble special was the seashell-pink brushed silk of which it was constructed, a color that bespoke utter femininity even before the matching, fingerless lace gloves and patterned silk stockings were slipped on, as well.

She'd turned to where she'd laid those accessories out, on the foot of her bed, when a commotion from the stable yard snatched her curiosity. Kira crossed to her bedroom's corner windows rather than the window seat, in order to push the modern panes outward and get a better peek at the excitement. If the ruckus had to do at all with the new gray stallion, she knew Damien would wish for as detailed a report as she could give—

Unless, of course, the man participated in the action firsthand.

Which was exactly the scene she encountered as she peered out now.

With a scowl falling somewhere between perplexed and dumbfounded, Kira beheld a washed and smiling "George" making his encore appearance at the Scottney Hall stables today. Also on stage for a second time pranced an agitated dapple gray stallion, this time with ears pinned back and a countenance intent on murder toward anyone who approached him other than "George."

Kira's frown broadened into a captivated smirk. It seemed "George" had become a valued commodity on Tom's stable staff—a fact she didn't protest in the least. As a matter of fact, she elected to hitch one hip against the window ledge and take full advantage of this opportunity to witness the combination of firmness yet gentleness expressed so eloquently by that man and his body. That body she ached and yearned to touch and caress, to explore and fondle...

"Well, look who's feeling better!" a voice called amiably from the door. Kira waved Ally further into the room, though she didn't shift from her position at the window. The maid bustled to her side, and joined her in perusing the scene below for a minute or two before murmuring, "A beautiful beast."

"Mmmmhmmm," Kira replied softly. "Seems like a nice man, too."

"I was talkin' about the horse."

"Oh." She flushed furiously as Ally giggled.

"But now that ya mention it, the other 'animal' is quite fine, as well," Ally ventured, a lilt of womanly interest deliberately inserted into her tone. "I wonder if he'd like to take some *fillies* around here for walks, too."

"He would *not*," Kira rebutted, and again endured her maid's teasing chortle.

This time, however, she joined her maid in the mirth, as a feeling of peace and rightness suddenly washed through her. Oh yes, her heart concurred with her mind, all of this *did* feel right, in a way she'd not felt during all her travels in America, through all those towns and cities which had never really been *home.*

But here...oh God, she belonged right here, in this land that surpassed beautiful, gazing upon the man she loved without limits, sharing a moment with a true friend that surpassed perfection...almost. If she closed her eyes, Kira determined, her imagination could fill in the gaps the scene still lacked: Damien would be Damien instead of the mysterious "George," and her love—now her husband—would be down in the stables working with one of Scottney Hall's horses simply as a favor to Father, before he and she mounted Dante together and returned to Hyperion's Walk for dinner and an evening of lovemaking. She was up here in the bedroom with Ally merely catching up on old news, chatting in the ways old friends did those things—

Her eyes slammed back open as a scream resounded through every room and corridor of Scottney Hall.

"My Lord Scottney!" The frantic, shrill wail belonged to Amy from the downstairs staff—and she sounded like somebody had rammed an ax into her belly. "My Lord Scottney, he's done it again! Damien Sharpe has murdered again!"

CHAPTER TWENTY-SEVEN

Kira nearly tumbled down the main stairway in her horrified haste. But once she stepped onto the floor of the foyer—the floor smeared with a haphazard path of clotted, dirty blood—her legs went horrifyingly cold and numb.

Still, she forced her stare to follow that crimson trail, until it ended at Amy's crumpled form. The maid moaned and chanted unintelligible words as she rocked and clutched a young woman in her lap. Several gaping wounds dominated the corpse's torso; her eyes stared out at the world in lifeless, pleading terror. Her last breaths had been clearly taken with the certainty she was about to die.

"*Bozhy...moj*," Kira choked, swaying from a flood of dizzying nausea. She gripped the banister with shaky arms as her legs gave out and she slid to the floor, tears rolling down her face at equal velocity. "Oh, my God...oh, Amy...who is she?"

The only answer she received from the maid was a raging scream, reminding her of an animal in pain who could express itself no other way. Everybody in the increasing throng gave Kira stares verging on silent accusation, until a strong and reassuring hand curled around her shoulder. She looked up into her father's taut face, and ended up staring at him a half minute longer than she'd planned. Astoundment was her impetus. She'd spent several hours last night in the library with Nicholas, but between then and this moment, he looked like he'd aged at least ten years.

The next moment, he supplied the reason why. "She's Laura Kincaid," he said in a guttural grate, indicating the dead woman with his eyes. "She's Amy's daughter."

No. No! NO! Her mind shrieked the word, but her throat gurgled out nothing but a string of anguished keenings. But only her ears heard the sounds. Nicholas's statement affected Amy like the crank of a torture rack, and the woman's reacting wails echoed to the end of the Great Hall and back.

"My baby," the maid sobbed. "My baby...my girl...my little girl!" She wrenched wild, tear-stained eyes up at Nicholas. "This is what that bastard has done to her, my lord! My girl... my girl!"

"I know, Amy," her father replied, his lips such a grim line, his mustache hardly moved. His nostrils flared wide, though, as he inhaled great, furious breaths and his chest quaked with the effort of maintaining composure. "I know," he repeated, "and by God, that beast will *pay* for his evil this time."

"I'm with ye, m'lord," a low male voice interjected then. "The bastard's depraved, and we won't let him go unpunished this time."

"We shouldn't have let it happen the *first* time," another growled.

"Amen," threw in another.

"But the others at Hyperion's Walk will believe us now," the first voice asserted. "And then they'll help us find the bastard."

"Then they'll help us hang the bastard."

"*No!*"

The foyer fell quiet as Kira's panicked outcry exploded over them all—as she realized they were speaking of doing these things to Damien. Not needing the banister's help this time, she lurched to her feet and swept the mob with a convicting glare of her own.

"Damien Sharpe didn't kill this girl," she leveled with conviction that surprised her, considering the foreboding throb of her heartbeat and the way her knees threatened to once more become nothing but packs of weak crumbs. "He didn't kill Rachelle, either."

Some of the glares upon her now turned to stares of stunned pity. Many in the crowd looked away from her completely. But no matter what they did, all of them accompanied their actions with murmurings and whispers following the same loose script. *The chit's barmy...can't see the writing on the wall in front of her...his poor lordship; just found his little girl and now he's lost her again, if you know what I mean...*

"My Lady Kira," a man finally waddled forward to assert past the long mustache he twirled with one hand, "we don't fault your demand for justice—we even admire your American spunk—but we're *certain* about this. The proof—"

"*What* proof?" Kira charged, now using the banister as a point to slam her hand down. The motion perfectly aided her goal of forceful emphasis; a dozen members of the throng jerked backward by quick half steps. "You have no proof, do you? No proof but gathered suspicions and rumors!"

Only one voice rasped through the crowd in reply to her then. A voice from the area at their knees. The voice of a mother strangled by the clutches of pure grief.

"Proof," Amy whispered, lips trembling. "You want *proof,* yer ladyship?" Somebody had gotten a blanket, gently draping it across the form in her arms, but now she tore back the covering, revealing once more her daughter's blue-tinged face. "Here's yer proof. *Look* at yer bloody proof. *Look* at it, damn ye; oh God, look at it!"

More sounds spilled from Amy's lips, but the words were a mashing of Gaelic and English and sobbing and screams. Her friends fell to the floor with her, embracing her with tearful croonings of condolence and sorrow, but the woman's anguished shrieks penetrated their midst just like a killer's knife had gashed open her child.

Especially the single comprehensible sentence she emitted before unconsciousness finally gave her a measure of ease.

"Sharpe has to pay for this!" Amy cried out, her body vibrating with the effort. She threw her head back; tears and spittle slid down her face. "Make him pay! Make—him—pay!"

She went limp then, collapsing atop her daughter's body, but the mob guaranteed her labor wasn't spent for naught. Not allowing an instant's pause to diminish the potency of their friend's hate, Amy's friends took up her outcry with the varying but vehement volumes and pitches of their voices. Their din spurred several men forward, one of them stomping even further than the rest, coming to stand directly before Kira.

"With all due respect, Lady Kira, get outta our way!" he bellowed, his deep-timbre words identifying him as the same man who'd first agreed with her father's assessment. Kira grimly surmised that was why Nicholas stood rigid and silent to the side now. "We're off to find a killer!"

"That won't be necessary, Roland."

The proclamation filled the foyer more powerfully than a burst of royal drum rolls and snapped every gaze the direction of the entrance portico. But in the instant after that, only Kira's eyes widened in comprehending horror.

A man walked in with presence nobody disputed, his

dark uniform and high boots marking him as somebody governmental and important. Following him were Tom Montgomery and one of Scottney Hall's carpenters, Sidney Freemont.

The two of them held the horse trainer everyone knew as "George."

At a small jerk of the lawman's head, Tom whisked away "George's" hat and head wig.

"*No!*" Kira entreated, rushing forward. Somebody's hand caught her by the elbow, forcing her back.

Tom ripped away the false eyebrows, mustache and beard. The throng gasped as one with their concurrent recognition then realization.

"It's *him.*"

"Sharpe's been lurking among us all this time!"

"Heavenly saints, I fed him apple tarts."

"Heavenly saints, *I* flirted with him!"

"I've been duped by a killer."

"We've *all* been duped by a killer."

"You've all been duped by *yourselves,*" Damien at last snarled, lunging once against his captors, only to be subdued by a pair of thick iron wrist cuffs and a debilitating blow to the back of his knees. As he fell hard to the marble floor, grunting with pain, Kira's body lunged forward again, sheer instinct pulling her. For the first time, she truly understood the torment of wildcats' howls when separated from their mates.

"For God's sake!" she heard herself lash, though again wondered how she formed lucid words when a predator of such savage fury stalked her every thought, her every breath. "Listen to him! You're arresting the *wrong man!*"

The man in uniform turned a politely steeled stare upon

her. "My good woman," he stated, sighing as if dealing with nothing more than a sulking child, "will you pray let me do my job?"

"You stiff-spined bastard," Kira spat. "If you were doing your job, Amy wouldn't be sitting here in her daughter's blood!"

"Kira!" came an abashed gasp from behind her—from the person, she suddenly realized, who wielded the clamping hold on her elbow. With new awareness—and the horror that jolted her heart to a stop as a result—she looked to that person now.

And glared with more hatred than she thought she'd ever have to feel in her life.

"Aunt Aleece," she charged from clenched teeth and a convulsing throat. "You're the one, aren't you? *You're* the one who betrayed Damien to them."

She received all the answer she needed, however, in the single vacillating moment Aleece took before speaking—a hesitation taken by a woman who never hesitated. "Kira," she rasped, "I—"

"Betrayed him," she lashed, wrenching her arm away with a vehement twist. "You betrayed *me*."

More like the Aleece she was used to, the woman pulled up her shoulders, leveled her jaw, and set her lips in a primly determined line. "Kira," she proclaimed, "One day, you shall thank me for this."

Beyond her control, a lunatic's laugh burst off her lips. The woman spoke as if telling her how to correctly pronounce "destroy" in French, not comprehending she'd done just that to her niece's heart—and life.

"Thank you?" she said on the mirthless remnants of that laugh. "My *good woman*, I have no plans of ever *speaking* to you again."

Before Aleece could so much as sputter in reaction to that, Kira whirled on her. She did so not only to rid her sights of the face she yearned to modify in a deliciously brutal manner, but to focus her attention on the more exigent catastrophe at hand: the fact that two more lawmen had now entered, and took Damien from Tom and Sidney as if they handled a stuffed mannequin about to be burned at a Guy Fawkes Day parade. On second thought, they'd probably give the mannequin gentler treatment.

Kira, now untethered and enraged, charged forward at them with the full force of her bared teeth and tearing hands. "Get your hands *off* of him!" She ripped at their arms, digging at their flesh as much as she could through the wool of their uniforms. "You animals, you're hurting him!"

One of the guards relented to her, jumping back with a gritted obscenity and sucking the wrist she'd just broken skin on with the force of her fury and a lucky twist of a finger nail. His comrade, however, only laughed harder as she attempted the same on him.

"Hey," that bastard drawled to Damien now, "ye've got yerself quite a little bird here, Sharpe. Comely little warbler indeed, singin' fer ye like this. I don't blame ye fer keepin' her around instead of slicin' her up."

She thought she'd seen the force of outrage on Damien's features when they'd first taken him into custody. That expression was a lover's glance compared to the glare he drove into his captor now, ordering the guard in a gritted baritone, "Leave her the hell out of this."

"Ohhhh." The guard lilted the middle of the word in mock fear. "Pardon my humble self fer offendin' ye, *Mister* Sharpe. Perhaps I should go place the warmin' bricks in yer coach now? Or fluff the pillows on the squabs? Anything to make ye nice 'n' cozy, *Mister* Sharpe."

The guard's taunting sarcasm induced an abundant enough chortle in his comrade that the small injury she'd inflicted now went forgotten. With seething senses and coiled fists, Kira listened to their shared laughs, fighting the yearning to have another go at them both, to claw away every inch of their skin this time. By every saint she knew and then some, she *fought*—and she forced herself to win, because one shared gaze with Damien confirmed in her heart what she'd felt in her gut: that he'd warned the guard away from her out of more than just masculine protectiveness.

He was determined to keep her out of this mess entirely. Determined her name would not be remotely linked with his, now tainted again by the blood of a murdered woman.

A woman you didn't murder! she screamed at him with her stare, letting her tears brim over and slide unheeded down her cheeks, past her trembling lips. *You didn't do this, Damien, and I know it. Because I know it, I'm a part of this, whether you like it or not.*

Because you're *a part of* me, *Damien.*

Because I love you, Damien.

I'm not going anywhere, Damien.

She watched a leaden swallow vibrate the throat beneath his jaw; the jaw now reddened and raw where Tom had ripped off his false beard—a perfect representation of the way they'd torn away a precious layer of her heart, too. Though Damien did nothing and said nothing else, she knew he endured the same torture inside, as well; a double apportionment of pain for him.

But she also knew his heart had heard the declaration of

hers. She'd seen the comprehension in the backs of his eyes, in the fast flares of intense blue light there, before the two guard-idiots had twisted at his chains, jerking him away.

In that moment, she saw he truly wasn't happy about her message—but she also saw he'd hoarded every silent syllable into his soul, greedily storing her promises and love like a boy collecting fireflies...creating his private supply of light to use in the lightless place for which he was now bound. Behind bars again. In chains again. As helpless as Rico and the others had been...hungry and lonely and heinously mistaken as a murdering beast.

By a mob who far better deserved the name than he did.

Kira cut into that pretentious herd now with her own foyer-filling outcry. First kindled by fury, the sound went fueled on by despair; it was a keening that both hated and pitied these people, a condemnation of the judgments they'd already reached, and a mourning of the chains she wouldn't be able to simply find in a hidden cabinet, and unlock from Damien's feet.

Damien. *Damien.*

The beautiful majesty of his name resounded in her heart as the lamenting sound continued to pour off her lips, as she chased the prison wagon now clattering out of the Main Courtyard, then watched it disappear from sight. And though that outcry dwindled to rasping sobs, she didn't move from that courtyard for a very long while. For hours into the grieving quiet of the night, she stood there and stared at the gate, at the huge amber walls of what was now her own prison, at the empty sky full of cold stars...the night sky that had no meaning any more.

Only then, long after she'd pressed her lips into a dry,

cracked line and her throat could form nothing more than a strained rasp, did she truly join the pain in her soul to the matching hole in her heart, and give a defining word to the resulting agony.

Once—just once—she pried her lips apart and forced out from her parched vocal chords, *"Damien."*

★ ★ ★ ★

"Damien."

She woke him from sleep with the utterance this time, sounding so soft, so sad, so *real*, Damien swore he'd open his eyes, reach out his arms and be filled with her life and warmth and passion again. The last twenty-four hours would have been just a hideous nightmare. He would be just a brooding grouch passing himself off as a modest bloke named "George" once more; Kira would be just a hoyden-nymph who'd barged into his forest and decided to give him dreams for the future once more. They'd laugh and love deep into the night, talking about all those dreams together...

But one of his guards let out an oath then, followed by the frustrated slap of playing cards against a wood table. Another guard snickered—Luke, the tall bastard who'd tempted him to really become a murderer during his arrest—and before his eyes opened by a crack, Damien realized nothing awaited his embrace except a straw mattress, a cup of stale water, and a cell full of even more stale air.

And memories. Hours upon hours of memories. The incredible moments Kira had given him, each a diamond he'd dismissed at the time as merely a pretty rock, that now plagued his waking thoughts and twisted through his sleep. His heart begged for release from the torment, but his soul pleaded for more like a condemned man cherishing every morsel of his last meal.

Indeed, Damien didn't know what hour would bring the beginning of his end—and this time, he suspected with certainty, the trial would be the end—so he let his soul triumph, forcing his heart to endure the onslaught of every sight, sound, smell, and sensation his mind could produce. When conscious, he could control those thoughts, so his lips curled in a giddy grin as he recalled the wet rebel stomping her way up a stream bank at him, the golden-skinned enchantress he'd danced with at a long-ago ball, the lover who gave herself so freely, she only had to glance his way to make him hard for her.

But in his dreams, he had no authority over the images. In his dreams, his heart waged violent battle against his mind. The nightmare always progressed the same way, not seeming a nightmare at all...first, she came to him wrapped in nothing but her unbound curls, the tresses spiraling in wonderful ways around her full breasts and the alluring triangle of her womanhood. But as soon as he'd reach for her, she faded into banks of thick black smoke...into darkness so impenetrable, he could only search for her by listening to her. *Kira!* he'd call, choking and tearing from the smoke. *Kira...Darling, you've got to help me! Where are you? Where...are...*

That was when she'd answer him. She'd call to him, pleading to him with her desperate sobs...her curse-laden weepings...and her unimpeded screams.

Ah God, her screams.

Please, God, he'd beseech the black void around him, *please help her...because I can't. Please help stop her screams.*

But they didn't stop. Her agony-filled cries drowned every

other sound from his senses until he'd jerk awake in a frantic sweat. Sometimes even after that, they'd penetrate his mind. Her voice would assault without warning during some stupidly unguarded moment, then echo for hours through his being until he could only pace his cell with frantic speed, warding off the sleep that would only make the torment worse.

Pacing. Sleeping. Waiting. Pacing some more. As the days stretched on, Damien sardonically ruminated, he was really becoming the animal everyone believed him to be.

Or perhaps this was merely what the onset of insanity felt like.

He sat with knees to his chin one morning, tugging absently on his hair as he contemplated that theory in any detail his mind could still garner. But in the middle of a scowling pursuit after the twelfth—or was it the fourteenth?—thought that squirmed its way free from him, a clang of metal against metal brought his head jerking to a semblance of attention.

He watched Luke shove open his cell door with a derisive leer. "Rise 'n' shine, pretty thing," the guard said. "Yer day in court has arrived."

Damien surprised them both by laughing, really laughing, at that. "Day in court," he explained in a hoarse croak. "That's a good one, mate. I can go to the gallows now knowing I've heard the joke of the century."

His remark found overwhelming justification in the scene they came upon in the courtroom. If half of Yorkshire had showed up for his first trial, then the other half joined them this time. Even a half dozen steps prior to stepping into the room, Damien witnessed an impromptu badminton match between opposite sides of the gallery, heard two jokes told at his expense, and spied four separate sets of male hands wandering up an equal number of obliging skirts. Ah, York, he thought while Luke stopped him to check the security of his wrist cuffs; a city with history traceable to the seventh century, the onetime center of the Roman empire, the favored Northern outpost of English monarchs throughout history...

Now, its main courtroom reminded him of a circus.

Especially because it came complete with the most beautiful circus gypsy performer he knew.

He'd expected she'd come...he'd prayed she wouldn't. But now that he saw Kira wedged in at the front of the gallery, shoulders held straight beneath her cloak and stare directed unswervingly ahead, he surmised it would have been less painful to rip his leg off than wish her anywhere else. Merely by beholding her, his body surged with strength and heat anew... and more amazement, too. Amazement at the coalescence of all his feelings for this woman who stood like a goddess among those buffoons...and who stood in a part of his heart he never knew existed. A part of his heart filled with all the good things about his life. With happiness and life, with trust and honor, with dreams and—

Love?

"Holy God," Damien uttered on a throat suddenly too dry for audible sound. God, *God;* could it be possible? Could *this* overpowering, careening, astounding feeling be what Kira spoke of when she'd told him she loved him?

When she'd told him she loved him, he reflected...so many countless times now. When she'd told him without ever expecting an answer, but always hoping for one.

And he'd never given it to her. He'd never given it to her, and now—

Now, a young woman at the fringe of the crowd caught

sight of him, and shrieked out the advent of his arrival. The news swept across the courtroom like a winter wind across a high moor, stilling and silencing all the beasts as they waited... and watched. In response, Damien latched his eyes to the front of the room.

The judge entered, his powdered wig and formidable jowls flapping at the same rate. He was Horton Plighton—the same judge who'd presided after they'd buried Rachelle, too. *Wonderful,* he snarled inwardly. *Just bloody wonderful.*

Then Luke shoved him forward, and the farce officially began. Damien paced forward beneath the resounding echoes of his bootsteps, the accusing intensity of a thousand stares, and the crushing weight of his heart's all-too-late realization— and remorse.

Because of that, he didn't allow himself a single glance more even in Kira's general direction. Christ, how could he? How could he pursue the disaster of meeting her gaze once, of subjecting himself to that sienna-flamed magic, of knowing, really knowing now, what the soul beyond that stare felt, and not being able to tell her? Not being able to stride to her, pull her over the rail, crush his mouth to hers, and profess before the entire bloody county that he loved her; *he loved her.*

But he was no fool. He'd slept little and eaten even less over the last collection of days. He had few physical stores to aid the depleted mess of his mind and emotions, and he knew he'd be at that rail inside of three strides if ever those forces became allies and decided to revolt against him. He'd selfishly drag her name, her reputation, and her honor down into the same sludge of shame as his, and he'd abhor himself for it afterward.

He refused to do it. He refused to *think* about doing it.

No matter how arduous the next three days became, Damien kept his eyes riveted forward, his expression meticulously neutral and his emotions under painstaking tether. He didn't waver even as "witness" after "witness" took their place on the stand against him, most possessing faces he'd called "friend" as recent as a year ago. Now, they all had their own stories to help the prosecuting barristers unravel the story of how he'd done away with his second victim in eight months—of how "George" had seemed so fond of the young Laura Kincaid... yet how strange everyone agreed he was, not choosing to live at Scottney Hall with the other stablemen...of how Laura's barbarically-murdered body had been found in a meadow at the edge of the forest...*his* forest.

At last, the barristers called up their last witness. Damien listened for the name with the same curiosity he'd given the previous fifty individuals. He just didn't expect his composure to receive its most shocking beating at this point in the trial.

"Your honor," the barrister announced with knelling, nasal surety, "the prosecution calls Rolf Pembroke to the stand."

Kira's stunned gasp sliced through the air behind Damien. Every nerve in his body yearned to second her sentiment with decidedly more vehement emphasis, but after he swept a glance over the smug profiles of the barristers, a grim resignation settled over him. He'd seen the phenomenon happen in dying wolves and horses, and now he understood it... understood it, and accepted it. He was *already* dead. They'd more than succeeded at killing him, and now Rolf had merely been called in to help them make sure the deed was done with complete finesse.

He didn't let the bastards down, either. *Very nice work,*

my friend, Damien commented caustically via his glare as his "mate" convinced the courtroom his testimony was given only after great personal conflict; that he really didn't *want* to tell all of Yorkshire about Damien assaulting him the night of the ball, then leaving him sprawled on his back in front of a burning building, fearing for his life. He didn't *want* to relay any of it at all...which was why he accomplished the feat in such vivid detail.

In the end, Damien let his shoulders sag and his head fall back, merely grateful the end *had* at last come. The illustrious Judge Plighton had once more been appointed his defense counsel, which, if precedence followed itself, meant absolutely nothing. Damien hadn't prepared an argument of his own, either. He knew better this time. As Rolf stepped down, he merely closed his eyes, surrendered to his exhaustion, and waited for his "devoted counsel" to dismiss the court for the day, giving the prosecution the evening to sharpen the nails of accusing rhetoric they'd drive in to his coffin tomorrow.

"...and so the prosecution rests," Plighton droned, true to form. He swiveled his jowls and wig Damien's direction. "Mister Sharpe, I presume that in refusing to cross-examine any of the witnesses so far, you also do not have any witnesses of your own to present." Pausing by only half a breath, he hurried on, "Therefore, I shall hear the prosecution's closing—"

"Wait!"

Inquisitive murmurs broke out across the courtroom as cold sweat broke out the length of Damien's body—pumped out by a heart suddenly thundering in alarm. Yet unlike every other person in the room, he didn't turn by an inch toward the source of the strident shout that had cut Plighton short. He adhered to his vow not to look at *her.*

That, he decided during the short but tense silence that followed, had been a *good* vow to make. Because right now, he didn't know if he was more tempted to kiss the intrepid hoyden, or strangle her.

"Lady Kira?" Plighton's perplexed tone adequately represented the consensus of the crowd's mood. "Do *you* have information to take up with the court about this matter?"

Her reply came as distinct and dulcet as the ring of a crystal bell. "I do, Your Honor." She cleared her throat with steady purpose. "I would like to call myself as a witness for the defense."

The murmurings erupted into scandalized gasps and outcries. A number of people in the crowd chortled, admiring Kira for her "juicy prank." Plighton subdued them by threatening eviction for further outbursts, but voiced his own shock with such a forceful combination of humph and growl, "outburst" was a kind term for the sound. Not that anyone in the room seemed eager to inform the man.

"My Lady Kira," he stated then, "with all respect, this is highly irregular, and usually not done."

"I know, Your Honor," she replied, still so serenely sure of herself, "but I have information that will disprove what all those other people said."

Banned into silence, the rest of the gallery could only surge forward as some sort of a combined physical being, their anticipation forming a nearly visible haze and a very tangible tension.

Damien slid his eyes shut and prepared himself for—
What?

Damn it, Kira, he snarled at her from the hungry, dizzy chaos of his senses, *what the hell* are *you up to?*

"Lady Kira," Plighton issued in an ominous baritone, "this court will not let itself be dallied with like—"

"Your Honor," she interjected, now shoving into the front section of the courtroom despite the guards who paced forward to grab her, "is it correct the prosecution has convinced you Laura Kincaid was murdered the night before they found her in the meadow?"

Plighton swept up a large hand. "Young lady, your father may be Nicholas Scottney, but I will not tolerate—"

"Damien Sharpe could not have murdered the woman that night, Your Honor!" Her intensifying tone yet stop-and-go pronunciation indicated the guards had gotten to her. Damien gritted every tooth in his mouth and locked every muscle in his body not to interfere unless he heard them hurting her.

If you bastards hurt one hair on her...

"Lady Kira," Plighton boomed, "that will be enough!"

"Damien couldn't have murdered her, because he was with me!"

This time, the crowd didn't even move. Damien didn't think they breathed. *He* didn't breathe. For the first time, Plighton had the courtroom peace he'd so exigently demanded, but the man appeared in dire need of a nice, diverting riot while *he* remembered what to do now.

Thirty interminable seconds turned into an eternity of a minute, until at last, the judge stroked his jowls contemplatively, and asked with quiet calculation, "Do you have proof of this, Lady Kira?"

A light spattering of the chuckles returned—until Kira supplied her equally secure answer. "Yes, Your Honor, I do."

Plighton's gaze narrowed. "Where is it, then?"

"Before your eyes, Your Honor. *I* am the proof."

"You—?"

"I am carrying Damien Sharpe's baby."

CHAPTER TWENTY-EIGHT

Kira smiled as a deafening din broke out around her. At last, she thought, they'd all listened to the *truth*. At last, all these pompous *vols* in their silly wigs had been forced to hear what Damien was really doing that night—for at last, this very morning, Ally and Cook had confirmed she was carrying the evidence to prove it.

Damien's baby. She was going to have Damien's baby.

That simple knowledge widened her smile to giddy proportions as she now looked to Damien, knowing she'd have no trouble getting him to return her gaze *this* time. Certainly enough, her love's stare already waited when she turned to him, his stubble-shadowed jaw intense, his eyes in motion with a million midnight hues, yet asking her just one fervent, silent question.

But before she could return even a nod in answer, Plighton's bellow stormed across the room. "Order!" he charged at the crowd. "I shall have order *now*!"

The crowd sat back down, but their excitement made their previous silence impossible. Kira glanced at them with gratitude for that. Their enthralled gasps and frantic chatterings effectively muffled the roaring maelstrom of her heartbeat, lending her composure she suddenly didn't have in abundance any more.

But she also turned back from that glance with a twinge of disconcertment. As she scanned the crowd, one distinct face stood out along the wall far to her left. She'd instantly noticed the features because they didn't jabber or gasp or swoon with or at anybody in the room. No, the strangely blank stare on that face was only directed at one person in the room: her.

Kira hadn't reciprocated her father's look. She wouldn't have known *how*. She swam in confusion over his presence, not sure whether to be infuriated or indebted by it. She did *not* need this dilemma at the moment, but she couldn't ignore the situation. She couldn't run away from wondering if Nicholas were here to help or hurt Damien's case. How she wished Mama or Sheena were here, with one of their crystal balls nearby!

Crystal ball or not, it seemed she'd have the answer to her confusion soon enough with Judge Plighton's help alone. The man stood as he addressed the courtroom once more, signaling the importance of his message.

"Lady Kira's announcement has certainly cast a new light on this case," he proclaimed, "which I find I must review in private before rendering a final decision on Mister Sharpe's verdict. Therefore, we shall reconvene in precisely one hour."

One hour. Kira shot her sights to Damien again, and discerned the words had impacted him with the same double-edged irony. One hour...it would be the longest of their lives; it would be the shortest of their lives.

She thanked every saint she could remember when it seemed his guard comprehended that, too. The bastard might have handled Damien like a slab of meat before, but over the days of the trial, the brutality had given way to a gruff politeness. Now, the feat of fathering a child appeared to have raised Damien a few more notches in the man's esteem, especially when the guard began to lead Damien back out of the courtroom, and jerked his head quickly her way, too.

Kira needed no further enticement. Eagerly and wordlessly, she followed them down a long dark hall, until the guard shoved open the door on a small holding cell. "It's not the palace," he muttered to Damien, glancing around to make certain nobody saw him unlock the wrist cuffs, as well, "and I can't shut the door, but—"

The man interrupted himself with a chuckle, knowing neither of them listened to him beyond the instant she rushed past him and into Damien's arms, laughing and crying at once. In return, Damien's harsh breaths vibrated through her, his trembling arms crushed around her, his thundering heart pounded against hers.

Suddenly, however, he pulled away, his gaze cast downward, his hands recoiling against his sides. "I'm filthy," he muttered apologetically. "And you're gorgeous. Ah God, Kira, you're so damn—"

"Furious!" Kira hissed. She pressed her hands to the sides of his face and wrenched his gaze up to meet hers. "*Shto s taboj*, you idiot!" She laughed then, and kissed him hard, then harder for a second time. "Damien...oh Damien, you beautiful, beautiful idiot, kiss me," she ordered. "Touch me...hold me!"

With a surrendering groan, he met, then exceeded her demand. He took her with his mouth and he tantalized her with his hands, pulling her fichu out of her neckline and teasing both her sensitive nipples with the tips of his exploring fingers. Kira gave herself over to his ministrations with desperate, throaty mewls, her own hands making short work of his shirt buttons so she could feel the bare expanse of his chest.

He felt wonderful. Oh God, *this* felt wonderful. Coherent logic still aided her enough to understand their absence from each other, perhaps both before *and* after today, did comprise a heady aphrodisiac—but that reasoning still didn't open all the windows of meaning to this moment.

The only way she peered into those windows was by gazing into Damien's eyes...especially as his hand moved from her breasts down to her abdomen. Kira swallowed back tears as he flattened his fingers there. The tears came back, anyway... when she saw a discernible, wonderful glimmer appear in his own gaze.

"Is...it true?" he finally whispered. "Kira...were you really... *are* you really..."

"Yes," she rasped, and slid her fingers into the spaces between his. "Yes. Your child is growing inside of me, Damien."

"*Bozhy moj,*" he grated then, and again they laughed together as he covered her mouth in a long, consuming, soul-searing kiss.

During that kiss, even though her eyes were closed, Kira knew she looked into yet another window of meaning to this moment...to this man. Oh yes, she assured herself, something had changed in Damien since they'd dragged him away from Scottney Hall last week; something making his kisses even more delectable and his gazes even more magical.

She beheld that secret, magnificent force even now, as he drew reluctantly away. He didn't pull back very far, though; one of his hands cradled her face, while the other still pressed tenderly to her belly.

And suddenly, as he leaned and kissed the tip of her nose, Kira knew exactly what window had been thrown open inside Damien. Her lips parted on a joyous smile because of that knowledge.

He loved her, too...and now he knew it!

His own mouth broadened on a smile then, too, though the edges of his lips possessed gentle intent. It was the look a lion got when smitten by his lioness, Kira reflected...though the great beast had gone willingly and happily to his passionate doom.

Surely enough, after Damien lowered one of the sweetest, wettest kisses to her lips, he continued caressing her with his gaze, alight again with those beautiful deep blue flames. "Kira," he whispered to her then, "Kira, I—"

"Hey, Sharpe shooter." The term was obviously a nickname wielded with amity, but rough regret underlined each word of the guard's interruption, too. "Apologies, Damien," he murmured, looking away as both of them righted their clothing, "but they're ready for ye again."

Kira voiced the reaction clearly foremost on all three minds in the cell. "It surely hasn't been an hour."

"No," Damien returned, "it hasn't." Like the face of a mountain subjected to a sudden Spring storm, the warmth of his features reverted back to hard, cold angles as he extended the wrist cuffs for his jailor's key again. "Which means the man has either been astoundingly convinced, or astoundingly paid."

As they paced back to the courtroom, Kira struggled not to dwell on how Damien enunciated his latter conclusion with such leaden certainty. Or how easy her own instinct found it to believe him.

She had to hope. *They* had to hope.

An expectant round of shufflings and murmurings hailed them into the courtroom. Kira tamped the urge to emit an ironic laugh. If she closed her eyes then let herself smell the spice of sausages mixed with the honesty of sawdust rather than the dampness of old wood and the deceit of marble floors, she would have sworn she entered an arena to begin a performance. She doubted anybody in this crowd would know about the difference in the two spectacles, either. Or care.

The crowd's furor calmed in respectful fear as Plighton made a production of entering again. Reluctantly, Kira scooted her way into the front row of the gallery once more, her heart thrumming in her throat as she noted the judge didn't take his own seat. Plighton was ready to give his verdict quickly, then make an equally fast escape from the stand.

But what in tarnation does that mean? her senses urgently screamed.

"Damien Sharpe," Plighton intoned then, rolling an imperious glance at the man she loved. "Please stand now." Damien did so, and there in his half-washed, uncombed and disheveled state, Kira concluded she'd never thought him more her dark, proud, remarkable prince.

"Mister Sharpe," the judge began, "I am faced with quite a conundrum. You have been accused of murder for the second time in one year—though as civilized members of society, we all know an accusation does not always equal guilt. And while the evidence in your case, along with Lady Kira's testimony, has been"—he swung his stare to the prosecuting barristers while stalling to select the term he wanted—"compelling; yes, quite compelling, it is all still, I am reluctant to say, evidence that brings insufficient resolution."

Kira pressed both her hands over her lips as reacting gasps turned the air behind her into an odd wind storm. For the first time, she dared to permit herself a shred of true ecstasy. Much of what Plighton said, complicated by his thick accentings and the resonance of his jowls, was still a baffling mess to her brain, but when the first wave of relief poured off Damien's sagging shoulders and made its way to her, she knew the hope in her heart was more than wishful thinking or misplaced instinct.

But the ordeal wasn't over. Plighton pointedly cleared his throat, adding a glare to indicate he hadn't dismissed *anyone* from the court yet. The room fell silent.

"This evidence, however, cannot be ignored either, Mister Sharpe. Two fine women of this county are now cold in the ground because, it seems, of you." The jowls made audible slaps as the man shook his head vigorously. "This court cannot, in good conscience, release you from the responsibility of this—nor set you free among the good people of Yorkshire again.

"Therefore, it is the court's decision to deport you to Our Majesty's New Zealand colony at the first possible opportunity. There, you will pose only a threat to cows and sheep for the remainder of your days. You shall be transported to London on the morrow's train, and remitted to the hands of the prison authorities there for further deportation processing. That is the final verdict of this court in this case. Court is dismissed. God save the queen."

In an eye's blink, Plighton fled from the courtroom—not even pausing to accept the roaring cheer he received from the crowd.

Not even pausing to look at the man he might as well have sentenced to death.

In a haze of disbelieving shock, Kira fought her way to Damien and let the guard rush them both out of the courtroom, dodging catcalls and rotten oranges as they went. Back in the holding cell, she clenched back tears as she pressed herself to him again, wishing she could clutch him tight enough to take all of him inside her, then simply walk out of this place without anybody being the wiser.

But even her love couldn't alter the cruelest joke the universe played on humankind: that one true love couldn't share one body. It took two...and that meant pain.

Dear God and all the saints, that meant pain.

She held him yet tighter, and despite her intense, shaking effort, the tears came, drenching his neck. Damien responded with his own embrace, but his arms were slack against her body, defeated and exhausted and battling, she knew, the fear of holding her any closer. If he did so, he'd succumb to his own avalanche of emotion—an avalanche he had difficulty restraining as it was.

Finally, with an effort of taut determination, he slid his hands to her elbows, and set her away. But she'd stepped no more than a foot back when he brought her back by framing her face with his hands, and kissing her desperately on the lips. In a flash of a second, they entangled tongues and moans and souls, grasping each other as if the rest of the world had crumbled away and they stood on the only secure rock left from that catastrophe.

In a way, Kira thought, the image wasn't such a fantasy, either. For in all the unsure wanderings and travelings of her life, she'd never known what a rock could feel like. She'd never known the desire to have a home with big, carved beds and nights by the fire and walks on the moors...and a man who saw all that she was, and loved her, anyway. A man who wouldn't mind if she decided to erect a few circus tents on that rock from time to time...

A man they were putting on a train for London tomorrow, and a ship for New Zealand next week.

This time when Kira opened her eyes and met Damien's gaze, she truly comprehended the pain she saw in those black, sad depths.

"Oh, my love," she rasped, stroking his brow, his jaw, his hair, "they might as well have put a bullet through your brain."

Damien closed his eyes and nodded. An oath growled up from his gut, but came out a whisper from his lips. "I'm sorry," he grated after that. "Good Christ, Kira, I'm so sorry...for everything..."

"Ssssh," she gently reprimanded him. "Ssssh."

At that, she coaxed his gaze back to hers. They stared at each other for minutes they had to make into hours, perhaps months, perhaps years. So many words clamored in her brain, so many promises she had to make to him...I'll *wait for you to send for me...I'll come to you after our baby's born...I love you, Damien; I love you, Damien...*

But all those syllables went silent somewhere between her heart and her throat, as she stood and shared his agony of knowing he'd never see his home again, or stand on British soil with honor again. He was thinking of his father, she discerned, and the ultimate disappointment he'd at last dealt Kenrick Sharpe. He was also thinking of their child, and the home that little boy or girl would never have to grow up in...the heritage they'd never be able to claim. Kira swallowed back the pain inundating her own soul as she experienced every stabbing, excruciating moment of his torment—

Until the instant Damien's stare changed.

At first, only the edges of his eyes flinched, and he blinked. But peering closer into his gaze, Kira witnessed a transformation of the thoughts *behind* those eyes—the thoughts that grieved no more, but plotted; the mind immersed no more in resignation, but decision. The soul that told her now, in calmly resolved certainty, *I'd rather be dead than deported.*

★ ★ ★ ★

As soon as her mouth popped slightly open and her eyes widened in comprehension, Damien prepared himself for anything from Kira—or perhaps nothing at all. He'd just advised her of his intention to become a true outlaw instead of a true convict; he couldn't expect or even ask her to join his quest. She would have to come by her own choice.

Elation soared through his heart when she relayed that choice to him via a dazzling, devilish smile.

She didn't give him much time to enjoy her beauty, however. Kira's expression swiftly reverted to a stare of solemn concentration, now directed out into the hall at Luke. After one more moment of contemplative consideration, she jerked back from Damien on what sounded like a pained shriek. The outcry, and her accompanying crouch over her leg, pitched with so much distress that *he* moved forward, not sure what or even if his little hoyden was up to now.

"Yer ladyship!" Luke dutifully dashed in, his eyes fixed so solidly on the perfect ankle and shin she now exposed, he never noticed he dropped to the floor directly between them. "What the bloody blazes happened?"

Kira swung her arm as if in dramatically-sized pain. In reality, she motioned to Damien that the guard occupied a perfect position to collapse gracefully to the floor. "Oh!" she gasped. "I think something bit me! Something big and—and hairy!"

"Well now, ssshh, m'lady; the best thing to do is stay calm and—oooog!"

After that short, stunned sound, the guard rolled to the floor like a napping baby.

Damien shook his fists out as Kira shoved Luke onto his back and wrested the ring of keys off his belt. "Sorry about that, mate," he muttered, and meant it. "But this way, at least you're not an accomplice."

By that time, Kira clicked him free of the cuffs, which they set gently on the floor, not wishing to disturb Luke's nap—or anyone else still in the building, for that matter.

With equal care, Damien grabbed her hand and led her on tiptoe from the same rear entrance he and Luke had used each morning and evening. Only *this* evening, he thought while taking a full breath of the twilight air, he wasn't bound for prison again. He was free.

He was also very much still in danger.

They were in danger.

Motioning for Kira's continued silence, Damien pulled her up a steep side street, then down into a narrow alley. The labyrinth of these sparsely-populated lanes would have to serve as their escape route—if his memory didn't fail them and take them down a time-eating impasse. He concentrated as completely on the task as he could while still listening for any shouts or whistles that would denote their disappearance had been detected.

Steadily, they progressed through the city. Miraculously, only the sounds of early evening rituals filled the air. Mothers hummed. Teapots whistled. Dogs whined at back porches for permission to enter warm kitchens. Damien's heart began to pump with gradual exhilaration. They were actually going to get out of York without having to run.

"Hey!"

His heart halted and the heat streamed out of his veins. Where the bloody hell had this little girl come from, with her nose full of freckles and eyes full of mischief? And eyes full of determination, too. Oh yes, this eight-year-old-going-on-eighty had decided they went *nowhere* before talking to her.

"Hello, there," Kira said to the imp, though the wobbling breathiness of her voice betrayed her own trepidation about this sudden interruption.

"You're a pretty lady," the girl declared, exposing a mouth of healthy white teeth. That aspect alone revealed her as a child of York gentry, at least.

"Th-thank you," Kira rushed in return, "but we're in a bit of a hurry, little one, and—"

"I saw you before," the imp went on with rapacious eagerness found only in a child. "I saw you at Mister Rolf's ball, in your green dress. And I saw you with your monkey. You're the monkey lady! Yeah, monkey lady!"

This "interruption" had just become a fatal mistake. "Let's *go*," Damien commanded, clamping Kira's hand hard as he jolted into motion. They were going to leave the city at a run, after all.

Thanks to the imp, it now sounded like they were going to have company, too.

Whistles, shouts, bugle blasts, and even hound dog howls seemingly erupted all around them at once. Damien no longer cared about what streets or alleys they utilized, as long as crowds of lanterns and gleaming police badges didn't illuminate their way. But the police and accompanying bastards seemed to multiply like rabbits, closing in tighter on them—and worse, forcing them back into York, instead of away from it. But each time either of them slowed, tempted to give in to defeat, the other took the lead, pulling them on, around countless corners and down what seemed a thousand alleys.

Kira had just jerked her way into such a lead when a burst of shouts erupted behind them, at the opposite end of the narrow alley they'd paused to rest in.

"There they are!" a voice boomed, as their lanterns flooded the lane with garish light.

"We've got 'em now!" bellowed a thick Cockney accent.

"Halt in the name of Her Majesty Queen Victoria!"

"Damien Sharpe, halt now!"

"Halt!"

Kira cried out something frantic, fast and Russian then, but the terror of her voice was drowned by a sudden series of sharp cracks, like a large log popping from extreme heat.

Heat similar to the fire erupting in Damien's lower right leg now.

Before the telltale wetness began to ooze from his shin, he squeezed his eyes shut and swore. But he didn't let go of Kira's hand, and he didn't break his pace in keeping up with her. *Keep running*, he commanded himself, *keep running, and pray for a miracle.*

His prayers didn't quite include a carriage barreling across their path, then stopping. From the vehemence underlining each syllable of Kira's curse—in English this time—the vehicle's interference warranted the kind of rage she usually saved for forest does and lion cubs in chains.

With her ensuing snarl, filled with nothing but disillusionment and hatred, Damien clearly assessed why.

"Father," she cried. "Damn you, Father!"

CHAPTER TWENTY-NINE

"Get in!"

Kira stood glaring at her father for preciously valuable seconds after he snapped the order, only increasing her fury with him tenfold—

Until she realized he'd punctuated the command by motioning to both she and Damien. And that he'd done so clothed from head to toe in the green and gold livery usually meant for his footmen.

Still, she hesitated. Intensifying her glower, she demanded, "What the hell is this about, Nicholas?"

Her purposeful use of his proper name usually expanded the man's nostrils in lordly pique and stiffened his spine to resemble one of the battle lances mounted on the Great Hall walls. But this time, Nicholas merely slammed his leather-gloved hands on his livery-clad waist, and glared back at her. Hard.

"This is about saving your arses," he answered, hurling the salty words with shocking ease. "And perhaps this bastard's leg, too."

Kira whirled at his indicating hand motion. Her eyes locked to the red stain blooming against the right leg of Damien's breeches. "My God," she gasped. "Damien!"

But no time remained for questions or their answers, for further reluctance or persistent pride. The search party had sent out messengers for reinforcements, and now shouting, jostling mobs advanced on them from two directions. Kira snapped her head one direction then the other, peering at the dual predators approaching with their undulating yellow lantern eyes.

Then she looked back to her father, with his gaze the color of a deep copper sunset…his gaze that suddenly told her everything she needed to know.

This is not easy for me, daughter, that gaze said. *But if you love this man, then by God, I'm going to help you save him.*

This *time, I'm going to be here for you, Kira. You can trust me, Kira.*

Kira flashed him an uncertain glance just before she dove into the carriage behind Damien. As the vehicle lurched into motion, bullets pinging against the wheels and thudding against the side panels, the words of one refrain also ricocheted around the confines of her mind. *You can trust me, Kira.*

"Father," she muttered tautly beneath her breath, "you haven't given me much choice."

★ ★ ★ ★

Under ten minutes later, they clattered out of York with nary a glance from the gate guards who'd been alerted to watch for a man and woman on foot, not a seemingly empty Scottney family carriage. Nicholas still didn't slow their pace, however. He only did that after they cleared Harrogate, and then only by a degree necessary to thank the horses for their outstanding efforts.

"He's got a destination already in mind," Kira at last deduced—though her tone transcended the darkness of where she and Damien curled on the carriage floor, amply conveying the scowl she attached to the statement.

She felt Damien's head nod into the crook of her shoulder. He moved with careful economy, the wound in his leg obviously depleting him of the scant strength he still had. Nevertheless, he said through gritted teeth, "I've got a—good idea—of where—that is."

"Newgate?" she sneered.

Damien snorted his dispute of that, knowing she'd only been half kidding about it. "Kira," he rasped, "your father—won't hurt—you. Loves—you."

"Ssssh," she gently chastised him, ashamed to admit her exploitation of his injury as an excuse to quell him—and the disturbing words he suddenly rendered in Nicholas's defense. "Rest now."

Damien stubbornly shook his head again. "Not—yet. Not—until I—tell you—"

"Damien, you've got to preserve your strength!"

"*I*—love you, too—Kira."

Her breath caught on a small, halting cry. She found his face through the near-black shadows, and ran the back of her hand along his firm, beautiful jaw. "Damien," she whispered reverently, and leaned to softly kiss him.

Until she realized the dolt had finally chosen to obey her, and now snored quietly in her arms.

Eventually, Kira's own eyes slid shut and her head drooped atop his. Exhaustion and slumber consumed her so completely that when the carriage door opened and her father's smiling form appeared, she had no idea how much time had gone by, or where they had finally stopped.

Her start of surprise jerked Damien awake, as well. He grimaced when shifting his leg, along with the makeshift bandage formed of her petticoat, but no other expression altered his features as he, too, looked to the moon-illuminated scene beyond Nicholas. His brows didn't leap as hers did. His mouth didn't fall open in stunned bafflement.

As a matter of fact, he looked like he not only accepted, but approved of the fact Nicholas had parked them in the middle of the Scottney Hall stable yard.

"Close your mouth, Kira," her father advised in a stage whisper. "Flies still love stables, even at midnight."

"But—" she stammered, "but what are we doing at *this* stable tonight?"

"Last place they'll look," Damien supplied then, accepting a brusquely grateful nod from her father for the support. Directing his gaze back at her, he quipped, "They may think I'm a killer, my love, but they don't think I've got balls. Not the balls to do *this*."

That comment drew a reluctant but sincere laugh out of Nicholas. The reaction lasted an all-too-fast moment before he stuffed it back beneath his veneer of sober concentration, but during that moment, Kira watched both men, enchanted by what she saw. She witnessed the friendship this pair had once shared as two proud and powerful men...perhaps, she yearned, the friendship they'd form once again.

"Besides," her father continued then, "here, we'll blend right in while we take care of Damien's leg properly. I'll do that while you go fetch your pet and your other valuables. Then we'll move on to Belford."

"Belford?" Damien reiterated, straightening despite the wince with which he finished.

"Belford?" Kira also echoed, though pondering why the name did sound a bit familiar.

"My holdings further north," her father explained. Again appearing anything but the formidable lord he'd presented to her until now, he braced both elbows to the top of the carriage door and gave her a sheepish smile. "It's not Scottney Hall," he qualified, "but it can suffice as home to you two until..." With that, he flicked another ambivalent glance Damien's way. "Well, until we get this whole mess straightened out," he muttered.

Kira only had to look at Damien to understand the full import of what her father had just offered—not only with the keys to his home, but the keys to his trust, as well. On her love's face, she beheld an expression she'd only seen once before: on the afternoon she'd declared her own belief in his innocence.

"Thank you, Nicholas," Damien said then. His hand, extended with firm purpose, underlined his appreciation for the Belford home. His voice, rough with emotion, offered his gratitude for the bigger gift Nicholas had bestowed to him.

At that moment, Kira didn't know if she could manage even those brief words. She thought of the first time she'd met her father, in that dim room back in London, now seeming a forever ago. She thought of all the betrayal and anger she'd felt; of the disbelieving disdain she'd given him as he'd sworn to try and make all those lost years up to her. Then she remembered her deeper, stubborn scorn as he'd urged her to see "his England."

With that memory, words now welled to Kira's lips. But before she uttered them, she turned to Nicholas Scottney through a gentle haze of tears, and lifted a soft kiss to his handsome cheek.

"Father," she told him then, "tonight, you've truly showed me 'your' England. And you're right...it's beautiful."

She kissed her father's jaw one more time—and the tear she found there—before promising both men she'd be back within the half hour, Fred and her valuables in tow.

Her material possessions packed easily and quickly. Kira selected only warm, simple garments as her "Belford wardrobe," gladly leaving every one of her corsets and crinolines behind. She also packed the beloved books Father had given her: several tomes of poetry, Mary Shelley's deliciously morbid *Frankenstein*, and an album of color paintings depicting exotic birds. On her reading table, she gleefully abandoned *The Mirror of the Graces*.

Fred, on the other hand, had decided to play a maddening game of late night hide-and-seek with her. Calling out his name in as loud a rasp as she dared, she checked the maids' sewing room with the extra ribbons he so loved, the music room and even the kitchens, which usually held no interest for him in their unproductive hours. No mound of rebellious brown fur greeted her in any of those locales.

She snapped her fingers in triumph as she scaled the servants' stairway for a third time. She spun happily on her tiptoes and rushed back down the steps, out of the Main Hall and across the Main Courtyard. She should have remembered her pet had developed a crush on a new arrival to the Scottney Menagerie, a green vervet monkey from the Caribbean island of Saint Kitts. Everyone had taken to calling her Frederika, in honor of her new enamorato. Kira grimaced now as she approached the building, regretting she'd have to break up the happy couple—also dreading her own leavetaking of her beloved wild friends.

"It'll only be for a few months," she vowed with conviction to both her pet and herself. She added in a whisper directed straight toward heaven, "Please let it be only for a few *fast* months."

During her walk up the glass-stoned entrance walk to the Menagerie, her scowl deepened. She didn't want to reprimand Fred while dragging him away from his little green lady love, but with every step she neared the Menagerie, she grew more certain she'd have to do just that. Restless rustlings emanated from all the animals inside, the birds flapping, the monkeys chittering; even the two wildcats released long, threatening *mmmrrrowls* from deep in their throats. At this time of the night, those sounds could only mean one thing: Fred wanted to play, and everyone else wanted to sleep.

"Ohhhh, Frederick," she groaned, "why do you have to be such a brat, on tonight of all—"

A distinct series of happy gruntings came from the shadows to her right, nullifying her complaint and stopping her cold in the center of the path. Surely enough, Kira knelt and welcomed her chimpanzee as he sauntered over from the bushes, proudly showing off his new fur accessories of twigs, leaves, and one fat caterpillar.

"Well, hello, my friend," she greeted, though equal parts warmth and confusion mingled in her tone. While Fred toyed with the ribbon at the neck of her cloak, she turned a puzzled glance back toward the Menagerie—and the creatures still shifting uneasily inside.

If Fred didn't provoke their agitation, then what *was* the problem?

She told herself the matter wasn't her concern. She told herself Damien and Father awaited her, and every moment carried the value of an hour right now. She told herself the animals merely sounded restless, not alarmed, and that she always overreacted to intuitions like this.

She told herself all those things as she marched up the rest of the walkway, and jerked open the Menagerie door.

She promptly forgot all those things as she confronted a sight more astonishing than her overactive imagination could have fathomed.

There on the iron bench before the waterfall, half-clothed bodies twined in a carnal embrace and tongues locked down each other's throats, were her Aunt Aleece and Mister Rolf Pembroke.

CHAPTER THIRTY

Neither of them heard her open the door over the spattering of the waterfall, which meant they subjected her stare to a long, minute's worth of their lusting gropings before Fred cackled a salutation to Frederika. Kira gladly released her pet to his assignation, freeing her hands to clamp swiftly over her mouth as the pair on the bench broke apart.

"Oh, my God!" Aleece sobbed, yanking her gown back over her exposed breasts and legs.

"Oh, my God is right," Kira countered, seeking balance against a building support beam. A wave of dizzy nausea assaulted her; due no doubt to the child in her body, the controlled heat in the room, and most overwhelmingly, the scene she'd just interrupted.

Not surprisingly, the only being in this room who seemed unfazed by this confrontation was the man who deftly smoothed his hair, refastened his breeches and approached her as if welcoming her to a garden gala. "Lady Kira," Rolf murmured, indeed as if he'd almost expected her arrival. "What a pleasant coincidence." He motioned to the seat where Aleece still tried to fix her clothes and deep breathe her face back to a normal hue. "Won't you please join us?"

Kira blinked up at the man once; twice. She peered for the fissure in his composure; the tiny sign telling her he didn't mean his invitation seriously.

"No," she finally fired back at him. "No, I will *not* please join you." Feigning exhausted grief, she pushed away from the support beam. "In case you've forgotten, Mister Pembroke, you gave testimony today that helped deport the father of my child to New Zealand. I don't wish to 'please join you' anywhere, anymore, at any time."

"But I think you do," came the assured reply. Kira should have just kept walking, gladly leaving this silly man and his arrogance to Aleece, who was obviously happy with her "animal." But she couldn't. She *wouldn't* let the bastard get away with such suave audacity—

Until she spun back toward Rolf, and saw his "audacity" came at the end of a loaded pistol barrel, aimed directly at her stomach.

The panther six feet to her right broke out in a threatening rumble of a growl. The cat smelled her sudden rise of fear, she comprehended, and for the animal's sake—for *all* their sakes— Kira breathed deeply several times, battling the physical manifestations of having a gun jabbed at her unborn child.

"Well," she leveled, reasoning a touch of humor, however forced, couldn't hurt the effort, "I do love a good party."

Not an inch of Rolf's silken mien fluttered, except to jerk the gun once in Aleece's direction. "On the bench," he calmly ordered Kira.

During her journey to her aunt's side, she observed Aleece's shock and perplexion at this strange change in her lover. "R-Rolf?" the woman faltered, staring dazedly at the pistol, clearly battling a tumult of emotions ranging from disbelief to heartbreak. "Rolf...my sweet...what on earth are you—"

"Shut up, Aleece."

Aunt Aleece's chin, still flushed a mortified crimson,

trembled. "Wh-what?"

"I said shut up." The man still spoke with the mildness of a minister. "I want to hear from our dear Kira right now."

Still conscious of the two pacing wildcats behind him, Kira concentrated on keeping her heartbeat steady and reining herself back from confronting Rolf's gaze. Tarnation, how she wanted go glare-to-glare with the bastard. How she wanted to find out why, all of a sudden, he chose to show the reality beneath his gentleman's façade...the reality she'd caught glimpses of before, in the moments the man had made her truly shudder.

And what that reality had to do with the necessity of her presence at the end of his gun.

"Really, Rolf," she retorted, "I don't understand what *you* want to know from *me*."

"Everything," he snapped, irritated. "I want you to tell me *everything* you know."

She sighed, equally and truly frustrated, as well. "About what?"

"You *know* what." He—and the pistol—took a slow, practically sensual step closer. "You were screwing Damien, my *lady*. He told you things, didn't he? He told you about Rachelle...and me."

Kira's brows jumped into startled arches, but this time, Aleece bested her at firing a response at their "gracious" host. "What *about* you and Rachelle?" she demanded, her spine going erect.

Rolf snaked a provocative smile at the woman. "Come, come, Aleece," he chided. "Surely you knew, my dear."

"Knew...what?"

"Of the intentions I had to court her. Of my intentions

to court her then marry her, then build Scottney Hall into an empire that would dwarf Hyperion's Walk in comparison!"

He bared a wider smile at them both then—a smile that stretched too far, so that in the space of one bizarre moment, his face transformed into the exact opposite of the suave, man-of-ultimate-presence Rolf. Now, his face looked wild and weird and demented.

Kira vacillated about what to say to him next. The panther and the tiger, now definitely discerning the threat of an uncontrolled human nearby, both increased their wary pacings, their huge paws shooshing across the floor. Her answering animal's instinct exhorted her to turn Rolf's thoughts away from talk of a long-dead woman named Rachelle. But her woman's heart wrenched her to push Rolf just a little farther—to learn what the man's thwarted plans of years ago had to do with Damien now. With Damien and *her*.

With one eye fixed on the wildcats, she took the risk of following her heart—for just a while longer.

"But...you didn't court Rachelle," she prompted Rolf then, hoping the remark convinced him she "knew" what he assumed she "knew."

"Obviously *not*," the man spat back.

"Because Damien came back," she said with slow, dawning realization. Dear God. Perhaps Rolf was right. Between the chunks of information she knew and the chunks *he* filled in, a tower of a story began to gain height...

A tower of an astounding story.

"Because Damien came back," Kira repeated then, enunciating the words with more conviction, "after you pulled him from that alley in London. You thought Kenrick Sharpe would finally be disgusted with him because of the incident, would disinherit him, but Kenrick didn't. Damien and Kenrick reconciled, and that's when Damien made the decision to court Rachelle himself."

"Right on the bloody money!" Rolf exclaimed, though the sound reverberated with no ecstasy—only agony. Only the agony of a man who now gazed up into the heights of the aviary behind the bench, looking as if he wanted to shoot every one of those birds down out of sheer malice. "She was the bride that should have been mine," he snarled. "But that was the way things always happened between Damien and I. He *always* got what should have been mine."

That was the moment comprehension struck Kira in a single, horrified wave. She didn't know what precisely triggered the blare of knowledge; whether it was the way Rolf stared at the creatures behind her but saw nothing but pawns for his rage, or the blood-thick bitterness of the words he uttered as he did so—but the realization was thorough in its logic, if heinous in its rightness.

"You," she stated, accepting the calmness of her voice as completely right for this moment, as well. "*You* were the one, weren't you, Rolf? You killed Rachelle because you wanted Damien to feel your hatred, and killing *him* wouldn't let you enjoy the deed at all. You wanted to watch him suffer."

"Damn *right* I wanted to watch him suffer!" Rolf didn't lower his sights from the aviary, but Kira also saw the glazed sheen in his eyes, showing his mind had journeyed to another place, another time. Perhaps, depending on how much his hatred had devoured of his soul, he'd gone there permanently.

"Yes," he hissed then, and finished with a laugh that unraveled from his lips the same way his sanity unraveled out of the charming, sophisticated, tragically fragile shell of his mind. "Yes, I killed her. I killed the pathetic little thing; is that what you want to know?"

Aleece didn't say a word, but began to quiver violently next to Kira. She wrapped an arm around her aunt; in truth, needing the woman as much as Aleece needed her. She squeezed her aunt's shoulder, fastening her attention on that point of human contact rather than the *un*humaness of the monster standing before them—the monster still holding them both at the mercy of his cocked pistol.

The monster she still forced herself to speak to in a statement instead of a scream.

"A wise career move, then," she ventured to Rolf in, unbelievably, a tone that could be termed conversational. She had no idea where her composure came from, but she made a point to thank that force when she got out of here. *If* she got out of here. "Is that what it was, Rolf?"

He rocked back on one heel and nodded confidently. "Yes," he returned. "Yes, I'd say so. I do like the sound of that. A wise career move."

Aleece jerked tearful eyes up at him then. Kira watched in agony as her aunt's gaze searched the man's twitching, snarling features, frantically looking for the man she'd adored...the man who couldn't have possibly murdered her little girl. "And—and me, Rolf?" she rasped. "What about me, Rolf? When you came here after the murder to comfort me, to hold me, to love me...was all of that a...a career move?"

Rolf considered her question for all of ten seconds before hiking his foot to the bench and drawling, "Well, my dear Aleece...yes."

"Of course," Kira filled in, preventing herself from succumbing to a savage tone only by fixing her gaze to a point in the man's forehead—right between his eyes. "Now that Damien was properly pushed away into his forest and you were in full possession of Hyperion's Walk, you decided it wasn't enough. If you had Scottney Hall, too, your kingdom would be complete—and Aleece was your key to gaining that. As soon as you'd 'taken care of' Nicholas in one of your 'unique' ways, she'd gladly sell the Hall to you for the simple price of a wedding band on her finger."

"Well, well, well," Rolf responded to that on an impressed chuckle. "Very nice, my lady. Very nice, indeed."

"Forgive me if I don't return the sentiment," she leveled.

"I plan on forgiving you for nothing."

His lethally low tone, combined with the renewed, controlled grace he employed to return to his feet, were enough impetus to crash Kira's heartbeat against her ribs at last. She silently begged the wildcats to understand as sweat trickled down her temples, sharp pinpricks attacked her nerve endings—and yet another flood of comprehension inundated her brain.

I plan on forgiving you for nothing.

The echo of his promise in her mind came punctuated by the cold press of his pistol barrel against the base of her neck.

"It truly was such a shame we couldn't get along, Kira," he said with a melodic undertone of regret. "I wouldn't have minded at all if you'd been my Scottney bride, instead." Slowly, he lowered the pistol's barrel down between her breasts. "God, I would have enjoyed giving you some good screws." His voice hardened as he pulled the gun back out, and rammed it hard to the center of her chest. "But I guess Damien got that privilege instead of me, too."

Kira struggled to calm her breathing; to hide her terror

from all the lethal beasts in the room, this one on two legs, the others on four each. Yet though she measured some success at that, her voice wobbled wildly as she stammered, "Rolf—Rolf, now—"

"Now is the time for you to rise, my lady. *Up*," he stressed when she didn't move, hauling her away from a near-catatonic Aleece with a brutal jerk. "I said stand up!"

He didn't ease his bruising hold as he pulled her across the foot bridge, to the other side of the Menagerie. He stopped only when they stood at the door to the panther's enclosure. In sickening contrast to his grip on her arm, he grinned through the bars, and emitted a string of juicy kisses at the big black creature.

"Hello, kitty kitty," he greeted. "Awww, why the sad face, kitty? What's that? You say a few folks have neglected to feed you lately? I'm sorry about that; so sorry. You've got to understand things have been a bit hectic around here lately." He yanked Kira closer to him, stroking the side of her face with the pistol barrel. "Well, don't worry now, kitty. I don't think you'll go hungry for much longer."

Kira's senses swam in vertigo as she felt a ring of keys thrust into her hands. "Open it," she heard Rolf dictate, the serenity of his voice now marred with guttural inflection. But her hands hung cold and numb around the collection of steel forced into them. "Open—it!" her captor repeated, seething now, curling her right hand around one of those steel pieces as he shoved cold metal harder against her forehead.

Somehow, Kira's brain surrendered a decision for her. She remembered Laura Kincaid's slaughtered body on the foyer floor, as well as the confession Rolf himself had given of Rachelle's murder, and realized this sad but dangerous man would think nothing of squeezing a trigger and exploding lead into her head. Given the choice between facing his gun or the wildcat who was familiar with her voice and scent—

She stepped forward and unlocked the cage door with jerking speed.

As she did so, Rolf began to pepper the air with a string of laughter. The sound grew in intensity until *she* thought she'd join him in his lunacy. She glared at him then, really stared, unsure which of her emotions took precedence on her face: loathing, confusion, sorrow, rage, or simple pity. Or perhaps all of them. It didn't matter to her. She was certain it didn't matter to Rolf.

"Oh, come, come, Kira," the man let up from his mirth long enough to playfully reproach her. "Don't you see the lovely beauty of this? Don't you see how people will talk in their salons and ballrooms about you? Why, you'll be *famous.* 'What a shame,' they'll say. 'What a terrible shame that darling Kira Scottney died beneath the teeth of those beasts she loved.'"

He chuckled a few times more, but discarded the mirth when he saw Kira refused to join him. "All right, then," he pouted. "If you insist on being no fun, then I suppose it's time kitty has *his* pleasure." He shoved the pistol back where he knew she'd receive his deadly intent the clearest: at the center of her belly.

"Into the cage," he ordered her. "Now."

★ ★ ★ ★

"Don't take a step further, Kira."

Damien heard his voice call out the command, strong and steady in every syllable, but the icy grip of terror around his senses wouldn't let him believe that intent. Not for an instant. Not while that madman in the body of his onetime mate still dug a pistol barrel into the belly of the woman he loved—into the future brain of his child.

Get angry! he ordered himself. He knew anger; he'd been lovers with anger for months; he craved every hot, invigorating drop of sustenance it would give him now. But frantic searches through his body yielded nothing but this debilitating ice...this hideous, nauseating sensation called fear. Real fear.

Dear God, he didn't know what to do. What to say. How to save Kira. *Dear God...Kira.*

But in that instant of frozen, thought-deprived desperation, he looked into Kira's face. And there, along the planes of beauty he'd kissed and touched and fallen in love with, was given the answer to his dilemma. Because *she* gave it to him.

She barely moved her lips, but the two words she mouthed to him were, to his dread, effortlessly comprehensible. *Trust me*, she asked of him.

Trust me.

And it seemed, Damien realized within the next minute, he had no other choice. Kira darted her eyes swiftly to his right, where he looked with equal alacrity to see the panther's cage door was still unlocked. But Kira, as the wildcat's intended meal, was the closest of them all to the door.

In order to save her, he really did have to trust her. To believe in her.

Damien looked to her again, hoping she saw his trust in the intensity of his gaze. Hoping she also saw how much he loved her. Christ, he loved her.

But his mooning gaze did nothing to help her situation.

The moment Rolf noticed their exchange, he rammed the pistol harder beneath Kira's ribs. "Well, isn't this sweet," he crooned, albeit past gritted teeth. "And so very convenient." A feral smile curled his lips. "You've picked the perfect time to play outlaw, Damien. Now I can do away with the old bitch, as well, and let you handle the criminal conviction honors once more. You've made it so easy, my friend. I suppose I should thank you. Forgive me if I don't."

Damien remained still and silent, surreptitiously looking to Kira for a signal of their next move. She gave it to him, pressing her forefinger and thumb together, as if stretching on a string. He had to supply her with more time.

"Bloody hell, Rolf," he muttered. "We were mates—"

"We *weren't* mates!" came the ferocious burst of a retort. "Mates get to share things, Damien. Mates means everybody gets to have the same damn things!"

The final three words escalated Rolf's voice to a vehement yell. In response, however, Damien took a long, deep breath—and with that inhalation, was filled with a strange, chilled calmness. "Was that what it was about to you, Rolf?" he returned quietly. "The *things* we had?"

The man sneered derisively. "Don't take that high ground with me, Damien. You can stand there and pontificate because you were the one who had it all! You were the one—"

"Who would have gladly shared," Damien stated. "If you'd only asked."

Rolf's reaction to that didn't take the form he expected. Damien steeled himself for another incensed eruption; he even welcomed the man's anger, hoping to goad Rolf into an attack on him. Then Kira and the baby would be safe—and for that reassurance, he'd gladly take a bullet in the gut, or anywhere else.

But Rolf didn't lash out at him again. The man's eyes, craftily assessing Damien's face, seemingly had the power to read his thoughts, too. Because instead of seething or yelling, Rolf now broke out into a long, savoring laugh—as he pulled Kira intimately close to him.

"But you see, Damien," he murmured then, "I don't *have* to ask now. I've already taken from you...just as you always stole from me."

Damien twisted every muscle in his body tight as the icy terror suddenly ignited into a fire storm of rage. He coiled his hands, yearning to stalk forward and plant a fist in each of the sockets housing Rolf's eyes. Then he'd take the bastard's pistol from him and use the bullet on the brain which had obviously festered and gone rotten long ago.

"So how does it feel, Damien?" Rolf snarled then. "How does it feel to see me with *your* possession? How does it feel to watch my hands fondle your woman? To see me enjoy her in the way only you should?"

Damien glared hard and intently—at Kira. With his eyes, he begged for mercy from this torture; he pleaded her to save herself from the grip Rolf wielded around her body, to save *him* from the hold Rolf wielded around his mind.

I can't take this much longer, Princess. Please let me kill this bloody bastard!

"Now, my good friend"—Rolf's inflection thickened in a sardonic parody of affection—"it's time for you to watch me dispose of your pretty little property, too!"

Before Damien could form a thought in reaction, let alone command his body to move, Rolf hauled Kira back and swung wide the door to the cage behind them. The huge black panther within released a peeved snarl at their intrusion, but held its position atop a mossy log. It warily dipped its sleek head toward them, its golden gaze hungrily sizing up the closest piece of warm-blooded meat:

Kira.

"In," Rolf ordered her, emphasizing with a hard poke of the pistol in her ribs. As Kira hesitated, skidding only a step further, the panther cleared a huge, darkly graceful leap off the log, then strode directly toward her—walking right out of the cage.

Damien watched in clenched agony as the woman he loved and a seven-hundred-pound panther locked gazes just three feet from each other.

But the next moment, he found himself scooting aside the agony to make room for his astoundment. He felt nothing less as he watched her extend a hand toward the wildcat, then murmur musically, "Hello, beautiful one. Are you confused by all this?"

"Confused!" Rolf spat into her ear, beginning to shake with flusterment and agitation. One of the performers in his scenario wasn't behaving on cue. That performer just happened to be a panther with audible hunger pangs sounding from its abdomen. "He's not confused, you little imbecile; he's hungry! Now get into the bloody cage!"

Raw antagonism erupted out of him as his control slipped further, and fear pounced into his brain in its place. The distraction occupied Rolf long enough for Damien to act. In two strides, he'd moved behind the man and snatched the pistol away. Rolf roared out a furious snarl as he clawed the air for the gun, but when he recognized his effort was futile, he brought that hand down around Kira, instead. He curled a vicious and unrelenting grip into her arm, causing her to shriek out in pain.

That cry was the only motivation Damien—and the panther—needed.

Damien pulled her hard against his chest in the moment the wildcat's front paws slammed into Rolf's face. As Kira screamed, he bellowed for Nicholas, who raced in and helped an incoherent Aleece escape from the building.

The four of them ran out into the night, hurling the doors closed and locking them—though the action didn't completely muffle the mortal shrieks and voracious roars tangling in an age-old ritual of death from inside.

But as deep as his sorrow delved for the man who once had been more than a mate—Rolf had been a *friend*—Damien clutched Kira closer and staunchly turned his back on the Menagerie. It was time to think about life now. About starting again now. About hoping and dreaming and being free now.

No, he corrected himself the next moment. He didn't need to learn any of those things—because the woman in his arms had already taught him how.

She'd taught him when she'd ignited his heart with the sweet, wondrous flame of love.

CHAPTER THIRTY-ONE

"Kira," Damien called gently, shaking his head with a knowingly amused smile. He supposed he'd have to get used to finding his wife crawling around in stable hay...he just didn't think he'd also find her doing so in her wedding gown.

And what a wedding gown, he concluded once again. When she'd appeared at the end of the Scottney Hall chapel in the creation, he'd seen why Nicholas had employed *three* of London's most eminent designers for the task of completing the creation in four weeks. The dress combined present-day femininity with a primal tribal flair, a perfect representation of the woman who filled it with beauty that had stopped his breath in his throat—and still did so. His sentiment, he'd noticed during their brief and intimate ceremony, had been echoed by every member of the small crowd they'd invited.

But now, the rest of Yorkshire waited on them—while his bride seemed intent, for some reason, on finding a needle in a pile of Scottney Hall stable hay.

"Kira, darling," he coaxed again. "Everyone's left for the gala over at the Walk. We're expected..."

"I know," she replied distractedly, "but—ah ha!"

Her face, framed by an exotic arrangement of white roses, white bird feathers, and her own beautiful curls, beamed him a triumphant smile. With a dramatic flourish, she produced not a needle, but a squirming green vervet monkey.

Damien couldn't help his answer of a hearty laugh and

heartier applause. "Perhaps you should enroll in the Sharpe Troupe as more than *grand dame du cirque,*" he teased. Approaching her—unable to stay more than three feet away from her, actually—he suggested, "Company magician?"

His new bride emitted a musical laugh of her own. She sighed, a light and content sound, while petting Frederika. "Fred refused to even approach the carriage without her. Er— Damien, I'm afraid we're spoiling our children already."

A wondrous, warm sensation filled him like summer's first breeze. *Our children.* Their children, who would have a heritage now—dualfold. But most of all, who would have lives filled with adventure and daydreams, of learning how to ride their horses then perform somersaults on them, of learning fencing *and* tumbling, of having tigers as family pets and, occasionally, half of England traipsing across their back lawn to view the most spectacular Circus and Menagerie in the land.

Their children, who would have lives filled with love. The love he'd never believed in...or perhaps had stopped hoping for.

An even stronger rush of amazement came at his senses then. And desire. Overwhelming desire for this woman who was now truly his, in all her flowing white gauze and feathers and gypsy baubles—and bits of hay. With an effort, Damien quelled the urge back. He turned his thoughts to a safer subject in hopes of accomplishing the same with the hard swell at the front of his breeches.

"Did you check on Aleece?" he asked while plucking strands of straw off Kira's shoulders.

"Yes," she replied softly, and a slight furrow marred her brow. "There's no change. She hasn't said anything since that night. But I think, perhaps, she's in a more peaceful place, even if it is in her mind. I can see she's happy, in her own way."

Damien found himself shaking his head once more; this time in soft awe. "Mrs. Sharpe," he murmured, bestowing a gentle kiss to her forehead, "you're a remarkable and wonderful woman."

He accomplished what he'd hoped with the words. A joyous smile erased the moment of troublement from her features. But as she directed a gorgeous smile up at him again, he found himself in a more precarious predicament. He wanted her again—with unignorable intensity. And this time, he saw Kira was aware of it, too.

"Damien," she warned—albeit while she let Frederika scamper away, then wrapped her arms around his neck. "Aren't we 'expected' somewhere?"

"Mmmmhmmm." He growled it in the moment before he took her mouth with wet, wanting desire.

"Oh," she breathed when they dragged apart many minutes later. "Oh, that's what I thought..."

But those were the last lucid words she uttered for a long while after that. For as they sank to the hay together, the beasts around them shifted restlessly, feeling the heat of the passionate fire they emblazoned as the beginning of their shared life, their shared love.

A fire that now climbed to touch Heaven itself.

Continue the Lords of Sin with Book Five

Surrender to the Dawn

Keep reading for an excerpt!

CHAPTER ONE

February 1891
The Saint Jerome's Home for Needing Orphans
London

"Miss Gwen? Miss Gwen, I'm sorry fer bargin' in so early, but—"

"Nonsense, Tessie," Gwendolen Marsh assured, turning from the rain-splattered window three floors over the empty East End street. "I'm awake. Come in."

She forced a smile to her lips for the dark-haired girl still fidgeting in the doorway—thankful the action also helped whittle the tearful lump swelling her throat.

One would think she'd learned by now, she reproached herself. As many times as she insisted on extending her volunteer's duties at Saint Jerome's for a fevered or needing child, so numbered the dawns she'd had to endure as this. Gray. Silent. Solitary. Nothing for company but her breath on that window's glass, and the fairyland of a life she envisioned in that haze again.

Yes, that world had once been hers. She had not just dreamt it, no matter how faraway the fairyland seemed now. No matter how distant the ballroom where she'd met a dashing rogue named Lloyd Alexander Waterston; no matter how fleeting the sweeping waltzes, balmy summer walks, and romantic hand squeezes of his courtship. No matter how much a stranger the laughing, flirting Gwen of those days seemed now.

She wiped the mist away, swallowing against the flood of pain, then left the window behind. "What is it, Tessie?" she asked. "What do you need?"

"Well, I—well, there—" The girl twisted her index fingers together. "There be *visitors* here for ye, Miss Gwen."

"Visitors?" Gwen glanced at the clock on the wall. The early hour of seven-thirty didn't amaze her as much as the fact that she had guests. No one had formally called on her in more than two years. Not since the "incident," as Aunt Margaret tersely phrased it. Not at the town house Gwen shared with the somber woman on fashionably proper Devonshire Street, much less here at Saint Jerome's, where, Aunt Maggie further *humph*ed, Gwen persisted in "consorting with who-knows-what-kind of rabble in the name of Christian charity."

"Aye, miss," Tess blurted on. "Visitors. Two gentlemen." A shy smile flitted across the girl's lips. "And one rather comely, if I may say so. He smiled at me, and bowed. Like I was a lady, I was. He bowed like this."

During Tess's demonstration, curious pricks alternated with tense knives down Gwen's arms and legs. *Lloyd*, a secret, special voice whispered from inside, *are you at last here, finally here, finally back? Is God at last listening—and answering—me?*

Her right hand flew to her left, straightening the

meticulously-shined engagement ring there. For the first time in months, the emeralds looked to twinkle, not taunt. Gwen felt her lips curl upward on their own volition.

Her smile dropped at the same moment as her hope.

Two men. Suddenly, she remembered Tess had said two. That eliminated Lloyd, leaving behind only one terrible conclusion.

Helson. It had to be Inspector Helson.

Her heart climbed to her throat again. Why couldn't he leave her alone? She'd told him—and what seemed half the Metropolitan Police—everything she could recall before her world had been changed in those black, blank hours on that cold, foggy night. And now she didn't want to remember any more. She wanted to forget the night of January 5, 1889, had happened at all.

In short, her heart retorted, *you want the impossible.*

A touch beneath the curls at her right temple served testimony to that fact well enough. Yes, she discovered with the usual jolt of dismay, it was still there. Almost as thin as the strands of hair hiding it, just over three inches long and hardly discernible to an eye not looking for it, but there. The reminder. The scar, and the event it represented, that might as well have been the spots of leprosy to the society she'd once called friends.

Gwen forced her hand to her side. She spread her fingers into the skirt of her burgundy house gown instead. Pausing a moment to check on Gertie, her now peacefully resting patient, she followed Tess down the main stairwell, commanding each step to restore her composure in place of the fuming frustration. The bitterness only tangled her like iron shackles when trying to escape the torture of Inspector Helson's calls.

She stopped at the door to the parlor, fidgeting again in an effort to hoard a moment's more time. "Dear Lord," she murmured, running a nervous finger along her lace collar, "Dear Lord, help me through this ordeal...again."

She took one more deep breath and pushed the door open.

She almost laughed aloud when she saw the real ogre she'd been dreading to confront. With his top hat cocked a jaunty angle over his sandy hair and a mustard-yellow suit tailored well to his lean frame, Bryan Reginald Corstairs presented as opposite a picture from stuffy Inspector Helson as anyone on the earth could. His light-blue eyes sparkled when he saw Gwen; a lopsided grin formed beneath his mustache.

How many times had she turned to that smile for support and reassurance in the last two hellish years? Gwen lost count long ago. Yes, despite Aunt Maggie's scandalized declarations of, "But a reputable young lady is not just *friends* with a *man*," Bryan Corstairs was the best of the few remaining friends she had.

"Ah," he exclaimed with a dramatic sweep of his hand. "What light through yonder doorway breaks? 'Tis certainly the east, and sweet Gwen the—"

"Bryan, you incorrigible fox." She approached him with fingers wagging in admonishment. "You nearly had me slinking down the drain pipe like a housebreaker. I feared I was doomed to Helson and more of his horrid quest..."

Her statement fizzled away as a form shifted just beyond the realm of the room's single gaslight. The form emitted a cough, low and controlled. Gwen leaned and peered into the shadows.

She gasped and jerked a step back.

He was still dressed in his heavy black rain cloak, one

unbuttoned flap pushed behind the crook of his right elbow. The other arm leaned at a dominating angle across the mantel, almost blocking the shelf completely. An errant swag of dark-brown hair brushed at his shoulder, trailing from where he cocked his head at her, features still just a teasing inch from the light. Silently, steadily, he continued to appraise her.

Just as she stood in numb shock at the sight of him.

Her arms succumbed to the impact first. Her hands plummeted into the folds of her skirt. She felt the smile drain from her lips. The air whooshed from her lungs as she struggled to speak.

"Oh," she finally blurted. "Oh, Lloyd."

The relief, the utter victory of comprehending that he stood here waiting for her filled her like the glory of a bower of roses on May Day. For a long moment, she didn't move. Then she laughed. She laughed freely and joyously.

"I knew it," she cried. "I knew you'd be back. I knew you were bigger than those ridiculous rumors, darling...I knew you wouldn't listen or care! We're going to show them, Lloyd; we're going to show them all what they can do with their gossip and their lies—"

"Gwen."

Bryan's interruption echoed his soft but insistent touch at her shoulder. As distant thunder rumbled outside, she felt the May Day roses sagging.

"Gwen," Bryan continued, "I believe there are some introductions to be made."

"Introductions?"

Long, booted legs stepped from the shadows.

Gwen looked up.

The peaceful lake-blue of Lloyd's eyes didn't meet her

scrutiny. Instead, an explosion of color seared her: a riot of gold, green, copper, and even touches of black bordered by unblinking dark lashes. Where Lloyd's features made a noble, aquiline profile, this stranger's nose jutted out a prominent edge—too prominent. His jaw rose so rugged above a neck three shades too brown, even beneath a cravat the color of creamed coffee, Gwen wondered which dock Bryan yanked him from.

Indeed, the only trait Lloyd shared with this person was the thick dark-brown hair which had fooled her in the first place. Now Gwen perceived the incongruities even in that presumption. Her betrothed never missed his twice-monthly appointments with the barber; the shoulder-length waves before her now only deepened the conception that she confronted a half-blooded Celtic warrior...perhaps a full-blooded one.

With horror, she realized she still stared at the stranger just as he examined her: curiously, intently—brazenly. She ripped her gaze away and fixed it to the safety of the wall, before managing to blurt, "Wh-what's going on?"

His scrutiny only continued in quiet intensity, making her abnormally self-conscious...disturbingly warm. By high heavens, one might even think the reprobate *liked* the way she looked.

Nonsense. How in the world could she think he'd ogle anything than what everyone else gawked at? How could she think the long-haired infidel interested in anything but *that?*

She should be used to such leers by now. She *was* used to it, she corrected, even if she no longer chose to endure the perverted distraction she provided people at parties, the probing glances trying to violate the coifed curls at her temple, struggling to make out the manmade damage from her natural hair line. Even if she no longer battled to ignore the pointed fingers, the arched eyebrows, the whispers and the gasps—some discreet, many not so discreet—all brandished as if on January 5, 1889, she'd been transformed from a human being into a circus side show freak.

"Gwen," Bryan interjected. "It's all right. I'm sorry we startled you. We were on our way back through this neighborhood, and I remembered your aunt telling me you were here tending one of the girls for the week—"

"On your way through?" She reclaimed her voice to aid her perturbed thoughts. "At seven in the morning? Just blocks from the most popular brothel in the East End?"

At *that*, the stranger's eyebrows shot up. Bryan cracked a knowing smile. "What did I tell you?" he said to the warrior. "Now do you think she's strong enough to do it?"

"Do what?" Gwen demanded—more than aware of her suspicious tone.

An uncomfortable pause stretched as her only reply. Gwen coiled her arms across her chest and threw a glare from the stranger to her friend.

"Bryan, if neither you nor your stone-faced lackey wishes to let me in on your dandy little secret, I've got a sick little girl upstairs who cares about what I do with my time." She set her sights toward the door, following quickly with her feet. "Good day, gentlemen."

Only a step more separated her from the door when a voice stopped her. A gripping, yet stroking voice; power gleaned from conviction, not volume.

"The Lancer attacked his eighth victim last night, Miss Marsh."

Her knuckles went white around the door knob. "God have mercy. Is she...?"

"No. She didn't survive."

"Dear God."

She slowly turned—to where the tall stranger's gaze awaited her. "Who?" she heard herself rasp.

"Lady Veronica Spencer, of Middleham," Bryan supplied. "I believe you knew her, Gwen."

She stumbled, watching her hand grasp for something—anything—to steady herself against the flood of pain. One of the room's spindly chairs reeled into view. She fell onto the seat with a shudder.

"We played together as girls," she murmured. Her voice echoed with memories too long neglected. "We'd take turns pretending to be Queen Victoria. There was a medieval bench in her mother's garden. It was our throne. Oh, Nicky—" Her throat caught on the nickname. "Dear Nicky."

Out in the front hall, Saint Jerome's prized table clock called out eight o'clock. The last knell faded away into a heavier deluge of violent rain.

"Eight bells," came the stranger's voice again, a muted sound when set against the torrent outside. Gwen looked up and concluded the same softness didn't hold true for his profile. His eyes drove a hard glare out the rain-soaked window; his jaw line grew even harsher as he clenched and unclenched the muscles beneath. "Eight bells for eight victims. Eight women defiled by that bastard."

If Aunt Maggie were here, Gwen would have been dragged from the room at the first syllable of such language. But in this moment, she found herself silently thanking the man for the words she'd yearned to scream herself so many times in the last two years.

She supposed he sensed that, for he turned back then, straight eyebrows lowering in a more profound study of her. Every ounce of reason told Gwen to look away, to escape that disturbing, disconcerting, even crude scrutiny from across the room...she couldn't. In his gaze, she saw something she never thought she'd find in another human's eyes.

A pain as deep as her own.

"Eight victims, Miss Marsh," he repeated lowly, "and you, his third, still the only one of them who survived."

She didn't know how to respond to that. She gripped her hands together in her lap and watched the warrior stalk across the rug, shined leather boots reflecting the lamp light with each measured, steady step.

As she dreaded, he stopped beside her chair. Gwen closed her eyes, alarmed by the effect his nearness had upon her. The shivers from the scratch of his coal-colored trousers against her arm. The unfamiliar scent of spiced men's cologne mixed with early-morning rain.

But worst of all, dear Lord, the feeling that despite his size and strength and strangeness, she...trusted this man. Despite the screaming dissent from her logic and sense, her heart went effortlessly into the security of his attention, the broad strength of his nearness.

She was in trouble. And she had no will to struggle away from the danger. When he took her right hand, pulling her to her feet, she went without thought or protest. His fingers surrounded hers, warm and large. Her left hand, and Lloyd's engagement ring, felt cold and far away.

"Miss Marsh," he told her then, "my name is Taylor Stafford. My wife, Constance, was victim number four."

This story continues in Lords of Sin Book Five
Surrender to the Dawn!

ALSO BY ANGEL PAYNE

Lords of Sin:
Trade Winds
Promised Touch
Redemption
A Fire in Heaven
Surrender to the Dawn

The Bolt Saga:
Bolt
Ignite
Pulse
Fuse
Surge
Light

Suited for Sin:
Sing
Sigh
Submit

Honor Bound:
Saved
Cuffed
Seduced
Wild
Wet
Hot
Masked
Mastered
Conquered
Ruled

Misadventures:
Misadventures with a Time Traveler

Secrets of Stone Series:
(with Victoria Blue)
No Prince Charming
No More Masquerade
No Perfect Princess
No Magic Moment
No Lucky Number
No Simple Sacrifice
No Broken Bond
No White Knight
No Longer Lost
No Curtain Call

Temptation Court:
Naughty Little Gift
Pretty Perfect Toy
Bold Beautiful Love

Cimarron Series:
Into His Dark
Into His Command
Into Her Fantasies

Shark's Edge:
(with Victoria Blue)
Shark's Edge (Coming Soon)
Shark's Pride (Coming Soon)
Shark's Rise (Coming Soon)

**For a full list of Angel's other titles,
visit her at AngelPayne.com**

ABOUT ANGEL PAYNE

USA Today bestselling romance author Angel Payne loves to focus on high-heat romance starring memorable alpha men and the women who love them. She has numerous book series to her credit, including the action-packed Bolt Saga and Honor Bound series, Secrets of Stone series (with Victoria Blue), the intertwined Cimarron and Temptation Court series, the Suited for Sin series, and the Lords of Sin historicals, as well as several standalone titles.

Angel is a native Southern Californian, leading to her love of being in the outdoors, where she often reads and writes. She still lives in Southern California with her soul-mate husband and beautiful daughter, to whom she is a proud cosplay/culture con mom. Her passions also include whisky tasting, shoe shopping, and travel.

Visit her at AngelPayne.com